Omdurman

Book 3 in the
Soldier of the Queen Series

By

Griff Hosker

Omdurman

Published by Sword Books Ltd 2023

SWORD
BOOKS

Copyright ©Griff Hosker First Edition 2023

Omdurman

Dedication

To Sword Books and all the people who help me to fulfil my
dream of writing the stories that still fill my head: Eileen, Dave,
Vicky, Sarah and now Eliza.

Contents

Prologue

When I reached England along with Troopers Richardson and Coupe, we all found the mood at home a depressing one. The failure of Sir Wolsey Garnet to relieve Khartoum resulted in the fall of that city and the death of General Gordon. It was seen as a failure. When we descended the gangplank at Southampton it was in contrast to the way we had left with tearful wives, bands playing martial music and Union Flags flying.

Out of the three of us, my wound was the one which had almost resulted in death but Jamie's was the most serious. On the voyage home, while Syd and I recovered and were able to walk around the deck, Jamie found he could barely walk, let alone stroll. The doctor who accompanied us on the troopship was not hopeful. "You may make a full recovery, but I doubt it. You will have to attend a medical before you return to Egypt at the end of your three-month leave. In your case, Coupe, it may well be to give you an honourable discharge."

As we headed for the station to take our trains home Syd and I tried to be positive. Jamie himself was putting a brave face on it. "Being back in England with decent food and no heat will help. Don't you worry, Sergeant Major, I will be back with you in three months."

We all caught the same train from Southampton to London. We were lucky in that there was a train waiting to depart when we reached the station and we even had three seats together. It was in London where we parted. Syd and I had to head to different stations. Jamie headed for a horse-drawn omnibus and, as he went, I noticed his pronounced limp.

I clasped arms with Syd, "You take care."

He nodded, "I am guessing your train will get you home quicker. It will be dark when I get home."

I laughed, "After the dark and danger of the desert, I don't think you will worry too much about the north, eh?"

He agreed and then waved an arm around the crowded streets, "A different world."

When I had fought at Rorke's Drift, almost seven years earlier, I had thought I would end my days in the 24th. Events and certain officers had conspired against me but I was now, unlikely though it had seemed when we were about to be massacred by Zulus after the disaster that was Isandlwana, a Sergeant Major. It was as high a rank as I could hope for. I also served Major Kitchener who had new ideas about the way the army should operate. Our small unit which, until recently, had been just a dozen men strong, operated close to the border and we rode camels. Life was dangerous but exciting. As I settled down in the train for the long journey north to Liverpool, I wondered if the life I had chosen was the right one. My son, Griff, depended on me and putting my life in danger, as my recent wound had clearly demonstrated, was not fair on him, my mother or my Aunt Sarah. They cared for Griff while I served the Queen but neither was getting any younger. Major Dickenson was a good officer and if I made the case I am sure he would allow me to leave the detachment early. The recent reforms meant that I could transfer to a local regiment and just train men. I knew I had the skills. As I watched the green countryside of England fly by, I had to decide if I had the mentality. I had been given a three-month leave and that leave began when I stepped from the troopship. I would take advantage of every day back in England.

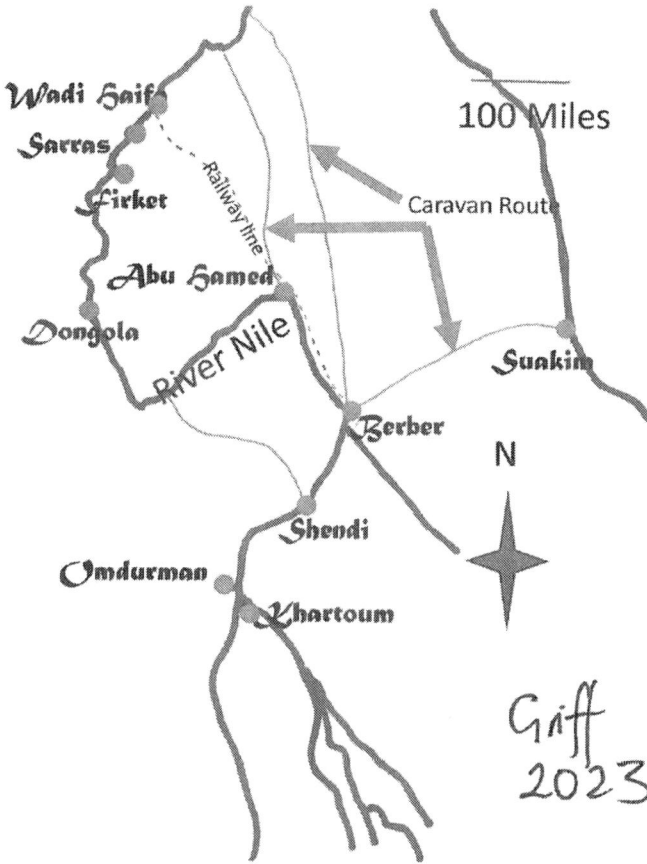

Egypt after the fall of Khartoum

Chapter 1

Griff had grown so much since I had last seen him that I barely recognised him. I had not sent a telegram to warn them of my arrival for the simple reason that the arrival of a telegram often made people upset before they had even read it and, in addition, I was unsure of the time of the journey. So as I walked down the road with my kitbag over my shoulder, I saw a group of boys playing and it took me some minutes to realise that one of them was Griff. He had grown. I leaned against the wall to watch them for a moment. They had wooden sticks for guns and it was clear what they were playing. I heard my son as he barked out orders. "We must hold them until relief comes!"

Another little boy, a head shorter with long unkept hair said, "But there are too many Zulus!"

"We can do it, boys, we are soldiers of the Queen!"

I laughed. They were playing out Rorke's Drift. Just then my mother came out. She was wiping her hands on her apron. She was about to speak to Griff when she saw me. Her hand went to her mouth and she croaked, "Jack!"

The boys turned around and saw me in my uniform. Griff recognised me and he ran at me. I dropped the kitbag for he threw himself into my arms. "You are home," he whispered in my ear.

"That I am, son and for three months."

The other boys formed two lines as, with Griff in one arm and my kitbag in the other, I walked to Aunt Sarah's house. Griff swelled with pride. His friends all stood open-mouthed. I guessed that there were few soldiers in the street. My red coat was distinctive. I knew that when I returned to Africa my red coat would be hung away for formal occasions. We would be wearing khaki.

Griff stroked the wool and then his hand went to my stripes. "Alan's dad says that a sergeant is an important man."

"That he is, son."

He beamed and held his head even higher. The neighbours had popped their heads out of their front doors at the squeals from the children and I was studied by women who, like my mother had come from the kitchen and were wiping their hands on their aprons. I had not spent much time at home and, unlike St Helens, while I was known by sight that was as far as it went. I knew that I would be the subject of much conversation that evening when the men came home from work. I was a diversion from the normal rhythm of the day.

I had to duck beneath the lintel of the door to avoid striking Griff's head. I dropped my kitbag to the ground as my mother closed the door behind me and, kissing Griff on the cheek, I lowered him. I was home.

As she put a hand on my back to direct me towards the kitchen, she asked me the inevitable question. Every soldier had it. "How long are you home for, Jack?"

"A full three months."

My mother was clever. She liked to sit with Aunt Sarah and do all sorts of puzzles. She knew that three months' leave meant a wound. She was silent but her head turned, and she studied me. Griff was dragging my kitbag behind me. He knew that I would have gifts for him. My mother sighed, "Let your father get through the door before you pester him for your present."

"Yes, Nan, sorry."

He was polite and obeyed orders. The soldier in me liked that. I sat at the table and helped him pull the bag closer as my mother lit the gas under the kettle. "If I had known you were coming I would have got something special from the butcher. As it is you will have to make do with lob scouse."

I could not help grinning. Made with meat left over from the Sunday roast, packed with potatoes and vegetables before being thickened by the leftover gravy, lob scouse was like a feast. I dived into the bag. My wound meant that I had no opportunity in Egypt to visit the souk and buy a present. I had been treated as an invalid by the medical staff. Luckily, I met an old sailor on the ship, he had been a ship's carpenter back in the day of wooden sailing vessels. He carved ships from wood and I commissioned two ships from him. Ironically, they were the first iron-clad ships in the Royal Navy, HMS Warrior and HMS Black Prince, but as they had sails it did not matter. The two replicas did not cost much but the work on them was exquisite. They had been rigged and had sails. Albert, the sailor, had painted the ship's hulls, decks and guns. They were magnificent and while I knew that Griff wished for soldiers, he would be happy with the present. I had wrapped the two vessels well and I brought them out one by one. He was intrigued as I removed the wrappings and when his eyes widened and his mouth opened in delight, I knew then I had made the right choice.

"Now, like the soldiers I brought for you the last time, you can play with these in the house but be careful with them. I have not the skill to repair them." I held one up, "This is HMS Warrior and was the first British ship to have a metal hull. The other is the Black Prince, her sister ship. When these were launched they were the most powerful ships in the world."

"Have you seen them?"

I shook my head, "These ships sail the world's oceans protecting the Empresses' Empire."

"Can I really play with them?"

"Of course."

He sat on my kitbag and began to move them as though the kitchen floor was the Atlantic Ocean. I said, as my mother poured the water into the teapot, "He has grown so much I barely recognise him."

"Sarah makes sure he eats well and gets lots of fresh of fresh air. We have him study each night. Mr Myers is really pleased with him. He says he could easily pass the scholarship into the grammar school."

I looked at my tousle-haired son. A grammar school was only for the best of students. Those with money paid for their children to go there but ones like Griff could, if they passed an entrance exam called a scholarship, win a place there.

I nodded and took out my pipe, "If he does then I shall make sure he has everything he needs. I will not have him going there as a pauper."

She laughed as she swirled the tea in the pot, "That is another five years off. Mr Myers sees Griff as a special child to be nurtured. He has no children of his own, you know. His wife died in childbirth, and he has dedicated his life to the school. We are lucky."

I had filled my pipe and, taking a taper, lit it from the gas. I held it over the pipe suddenly aware that Griff was studying me.

I smiled. I had grown up watching my father and men like Trooper smoking a pipe. Griff lived in a house of women. For him, it was a novelty. I tamped down the pipe once it began to draw.

"Doesn't that burn your fingers?"

I shook my head, "My hands and fingers are gnarly old things."

My mother poured the two teas, hers in a cup and mine, as she knew I liked it, in a mug. She sipped hers and then said, quietly, "Where were you wounded?"

Even though she had said the words quietly, the sharp ears of Griff had picked them up, "You were wounded?"

I saw the look of annoyance on my mother's face. She was angry with herself. There was little point in lying about it. I nodded, "Just a couple of cuts. They have healed and I will be fine."

"They don't give you three months of leave for nothing."

I took the pipe from my mouth and leaned over. Nodding in Griff's direction I said, "Later, eh?"

She smiled, "You are right." She looked at the old clock on the mantelpiece. "Well, your Aunt Sarah will be home in an hour. I had best get on with the tea."

I drank my tea and smoked my pipe. Griff was distracted by his ships but still kept up his questions. The young always did. "Did you see much fighting in Africa?"

I sighed. How did I explain what we did in such a way that he would not fear for my safety when I left him once more? "Most of the time it is routine. We patrol on our camels and watch more than anything else."

"You ride a camel?"

"I do."

"What are they like?"

"I am lucky, Aisha, that is my camel, is a good one. She doesn't spit and she is fast."

"And is it hot out there? Mr Myers says it is."

"So hot that you have to ride early in the morning and then spend the hot part of the day finding whatever shade you can." I lifted my mug of tea, "And you learn to appreciate water. There is so little of it in the Sudan that it is more precious than gold."

He looked at the tap. I remembered when we had to go outside to a tap but here there was plumbing and we had water at the turn of a tap. "Water?"

"Aye, water."

I spent the hour before my aunt returned describing not the fighting but life as a soldier of the queen.

The women in the street had forewarned my aunt of my arrival and she almost burst into the kitchen, "Where is he? Where is little Jack?" I stood and she threw her arms around me, hugging me and kissing my cheeks. It was her way. Aunt Sarah was the most practical woman I knew but I felt tears on her cheeks. She quickly brushed them away, "I am a silly old woman. By, but you look well. Look at the colour of you. How long?"

My mother, stirring the lob scouse, said over her shoulder, "Three months."

Aunt Sarah stepped back, "But three months means…"

"Later, our Sarah. Jack, do you want to take your kit bag upstairs? You can have the box room Griff normally uses. He can go back to sharing the bed with me."

"I can sleep on the settee."

"You will do no such thing! Griff doesn't mind do you?"

"No, Aunt Sarah."

I picked up the bag and headed up the narrow stairs. Griff followed. The room was called a box room because of its size. There was a single bed, a tiny wardrobe and a small chest of drawers. There was room for little else. I put the kit bag on the top of the wardrobe after taking out my shaving kit. I would unpack properly later.

Even as we descended the stairs I heard Aunt Sarah shout, "Tea is on the table."

We ate in the kitchen. It was cosy and meant no one had to go far to fetch what we needed. There were jars of piccalilli and pickled beetroot on the table as well as bread. Those were things I missed. We did not starve at Fort Desolation but army rations were dull. When we acquired a jar of pickles it was as though we had won a sweepstake.

My mother said Grace and then I dived in. As I mopped up the last of the gravy from around the plate with my bread I studied my family. This was why I was a soldier of the queen. Not to defend an outpost of the empire but to provide for my family. As a Sergeant Major, my pay was more than adequate and I was frugal. Apart from buying tobacco most of my pay went directly to my mother and my son. If I left the army would I be able to earn as much?

I told them, as we drank tea and I smoked the pipe, of my life. I told them of the Arab slavers we had encountered and they were shocked that such things went on. I described how Sam had built a bread oven and his passion for baking. The fighting and the flights for life I omitted. There was no need to give any of them bad dreams.

"And how is our Billy?"

"Oh, they are doing well. They have a new house out Walton way and it is lovely and little Jack is growing well. Elizabeth is expecting again and she hopes for a girl this time."

"Good."

"He is doing well at work too." Aunt Sarah shook her head, "When I think back all those years when I first took him in to be a clerk...he is senior now. He is earning so much money that they bought a much bigger house."

My mother turned and shook her head, "I didn't know why they did that. It is too expensive. Why leave that lovely house? He needs to watch his pennies, does our Bill."

"The company is expanding, Mother. Our Jack here and the other soldiers of the Empire have done such a good job that the bosses are setting up offices abroad. There is one in Halifax Nova Scotia, a second one in Cape Town and they say that there will be one at Suez."

I looked up, "Suez?"

"The canal is such a success and shortens the journey to Australia and India that the bosses think we can make a fortune. It means more jobs over here and more pay for men like Bill."

"What about you, Aunt Sarah?

She laughed, "I am a relic. When I began there we had less than ten people in the office. Now there are more than a hundred, not to mention all those who work in the factories. One day they will decide that they have had enough of me and retire me."

I was shocked but then Aunt Sarah, whilst younger than her sister, was no spring chicken. "Will you get a pension?"

She and my mother were washing the dishes and as she put the last dish in the cupboard she shook her head, "I honestly don't know. I would like to think so. I have been saving and I have some money but..."

I said, "Surely our Bill can do something if, as you say, he is so well thought of."

"I think they have only kept me on for so long because of our Bill. Don't you worry about it, Jack. When I am finished at Hargreaves and Winterbottom I shall enjoy life here. No more ten-hour days, six days a week."

My mother shook her head, "You will be bored beyond belief." She wiped her hands, "Now then, Griff, time for bed."

Still clutching his two ships he said to me, "Can you read me a story?"

"Of course I can, son."

Aunt Sarah went to the small bookcase where the books were kept. She handed me, *'The Coral Island'*, "This is the one he is reading at the moment. I have marked the page we are up to with a book marker." I saw that it was a crocheted one. "Just a chapter. He has school in the morning."

I was pleased that Griff was able to wash and undress himself. He donned pyjamas and climbed into my mother's bed. I lay next to him and then read the chapter. When I was young I had not enjoyed such things. With my arm around Griff, I wondered if my life would have been different if my father had done this with me. I dismissed the idea immediately. You cannot change the past and it is foolish to do so. You can only learn from it.

Closing the book, I pulled the sheet up around him and kissed him on the forehead, "Good night son, it is good to be home."

He smiled, "And I am glad that you are here too. We shall have such fun."

My mother and my aunt were sat before the fire in the small sitting room. Both were sipping the inevitable cup of tea and they had left the best chair for me. There was little point in objecting. I was the head of the house and it was my right as they saw it.

I took my pipe and lit it. My mother said, "Sorry, there is no beer in the house for you."

I shook my head, "No matter, I will go to the off-licence tomorrow. Tonight," I waved the stem of my pipe around, "this is enough."

They let me get the pipe going before Aunt Sarah said, "Now, tell us about your injuries."

There was no arguing with Aunt Sarah and I told them of the wounds. I saw them looking at my stomach and I smiled, "I am over them. In truth, I do not need the leave but I will take it nonetheless." I then told them about Jamie. "His wound may end his career and he is a young lad who wants to be in the army."

"Surely he could get something else."

I shook my head, "It is not as easy as you think, Aunt Sarah. In the army, you have men around you who are as close as your family, In some cases closer. Dad and Trooper have been dead so long that I can barely remember them and our Bill, well, it is different but the men with whom I eat, sleep and serve are like brothers. You don't find that in a factory. What we do is specialised. You can't simply transfer what you have learned from the army to civilian life. Jamie may struggle to make a living."

"And you, Jack, what about you? Is the army going to be your life? Will Griff grow up with a father living halfway around the world?"

I didn't answer for the simple reason that I had no answer.

The next day I walked Griff to school. I wore old clothes that did not mark me as a soldier. Griff was disappointed. My gait, however, told everyone what I was, a soldier. I chatted with Mr Myers. I liked that he greeted every child each morning. The prompt ones would be greeted with a smile but the tardy ones and their parents would be subjected to a withering glare.

"Griff, run along inside."

"Yes, Mr Myers. Will you be here to pick me up?"

I snapped a salute, "Of course, sir! Yes sir!"

Giggling my son ran off.

"Your son is gifted, Sergeant Major."

"It is Jack."

The teacher shook his head, "You have earned an honourable title and I respect both you and your uniform more than you can know." He nodded at another child who arrived and ticked their name off on the register. "Yes, your son devours knowledge like others do food. He grasps difficult concepts quickly and is so far ahead of others that he often helps those who are slower at such things. Even there he excels for he is both kind and patient. Those are rare qualities in one so young." He sighed, "If I had been granted a son I would hope for one like Griff." He smiled, "How long are you home for, Sergeant Major?"

I knew they meant well but each time the question was asked I felt as though they were trying to get rid of me. I knew it was not what they intended but that was the way it felt. "Three months."

"And then back to Africa." I nodded. "Can the Mahdists be defeated? When General Gordon was abandoned it caused great sadness here in England for he was a righteous and noble man."

"It was not the fault of the soldiers. We did all that we could to save him but we are directed by politicians. It was the policy of the Government that caused the fall of Khartoum but I am confident that we have the men to undo the work of these Dervishes if those in London have the will."

He held out his arm, "Let me shake your hand, Sergeant Major. Know that there are many of us in this great land who also thank you for your service. I only know what goes on because of what they write in newspapers and, as we all know, journalists have their own agendas. It is good to talk with someone who speaks the truth."

My aunt told Bill that I was home and that evening he sent a message via my aunt that the whole family was invited to his house for a Sunday lunch. I smiled at the wording of the invitation. It was as though Bill was the head of the family and not my younger brother. I did not mind. I was the one who had chosen to be absent. It would be good to see my sisters and their families too.

My mother and son insisted that I wear my uniform when we went to the suburbs to see my brother and his family. He lived in Walton, close to Stanley Park and so close to the countryside that you could see the farms. We had a bus ride and a walk to get to it. I smiled when Aunt Sarah told me that my brother had recently bought one of the new safety bicycles and he cycled into work each day. The house was not as grand as most of those we saw but it had a front and rear garden and stood alone. More importantly, it was quiet. One drawback was its semi-isolation and my two sisters, Alice and Sarah, had declined the invitation because their husbands both worked and they had young children. My mother decided to host a gathering at Aunt Sarah's before I returned to Africa.

Griff was delighted that there was a bell that you pulled. Billy looked prosperous when he opened the door with a fine waistcoat, watch and chain, good suit and now sporting a rather serious-looking moustache. I guessed we would be the only ones who called him Billy. William or Mr Roberts would be the more likely appellation. I saw why my mother had insisted upon the uniform. The clothes I had worn since returning home looked shabby by comparison.

"Jack, how splendid to see you." I grasped his hand and shook it as firmly as he did but I kept the smile from my face. He sounded twenty years older than I knew him to be. He looked down, "And Griffith, how you have grown."

Griff looked as though he did not know what to do and so I said, "Shake your Uncle Bill's hand."

Griff did so.

"Elizabeth is with Jack. Now that he is a toddler it takes her all her time to keep an eye on him and with the new baby just a couple of months away…"

My mother said, "Jack is home for three months. I could come and stay with you until the baby arrives."

He hugged my mother, "A kind offer and I will put it to Elizabeth." I noticed that he no longer called her Bet. The promotions had changed Billy. He put his arm around my shoulder, "It is a shame that Sarah and Alice could not make it, eh, brother, still, it will be cosy."

"You have a fine home, Billy."

"I thought when I bought it that I would struggle to make the repayments but my promotions now mean that I am one of the best-paid men in the company. The chairman took over the mortgage and made it a company loan. The rate of interest is quite low and the house will be ours five years from now." He leaned in, "I have some shares not only in our company but others and they bring in an income that is greater than the money Aunt Sarah earns." He frowned, "Best not to mention that, eh?" He ushered us towards the main room. I will get us some drinks while you greet my wife, eh?"

There was a large sitting room and the luxury of a dining room. It was not large and I reflected that if my sisters had come we would have struggled to fit. Elizabeth was in a nursing chair and Jack was playing with a puppet of some description. He saw Griff and squealed. He said something but I made out not a word. Griff didn't seem to mind and he squatted happily next to his cousin, the two of them playing as though it was the most natural thing in the world.

"Congratulations, Elizabeth."

She smiled, "It is still Bet." She shook her head, "Money and comfort have not changed me, Jack." I bent to kiss her on the cheek. "You look well. The African sun suits you. It is hot is it not?"

I nodded, "Unbearably so. You have to make your life function around it." She cocked her head to one side. "When you are able you stay indoors between noon and three. We soldiers do not have that luxury but we learn to adapt."

Aunt Sarah asked, "How?"

I shrugged, "We have a puggaree, a sort of cloth which goes around our helmet. We can use that to cover our faces. I sometimes use a keffiyeh, a cloth which can wrap around my helmet, neck and face. There are all sorts of tricks. Now that we are no longer constrained to wear red wool, life is easier."

Billy had re-entered, "I think that is a shame, Jack. The red tunic marks our soldiers as British."

I sighed, "And here in England, it is comfortable to wear but if you are trying to keep hidden from enemies it is more of a hindrance."

He handed me a glass of beer and gave glasses of what I took to be sherry to my mother and aunt, "But the British Army does not hide. We stand and fight."

I controlled my temper. On the train north, I had heard such views expressed by civilians who had not the first clue about war. He was spouting what he had read in the newspaper."

Aunt Sarah recognised the problem and she smiled and changed the subject, "You have made this a lovely home, Elizabeth."

She gave Billy a curious look and just said, "Oh, I try. I do miss working though. I enjoyed the company of the other girls."

"The wife of a senior manager does not work. You know, Aunt Sarah, that I am the only manager who does not have servants. It is too bad but Elizabeth does not want them. We could easily afford them. Still, it won't be for long before there will be huge changes."

The words jarred for the three of us and we all stared at my brother. He grinned, "I cannot contain it any longer. I intended to tell you when we dined but I shall tell you now." He paused and said, dramatically, "I am to run the African part of the company. The chairman himself said I was the perfect man for the job and young Mr. Hargreaves is very keen for me to go. He is the future of the company. I leave," he looked at me, "Well, around about the same time as you, Jack. I will get the house and servants sorted and then Elizabeth and the children will follow. Isn't this grand news?"

Elizabeth's face told its own story while my mother and her sister simply looked shocked. Aunt Sarah recovered first, "I knew that an office was being set up but I did not know an appointment had been made."

"It has all been done in secret, Aunt Sarah. The chairman did not want our competitors to get wind of it. There is a house for me in Alexandria and there will be an office in Suez." He nudged me with his elbow, "I shall need to pick your brains before you leave, Jack."

I shook my head, "Alexandria is not the place to bring up children, Billy, and Suez... it is perilously close to where there is danger."

"Nonsense. The chairman has been assured that Egypt is now British and as we hold the canal then it is important that there is an office there. I believe they have finished the railway line from Alexandria to Suez?" I nodded, "Well there you have it. When I need to visit the office in Suez, I shall catch the train." I could see that he was disappointed, and it was confirmed when he said, "I have to say I thought for a better reaction to my news. Your son, Mother, is rising like a star. Who knows where it will end? I can make my fortune there and when I return, I shall be rich beyond measure. I have spoken to others who worked for the East India Company, and they have told me of the bounty that can be made. A few years, while the children are too young to go to school, will see me rise even higher."

He did not see it. He had no concept of the danger in which he was putting his wife and children. I knew there were fine sections in Alexandria where other Europeans lived but Elizabeth would be largely on her own. I looked around the well-furnished home. Here she was alone too.

"And you cannot get out of this, Billy?" I was still the elder brother and I had advice to give.

"And why would I want to?"

"Because I have to be there as a soldier of the queen and I have no choice. You do."

His scowl told me that the conversation was ended.

There was a damper put on the whole visit. The food was delicious. Elizabeth was a good cook and both Jack and Griff behaved impeccably but my mother was upset and Billy seemed to think that it was all my fault. When we had finished the meal and the two of us went out for a smoke, I decided to clear the air.

"Billy, have you really thought all this through?"

He sucked on his cigar almost angrily. I waited for him to blow out the smoke and answer me, "I have, brother. We are no different you and me. You wear the uniform and fight with a gun. I wear this," he gestured to his suit, waistcoat and watch, "I fight, not with guns, swords and bullets but with money. We both serve England but do so in different ways. I know that life will be different in Egypt but we shall have advantages there that we do not have here. There will be a palatial house, servants, a tutor for the children and we shall be rubbing elbows not only with other merchants such as me but lords and their families. This is a step on the ladder to a better life."

I did not pick him up on the fact that if I failed I could lose my life. He would just lose money. "I do not think Elizabeth sees it the same way as you."

His face hardened, "She is my wife and she will see, eventually, that it is for the best."

"And Mother? Aunt Sarah?"

He turned and almost spat the words out, "You hypocrite. You chastise me for going abroad. You abandoned your son and rely on my mother to look after him and yet you have the gall to tell me off."

I felt my fingers clenching into fists. It took all my self-control to hold in check the desire to punch him hard. He was my little brother but he had stepped over the line. In that single moment, our relationship changed. I realised that people like Jamie and Middy were closer to me and the way I thought than my little brother.

"Very well." I tapped out the pipe and tucked it in my tunic pocket, "You want to know how to prepare for life in Egypt? Buy yourself a gun and learn how to use it. While you are in England buy cool and light clothes. Find a good solar topee. Acquire as many medicines as you can: quinine, antiseptics, and antacids. The food and the drink you will endure are totally different from what you are used to. Most of all, our Bill, realise that you are going to a completely different world."

He laughed and smiled, "If you can handle it then so can I, our Jack."

I did not think he was right. For one thing, I had not endured Africa alone. I had the regiment around me. For another, I knew who my enemies were. Jack was in the world of business and who knew what your enemies might do.

As we headed home the three of us were silent. Griff chattered away for he had been oblivious, as all children were, to the tensions in the house. Mother and Sarah had spoken with Elizabeth when I had been in the garden with Jack and I think they had plans in place. As they say, the best-laid plans …

Chapter 2

The visit to my brother effectively ruined my leave. He had planted unwelcome thoughts in my head. He was right, I was using Aunt Sarah and my mother. He also made me think about my mortality; I could live my life knowing that Griff was cared for but what would his life be like if something happened to me? Even though I smiled, laughed and was generally affable, especially with my family, inside, turmoil boiled within me.

When Griff was in school then my mother and I could discuss the problems my brother's decision had created. Of course, she would go to live with Elizabeth once Bill left for Africa and despite his words, he would be leaving before I did. That became clear within a couple of days of Aunt Sarah returning to work. She was to be retired. She was old enough but I knew that she was not ready. She had a month to work and then would retire with a small pension. It was less than a third of her pay and whilst that was far more than most received, she was not happy about it. She discovered, when she had the meeting, that it was Bill's doing. He would now be leaving England a fortnight before my leave was up and he wanted another in place at Walton and that would be my mother. My little brother had changed and was making his world suit him. Aunt Sarah's retirement would remove her presence from the office and ensure that Elizabeth had all the help she needed.

After Griff had gone to bed we sat and discussed the future. My mother was torn, "I cannot leave Elizabeth and two bairns on their own. I don't know how Billy can."

Aunt Sarah smiled less these days, "He has changed. I should have seen it but after he was promoted, two years since, I have had little contact with him. He has been seduced by the board. He is clever." She smiled at me and patted the back of my hand, "Not as clever as you, Jack, even though he thinks he is cleverer. He has learned to be ruthless. He had two girls sacked because they didn't meet his high standards. I think they are sending him there to make as much money for them as he can."

I lit my pipe. Mother said, "Poor Griff, when I go to Walton he will think I have abandoned him."

Aunt Sarah shook her head, "I have a month to work and then I shall be home. The one good thing about this untimely retirement is that I can spend more time with Griff. He will not be neglected, Jack, that I can promise."

"Perhaps I ought to get a transfer to a home depot."

Aunt Sarah shook her head, "And uproot, Griff? Take him to, God knows where? It is not fair on him, Jack. He likes the school. He has his friends and this is his home. I will be here for him." She patted my hand again, "And for you. Of course, if you left the army then you could be here for him but I don't think you are ready for that yet, are you?"

She knew me as well as anybody and I shook my head, "Not yet. I left a job half done and that is not my way."

When my sisters and their families came on Sunday, for lunch, we told them all. We had to. Bless them, they rallied around immediately. Alice and Sarah still lived in St Helens but the railway service meant they could get to Liverpool easier than getting to Walton, which needed a good walk.

Alice was practical, "Anyway, it is only for a few months until Bet can take the children and join Billy in Egypt."

I shook my head, "You have no idea of the journey. With two young children? It will be a nightmare."

Aunt Sarah said, "I hear that Billy has advertised for a nanny." We all looked at Sarah who shrugged, "He did not tell me but one of the typists from personnel had been asked to type out the advertisement."

"And then there is the house. What will they do with that?" My mother loved the house and could not understand why anyone would want to leave it.

"He will probably rent it out." Billy had told me that he would not lose money on the house and when his time abroad was over he would come back, sell it, and buy a bigger place. His ambition had not ended with Africa.

One effect of all this upheaval was that I became far closer to Griff. I made sure that every moment we had together was used well. The school holidays were approaching and I determined that we would take trips out. I planned to go to Southport and Formby where we could play on the beach and in the sea. I would take him to Chester and, perhaps, to Rhyl. A holiday was rare for most people but I had my pay and we had the time. Those days alone with Griff, for Aunt Sarah and my mother had to spend increasing amounts of time with Elizabeth, were joyous. I was able to teach him practical things. When we went to Formby I showed him how to make a windbreak to protect us from the wind. I had learned to do so in the desert. I taught him how to walk in the sand and even how to follow tracks. When we went to Chester I told him of the history of the place and how the Romans had used it. He was like a sponge and soaked up information so quickly that I could barely keep pace with him. I even taught him some Arabic and a little French. He had a natural ability with languages.

Little Victoria was born just a few days before Billy left for Africa. Mother and Aunt Sarah were with her at the time. Mother stayed on and when Aunt Sarah returned home she was seething. "He does not care about his family. He barely notices little Jack and all that concerns him is getting to Africa. He was prouder of the fact that he was being accommodated in a fine hotel in London and then another in Southampton before the ship took him to Alexandria than he was about his poor wife. She had a hard time."

"But mother and baby are well?"

"They are and the nanny that has been hired, Jane, seems competent, although a little young in my view."

I got to see all of them a few days later. It was the day that Billy left. He had a trunk packed and a hansom cab was there to take him to the station. Unlike me, he was travelling first class and would have a couple of nights in London where the chairman of the parent company would wine and dine him. Billy had changed. As he climbed into the hansom cab he gave a perfunctory wave and was gone.

The last week before my leave was over I did not sleep much. I was worrying not only about Griff, my mother and Aunt Sarah but also about Elizabeth and her children. I liked Bet and she did not deserve this. Jane was a help but I was not sure how the young girl would cope in Africa, how any of the four of them would cope. I said my farewells to Bet two days before I left. It would also be when I said goodbye to Mother.

Bet was a little healthier now than she had been after the birth and was no longer bed-bound. She held my hand, "Jack, if you are able then I would have you visit me in Alexandria." She said the words as though she was talking about a hospital or madhouse.

"Of course, but I am a serving soldier and…"

She squeezed my fingers, "Jack you are a good man. I know that you will try and that is enough for me."

I smiled, "Then I am at your command. Do you have the address?"

She had already written it out in that incredibly neat hand of hers. She handed it to me. "And if you can, keep an eye on Bill. This is a temporary madness. Money and power have not changed him, not really. I believe that underneath it he is still the same man I married and Jack and Victoria are the embodiment of the man he was."

The night before I left, after Griff had helped me to pack, I tucked him up in the bed he now occupied alone. "It will be strange to have you leave again for I have enjoyed all that we have done and Nan, I miss her."

"It will not be for long, Griff. When Aunt Bet goes to Alexandria, she will be home and you have Aunt Sarah."

He nodded, "Aunt Sarah is very strict."

I knew that already from my mother but since she had retired from work she had mellowed. Perhaps she saw traits in Billy for which she blamed herself. I just knew that she seemed a little gentler with Griff and did not push him as hard.

The train I would take left on Saturday morning. It was early but Aunt Sarah and Griff insisted on seeing me off. It was a fast four-hour train and that was important. I had left my departure as late as possible. I should, really, have left the day before to ensure that I would not be absent without leave but I gambled that the train would be on time and there would be no delays. The London train was already waiting at the station and I found an empty compartment and hurled my bag inside. I kissed and hugged Aunt Sarah and, as the guard blew his whistle, squeezed Griff so tightly that he moaned. "I love you, son, and I will get back to you as soon as I can."

"I know, Dad, but take care, eh? I don't want to lose you. This world is not the place to be alone."

"Get aboard Sergeant Major, eh?"

The guard said it in a kindly manner but it hurt to release Griff and get into the train. The door slammed as Aunt Sarah put her arm around my son. I wanted to say more but feared to do so. I did not want my voice to break. I saw the tears welling in Aunt Sarah's eyes and I just saluted. Griff snapped his heels together and saluted back. The train chug chugged its way from the station. I was going back to war.

It was late afternoon when I reached Southampton. I made my way to the dock. There was a troopship leaving the next day and provosts were patrolling the dock. A corporal was checking names and allocating berths. He found my name. "The East Sudanese Exploration Group, Sergeant Major? That is a new one for me. Oh, hang on, there are two more of your lot aboard, A Major Dickenson and a Private Richardson." He nodded to my medals as he ticked my name, "I can see you have done your bit already."

"Berth?"

He wrote the number on a slip of paper and I hefted my bag on my shoulder and strode towards the troopship. Most were bound for India but there would be replacements aboard for units in Egypt. There would be ones like me who would serve with the Egyptian army and receive a promotion. The risks of serving in Africa were outweighed by the pay and promotion which would give a better pension. They had given me a two-berth cabin and I guessed that I would be sharing with Syd. I hoped so. I got on with most blokes but the East Sudanese Exploration Group was a tight little unit. I was comfortable with Syd.

I went on deck to watch the loading. I would be saying farewell to England for... I knew not how long. Syd barely made the ship. I saw the figure racing towards the hut in which sat the corporal with the list. Stevedores were standing by the hawsers that tied us to the land. The tide waited for no man and as soon as Syd had raced up the gangplank it was removed and the hawsers released. I waited at the tumblehome, "Nearly absent without leave, Trooper."

He grinned and saluted, "Bloody signals at Newark nearly did for me. I should have been here more than an hour ago, Sergeant Major, but I missed my connection. I had to run." He held up the slip of paper, "Where is this, Sarn't Major?"

"You are sharing with me."

He looked surprised, "NCO sharing with Other Ranks?"

A familiar voice behind us said, "Yes, Lance Corporal Richardson, as you know we do things differently in the East Sudanese Exploration Group."

We turned and saluted Major Dickenson. "Sir." I took in what he had said. "Lance Corporal, sir?"

He nodded, "We are a bigger unit than when you left." He looked at his watch. "Dinner is in an hour. What say I meet you two by the stern and we can have a chin wag?"

"Sir." He strode away to the officers' section of the ship. We descended into the bowels. The porthole we had would barely afford us any light while the major would enjoy a much larger one on the main deck. Such were the privileges of rank.

"Congratulations, Richardson."

He grinned, "I won't lie, Sarn't Major, the pay will be welcome." As we entered the cabin and he began to unpack he suddenly stopped, "Jamie? Where is he?"

I thought back to my conversation with the corporal. "His name was not on the list. Perhaps he is still recovering."

Neither of us believed that for a moment but until we knew otherwise, we would deceive ourselves. This was a troopship and, as we entered the English Channel, the bugle blew to summon us to the mess. There were three for rank was all. The officers enjoyed the smallest one and the best service but the one for the NCOs was also intimate. The one for the other ranks was huge. The steward, a small man from the Catering Corps looked contemptuously at Syd as we neared the entrance, "Other Ranks are on the deck below."

I snapped, "Lance Corporal Richardson has not had time to sew on his stripe." I leaned forward to the weasel of a man, "I take it my word is good enough?"

"Yes, Sergeant Major." He waved an arm and we swept in.

The food was good but then again we had just left Southampton. The quality would deteriorate as we headed south.

24

The best that we could hope for would be that we would take on fresh provisions at Gibraltar. Billy would have had a more luxurious diet and accommodation. His was not a troopship but a liner. Whilst he would disembark at Alexandria there would be others heading through the Suez Canal to go to the antipodes and the Indian sub-continent. Victoria's Empire was huge. I did not know anyone other than Syd in the mess but that was no surprise. As far as I was aware the 24th battalions were not heading to either Egypt or Sudan. As we entered the mess I saw curious looks at the medal ribbons on my chest. Most of those on board had none yet. Syd and I were the veterans.

"How was your leave?"

Syd shrugged, "I forgot that as well as seeing my family I would be likely to bump into her. I did." He grinned, "The bastard she left me for has lost his good looks. Broken teeth do that. I don't think I will bother going home again. My parents are more concerned with my brothers and their family. I left home…" he shrugged, "I am forgotten. And you?"

I would not spill family secrets and I just said, "Good to see my son, my mother and my aunt. It was interesting." He gave me a look that invited more information but I kept a straight face.

When we finished, we went aft for a smoke. I suspected that there was wine and the like in the officers' mess as the major did not appear until I had finished my first pipeful. From his rolling gait, I assumed he had drunk well. He had that rosy glow that comes from a glass of port too many.

"Ah, comrades! A good leave I hope?"

We gave the only answer we could, "Yes, sir."

He had a cigar in his fingers. It had gone out. "Have you a light, Sergeant Major?"

"Yes, sir." I lit it for him.

"I only had a month's leave but I am ready to get back. I miss Fort Desolation."

I smiled, "Then we are still based there, sir?"

"We are but you will see some changes since you were there. We have twenty troopers and Colonel Kitchener found us some Sudanese soldiers to act as cooks and do sentry duty. Life is much easier than it was."

"Coupe, sir?" I had to ask the question.

He shook his head, "The doctors said he would be crippled and could not serve. There was a time that might not have made a difference but since the reforms, we have to look after every soldier."

"I bet Jamie wouldn't see it that way."

He nodded, "Prescient of you, Sergeant Major. He appealed. That is why I was given leave. He asked for me to make a case. I tried but failed. He is honourably discharged and will have a pension."

I said nothing but knew that this could be the breaking of Jamie. Riding and the life of a soldier were all he wanted. But he was left with nothing.

"And Lieutenant Hardy has taken a promotion to serve in the Egyptian army. He is now a captain."

Syd asked, "Do we have another officer then, sir?"

"Not yet." He nodded to me, "You and I will box and cox, Sergeant Major, until we find a replacement. The men you left are busy training the replacements. Smith was promoted to sergeant." He looked at me, "Your recommendation, Sergeant Major."

I nodded, "Yes sir."

"Dunn has been confirmed as a corporal and the others, like you, Richardson, are lance corporals."

My pipe had gone out and I tapped the ash over the stern before slipping it into my breast pocket. "And our role, sir, has that changed?"

"Colonel Kitchener is keen for us to become as familiar with the border as we can. He sees a time when the Government will have to retake Sudan if only to protect the Suez Canal and Egypt. The original squad are the experts and the new boys are real novices. By the end of the year, they should be fully trained and next year... We shall see." He stretched, "I enjoyed our little chat. It will take us two weeks to make the voyage, what say you that we meet here after dinner each night?

As I lay in my bunk that night, comforted by the sway of the sea, I drifted off to sleep but with a mind filled with turmoil. I wondered if the major had been the right man to make the case for Jamie. I dismissed the idea immediately. He was an officer and even had I been summoned I doubt that my words would have held much sway. Was Jamie a foretaste of my future? Would I be discarded if I had an injury that might prevent me from earning a crust for my family? Perhaps I should get out before that happened. I could not see any job for which I was suited but I was hard-working and for my family, I would do anything.

I got off to sleep quite quickly but was haunted by dreams, not of me or Griff but of Elizabeth and her children. The result was that I woke early. Syd was still snoring and so I dressed myself in my off-duty khaki and headed to the deck. The messes were just being prepared for breakfast so I took a turn around the pitching deck. The Atlantic was never benign but the waves from the west were not as big as I had seen them. I was greeted by the crew. The ship regularly made the run and the crewmen were as tanned as I was. They recognised that I had served in Africa and that bonded us a little. I chatted with a couple and took the opportunity to ask about other ships that might make the run. It turned out that despite his first-class transport, Billy would not make the run any faster. All the steamships travelled at about the same speed, ten knots. I don't know why but that made me feel slightly better. That, and the walk around the deck, gave me an appetite and when I passed the mess I saw that they were almost ready to serve. I went to the cabin where Syd had risen and was dressing.

"If you get a move on, we can be there when they open."

That was enough to encourage Syd to finish dressing. First in the queue meant hotter food, tea and a choice of seat. We arrived just in time and walked in, picked up our trays and had hot bacon, eggs, sausage and black pudding placed on our plates. With freshly baked bread and a mug of steaming tea, I doubted that even Billy would have enjoyed a better breakfast. We ate alone for the others who arrived early chose other tables and we left before the mess had begun to fill up.

We had days to fill and Syd asked, "What is the plan, Sarn't Major?" On previous voyages we had been tasked with learning Arabic, studying maps and training new men. We had none of that to do. I had thought out a plan on the journey south to London. "I thought a smoke while it is quiet and then enough laps of the ship to give us five miles of exercise." He nodded at the wisdom of that. A three-month leave and a wound had left us both a little unfit. "Then I have a book I would like to read until lunch. The same after lunch. We have to keep active."

Syd and I were of the same mind. There would be card and dice schools where men would win and lose small fortunes and they could lead to fights. Others would take solace in gin, rum and brandy. All three could be purchased from members of the crew who knew how to profit from soldiers. Soldiers liked to drink.

"What is the book?"

"It is called '*The Coral Island*' and I read it to my son but he had almost finished it when I got home. I know the end and I would like to read the beginning." Griff had enjoyed the book so much that he wanted me to share the same experience and read of an adventure. I had bought him the new book '*Treasure Island*'. We had only managed one chapter before I left. I had bought myself a second copy in the bookshop in Liverpool. I wanted to be able to share the book, albeit remotely, with Griff.

The pattern was set. Each night we would speak with the major. The first night was the one where he had imbibed the most. He confided in the two of us both his and Colonel Kitchener's plans. Over the course of the voyage, we learned that the Mahdists, now that the Mahdi himself was dead, were beleaguered from the south and west by the Belgians and the French and from the east by the Italians but that the only successes came from us in the north, using the reorganised Egyptian army. With British officers and NCOs, it was a formidable force.

"Still, it will take British soldiers to defeat them and give Sudan some stability. Our job is to become as familiar with the desert as we can. We made a good start at Fort Desolation and the colonel wants to increase our numbers." He chuckled, "He has little time for the red tape of the war office and uses his position at Suakim to divert some of the funds from there to pay for the fort, the soldiers and the supplies."

I suddenly became worried when the major mentioned that, "Sir, we are still part of the British Army, aren't we? I mean I know I served briefly with the Egyptian Army, but I want to go back to England one day."

He smiled, "We are. Let us just say that the colonel is a clever man and knows how to use figures to confuse the bean counters at Horse Guards."

We were both relieved. I was almost thirty-three and whilst I did not feel old I knew that I had another seven years or so of service before I could think of going home. I wanted to have earned as much money as I could by then and if I could rise to Regimental Sergeant Major then I would have a much better pension. I knew that our unit would never be a regiment. At the moment we were little better than a troop.

We learned that the colonel planned on expanding our numbers until there were a hundred of us. Trained by him and speaking fluent Arabic we would be the edge that the British army needed to defeat the masters of the desert, the Dervishes. He had also earned the new title of Pasha. It was a title from the Ottoman Empire, and I had no idea of its equivalent in the British Army but the major seemed impressed.

As Alexandria hove into view, I wondered if I had the time to find Billy. Almost as soon as the thought crept into my mind, I dismissed it. The major would want to take a train to Suez as soon as he could and I had no idea where the offices would be. Billy had made his bed and he would have to lie in it.

When I had first come to Egypt the railway had been in its formative state. It was still run by army engineers, but it was a much more cohesive network and ran with remarkable efficiency. The journey was unbearably hot and my desert kit was still at the fort. We suffered on the train. At Suez, we took the small steamship that kept the outpost at Suakim supplied. At least in the Red Sea we had a cooling breeze and we chugged our way south. It took five days to cover the eight hundred miles. Even when we docked we were not home.

While I sought our transport, the major went into the office of the garrison. When we had first come to Suakim it had been Colonel Kitchener and a handful of men who were the military presence. Now there was half a battalion of loyal Sudanese with British officers. The commander was a colonel but as it was of a Sudanese squadron he and the major were of the same rank. Syd and I headed for the stables. Colonel Kitchener was a very organised man and there were four camels waiting for us. The sergeant was English. He looked very young to be that rank but I guessed he saw a better chance of promotion that way. I had.

"There are new uniforms waiting in the QM's office, Sergeant Major, and the Lee Metford carbines that are being issued."

I frowned, "Lee Metford?"

"The army, the regulars I mean, have been issued with the Lee Metford rifle. It has a five-shot magazine. The carbine does too. They say they are developing an eight-shot one, imagine that?"

I nodded. By regulars, he meant the British army. "Is it any good?"

"Hard to say, Sergeant Major, we have not had time to use them for any length of time. They fire a .303 and the magazine makes loading easier but..." Like every soldier, we liked what we knew and were wary of innovations, "there is a rumour we are getting new sword bayonets too."

That would not affect us much. We rarely used them. I had a sword I had taken in battle and I would use that. My weapons were, I hoped, still in the fort. As the senior NCO, I had my own room, my haven.

The major having received his written orders, we headed along the caravan road to Fort Desolation. When we had first travelled there it had taken three days. With just three of us, it took two although my rump had to readjust to riding and a camel who was not as gentle as Aisha. I was pleased that the new men I would be leading did not see the discomfort of their sergeant major.

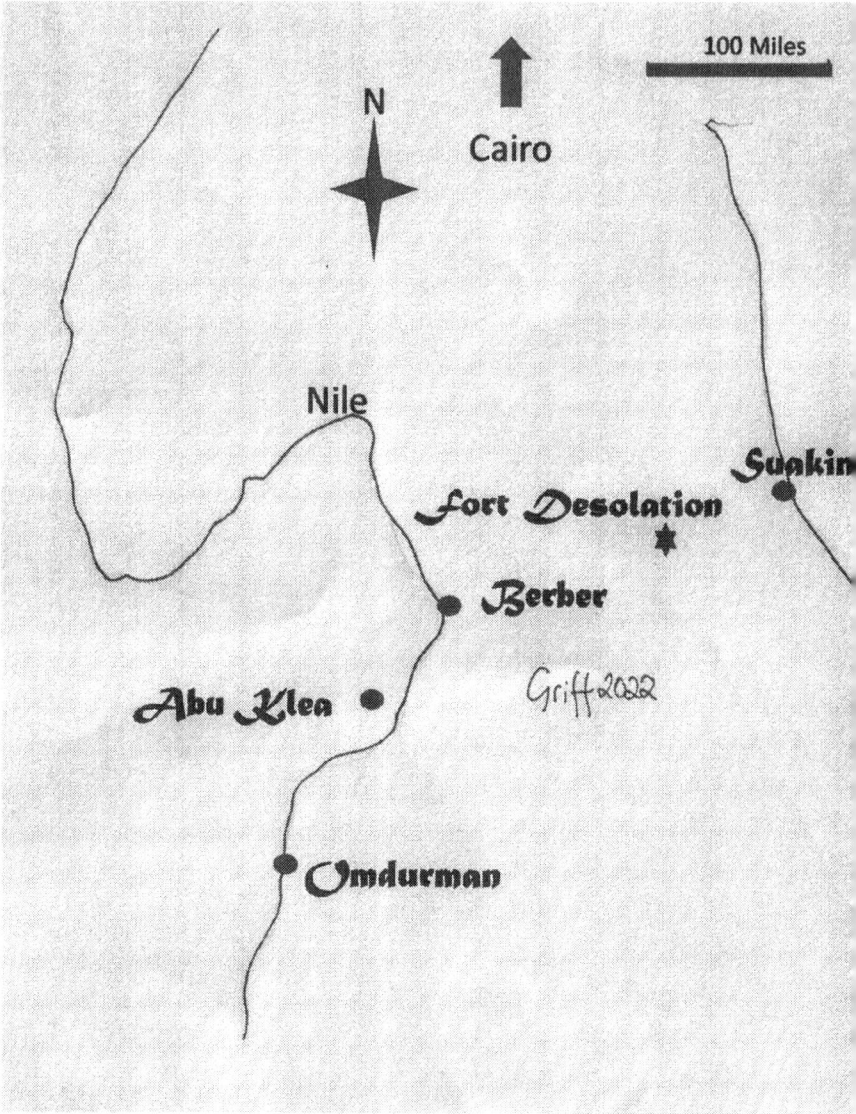

Chapter 3

There was so little green on the caravan route to Berber that even without the mud walls of the fort, it would have stood out just for the handful of palm trees and scrubby growth that marked the oasis. One of the first things we noticed when we arrived was that the only Sudanese who did not travel the desert with their herds of animals were the ones who clung to the precarious farms on the odd oasis. The flag flew from the old fort and there were sentries on the walls. They were harder to see because they wore khaki now but their presence was reassuring. The fort had been built close to a small oasis. It must have been fed from an underground spring for it was kept refilled and so long as it was not overused never dried up. It lay just a hundred feet from the walls of the square fort. The mud walls were old but we had repaired them. The tower, which had been in danger of falling down was now fully functional and the Union Flag, as well as the flag of Egypt, fluttered from it in the slight breeze. It felt like a place we could defend.

Saeed waved from the gatehouse. He was officer of the day. He had been a lieutenant in the Egyptian army but he had accepted Colonel Kitchener's offer to join our unit as a sergeant. The major knew that Sam Smith could cope running the fort so long as Saeed was with him. As we entered the fort, I could not help but notice how clean and organised everything looked. Before I had left we had made improvements but in the four months I had been away it had been transformed into a proper British outpost.

As we dismounted the newly promoted Sergeant Smith snapped a smart salute, "Good to have you back sir, you too Sarn't Major."

The major and I returned the salute, "And the fort, Sergeant?"

"I did as you ordered, sir. We kept the land four hundred yards from the walls closely inspected each day and we watched the caravan route. Other than that we just trained the new boys."

His report was delivered concisely and in the approved manner but I detected criticism beneath Sam's words. They were the ones I would have made too. The men could not be properly trained inside the fort. They needed to be out in the desert. Each trip I had made on Aisha had made me a better soldier and, as I looked at the new men, keen to see their Sergeant Major, I could see the inexperience etched all over their faces. The very nature of our unit meant that we had volunteers. Old hands liked the comfort of their own regiments and officers. It was the young and the adventurous who joined us.

The major nodded and looked at the sun. It would be dark within the hour. Sunset came far quicker here in Africa than it did in England. It was as though someone had turned off a gas mantle. "We will clean up and then, after we have eaten, I will hold an officer's call with the NCOs." He took a bottle of brandy from his saddle bags. "I can tell you our orders and then we can celebrate the return of our friends."

I could see that the rest of the original unit were keen to speak to Syd and so, after handing the reins of the camels to a waiting Sudanese private, I said, "Have the animals stabled. There are weapons and uniforms. Take them all to the Quarter Master's stores but don't unpack them."

"Yes, Sergeant Major."

I looked at the major, "We still have to decide who is to be the QM, sir."

"I know. It is on my agenda." He smiled and waved an expansive hand, "Good to be back, Sergeant Major?"

I snapped to attention, "Of course, Major." The truth was I did not know how I really felt. Billy's decision had upset the routine of my life. As much as I tried to hide it in the recesses of my mind, like a relentless spider it would emerge when I least expected and spin the cobwebs that confused me.

I had hefted my kitbag from the back of the camel and I headed for my room. It was as I had left it the day I went on the fateful patrol that had almost ended my life. Someone, probably Saeed, had kept it dusted and cleaned; the desert was constantly trying to reclaim the fort. I saw that my Martini-Henry and Remington, not to mention my pistol had been cleaned and oiled. I ran my finger along the firing mechanism, it had been done recently. I unpacked. Unlike the rest of the men who had foot lockers, I was like the major. I had a wardrobe and I hung my clothes up. I put my forage cap on the shelf and took down the helmet. It had been repaired while I had been away but just looking at it brought back the memory of the desperate fight with the Dervishes. My sword hung from its frog and I did not bother to test the edge. Like the rest of my equipment, it would have been sharpened and oiled.

I changed into an older uniform. I would need to wash my other for the journey from Alexandria had been a long one. Even as I took it off clouds of dust and desert dropped to the floor. I frowned. What had been clean a moment ago was now sullied. Such was life in the outpost. You never had a chance to be bored for you had to work just to maintain the status quo.

Colonel Kitchener ensured that the fort was regularly supplied. Its position was vital for the peaceful passage of the caravans. Suakim was the only British outpost for hundreds of miles and Fort Desolation was the last marker of the empire in this part of the world. Britain might have lost the Sudan but Kitchener was telling the Mahdists that it would only be a temporary loss. The smell of food drew me to the mess even before the bugle sounded. We were too small for separate messes and we all messed together. Before I had left we had all eaten at one table. Now there were three but one, the largest, was reserved for officers and NCOs. It was laid out with cutlery and metal plates. Syd and Sam were there already and they half rose as I approached.

"None of that, eh lads? Let us save that for the parade ground." They sat and I said to Sam, "Well-deserved promotion, congratulations."

"The major said you recommended it, Sarn't Major, thanks. The pay and the pension will come in handy."

Some of the other members of the unit had entered and I nodded to them, "What are they like?"

He smiled, "The usual. Some of them think that they are here to win glory and fame. There are a couple who are hiding here, and I don't know why yet but most are just like Jamie was, desperate for some action."

Just then Corporal Dunn came in. He had been a Midshipman who was always seasick. He was natural officer material and I hoped that we could win him a promotion. As a navigator, he was the best in this part of the world and could navigate across the desert sea by day or night. He beamed when he saw me, "Sergeant Major, welcome back."

"And how have you been, Middy?"

"Just waiting for your return, Sergeant Major. We have been cooling our heels in this oven since you left. As soon as we heard you were coming back we knew that patrols would resume."

I looked at Sam, "You haven't been out since…"

He nodded, "Aye, not since the lads bought it. To be honest we couldn't, not until these lads arrived and they have been too green to let loose."

"And are they ready now?"

The two of them looked at each other and I saw doubt on their faces. Sam sighed, "Probably, I mean, we have done our best and Saeed has worked like a Trojan, but you know how it is, Sergeant Major, out there the desert shimmers and changes in a heartbeat. One mistake and…"

He left unsaid that it had been Lieutenant Hardy's mistake that had cost our friends their lives. He was a good officer but had not been on as many patrols as we had.

The bugle sounded and, led by the major, the rest of the NCOs entered, followed by the rest of the troop. The grins from the last of the originals made me smile. Everyone stood to attention until the major sat. We all sat. I was about to head to the dixies to collect my food when Sam said, "We have orderlies now to do that." He gestured at the Egyptian orderlies who were bringing the dixies, "There are twenty men who act as the garrison and serve us food. They have a sergeant in command and Saeed keeps them straight."

As though on cue, the former Egyptian officer entered. He smiled apologetically to the major, "Sorry, sir, one of the sentries reported seeing a horseman. Mohammed has good eyes and I rode out to investigate."

"Alone?"

"I was within sight of the fort the whole time, sir. He was right. I found fresh dung."

The major nodded, "Then it seems that we have arrived back at the right time. Let us eat first and then we can talk."

The food was good but the influence of the Egyptians was manifest in the taste. It was spiced a little more than we were used to and also had fruits in it. It was a good taste but it was different. That alone told me that I was back in the Sudan. I listened more than I spoke as news and gossip was exchanged. The other four originals had not been home for a long time and Syd was able to tell them what England was like. I confess that I was studying the new men at the other tables.

I said to the major, "Are they all from cavalry regiments?"

He shook his head, "Half of the men are like you, from infantry regiments. Saeed has been working with them to make them able to ride."

"It would be easier on horses, sir."

He nodded, "I know but the desert is easier when you ride a camel. You know that, Jack." This was the mess, and I liked the slight informality. Eventually, Sam and the others would revert to 'Jack', when we ate. I discovered that we now had a bugler, Bill Brown. Jamie had been the bugler and we needed someone to give the commands in the heat of battle. A small patrol did not need a bugle but a troop did.

When the food was finished, we smoked and the major brought out his bottle. He turned to me. The orderlies had cleared the table. I stood. As soon as I did the mess fell silent, "Right lads, we have a busy day tomorrow so those who are not on duty tonight, off you trot. Tomorrow I shall get to know some of you a little better." I waited until they had stood and left before I sat.

Major Dickenson said, "Who is on duty tonight?"

Jake said, "Me sir."

The major poured out a glass for each of us. "Here's to those who fell. We shall not forget them."

We stood and raised the glasses in the air. "To Danny, Tom and Harry."

We sat and the silence was imposed by each of us as we remembered the three men who had died.

"Right, first things first. We need a Quarter Master and an armourer. Poulter, you are QM."

"Sir."

"Johnson, armourer. We have some new carbines but before they are issued, I want you to be familiar with them. You will not be on patrol tomorrow, and neither will you, Poulter. Have the new guns and uniforms unpacked. Whenever you need to, Johnson, just leave and do your duty."

He nodded, "I will sir, but first I will savour this brandy. Nights are cold here in the desert."

The major nodded, "Right then let us get down to it. The colonel is keen for us to press the Mahdists. He wants this enclave to be a place that they fear. The sergeant here," he gestured to Saeed, "has found evidence that needs investigation. Tomorrow, I want you, Sergeant Major, to take Sergeant Saeed, Corporal Dunn and ten of the new men. Investigate the rider and the land for ten miles to the north and south."

I looked at him, "That is a long patrol, sir."

He nodded, "Aisha has not been used since you left. She needs the exercise, and this unit has been idle for long enough." He leaned in, "Push the new men, Sergeant Major, and find what they can do. By the end of the year, we will be doubled in size." I nodded. "I will take Sergeant Smith and the other new men the day after. Poulter and Johnson can come with me. We will have one day of rest and then repeat. Colonel Kitchener wants aggressive patrols. Let us give them to him."

When the brandy was finished the major retired and that left me with the others. We would be able to talk. "Saeed, what is your opinion on the situation?"

"The ones who took over from the Mahdi are not as good as he was but no one has taken direct control. The Khalifa Abdallahi is the most powerful figure but that is because of his tribe, the Ta'aisha. So long as he has their support then he controls the land around Omdurman?"

"Not Khartoum?"

He shook his head, "That has been abandoned. Omdurman is across the Nile from Khartoum. They think that Khartoum has Gordon's ghost. The Mahdi thought that the general's death was a mistake."

I nodded and looked around the table. These men were as solid a group of leaders as I had ever known. They reminded me of Hooky, Cole and the others in the 24th but then we had a whole battalion. Here we had the smallest unit I had ever known. "It seems to me that we must become the eyes and ears. I cannot see us being able to fight off a Dervish army. Remember the last patrol to Berber?" The ones who had been on the patrol nodded. "We were seen off by less than fifty men. We have to train the men to ride hard and fast. They must use the skills of discipline and order." It was not mentioned but Lieutenant Hardy had clearly not displayed those qualities. I stood and pointed towards my quarters, "I am just behind that door. If you need to talk, to question, to doubt, that is where you do it. To me and no one else. Understand?" They all nodded. "You can moan all you like to me and I promise that it will go no further. Goodnight. See you in the morning."

I slept but it was a troubled sleep. The trip down the coast had shown me just how isolated we were. My body was now set to life in Africa, and I rose well before dawn while the night watch walked the ancient mud walls. The cooks had yet to light the fires under the food. I lit the oil lamp and dressed. My cosy chamber meant I had everything organised and to hand. I had cleaned all three weapons the night before. It was habit more than anything. The sword I had sharpened on the grindstone as I had my knives but it had not been really necessary. It was all part of the process of preparation to rejoin the unit. With my pouches filled with bullets, I donned my Sam Brown belt. I put my helmet under my arm and my cloak and keffiyeh over my shoulder and left the chamber. Outside it was still blissfully cool and it was there I donned my helmet and went to the stables. I had seen Aisha the day before. She had been well cared for but I could see that she needed exercise. I stroked her and gave her a treat then I saddled her and led her to the water trough. One of the duties of the garrison was to keep it filled up. As she drank, I draped my cloak and keffiyeh over her back and, when she was satiated led her back to the stables and tethered her. The smell of the fire told me that the cooks were up and about. I saw Sergeant Abdul emerge from the barracks and seeing me, he ran over.

"Good morning, Sergeant Major."

"Good morning, Sergeant. Today I want the ditch clearing of rubbish and the sides sharpening." My experienced eye had spotted the weeds that were clinging to the side of the ditch. In the grand scheme of things it was not much to worry about but the work would keep the men occupied and remind them that it was a fort and that fort needed to be defended.

"Yes, Sergeant Major."

I smiled, "We will soon get to know one another and if there is anything of which I do not approve, Sergeant, then you will be the first to know."

He nodded, "Yes, Sergeant Major."

"I take it they will have a brew on?" I gestured to the cookhouse.

Grinning he said, "Always, Sergeant Major."

"Good. Then let us have the first mugs."

Colonel Kitchener was well aware that the Egyptians who fought alongside us were Muslims and in deference to their religion, we did not eat ham. I had noticed chickens and knew that we would have eggs. The meat that would be fried would be dried goat or lamb. I was never keen on that and so, with the mug of tea in my hand I went to look at the porridge. It was being stirred by one of the cooks. The chief cook stood by nervously.

I said, "We have honey and dried fruits?"

"Yes, effendi."

"Sergeant Major will do. Make sure we have plenty and if we look to be running out let me know. The men need the fruit." I pointed to the table I would use, "Fetch me a bowl when it is ready."

Abdul brought his tea over and we sat in companionable silence. I would have loved a pipe of tobacco, but I was disciplined. Here at the fort, I would restrict myself to a welcome one after we had eaten. The tea was perfect. Sam had trained the cooks well in my absence. Soldiers who went on patrol after drinking a decent couple of mugs of tea were happier soldiers. We were like camels with their humps. We stored the tea to keep us going during the day.

"Tell me about the men."

He frowned and cocked an eye, "Sergeant Major?"

"Start with you, your background and your experience."

"Ah," realisation filled his face, "we were part of a battalion that was badly handled by the Dervishes at Alt Klea. The men here held when the others broke and ran. We were going to be disbanded and sent to other battalions but the Pasha, Colonel Kitchener, decided that we should be rewarded for our courage and he seconded us to his command at Suakim. We were part of the garrison protecting the port. Two months ago we were sent here." He smiled, "This is the last outpost and we see it as an honour." He seemed to anticipate my next question for he answered it while it was still forming in my head, "We have not fired our guns in anger since Alt Klea but we practise every day.".

I nodded, "The Martini-Henry?"

"Yes, Sergeant Major. Sergeant Smith says you use one."

"I do. It is a good weapon. Not the fastest rifle but an accurate one."

The bugler appeared at the mess and looked at Sergeant Abdul. He, in turn, looked at me and I said, "You are the officer of the night watch, Sergeant."

The sergeant gave a signal and the bugle sounded. The day at Fort Desolation was beginning.

I was more than a little nervous as Middy and I led the patrol from the fort. The gates slammed ominously behind us. Saeed was at the rear having identified for me the place he had seen the Dervish. Middy, Saeed and I all looked more like Arabs than the rest of the troop. They would learn. They had their neck cloths in place but their puggarees were still wrapped around their helmets. Middy, Saeed and I had ours around our faces and wore keffiyeh wrapped around our helmets and necks. Our eyes were the only exposed part and the brim of the helmet afforded them some protection from the glare of the sun and sand. Middy was the finest navigator I had ever met and he would lead us to the place identified by Saeed. We rode in silence. In the desert sounds carried a long way. Middy led us across the sand where he could so that the camel's feet did not make a noise. Rocks were also a dangerous place to cross. They might hide our tracks but animals could slip. Better to ride through sand or what passed for soil. The one piece of equipment we did not have was goggles to protect our eyes from the glare of the sun and the desert sand. When we had been in Suakim we were told they were on their way.

We had ridden for an hour when Middy pointed. I saw the stand of straggly palm trees struggling for life. We were three miles north of the caravan route to Berber. I held my hand up and we stopped. I waved it and Saeed rode up to join us. I could see no signs of life but that meant nothing.

"Sergeant, take four men and ride in a wide loop around the oasis."

"Yes, Sergeant Major. You four come with me."

The four men he selected wheeled and followed him north and east.

"Middy, we will approach from the west and south. Nice and slow. eh?"

"Yes, Sergeant Major." He turned in the saddle and said, "Be ready to draw your carbines and listen for the orders."

I could not help smiling. The diffident ex-sailor had grown into his role and command came easily to him now.

I kept my eye on the oasis for movement. It would take some time for Saeed to work into position. The dried-up river bed we were following would keep us hidden but I would be able to detect anyone who was moving in the oasis. There was no breeze and all was still. The palms hung limply. Middy looked at me for confirmation to turn when the wadi turned south. I nodded and our camels climbed up the shallow bank. As soon as we reached the top I saw that we were less than four hundred paces from the oasis and I saw, as soon as we reached level ground that there were watchers and they had seen, not us, but Sergeant Saeed and his four men. I was drawing my Remington even as the three riders galloped from the oasis. They were riding camels and, unlike ours, they had rested. However, ours were moving and I urged Aisha on. She was the best camel we had and soon had extended a lead over Middy. The troopers, new to this, were even further behind. I mentally made a note to do more training. Their riding skills had clearly been neglected. I realised that the Remington was the wrong choice and, after sheathing my carbine, I drew my longer Martini-Henry.

One advantage we had was that Saeed and his men were approaching from the north and we were from the south. The Dervishes, and I saw the patches on their cloaks identifying them, had to keep going in a straight line. Any obstacle would force them to turn towards one or the other of us. We were gaining although once their animals were up to speed then that lead would stay the same. A camel is a fast animal but it is not a platform for firing a weapon. The carbine's range was shorter than a rifle and the bouncing back of a camel would simply waste a bullet. The Martini-Henry was a breech-loader and I would wait until I had a clear shot before I fired.

It was the wadi we had used that came to our aid. We had left it when it had turned south but the Dervishes had to cross it. They had three choices: cross and continue heading west, turn north up the wadi or head south down the wadi. Either of the latter choices would bring them closer to us and they chose to try to clamber up the other bank. We were less than two hundred yards behind them and I stopped twenty yards shy of the wadi. Even as I rested my forearm on Aisha's back I shouted, "Keep after them, Corporal." I had trained Aisha to be still and she was. I aimed at the leading Dervish and, as he reached the top, fired. The .303 slammed into his back. He was holding tightly to the reins and my bullet must have killed him instantly for, as he fell he jerked the camel's head. The animal was fighting to keep its feet but gravity took over and it tumbled back into the wadi. It knocked the second camel to the side and the third Dervish had to turn to the right.

I chambered another bullet into the breech and then urged Aisha on. Middy knew we needed prisoners and the two Dervishes were not going to escape. Unfortunately, the troopers did not wait for the command and their Remingtons barked as soon as they reached the wadi. Even novices such as the new troopers could not miss and the two Dervishes died. I mentally cursed.

Sergeant Saeed and his men reached the bodies first and Saeed secured the two camels whose riders had been killed. The first camel had fallen awkwardly and I could see that its neck was broken. When we reached it I dismounted and, taking my Webley, put the animal out of its misery.

Middy was clearly annoyed, "I am sorry, Sergeant Major."

I nodded and turned to the men we had led. They were grinning and looking pleased with themselves. I shouted, "And who gave you the order to fire?" The smiles went from their faces. I pointed to the two men they had shot. One had been hit by four bullets. At least they could shoot straight. "We needed prisoners and now we have none. Major Dickenson will want to find where these Dervishes are going. If we had taken prisoners, then we would know already!" Silence filled the wadi. I gestured to the four men with Sergeant Saeed. "Those four obeyed orders. The rest of you. I want this dead camel butchering. We will use the meat and your punishment will be to ride back with dead camel meat."

"But Sergeant Major..." I turned to look at the young trooper, "We have never done this before."

"Well, Trooper?"

Middy said, "Atkinson, Sergeant Major."

"Well, Trooper Atkinson, this is your chance to learn." I turned, "Sergeant Saeed, they were heading west. Take your four men and see if you can pick up a trail. It will give the major somewhere to start."

Middy shouted as Saeed led his men away, "Make your camels sit."

We had already done so but the novices had much to learn. I went to the dead Dervishes. They were well-armed. They each had a musket or a rifle. The one rifle was a Martini-Henry. They had taken it from an enemy. They each had a sword with a crosspiece. They were wicked weapons when used in hand-to-hand combat and were feared by even British soldiers. They had daggers too. Their water skins were full and they had food. It suggested to me that they had only recently arrived at the oasis. I secured the weapons, skins and food. We wasted nothing at Fort Desolation. When Saeed returned we would head back to the oasis and examine the ground. There would be clues we could use. The stink from behind us told us when the troopers had gutted the camel. I smiled. They would learn to leave the bowels and stomach intact next time. One or two of them were doing a good job of butchering and they were taking usable hunks of meat. Some of the others were making such a mess that the meat they took would have to be cooked as soon as we got back.

Middy came over and shook his head, "Sam will be annoyed. We thought we had drilled into them the importance of waiting for commands."

I nodded, "The problem is, Middy, that this was their first contact with the enemy. They were excited and they saw me hit the first Dervish. The major sent me out today so that I could see what was needed and I have. They need lessons in riding and to learn to obey orders." I nodded at the blood-spattered uniforms, "They will all have to do some dhobying and that will help to reinforce the message."

Saeed returned an hour later. It would soon be noon. The butchery was largely complete. The rest of the carcass would be devoured by carrion. The bodies of the Dervishes we would leave. It would be a message for the rest. Fort Desolation was no longer inactive and passive. I pointed to the distant oasis. "You can give me your report there. We will walk the camels."

"Yes, Sergeant Major."

Middy and I led and we walked. We were not suffering as our puggarees and keffiyeh kept us cooler but I could tell by their gait that the new men were. The two miles or so walk would add to their misery.

The oasis was not a large one but its trees gave shade and the puddle of water would give the camels a drink. They would empty it but over the next hours, it would fill up again. While the men found what shade they could, drank from their waterskins and ate their rations I went with Saeed to examine the oasis. We found the fire that had been used, it was clear that the fire was one that was constantly used. The stones around it were blackened with soot. Saeed found the toilet they had used and, once again, it was clear that this was a regularly used oasis.

"The Dervish use this often, Saeed."

He nodded. "It is a good spot. You can see the caravans and the road from the fort." He shook his head. "That is how they spotted me the other day. I used the road."

"Lesson learned, Saeed but I don't think they will use this one again. The major will follow their trail tomorrow but the day after let you and I see if we can find another oasis that they might use." As we headed back to the others I said, "The question is, are they merely watching or is there another more sinister purpose to this?"

"Sergeant Major?"

"Why watch us? When we head back to the fort look for tracks. Have they been watching the fort at night? That would make sense. What are they planning? We needed prisoners."

Saeed shook his head, "They are fanatics and would not talk. They believe that a death in a Holy War against us guarantees them entry into heaven. They would die, even if we tortured them."

"And we won't torture them."

When we reached the shade of the trees, I unwound my keffiyeh and puggaree. I squatted and took a couple of sips from my waterskin. I took out some of the dried goat meat and chewed it slowly. When I had finished, I took another couple of sips. Middy and Saeed had done the same and I saw the others watching us. One shook his waterskin, ruefully, as he realised he had drunk more than half. We could have told them to husband their water but this way they would remember the lesson. By the time we reached the fort, they would have empty skins. The noon sun was beating down so fiercely that even in the oasis it felt as though we might melt.

"Middy, set sentries."

The men had all eaten and he stood, "Wyatt, Shaw, sentry duty. I will have you relieved in half an hour." The two men had been the first to fire.

As they trudged off Atkinson asked, "Sergeant Major, are all the Arabs enemies?"

"No, Atkinson. There are friendlies and that is why you always wait for the order to open fire."

"Then how did you know, Sergeant Major, that they were Dervishes I mean?"

"First of all, they ran." He nodded. "Secondly, they were all wearing the black patch. The Dervishes wear such a patch. It is not always in the same place, but you can spot it."

Emboldened by my lack of aggression he continued, "Sergeant Major, it is hot in the fort but out here..."

I nodded, "The fort has walls that afford shade. Those walls are thick and that means they absorb some of the sun's heat and that is why it is not as cold at night in the barracks as it would be if we were sleeping out here."

One of the others, I later learned his name was Lowe, looked around him at the rocks, "Sleep out here? At night? There are snakes!"

"Snakes, spiders, all sorts of things that creep, bite and sting."
I had to smile at Corporal Dunn's words for he had once been
terrified of the night. He had learned there were other fears that
were much greater.

We left the oasis when it was cooler. The chase had taken it
out of the camels. Had we not followed the Dervishes we could
have explored another five miles or so. As we neared the fort the
sentries waved a welcome and I was relieved. I was satisfied
with the patrol which had not been the disaster it might have
been. There had been mistakes but they were ones from which a
lesson could be learned. Not least we discovered, as we
approached the fort, not from the road but across the wasteland,
that the Dervish had been investigating the fort at night. Saeed
found tracks and camel dung where it should not have been. The
Dervish were here for a reason. They were searching for the
fort's weaknesses. Sometime in the future, and the near future at
that, there would be an attack on the fort and, in all likelihood, it
would be at night.

Chapter 4

While Middy and Saeed saw to the camels, the meat from the dead camel and checked equipment, I went to the orderly office. Sam and the major were poring over a map. Middy had made it when we first arrived and I knew that when he had a moment he would add details from today's adventure too. They looked up and the major smiled and said, "Well?" He gestured to a seat and I sat.

"Green as grass and they opened fire without being ordered to."

Sam frowned, "Sorry about that."

"They learned from it and the other thing is that they can ride but actively patrolling needs more skills than they possess. If I might suggest, sir, before you ride tomorrow you have Sam give them some pointers on how to make their camels work better."

"Good idea. And the Dervish?"

"Ah, that is the more serious issue. We found three of them but they were all killed so we have no prisoners. We discovered that they had been watching the fort not only from the oasis but also closer to the walls at night. I think that they are planning a night attack."

The major lit one of the cheroots he smoked during the day, "Is that why you had the ditch cleaned and sharpened?"

I laughed, "No, sir, I am not a fortune teller but it is good that we did. If they come to attack us they will have more of an obstacle than they expect."

Sam asked, "Should we keep fires burning on the walls at night?"

I shook my head, "It will ruin the night vision of the sentries and mark the position of those on the walls."

"Damn, then we will be blind."

"Not necessarily, Major Dickenson. If we use two or three men each night from the patrol that has been out that day to walk outside the walls then we can keep the Dervish on their toes. We only need to do it once a night but vary the time. If you like, sir, I can take a couple of lads out tonight." I smiled, "I think I have two perfect candidates."

"Well, it is worth a try. Where did you catch up with the Dervishes?"

I stood and went to the map. Jabbing my finger at the wadi I said, "Here. We chased them from the oasis and they were heading west. They would have escaped if we hadn't split the patrol."

"Then tomorrow, Sergeant Smith, we will ride directly to this point and see what we find. You go and change, Sergeant Major. If you intend to be up in the night then you need your rest."

"I will be fine, sir."

"Oh and ask Sergeant Abdul to come and see me. He will need to ginger up his men."

I smiled as I passed the washhouse where the men were washing their tunics. I went over to them. "Atkinson and Lowe, I have a special duty for you. Report to the main gate at two a.m."

I saw the question forming on both their mouths but I cocked an eyebrow and they thought better of it. They chorused, "Yes, Sergeant Major."

"You will need your carbines. And a coat. It will be chilly." Enigmatically I left it at that. Before I went to change, I headed for the armoury. Jake and Paul had a Lee Metford carbine stripped down to its component parts. It was the best way to understand a gun. Take it apart and then put it together. "Well, what do you think?"

Jake held up the magazine, "These are handy. The lads will have eight bullets to fire but we only have four magazines a man."

"I thought they only had a five-bullet magazine."

"These are eight bullet mags but with just four of them per man..."

"The major has an orderly coming with the next caravan of supplies. He will have chitties. We need at least ten per man. Get spares for the new men who aren't here yet." On the way to Suakim Major Dickenson had told me that along with the next men to join us we would have a couple of orderly clerks. Non-combatants who could deal with the inevitable paperwork of a garrison that should soon top a hundred. "Anything else?"

"We fired one and the range is slightly longer than the Remington. In theory, it is a handy gun but..."

I nodded, "The proof of the pudding will be in the firing. Take a couple with you when you go out tomorrow. There is no point in issuing them yet. The new boys have a lot to learn." I explained to them what had happened. Like Sam, they adopted guilty looks but they had no need to. What we were doing was new to everyone. We had learned hard lessons. They had cost us three dead friends and an invalid.

The camel meat was put on to cook as soon as we came back. The heat would soon spoil it and it could be a tough meat. We had left the offal with the carcasses. The hyenas, foxes and rats would gorge on the bounty and might even ignore the humans. When I had changed I went to the mess. There was always a dixie of tea and nothing refreshed more than a mug of tea. I had grown used to the goat's milk that was used. There was an awning that afforded shade and I used it. As I sat drinking the strong hot tea, smelling the cooking camel meat, I put my mind to the problems I had uncovered. The next batch of recruits was due in the next fortnight and we did not know when the Dervish would attack. What had surprised me was that they had not attacked before for they must have known how few we were. Waiting for an attack drained morale and made men jump at shadows but, by the same token, we needed more men to defend the walls.

I saw Sergeant Abdul leave the major's office and, seeing me, he headed across to me. One of the cooks fetched him a mug of tea and he sat. Shaking his head he said, "This is serious, Sergeant Major. I am angry that my men did not see the watchers if they were close to the fort. They were close then?"

I nodded and gestured with my thumb, "They got to within ten feet of the ditch. They will expect it to be as it was when I returned."

"The men need to be more vigilant."

"That will help but you know yourself, Sergeant, that the advantage is with the watcher. If men stare into the dark for too long they become night blind and all a watcher needs to do is to see the head of the sentry turn and then move and wait. They could sleep during the day so tiredness would not be a problem. Once they were close to the ditch then they would just be shadows. Do not dwell on the past. What is done is done.

Tonight, I take two men and we will walk the perimeter. Warn your men for I do not wish any watcher to be alerted."

He nodded and frowned, pausing with the mug almost at his lips, "Would it not be better to wait until tomorrow? The watchers were killed by your men today. They will not have any others in place."

"The circling birds in the sky will tell them that there has been a death in the desert. Even while we were sheltering in their oasis they would have investigated and even though we had left they would find our signs. There will be more men watching in the oasis but they will keep hidden." I smiled, "I do not mind a stroll in the dark. Before you came we had the night watch."

We chatted about our service in Egypt. The sergeant and I had fought in the same battles. As with every battle a man's memory of it differed. It was dependent upon his place in the battle line. Mine had always been in the hottest part.

The bugle for food came when we had just finished our tea and meant that the two of us were the first to sit. There was no hierarchy to the table we used although I tended to leave a chair for the major next to me.

Some of the tenderer pieces of camel were in the stew we ate but the bulk of the meat was bully beef. Beans and rehydrated dried vegetables were its main constituents. The camel bones would ensure that for a week or two we had better stock. While we ate we talked. The others, like me, were keen to use the new carbines. The ability to fire eight bullets in quick succession might have saved our three dead friends. In the time it took to chamber another round, a Dervish could cover ten paces and if he was mounted, twenty.

Jake had been given the role of armourer because he knew weapons. As Middy waxed lyrical about being able to keep firing Jake said, "The thing is, Middy, if every carbine empties its magazine at the same time then you have the same problem. Once you reload the magazine it is then that you are vulnerable and until we are able to order more we are restricted. We have the bullets but the troopers will need to load their own magazines. If they do it badly then the gun can jam."

He was voicing my thoughts, "Tomorrow, I will spend time out there," I pointed with my fork, "and we will see how the guns work. I think the lads will find that today was easier than tomorrow will be."

Middy was the officer of the watch and he retired early, as did I. The one pipe I had was the best of the day. It tasted sweeter and helped me to sleep quicker. He came and shook me awake, as I had asked and, after dressing, I woke Lowe and Atkinson. I took just my Webley. Middy had two of the Egyptians open the gate and we slipped out into the chilly blackness of a Sudanese night. I drew my pistol which hung from a lanyard around my neck. I waved Lowe to my right and Atkinson to my left. I had ordered them to fix bayonets to their carbines when we were in the fort and we began our perambulation. There were animals hunting in the dark and despite our attempts to be quiet they heard us coming and skittered out of the way. The two troopers twitched nervously when that happened. I was looking ahead and then glancing at the ground. I saw no signs of the enemy. Occasionally I stopped and sniffed the air. My two companions looked at me as though I had gone mad. I would explain when we returned. I had learned in Zululand that men smelled of what they ate and how they lived. My men had the smell of British soldiers. The Egyptians who served with us had the same diet and the same smell. The Dervishes smelled of camel and horses. Their sweat and their diet identified them as different too. I was sniffing to catch their smell on the air. There was none. It took a slow hour to do the tour and Middy himself opened the gates.

I shook my head as we entered, "No sign of them and that is a good thing. Saeed can take out two more men tomorrow." He nodded and returned to the walls and I turned to the two troopers, "You two did well. You weren't too noisy and you kept your nerve."

"It was scary Sergeant Major. Those noises…"

"Creatures of the night, Lowe. You will smell the enemy when they are close, not hear them."

Atkinson beamed, "That was why you were sniffing."

"You have much to learn but you have made a start. Now back to bed. We will be up again in a couple of hours."

Soldiers learn to fall asleep quickly. In my case I was also able to wake quickly and although I was not up as early as I had been the day before, I was still the first in the mess. While we ate, I said, "Middy, make sure you get your head down for an hour or two. I will take the men on a little ride to improve their riding skills. We will use the new carbines at about eleven."

Jack nodded, "There are twelve ready for you, Sergeant Major." He looked at the major, "What do we do with the Remingtons, sir?"

The major had clearly thought it through for his answer was prompt, "We issue them to the Egyptians. I know we don't expect the cooks and orderlies to fight but if we are attacked, as the Sergeant Major suspects, then an extra ten carbines on the walls can only help."

Sergeant Abdul smiled, "They would feel honoured, effendi. They cook for us but all of them joined the army as soldiers. They are not cowards."

I said, "Then I will leave the training of them in the use of the carbines to you, Sergeant. There will be twelve today and the major's men's carbines will be available tomorrow."

I had my men stand to on the walls of the fort as Major Dickenson and Sam led their patrol out. They had three lance corporals as well as the sergeant and the major. It would ensure that they had plenty of experience. They would head for the oasis first and then try to find the Dervish camp. Once they dropped from sight I said, "Saddle your camels and full gear. We shall have a little training. Yesterday was not your finest hour."

We spent two hours in the saddle. I had them move from a column of twos to double lines. Saeed and I had the troopers wheel. We practised stopping, dismounting and, using the camels as protection, dry-fired. Saeed was able to watch the men I could not see and he told them when they got something wrong. We were a good team. As we headed back to the fort I said, "And one last thing. Unless your superior officer is dead, you wait for the command to fire. Do you understand?"

"Yes, Sergeant Major." I smiled as the response came from every trooper together. They were becoming one.

When the camels were unsaddled and given water and food we headed for the armoury. Middy emerged from his quarters and joined us. I acted as QM and took the old carbines and stacked them for Sergeant Abdul to collect and then issued the

Lee Metford carbines, magazines and bullets. "Your first job is to load your magazines. Lance Corporal Johnson impressed upon me the need to do this carefully. Take your time and get it right. You only have four magazines at the moment." I patted the cartridge pouches on my belt. Each one held bullets. "The magazines are too big to go here and so they will need to be in your haversack. Now, find somewhere shady and load your magazines. We have half an hour before we get to use them. We will fire them now and then again when the sun is no longer making it impossible to move." I smiled, "You see, I am not completely heartless."

I slid the bullets into each magazine and then checked them to make sure that they were correct. I placed each magazine in the gun and then removed it. It was not, as yet, a natural action. My hands wanted to slip a bullet into the breech. I resolved to practise in my quarters until I could do it with my eyes closed and it became second nature. It was eleven thirty when I led the men from the fort. Abdul had issued the carbines to his men and they watched us as we marched just thirty paces from the ditch and faced the desert. I chose the side that was closest to the oasis. The major would have checked it but any watchers might have returned and while they could not see us they would hear the firing and I wanted their curiosity piqued. Curious men might investigate and we still needed a prisoner. All thirteen of us were in the same boat. None of us had used the weapon. While most of the bully beef tins were reused in some way there were always some that would be buried. I had collected twenty and, after the men had filled them with sand, I placed them in a line one hundred paces from us. It was just a rough target, but it would do.

I faced the men. "You will fire on Corporal Dunn's command. Listen to his words and obey every order."

"Yes, Sergeant Major."

Middy and I had discussed this with Saeed while we had eaten breakfast.

"Load."

We each slid a magazine into the gun.

"Present."

We raised our guns.

"Aim."

I looked down the sights. I had chosen my bully beef can already.

"Fire!"

The carbine bucked but I was expecting it. When the smoke cleared, I saw that I had hit the can but not in the centre. I adjusted the sights to compensate. Looking down the line I saw that only four cans had been hit. I knew that Middy and Saeed would have hit their targets and I wondered who the other good shot was.

Middy shouted, "Adjust your sights and then take aim."

Sweat was dripping down my face and I knew that we would only have the chance to empty one magazine.

"Fire."

This time my bullet smacked into the centre and when I looked down the line I saw that six cans had been hit.

Middy waited until the smoke had cleared and then said, "Take aim. Let us assume that the Dervishes are massing for a charge. When I give the command to fire I want you to empty your magazine and then reload but do not fire your second magazine." The silence that followed showed that their attention was on the corporal's words.

"Fire."

The rapid firing was deafening and this time the smoke swirled. There was not as much smoke as there was at Rorke's Drift and it did not totally obscure the target but we were wreathed in thin smoke. I heard the guns click on empty and I took out the new magazine. I heard four snap into place quickly and then there was a ragged series of clicks. I looked down the line and saw that Shaw was the slowest to reload.

I nodded, "Go and check your targets. See how many times you hit... or missed and remember what you need to do to adjust your gun."

We headed for the bully beef tins and I saw the eight bullet holes. I was pleased with myself. One or two of the cans only had a couple of holes. Each man would know if he had hit. Little would be gained from identifying them. They needed time.

The afternoon was spent getting to know the guns by taking them apart and putting them together. They were a well-made piece of kit but I still preferred the longer range of the Martini-Henry.

The major returned without having come into contact with the Dervishes but he had seen signs, at the end of his patrol, of hoofprints suggesting a large number.

"I think they are the Baggara tribe. Sergeant Major, take your patrol south tomorrow. We will get to know the carbines.

We headed south. In theory, it should have been a safer patrol for all the evidence was that the Dervishes were to the west and north of us but it paid to be cautious. We stopped, before noon at a small oasis. There was no water but the trees showed that occasionally there was rainfall. We used the shade and drank from our skins. Saeed and I examined the oasis while Middy added to his maps.

We found the signs quickly. Many riders had used the oasis. Some rode camels whilst others rode horses. It explained why the oasis was dry. Saeed said, "So, Sergeant Major, it seems that the Dervish have the fort surrounded."

"So it would seem and we must be making it easy for them. They see us leaving the fort and make sure we don't see them."

"Why do they not ambush us?"

Saeed had asked a good question and I could not think of an answer. They knew, from their one success, that their best chance of victory came in catching us in the open. "We will just have to be vigilant, won't we?"

My news disturbed the major. "Tomorrow, we take both patrols out at once. The orderlies have their carbines and Sergeant Abdul will train them today. Perhaps the sound of firing will make them think that we have more men than we do." He shook his head, "Until we get more men we are sitting ducks here. If Saeed is right and they have scores of horsemen then it is only a matter of time before they try to shift us."

We repeated the patrols for three days but then had to stop. The animals were becoming exhausted. We had a day of rest. The major had me lead some close-order drills to keep the men sharp and the next day I led my patrol out. This time Syd came with me. The major had decided to spread the NCOs out. I was happy for Syd and I, along with Saeed and Middy, were a good team and worked well together.

It was our turn to head south. The oasis was still dry and so we headed further west. According to Middy's map, there was another one four miles to the west. I estimated that, by leaving the fort just after dawn, we could be there by eleven and use it for shade during noon. I was pleased that the men had learned. Lance Corporal Poulter, as Quarter Master, was inundated with requests for keffiyeh. He only had eight and keffiyeh went on the lengthening list of supplies we needed. They now used their puggarees and ensured that the cloth at the back of their helmet was well attached. The new khaki uniforms came with puttees and whilst a nuisance to put on they were a godsend when we rode through thorn.

I still rode at the fore. This time I had Syd next to me and Middy rode in the middle, his notepad hanging from his saddle. His eyes were constantly looking for new landmarks and then his pencil would scribble away. As soon as we returned he would add them to the master maps. We saw no signs of traffic except where we expected to, on the caravan route and we passed that early on the patrol. After that, all that we saw were the tracks of animals. As we neared the oasis I had the men take out their carbines. The first patrol when we had startled the Dervishes had been a warning but when the birds took flight as we approached I knew that the oasis was deserted. Surprisingly it was relatively full and after we had drunk the animals gorged themselves on water. Syd set the sentries and we settled down to find a cool spot under the trees.

Every half hour one of us would get up and walk the perimeter to ensure that the sentries were alert. It was just before two in the afternoon when I was checking the perimeter that I detected a movement. Wyatt, the sentry, had not but that was not a surprise as it looked to be a shimmering shape in the distance. I recognised it for what it was, a rider or riders.

"Back to the others and tell Corporal Dunn I said to have the men stand to. There are riders coming."

He looked in the distance, "Why is that a problem, Sergeant Major? Perhaps they just want to use the oasis."

I nodded and said, patiently, for he was new, "Aye, Wyatt, but the trouble is these riders are coming from the west and not using a road. They might be innocent but better to look foolish and have a loaded gun than sit here and be attacked. Now run along."

I took my binoculars out. They were a precious gift and I looked after them. I raised them, the better to identify the riders. As I feared, they were Dervishes. I saw the black, red and green squares sewn prominently on their jibbah. More alarmingly they also carried a standard. This was a black one. It confirmed their belligerent intent. They meant harm to someone, in all likelihood, our fort. The cloud of dust obscured their numbers but it also was an indication that there could be in excess of sixty riders.

Wyatt returned and with him were Saeed and Syd. I pointed, "Dervishes and they are coming here." I nodded to Wyatt who was kneeling and aiming his carbine. "I would risk a run back to the fort but..."

Syd nodded his agreement, "Give them a bloody nose first, eh Sergeant Major? Empty a few saddles and then escape in the confusion."

"That is my idea. Lance Corporal, leave Middy and two men with the camels and bring the others up here." As he turned, I said, "And bring my Martini-Henry."

Saeed pointed to the last tree to the south, "I will anchor the line there."

Wyatt was looking up at me nervously, "Action, eh, Sergeant Major?"

Men, nervous men especially, will do that. They fill the silence with anything. Wyatt did not need an answer, just reassurance, "Listen to the orders and do everything I say. This is a test but I am sure that you will all emerge successfully from it."

I did not look around when I heard movement behind me. I had already laid the Lee-Metford to lean against the last palm tree behind which I stood and when Syd handed me the Martini-Henry, I just pointed it to the right. "Take the last tree to the north."

"Yes, Sergeant-Major. You lads, fill in the gaps between me and Sergeant Saeed."

They saw Wyatt already kneeling and as they found their own spot emulated him. I slid a bullet into the breech and rested it on the trunk of the palm tree. When it had been younger the wind had blown and made it naturally bend. As it grew more mature and stronger it became straighter. I used the curve. If nothing else it would disguise me. The red coats we had worn would have made us stand out but now we blended in against the sandy background. The Mahdists were now easier to see without the binoculars. There were fifty or so of them and they were fanned out. Some rode horses and some rode camels. I saw not only muskets but also rifles. I could hear the noise of their animals and I knew that it would frighten the men a little. Once they had something to do the fear would be forgotten but just waiting aggravated that fear.

"When I give the command to fire I want you to empty your magazine and reload but do not fire your second one until you hear the order. When you fire then aim. Your targets are bigger than the bully beef tins. I do not want a single round wasting."

"Yes, Sergeant Major." The chorused response was reassuring.

We had to wait until they were less than a hundred yards from us. I wanted the almost one hundred rounds to do some damage. That the Mahdists were not expecting us was clear from their formation. If they thought the oasis was occupied then they would have split up and come from two or three different directions. Their leader would be at the fore and if we could hit him then the others might lose heart and direction. With that in mind, I peered down my sights. The leader rode a magnificent black stallion. I could see sunlight glinting from his sword. The basket hilt told me that it had been taken in battle, probably from a Scottish regiment. He would be my target.

When they were two hundred yards from us I said, "Aim." The horsemen closed with us and I aimed my trusty rifle at the chest of the leader. His head was wreathed in cloth. The red square on his jibbah was almost central and I aimed at that.

"Fire!" I squeezed the trigger and was already loading a second bullet as the rider threw his arms to the side and fell from the stallion. The rest of the patrol did not have to reload and although more ragged than the first volley the sound of the bullets leaving the carbines rolled through the oasis. My second bullet smacked into the shoulder of a camel rider who, whilst he did not fall from the saddle had to wheel away. My third and fourth shots found their mark and as the last bullets were fired by my men I slipped the Martini-Henry over my shoulder and picked up the as-yet-unfired Lee-Metford. There were fifteen animals wandering around without riders and the Mahdists had pulled back. It was time to leave.

"Back to the camels." I raised the carbine and took aim. I had eight bullets and if I fired them then they might think we had not left. I could rely on Syd and Saeed to mount the men. I aimed and fired. The milling riders began to move away from the oasis. Three men reeled but did not fall from their saddles. I knew I had hit more and wondered at the power, or lack of it of the carbine. The Martini-Henry slammed into a man. Whilst my patrol's bullets had found flesh they had not had the stopping power of the Remington.

I turned and ran back to the camels. They were already mounted and Aisha was on the ground and waiting for me. I slipped the Martini-Henry into the scabbard and as I climbed aboard reloaded my carbine.

"Sergeant, take us home." I could rely on the vastly experienced Egyptian to keep a steady ground-eating pace. It would take some time for order to be restored and even then the approach to the oasis would be a cautious one. If we could establish a half-mile or even a mile lead then we could escape, even with novice riders.

"Corporal, in the middle. Richardson, with me at the rear."

Camels could gallop but they were most comfortable with a loping canter. They ate up the ground. The Mahdists who had horses might be able to catch us but in doing so would become exhausted. This was a race. The sun was still hot but it would be worse for our pursuers who had ridden during the hottest part of the day.

Syd must have been thinking the same thing I did for he said, "I wonder why they travelled in the heat of the noonday sun?"

"I wondered that too. Perhaps they intended to make an overnight camp at the oasis. It had plenty of water. They would need that for their horses." I glanced over my shoulder. There was still no sign of pursuit.

"They will know where we came from."

"Then the colonel will be happy. He wanted them to feel our presence."

The nearest riders to us were Shaw and Lowe, twenty feet away but Syd still lowered his voice when he said, "Aye, but it means that they will try to get rid of us all that bit quicker."

I nodded. "Let us hope that the reinforcements and supplies are sent sooner rather than later."

When we saw the fort, in the distance, then we knew that we had escaped. Syd and I had not seen any sign of pursuit, there was no cloud of dust following us but that did not mean they had not sent men after us.

As the gates slammed behind us I dismounted and handed my reins to Syd, "I had better report."

"I will look after Aisha for you."

I nodded. We looked after each other, that was our way and, as I headed for the office, I saw that the men I had led were also learning to do the same. The recruits were no longer novices. They had been blooded. Now they had a chance to survive this harsh environment.

Chapter 5

"This oasis, Sergeant Major?" He took out the map,

I nodded, "Yes Major Dickenson. It is less than fourteen miles away."

He lit a cheroot and nodded to the seat, "Sit down, Jack." I did so. "You can smoke if you wish."

"No thank you, sir."

He jabbed a finger at the oases marked on the map as he spoke, "They were here to the north. We found evidence of them here to the south and now you found them to the west. I am betting that if we went to this one," he pointed to an oasis to the north and west of us, "we would find evidence of them and in numbers. Was there plenty of water at the one you found today?"

"Yes, sir."

"Then it could easily support larger numbers." He leaned back. "I hate the isolation. The new officer and men could be on their way here or they might still be at Suakim."

"We could always send a rider back, sir."

He shook his head, "You know as well as I do, that it would have to be one of the originals and if we are attacked then we shall need all their experience."

Silence filled the office. I cleared my throat, "There is something else, sir."

He looked at me, "Something I have not seen?"

I pointed to the east of us and the last oasis that we had used on our journey west, "We have not patrolled to the east. Suppose they are there too? The reinforcements might be ambushed heading for us."

"Good God, you are right. I shall lead my patrol there tomorrow. While I do you had better check our defences. You have an eye for that sort of thing." He smiled, "Rorke's Drift, eh?"

I nodded but that seemed a lifetime ago. I was probably one of the last men still to be serving. Captain Bromhead and Lieutenant Bourne would still be soldiers of the queen but Hooky, Coley and so many others had left already. I doubted that I would know any of them. But for Harding-Smythe, the bully of

61

an officer I might still be in the Welsh regiment. I knew that if I was then I would have been unlikely to have risen above the rank of Corporal. It had taken secondment to the Egyptian army and then this new Kitchener-inspired initiative to get me to the heady heights of Sergeant Major.

"I will have Sergeant Abdul organise the Egyptians. They have the Remingtons but I am not sure that they have fired them yet."

"It can do no harm and we had better brief the NCOs. The officer of the night is an even more vital duty now." He smiled, "Go and get yourself cleaned up Sergeant Major. What is it that they say, 'If you don't have a sense of humour then you shouldn't have signed up'? How true, eh?"

The NCOs had already deduced that the night was when the Mahdists would attack and the briefing was probably unnecessary but it did no harm. I resolved to do without an hour of sleep each night and take a turn around the walls. We had delegated the examination of the exterior to the night watch. My body was now used to unsociable hours.

While Sergeant Abdul and I held a training session with the carbines Syd and Saeed had half of my patrol standing guard on the walls, while the other half, under Corporal Dunn, embedded stakes in the ditch and then covered the sharpened stakes with thorns. It would not stop a determined enemy but it would slow their progress. It was clear to me, after an hour of firing the carbines, that the cooks and orderlies were not the best of shots. The sergeant and I spoke as we sent the cooks back to their kitchen and the garrison resumed their sentry duties, "Bullets will be wasted if they fire at a distance of greater than fifty paces, Sergeant Major."

"I know. How about this then, Sergeant? The chief cook is used to commanding the cooks, we put him in command of all of the supernumeraries. You can spread his men out on the walls if we are attacked but you tell him he is only to order his men to open fire when you give the command. Twenty men adding their fire when the enemy is fifty yards from us might be just enough to give the enemy a shock."

"They are not cowards, Sergeant Major."

"I know but we will need to use them judiciously." I pointed to the walls, "Until we get reinforcements then the walls will not have enough men on them. There are just forty-nine of us and that means eleven men to a wall, three on the gatehouse and two in the tower. We risk being overwhelmed. We need the supernumeraries but we have to use them wisely."

He nodded, "I will speak to them." He saw my face, "You terrify them, Sergeant Major. It is your reputation that does it and not your manner. They are afraid to let you down. Perhaps if I am training them then they might improve."

When I left the Egyptian, I was disappointed, not in him but in myself. I thought I had modelled myself on Colour Sergeant Bourne, but we had never been afraid of him. I would need to try even harder.

There was relief when the major returned to say that while there was evidence that the Mahdists had visited the oasis they had not, as yet, visited there in great numbers.

"If I might suggest, sir?"

"Go ahead, Sergeant Major."

"Instead of sending out patrols where we have been how about a smaller daily patrol to the oasis? It is just a few miles away."

"Good idea."

I sent Middy and six men the next day on the first of the newer patrols. Each day that the enemy did not attack was a relief but we were still concerned by the non-arrival of the recruits and the supplies. If we did not receive more bully beef and bullets in the next seven days then we would have to send men back to Suakim and that meant leaving the garrison undermanned for at least six days.

I had taken a look around the fort and ensured that the night watcher was all in place. I had just come from the walls and was taking off my boots when I heard the cry followed by a shot and then the crack of a carbine. I began putting them on again as I heard the bugle. Sam had just taken over from me and I was confident that he would not panic but with just twelve men on the walls, he needed all of us as soon as possible. I attached my sword to the frog on my belt and my carbine. I had not removed my Webley. As much as I liked my Martini-Henry, I could guarantee that I would not need its length. I needed the speed of an eight-bullet magazine and so I took the Lee-Metford.

I hurtled from my chamber and entered the darkness of the night. It was lit by flashes from the walls. We had decided our places five days ago when we had held an officer's call. A senior NCO would be along each wall and the corporals and lance corporals at the far end. Major Dickenson would fill in where there was a weakness. As I ran up the stairs to the gate wall, I saw a face appear over the wall. There would be huge gaps between the sentries until the rest of us arrived. I fired from the hip and at a range of ten feet the bullet smashed into the Mahdist's face and threw him back. I had to fill in where I could and I raised my carbine and risked leaning over the wall. The bullets and musket balls slammed into the wall as I did so but I saw that there were two ladders guarded at the foot of the wall and men were ascending. I aimed at the nearest ladder and fired first at the men at the foot and then, as I emptied my magazine, moved upwards. One of the falling men took the ladder with him as he was hit and the ladder fell into the ditch. I was empty and I ducked behind the wall to reload.

Cooks, orderlies and the rest of our men arrived and as they passed me I shouted, "Clear the walls first and then the ditches. Try to keep your heads down and make every shot count."

With just three magazines left, I knew that I would have to be frugal too. I reloaded. I heard Saeed shouting in Arabic. He was clearly ordering the cooks and orderlies. I saw, as I rose, the flashes from the men in the tower. They had the advantage of being able to see further. If they had enjoyed Martini-Henry rifles then they might have been able to hit the riders who were relatively safe in the darkness. I had barely stood when the bullet came from the tower and the Dervish who was about to slash me with his sword fell back. I peered over the wall and aimed at the nearest ladder. The first one I had hit lay in the ditch. The other was full of men. Middy arrived and I said, "Take charge here. There is a ladder we need to shift. I will head down to the other end."

As I ran down the fighting platform I passed two men. One was dead and one was wounded. Both were Sergeant Abdul's men. It explained why they had nearly breached this wall. A face appeared next to me when I reached the ladder and rather than using a bullet I smashed the carbine's butt into the man's face. It was a powerful blow and, as he did not have a hold on the wall, he fell screaming to the stake-filled ditch. I leaned over and fired at the next man just two feet away. Middy was firing too and after four bullets the ladder was cleared. I reached over and pushed it to the side. As I did so a bullet splintered the stone just a handspan from it. My left hand was lacerated by the fragments. I ignored it. Looking down the wall I saw that the men had now all arrived but with two men down we had fewer men than the other walls. The one advantage that we held was that the two ladders were down and if they were going to be raised again we would have the chance to hit them. Major Dickenson was now at the gate. It was just a couple of feet higher than the rest of the walls and afforded more protection. There was a wooden roof. He did not have a carbine but his pistol was in his hand.

"Two men down, sir. One dead and one wounded."

He nodded and gestured over the wall, "They have come in numbers."

"Yes, sir, but we have stemmed their first attack. Now we need to hold our nerve. Daylight will show them the folly of their attack. There are dead and dying men in the ditch."

"Ginger the men up, Sergeant Major. It is your voice they want to hear."

He was being a realist and nodding I shouted, "Cooks and orderlies, stay behind the walls and save your bullets for when they get closer. ESEG, pick your targets and ignore the horsemen."

I knew that would be hard for the young men but it was vital that they conserved their bullets. The carbines might have the range but, in the darkness, they could not guarantee a hit. I was reassured when the rate of fire from my wall slowed. The men had heeded my command. The other walls reflected the discipline of two officers on every wall. I peered over the wall and saw that the only movement came from the ditches where wounded men writhed. They were not a threat and there was no point in wasting a bullet. I walked down the wall speaking to each group of men as I did so.

"You are doing well and we have beaten off their attack."
Nervous faces turned and smiled. "Good shot, Lowe. The
practice has paid off."

"Thanks, Sergeant Major."

I was halfway down the wall when the leader of the Mahdists
ordered the second wave in. They had clearly decided to
concentrate their forces on the gatehouse wall. We dared not risk
bringing men from the other walls in case they attacked there
too. We would have to rely on the men on the wall and the ones
in the tower. They brought men with rifles and muskets. They
knelt and took aim.

I knew what was coming and I shouted, "Take cover." The
pall of smoke from the muskets and rifles would effectively hide
movements. While the Dervish might be poor shots, they had
fifty muskets and rifles firing. As I had discovered, even
splinters of stone could wound. They fired four ragged volleys,
and I risked peering through the crenulations. Men were now
racing towards the ditch. Bodies lay at the bottom and the enemy
dead would give them a secure base in which to plant their
ladders. There were four ladders. "Open fire!" Resting the
carbine on the wall I took aim. My bullet hit one of the ladder
carriers and when he fell he put the others in disarray. One ladder
would be tardier than the others. Every enemy weapon fired at
the flash from my carbine but by then I was squatting below the
parapet. The mud wall would be pocked marked but it held. I
worked out that I had three bullets left in this magazine and
another two magazines. I was annoyed with myself. In the lull, I
could have reloaded my first magazine.

The ragged fusillade continued and the only counterfire came
from the men on the tower but once they closed with the wall the
ladder men were in dead ground. The muskets and rifles would
keep firing until the ladders were at the wall but they would have
to cease fire then or risk hitting their own men.

The major raced down the fighting platform, "I am doing no
good here. I shall go to the tower where I can see what is going
on. You take charge here, Sergeant Major."

"Sir." He was right. He was blind to the other walls and at the
top of the tower, he would have a better picture.

As soon as the bullets stopped hitting the walls I said, "On your feet. Here they come!"

I stood and leaned over. Bullets and balls still came at the walls but they were aiming high. Even so, something clipped my helmet. Ignoring it I leaned over and took aim at the man beginning to ascend. I hit him with my first bullet but did not stop him. My second one did. I fired the last bullet from the magazine at the man securing the foot of the ladder. Again, I hit him but he did not move.

I reloaded the carbine. The rest of the men were firing at the ascending figures but a cry from my right told me that someone had been hit. Some of the men climbing had rifles too and the flash from a muzzle struck Trooper Price in the face. The dead man was thrown back into the heart of the fort. His killer was just ten feet from me and a bullet to the head, even from a Lee Metford, was fatal. Price had been a quiet lad and now he was dead. I moved to the gap where Price had fallen and I fired obliquely at the next ladder. That way I had some protection from the walls and I could still hit the enemy. Atkinson saw what I was doing and he emulated me. Price had died because he had been looking directly over the wall. More men copied us and even the cooks and orderlies were able to fire their single-shot carbines at the climbing men. We began to take a toll on those who were climbing the walls.

The attack was beaten off and the men fell back. I shouted, "Reload your magazines. Corporal, have the wounded tended to."

I went to the wounded Egyptian I had passed when I had first arrived. He had bled out and was dead. I was not sure if we might have saved him but we could have tried. He had died alone and unnoticed. It annoyed me.

"Atkinson, Jennings, take the dead down to the parade ground."

"Yes, Sergeant Major." I looked to the east and saw the glow that signified a new day. Sunrise was relatively swift in Africa. I wondered what it would bring.

I saw a cook staring at the dead Egyptians as they were taken away, "Go and fetch some water. We all need it."

"Yes, effendi."

Glad to be doing something familiar, the cook laid his carbine down and raced off to fetch water. I was dry and knew that dehydration, even at night, was a dangerous thing. I walked down to Corporal Dunn, "We lost Price."

He nodded, "I know. Will they come again?"

I looked into the darkness, "They might but all that they need to do is to stay where they are. They are cutting off the main route to Suakim. Even if they don't know it we know that we are almost out of supplies. We are trapped here." I pointed to the trees where we took our water. "We can only risk going there to fetch more water at night. They will watch it and we risk losing men every time we go there."

"Then it is hopeless, Sergeant Major."

I patted my carbine, "While we have guns and bullets it is not hopeless and the men have done well. Keep up the men's spirits, Middy, eh?"

I looked up at the tower and saw Major Dickenson. He was holding my Martini-Henry. I waved at him. He shouted, "It looks like they are waiting for dawn, Sergeant Major. They have pulled back a little."

"I have sent for water. I will have the men fed."

"Good idea."

"Cooks, you can leave the walls. Fetch food and water. You all did splendidly." I repeated it in Arabic. They could all speak English but hearing their own language would encourage them. The walls thinned as the rest of the cooks left us.

I let the others drink before I did. I used some of the water to clean my wound. When I had time I would wash it with vinegar. The cooks had made corned beef sandwiches and they were most welcome. Eating seemed to be such a normal activity that the threat of death lessened. As the sun rose we saw the death in the ditch. Flies were already buzzing around the corpses. When the day became warmer so the stink would grow. I saw that the horses and camels had been moved further away. Perhaps they suspected we had artillery. We did not. They were three hundred yards from the walls and I saw that they had settled down to watch us. I now had a better idea of numbers. There had to be two hundred men close to our wall. Only Major Dickenson in his eyrie would have a better idea of the total numbers.

We had finished eating and the sun was climbing when I saw the twenty men detach themselves from the main body and scurry forward to some rocks that lay just a hundred and fifty yards from the walls. Their intention became clearer when their rifles began to fire at the walls. One of the cooks who was bringing water fell. The bullet struck him in the head and he tumbled to the ground.

"Take cover!" I had been slow. Colour Sergeant Bourne would have identified the danger.

With my back against the wall, I looked up at the tower. Major Dickenson had Shaw and Wilkinson with him. While bullets were aimed at them the walls afforded more protection. I saw that the major had given my Martini-Henry to Shaw. The trooper had shown skill and my rifle flashed as he fired. If nothing else it told the Dervish that we could fire back. I turned and rested my carbine on the wall. It was not a rifle and did not have the range of a rifle but I was a fair shot and having reloaded my magazine I felt more confident about using up my bullets. I waited until I saw a puff of smoke and aimed at it. My bullet pinged off rocks. As I had found flying stones could hurt. The fusillade that was returned splattered the wall where I had rested my carbine. I smiled. It would take time for them to reload and Shaw would be in position to fire at the first head that appeared. I heard the crack and then the cry. Once again there was another fusillade at the tower but all three heads had disappeared. As the morning passed a pattern emerged. Their marksmen kept up sporadic fire as they probed for weaknesses. They had marksmen at every wall but from the sound of their guns, we were the focus of the greatest numbers. The bridge over the ditch and the gate itself were tempting targets.

The cooks brought more food at noon. I had the men go in pairs to relieve themselves and to fetch more ammunition. I knew the temporary safety would help. I did not leave the walls nor did Dunn.

The firing was sporadic but rolled across the desert and when, in the early afternoon, I heard the bugle from the east I wondered what it meant. The major had binoculars and he must have used them for he shouted, "There is a relief column."

I knew that he was wrong for no one knew of our dilemma but any help was welcome. I took a decision. "On my command I want every man to rise and fire three rounds at the enemy. Everyone. Do you understand?"

The chorus of, "Yes, Sergeant Major", was reassuring.

What I wanted was to tip the balance in our favour. The Mahdists would be wondering what the bugle meant and the combined fire from the fort might just be the deciding factor. I held my carbine and stood, "Stand!" Every man on the walls stood. "Aim!" I pointed my carbine at the rocks. Already Dervishes' faces rose. "Fire!"

The three rounds from every man were all aimed at the marksmen. Some of the bullets found flesh while others splintered shards of rock to pepper the attackers and when one or two ran the rest followed. Some men disobeyed my command and emptied their guns but that was understandable. I saw the leaders gather close to their horses and when Shaw's bullet nicked a horse, making it rear, it decided them. They mounted and fled west. We had survived, but, as I looked at the bodies in the parade ground, I knew that it was at a cost.

Chapter 6

It was not a relief column but it was the reinforcements and the wagons with our supplies. It had been timely but we had been lucky. I saw that there were less than thirty men arriving with the four wagons. Had the Dervishes held their nerve then they could have attacked and destroyed the wagons and then taken the fort at their leisure.

The major descended from the tower and was waiting by the gate. I waited until I was sure that the Mahdists had gone before I shouted, "Open the gate."

The gates creaked open and the men entered. The faces of the men on the walls all turned to look at me. I shook my head, "We wait until we are sure that they have gone, eh?"

I walked down to Middy, "Take charge here and I will walk the walls."

"Yes, Sergeant Major. We were lucky."

"And then some."

I walked to the next wall. Sergeant Abdul was there. I nodded to the bodies, "Sorry that you lost men, Sergeant."

He stood to attention, "They died doing their duty, Sergeant Major."

We had only lost a handful of men and they had all been on the gate wall. Others were wounded but none seriously. Like me, they had suffered stone cuts and splinter wounds. By the time I reached Corporal Dunn a new trooper said, "Sergeant Major?"

"Yes…?"

"Trooper Golightly, Sergeant Major. Major Dickenson says you can stand down the men. The replacements will stand a watch. He wishes to see you in the office."

"Thank you." I saw the new men already climbing the stairs. "ESEG, stand down. Well done!"

They all cheered. I waited until they had all descended and their places were taken by the fifteen troopers and five Egyptians. We had more replacements than I had expected.

The trooper came with me to the office as though I couldn't find my own way there. As I neared the office I said, "Have the

Dervish bodies piled up outside the walls but make sure they are dead."

"Sergeant Major?"

The reddened skin told me that this was someone new to Africa. He had not transferred from a unit already serving, "They like to play dead and when you go near them, they stick you with a knife. Just be careful, eh?" I placed my carbine next to the wall.

"Yes, Sergeant Major."

When I entered, I found that there was a new officer. I took off my helmet, tucked it under my arm and snapped my heels together, "You sent for me, sir."

"Yes. This is our new officer, Lieutenant Foster. Lieutenant, Sergeant Major Roberts."

He was a young officer with handsome features and a waxed moustache. If he had not shown courage in sounding the bugle and emulating a battalion, I might have thought him a dilettante. I would judge him when he had shown me his true colours.

"Sit down, Sergeant Major, we need to talk about the attack and the lieutenant needs to know all that we know."

"Sir."

The major turned to the young officer, "You took a chance, you know, charging in like that. Had you been ambushed then we would have lost the fort."

The smile left his face, "Sorry, sir, but when I heard the firing it was the only thing I could think of."

"The sounding of the bugle was a good idea but the reckless charge was not. Anyway, that is in the past. Thank you for the bugle." He turned to me, "And the losses?"

"Three of the Egyptians and Trooper Price. There are wounded men but, from what I could tell, nothing serious."

He nodded towards my hand, "You had better get that seen to as well." He shook his head, "We have no doctor here, Lieutenant. We are too small to warrant one, as yet. I daresay that when we get to company strength, they will have to send one." He tapped the sealed orders that lay on the desk. "These may give us a better indication of when that is likely to be." We both nodded. "The defences held."

"Just, sir. The fact is that they got over the walls and none of us expected that. We need more men on the walls at night."

"You are right. The lieutenant brought twenty men in total as well as a couple of orderlies for the lieutenant and me. It is still not enough but it is a start. How do you suggest we organise them?"

The question was asked of me but the lieutenant began to answer, "Well, sir, I …"

The major shook his head, "You will be the adjutant, Lieutenant, and in the fullness of time you will know as much about Fort Desolation as we do but the Sergeant Major knows the troopers and NCOs better than anyone."

"Sorry, sir, I just wanted to help."

"And I am sure you shall."

I nodded, "We have thirty-four other ranks now, sir. I think we make seven-man troops. We have six NCOs and we will have a better organisation. We number them from one to five. Sergeant Smith can have Number One troop. If we mix the new men with the more experienced hands it will help."

He frowned, "That gives a spare NCO, Sergeant Major. Why waste him?"

"Sergeant Saaed can lead, sir, you know that. This way there are four of us who can take out the patrols. I know it will take the lieutenant some time to find his feet and so we can use me and Sergeant Saaed to acclimatise him."

The lieutenant coloured. "I have experience, Sergeant Major."

I turned, "In the desert, sir?"

"Well, no but I can speak a little Arabic and stood watches at Suez. I can ride."

I did not answer for it was not my place but the major did. "It is a different world out here, lieutenant. Now," he placed his hands on the table and stood. I did so too and the lieutenant a heartbeat later, "We have a fort to clean up and good men to bury. If you would care to take a tour of the walls, Lieutenant?"

"I took the liberty of asking Trooper Golightly to have the Dervish dead removed. Once the dead are buried we ought to send a patrol out to see if the Dervishes have gone."

He nodded, "You organise that. Today is a day to secure the fort. We will have an officer's call before we eat and a parade tomorrow." He tapped the orders, "By then we will know what is intended of us."

I headed for my quarters. I laid my carbine on the table and picked up my swagger stick. I emerged to find the fort a hive of activity. The cooks had cooked food and were waiting to serve it. The men who had been on the walls all night were in groups, talking about their experiences. With the lieutenant and the new men on the walls, and the Dervish dead gone, the troopers were idle and that was never a good thing. I turned to Trooper Brown, the bugler, "Sound NCO's call."

The strident notes rang out and every face turned to me. The three sergeants, corporal and three lance corporals all raced to my side and stood waiting for my orders. "Brown, go and get yourself some food."

"Yes, Sergeant Major."

"The lads do not need to brood. Get them fed. Sergeant Smith, have three graves dug as soon as men have finished. We need to get the dead underground as soon as we can. Their bodies are a reminder of how close we came to disaster."

"Where shall we bury them?"

"Next to Harry and the others." I had not been there but the men who had fallen when I had been wounded had been buried not far from the oasis. The simple wooden crosses were now bleached by the sun. "The major will say words over them. Then you and I, Saeed, will take seven men and see if the Dervish have gone or if they are regrouping. Sergeant Smith, you and the others can burn the Dervish bodies. Search them first. I doubt that they will have any papers but you never know. Take their keffiyeh. They won't need them and if the lads wash them then they will come in handy."

Soldiers like order and being given orders. They ate but we did not give them time to dwell on the dead. The major, having read the orders, conducted the funeral. The new men stood a sombre watch as the two Egyptians and Trooper Price were laid to rest at the oasis. It was still under the glare of the hot sun that we set off. We would normally have waited until it was cooler but we needed intelligence. Saeed found the trail and it did not head west, to Berber, as we had expected but to the north and east. The birds circling above gave us the direction they were taking and we found half a dozen bodies within five miles of the fort. They were the injured who had succumbed to their wounds. With the bodies we had seen at the fort then sixty Dervish had died. We stopped when we saw the cloud of dust ahead. It was the Dervish raiders and they were leaving.

We halted and I let the men drink from their water bottles. Sergeant Saeed and I dismounted, "What do you make of it?"

He shook his head, "I was expecting the threat to have come from Berber, in the west."

I nodded. Saaed was a former Egyptian officer, and he was intelligent. Sergeant Abdul would never have made the deduction. "It might explain why we had little warning. Our patrols to the west and south, as well as the north, had an effect. What is there to the north and east?"

He pointed to the east, "Suakim lies there but north? It is just an empty desert until Egypt. The river and the fertile land lie to the west."

As we mounted to head back to the fort I said, "Well, it is clear that we need to explore here. We need Middy's maps to give us a clearer picture."

We arrived back just as the bugle sounded for food. By the time we had unsaddled our animals and cleaned ourselves up almost half of the men had eaten and left. It was a good thing for the increased numbers made it a little crowded. We would need to use sittings from now on. Sergeant Abdul vacated the table as Saeed and I approached. "I will walk the walls with my new men. Now that I have a corporal some of the weight is taken from my shoulders."

Whilst the English reinforcements had all been troopers, I had seen the stripes on one of the Egyptians. We sat and ate. The supplies meant fresh food as well as canned goods. The fresh food would not last long but we would enjoy it.

The major looked up as I sat, "They headed north and east, sir."

"I don't like that." He sighed. "It means we will have to send an escort back with the wagons. If the raiders had gone west then there would not be a danger but east…" His eyes asked me a question.

"How about Lance Corporal Richardson takes his troop, sir?"

Syd said, "My troop?"

"Yes, Sergeant Major Roberts wants us to reorganise the men into five troops. I have my new orderly, Private Jackson working on that now." He smiled, "He seems a fussy type, but he is organised."

The lieutenant nodded, "That he is, sir. He does everything by the book. He is older than the others and I am not sure how much combat experience he has."

"That doesn't matter. We have men who can fight but what we need is someone to organise us. Right, Richardson, I will have my report ready for you to take back to Suakim to give to the colonel. There is also a request for the equipment we need." He shrugged, "We might not get it, but we can ask."

I shook my head, "We need to take from our enemies, sir. They are equipped for the desert, more so than we are. We should start to think more like Arabs."

The major nodded, "One more thing, Richardson, spend a night or two in Suakim. I am asking for more magazines and supplies. You can escort the wagons back."

"Right, sir." Syd knew that there would be opportunities for him and his men to use both the markets at Suakim and the dock to get things that we needed.

The major stood, "Right, my office in half an hour. I will let you know the names of the men in your troops and I will give you the colonel's orders." He smiled, "And there is mail from England. I will let you be the postmen. Jack, you and Saeed eat first."

"Sir."

I knew that letters from home would be more than welcome. Syd and I had been on leave but the others had been away from home for more than a year. I knew that not all the men would get letters. Every soldier had a different story. Some were like Syd whose marriage had broken and made him make a new start but there were others, like me, who were taking the extra money to provide for families. There were other stories and, perhaps, I would never know them.

The orderly, Herbert Jackson, was older than any of us. His uniform was immaculate but lacked medal ribbons. It confirmed that he was not a fighting man. He stood at the major's shoulder and had all the papers the major needed to hand. When he took them back, he shuffled them into a neat pile. That was Herbert, a neat little organised man.

"The colonel is happy with our progress and he hopes to send another fifteen men next month. That means we need to make room for them here. The new men will be English volunteers and my plan is to incorporate them into troops. Jackson."

The orderly handed over the five lists to the troop heads, "Here are your troops, gentlemen. I am having a noticeboard made so that I can pin orders up outside. I will ensure that you all have duplicates and I will make you your own list, Sergeant Major."

The major smiled, "As you can see Private Jackson is a soldier who knows how to organise. The other new face is Private Rose who is the lieutenant's orderly and servant. Like Jackson here, he will make sure that we look smart but unlike Jackson, Private Rose will accompany the lieutenant on patrol. It gives us an extra man."

Price had a replacement.

"Now, tomorrow…"

"Sir?"

"Yes, Sergeant Major?"

"Saeed and I thought to take Corporal Dunn and his troop."

Jackson coughed and said, "Number Two troop, Sergeant Major."

"Thank you, Jackson. Number Two troop. We need to know where the Dervish went. We have little information about the north and east. What worries me is that Suakim might be a target."

The lieutenant shook his head, "Colonel Kitchener now has a squadron of Egyptian cavalry there. I believe we are in greater danger than Suakim."

Major Dickenson nodded, "Good idea, Jack, and that will give the rest of us the opportunity to integrate the new men."

He spent an hour going through the plans for the future. Each day would see two troops out on patrol. It meant that we had more rest than before. The colonel wanted detailed information about the Dervish positions and that meant that once we had investigated the northeast we would head back to Berber. That would be a real test for the new men.

Before we left, we were given our letters. There was just one for me and it was from Aunt Sarah. I recognised the writing. It had been sent a couple of months after Elizabeth had given birth to Victoria, my niece. There was no mention of Billy but then again, like me, he was halfway around the world. I read it three times. Aunt Sarah gave me meticulous details about Griff and his ways. Jane, it seemed had not got on with my mother and had left by mutual consent. I suspected that Billy would not like that. He had enjoyed having a servant.

As I would be out on patrol I rose early and was there as the cooks prepared breakfast. There were smiles for although they had not had to do much actual fighting, they had been in harm's way and they now felt like soldiers.

"We showed those savages, did we not, effendi?"

"If they come again they will get more of the same."

They were ebullient. None had been hurt, not even a scratch and burying the three men had, somehow, made them feel better about their performance. Real soldiers had died and they had not. They ignored the fact that they had been sent from the walls to fetch food. I doubted if, now that we had more men, they would be needed again. As I ate my porridge Saeed joined me as did Middy. We ate in silence. I was working through, in my mind, what the Dervishes might do next. They had seen that they would lose many men taking an irritation like Fort Desolation. We just protected the road to Suakim and they could threaten that from other directions. We were, in the grand scheme of things, an annoyance. They would rather we were not here but we were too few to harm them. This day would, I hope, reveal their plans.

I wrote a letter home and gave it to Syd. He would see that it was sent home on a boat. It might take three weeks to get home but it would be news and tell my family that I was still alive. I wondered if Billy would do the same.

Middy's troop had two new men, Ashcroft and Lowery. I nodded with approval as Shaw, who was also in Middy's troop, showed them how to fasten their puggarees. He also gave them two of the keffiyeh we had taken from the dead. A few weeks ago he had been as inexperienced as they were and whilst he was not yet an old hand, he was getting there. Until the wagons returned, we still only had four magazines apiece. I still had my Martini-Henry with me and that might prove to be more important. We took extra dry rations in case we could not get back. I had told the major that there was little point in leaving a job half done.

Saeed took the lead with Middy and I rode at the rear. It gave me the chance to see how the new men rode. They had ridden from Suakim but as the other troopers had discovered, riding on patrol needed more skills than simply plodding next to slow-moving wagons.

We soon reached the place we had seen the dust cloud the previous evening. It was a small oasis and the Dervish had clearly camped there. They had drunk all the water. Until the rains came, or the spring refilled it then it would be a dry oasis. Our animals had drunk well at the fort and would not need water for a while. Saeed and I examined the tracks while Middy added the oasis to his map.

"They are still heading northeast, perhaps more east than north."

"I agree, Saeed, but where?"

He did not answer for, like me, he was in the dark. As we mounted our camels to continue to follow the tracks I said, "We will camp overnight tonight. We need to know where they are going."

"In the desert, Sergeant Major?"

"Yes, Ashcroft. That is why we brought extra rations and you have your greatcoat."

Shaw chuckled, "Don't worry, Ashy, the Sergeant Major knows what he is doing. He hasn't lost a man yet."

I took it as a compliment, but I didn't like Trooper Shaw's tempting fate.

That afternoon a dust storm blew up. We had to ride with our heads down to avoid being blinded by the sand. It soon blew itself out but the sand had insinuated its way into every orifice. The rest of the journey was more than uncomfortable.

We managed to make, with a long noon rest, forty miles that day. We had not passed a second camp and knew that they had pushed on. That told me their camp was close, just how close we would discover the next day. We did not find an oasis but a dry wadi afforded shelter. The land was riven with rocks and scrubby bushes. We would remain hidden from our enemies. Saeed, Middy and I took on overseeing the watches. Middy had three men on watch and Saeed and I had two each. I had the nervous Ashcroft with me. I knew he wanted to talk but I put my finger to my lips and whispered, "Sound travels over the desert. Don't talk and if you want to attract my attention then wave."

He nodded. Jarvis, one of the older hands, just grinned.

We heard foxes and other animals in the night and when we woke we saw the tracks made by snakes and other creatures of the night but they had avoided us. We pushed on but this time I had the men keep their carbines ready to use. We emerged from the wadi and continued following the tracks. The animal dung marked the trail as clearly as mile markers back home. The land began to rise but the tracks were almost arrow-straight. Not long before noon, I saw buildings in the distance. There were not many of them but they were clearly visible as were the trees and the tendril of smoke rising. Movement confirmed that we had found their camp but there looked to be far more men than we had chased from Fort Desolation. We stopped so that Middy could add the details to his map. We could have gone closer to discover numbers but there was little point for we might risk the hornets being angered and we were too far from home.

We turned around and headed back. We did not stop at the wadi but pushed on and camped at the small dry oasis the Dervish had used. We reached Fort Desolation in the mid-morning. The men were covered in dust from the desert and we all stank of camel. The major was waiting in the gateway with Lieutenant Foster.

"You had us worried, Sergeant Major."

"Sorry, sir, but it was a worthwhile patrol. They have a camp about fifty or sixty miles from here and there are many more of them than attacked us. Middy." Dunn proffered his map, I jabbed a finger at the spot. "It looks to me like it is just twenty or thirty miles from Suakim."

"Good work, Sergeant Major. The colonel should know about this." The major was a decisive man, "Corporal Dunn, you and your troop can escort me to Suakim tomorrow. The colonel will not be happy to have so many men on his doorstep. You and your men can have the rest of the day to recover. You will not be needed."

"Sir." He led his camel off and shouted, "Number Two troop, on me."

"How did the new men work out?"

"Nervous but other than that fine. We do need the goggles though, sir. We are blind without them when a storm blows up."

"They were on the requisition. I shall ginger them up." He turned to the Lieutenant. "The Sergeant Major can command tomorrow when you take out your patrol. Just make it a short one, Archie. Sergeant Smith knows his business and the purpose of it is just to make you acquainted with the desert, eh?"

"Right, sir. Don't worry I know I am the desert virgin. I will feel my way into the sand."

I smiled. The lieutenant was a poet.

Chapter 7

Syd returned two days later. He had passed the Major on his way to Suakim. He had no wagon but he and his troop led four laden camels. The camels meant we had remounts and we would not need to escort wagons east. There were magazines as well as some goggles and, most importantly, fresh ammunition.

Syd chuckled as he reported to the lieutenant and me, "The QM at Suakim wanted to know where the old Remingtons were. I said they were all broken; the wear and tear of the desert."

The lieutenant frowned, "Why didn't you tell him the truth, Richardson?"

"Sir, with respect, if he knew that we had given them to Egyptians he would have asked for them back."

I backed up Syd, "Yes, sir. I am not saying this of the Quarter Master at Suakim but some of the Commissariat are not above selling old guns to give themselves a nice pension. We kept them so that we were better armed."

He nodded, "I am learning. Anything else, Richardson?"

"Yes, sir. The colonel now has another two Egyptian cavalry squadrons. I reckon he is ready for a bit of action. Colonel Kitchener does not strike me as a man who just watches."

He was right. When the major returned four days later, it was with another ten recruits who swelled our numbers and also more orders.

The major slapped the orders on his desk as he faced his officers, "The colonel intends to ride to Handub."

"Handub?"

"Yes, Dunn. It is the name of the place where you and the Sergeant Major discovered the Mahdists. We are taking the war to the enemy. Sergeant Abdul will command the fort in our absence. There are another ten Egyptians on their way here. They are coming on foot so they will arrive just after we leave tomorrow. We are to rendezvous with the colonel twenty miles south of Handub. That is your job, Dunn. Get us there safely."

Dunn was far more confident than he had been. He grinned, "Yes, sir, I shall do my best."

Jackson would be left at the fort and I knew that he would keep Sergeant Abdul on the straight and narrow. When we left, before dawn to ride in the cool, I wore my goggles for the first time. They had a blue tinge to them which also helped the glare of the sun. Life was much easier.

Corporal Dunn and his troop rode at the front. His troop had the most experience now. They had been to Handub and also Suakim. Ashcroft and Lowery rode more like the other men in their troop and Ashcroft already had far more confidence than before. I rode behind the major and the lieutenant with Bugler Brown next to me. We still had no colours but it felt more like a squadron than a detachment. More importantly, we would be going to war and fighting alongside others.

We reached the rendezvous early thanks to Dunn's navigational skills. It was a high piece of ground. There was no water but it was a place that could be defended and there was some scrubby grazing. Being just twenty or so miles from the coast there were more rain showers and the air was marginally cooler. It was why the colonel had chosen the place. He was an organised man.

I had learned more about the lieutenant when we had shared the command of the fort in the major's absence. He had been a lieutenant in a yeomanry regiment, the Royal Gloucestershire Hussars. He had not got on with the colonel who saw the regiment as a way of impressing the locals. The lieutenant wanted to fight and after falling out with the colonel traded his rank to become a lieutenant in the ESEG. It showed me that he was a soldier and wanted to fight. The problem was the bad habits he had picked up in the yeomanry. The major was also aware of his deficiencies but saw in the young officer, raw clay that could be moulded into a soldier. Certainly, he was less stiff even after just a week with the ESEG but he still frowned when the major called me Jack. Like the major, he did not carry a carbine and I thought it was a mistake. His sword was a good one and he had a very expensive pistol but neither would be much good unless we were involved in a cavalry charge.

The men he had brought were a mixed bunch. The one common factor was that Egypt was closer to India than England and most of them had transferred from Indian regiments that

were about to be sent back to India. Now that General Grenfell
had taken over the Egyptian army they were considered almost
as good as the Indian regiments and so men who still wished to
be in the army transferred. There was just a six-year enlistment,
following the Cardwell reforms, and many wanted to leave the
army and return to England. Life as a soldier was less hard than
it had been but with English factories now paying good wages
and sending their wares to the far-flung empire, the army was no
longer the attraction it had been. There were, however, men like
Shaw, Lowe, Atkinson and Ashcroft who saw the army as a
place where they could make a mark. All hoped for promotion.
As we camped and I walked around the men I could see which
ones would be dependable and which ones would be likely to fall
short of our high standards. I shared my views with the other
NCOs and they would keep an eye on the ones who were
suspect.

Colonel Kitchener rode into the camp at the head of his four
squadrons of Egyptian cavalry. Three were mounted on horses
and one on camels. They were undermanned squadrons and there
were less than two hundred and fifty men in total but they were
well-trained and disciplined.

The colonel dismounted close to us. I did not expect
compliments, that was not Kitchener's way. He merely strode up
to the major and said, "Your chaps will be the scouts tomorrow. I
want you to scout the enemy out tonight so that we can attack in
the morning. I do not like the enemy so close to the port of
Suakim."

"Yes sir."

He nodded to me, "Good to have you back, Roberts. Sudan
seems to suit you."

I suppose the fact that I was noticed was a compliment in
itself.

It was good that we had arrived early as it meant the camels
were rested. We headed into the dark soon after sunset. I rode
with Middy's troop and Saeed at the fore. We went as the moon
appeared from behind a cloud in the east. As the stronghold was
on a plateau the troopers would be hidden in the dark by the
lower land. We could smell the fresher air from the sea as we
climbed the gentle slope that led to what had once been a

stronghold. We stopped when Middy nodded. He had a great sense of direction. We dismounted and, by the use of hand signals, the major had the men make a skirmish line. One-half of the troopers held the reins of the camels of those who had their carbines at the ready. Despite the lieutenant's objections, it would be Saeed and me who approached the camp. I think the young officer saw an opportunity for glory and recognition but this was a job for two old hands. I left my sword and carbine on Aisha and took just a knife in my puttees and my Webley. If I had to open fire then it meant we had been discovered and, therefore, failed. We both wore the ubiquitous cloaks with the hood and they hung over our faces. Saeed would lead so that if we were challenged he would act like a local. The language was a problem as although we could both speak it, we did so with a clear accent.

We headed along a slight depression that hid us from view. We could hear the noise of the Mahdist camp in the distance. Soldiers the world over sound the same in camp. There is a buzz of conversation that is punctuated with, sometimes the sound of joy and sometimes anger. This one was no different and we puffed our way ever higher. We knew that we were nearing their camp when we came across a squatting man who was clearly emptying his bowels. Saeed raised his hand in apology and mumbled something. The man grunted and we made our way around him. The smell as we turned the corner told us that we had stumbled upon their latrine and that was a stroke of luck. Two men emerging from such a place would arouse no suspicion. There were some natural steps that led up to the plateau upon which the settlement stood.

The stink of the toilet was replaced by the smell of woodsmoke and food being cooked. There were dozens of fires dotted around the vast camp and men were clearly in tribal groups. The Mahdists were not one tribe but many. The horsemen were the Baggara and as this was largely a force made up of horsemen then they were the main tribe, but there were others and they were recognisable by their weapons. We made our way through the camp in a meandering walk that would appear as though we were seeking our camp. It was getting late, for the climb had been a long one. What we had not come across were sentries. I suppose the elevated position of the camp made them feel secure and as they had yet to be threatened, they were more relaxed about their safety. We spied the buildings of Handub. There were the remains of what had once been a fort but the crumbled walls were not even man high any more. Around them were dotted six or seven buildings, and a couple of trees and shrubs marked what had been the heart of the original settlement. Saeed and I were both counting as the Egyptian led us in a meandering circle. They would be rough numbers only but would give the colonel a picture of the place.

I spied a couple of Remingtons as we moved through the camp but the firearms we saw were mainly old rifles and muskets. All were single-shot weapons and a few of the muskets were muzzleloaders. When they fired it would be preceded by a pall of smoke. Less than a quarter had such weapons and we heard the sounds of swords and spears being sharpened on whetstones. This was an army that liked to fight in close order.

We were almost back at the start of our tour when we were challenged. It was not a sentry, we had still to see one, it was a man who stood and almost stumbled into Saeed. The man had been at fault but, as his friends laughed, he turned and began to berate Saeed.

"You old fool! Can you not watch where you are going?"

Saeed shrugged and said, "When a man needs to rid his body of spoiled goat then he must hurry. I am sorry, my friend." He bowed and gestured for the young man to go ahead. Mollified the young warrior strode ahead of us. As we followed, I realised that he would be a problem and I slipped my long knife from my sheath into my hand. We found the natural steps we had used to ascend and passed two men returning to the camp.

The young man went further along the path. He suddenly turned, "You two, do what you must there. I will have privacy and not endure the stares of two stinking old men."

Saeed nodded, "Of course, and it is considerate of you to think of our old bones."

We both squatted as though we were defecating and waited. The smell from the young man reached us and then, a short while later, he emerged. As he neared us, he sniffed. "For one who was so desperate to use this cesspit you are having trouble, old man." He had neared us and I made a mistake. I glanced up and he saw my face. I saw his eyes widen and he said, "You are not of..." He got no further. My hand went to his mouth as I rammed the long knife up through his ribs and into his heart. Saeed caught his body. We dared not leave it and after sheathing my dagger I grabbed his legs and we stumbled down the slope. He was heavy. We carried him four hundred paces until we came to a jumble of rocks that tumbled to our left. We stopped and began to swing the body. I mouthed 'one, two, three' and on three we hurled him into the air. Even close to, we barely heard the noise as he hit the rocks and disappeared. I doubted that the camp would have heard anything but we took no chances and hurried down to the waiting troop. We mounted and, without a word being said, headed back to Kitchener's camp.

We waited until we neared our sentries before we spoke. "How many, Saeed?"

"I think, perhaps, four hundred, Sergeant Major. There looked to be four standards."

A standard was a unit of a hundred men. It was an informal arrangement. Standards were organised into a rub of perhaps eight hundred to twelve hundred men.

I nodded, "I agree. They are mainly Baggara, Major."

"Saeed, you can go back to the camp with the rest and the Sergeant Major and I will report to the colonel." Almost as an afterthought, he said, "Take charge, lieutenant."

Colonel Kitchener was many things but he was not a lazy man and his lamp still burned at his tent. He had a bodyguard of six warriors but we were recognised and admitted. The colonel looked up, put his fingers together and said, "Well?"

The major gestured for me to speak, "They have no sentries set, sir. They have a number of camps on the plateau and they are mainly Baggara. About a quarter have firearms and I estimate that there are four hundred of them. Sergeant Saeed concurs."

He nodded, "No sentries eh?"

"No sir."

"What is the approach like?"

"Saeed and I approached from the east. There it is relatively steep in places. Horses and camels would struggle but..." I looked at the major.

"But the west is a long slope. It could be crossed by horsemen and camels sir, but it would have to be in daylight. When the Sergeant Major and Sergeant Saeed inspected the camp I had Sergeant Smith explore that side too."

He beamed, "Good, then we can attack. We shall make the attack at two o'clock. They will be resting from the noon sun and the glare from the sun will help us."

I was not sure but then I was not used to directing cavalrymen.

"I want the ESEG to attack the enemy on our flank. Your task is to stop them from escaping, Major."

"Sir."

"I will send written orders in the morning, but you and your men will need to rest. You are dismissed,"

As we walked our camels back to our camp I said, "In the heat of the day, sir?"

He shrugged, "It is bold but the one thing we can guarantee is that they will not be expecting it. The question on my mind is why were they waiting? They had enough men to come back to Fort Desolation and take it."

"Then they must be waiting for reinforcements. Perhaps Suakim was the target."

"Perhaps."

Before the men retired to snatch a few hours of sleep Major Dickenson briefed the NCOs and the lieutenant. "Watch the new men. These are a dangerous enemy and they will not take kindly to a sudden attack. We will be outnumbered and the colonel is relying on surprise. If things go awry, gentlemen, then we will have to think on our feet."

"Sir."

As I lay down in my blanket and cloak, I reflected that this would be my first cavalry charge. I was a rifleman. I had a pistol and a sword but I was both less familiar and less comfortable with those than with a rifle or even a carbine. Our men would be even worse off. They had no swords. We would need to halt and fire a volley from our carbines. The Egyptian cavalry had lances as well as swords. I hoped that the major had thought this through too.

We had time in the morning to check our weapons and, in my case, to put an edge on my sword and my knives. The colonel sent his orders and our place was in the vanguard. We would lead the cavalrymen to the place where we would launch the attack. We left just before noon and, for the first time, endured the hot sun of the desert. It was brutal. We would have the chance to rest before we launched the attack, but the men would be suffering. I was just glad that we had taught them to cover up. Even the new ones had seen the wisdom of keffiyeh and puggarees. We dismounted when we were in position. The concave slope helped to hide us from the camp but the Mahdists had seemed oblivious to our presence. There was no glint from weapons on the plateau. The gentle slope to the western side of Handub would sap energy and so the colonel had us all dismount. We would walk our animals up the slope.

There were no bugles. Colonel Kitchener simply waved his sword and we walked our animals up the slope for the half-hour climb. We were on the right and compared with the cavalry squadrons seemed inadequately small. I knew that the men, especially the new ones were desperate to talk but they all obeyed the orders and remained silent. The raised sword was the signal to stop and then, when we watched the colonel climb into the saddle, we did so. The camp was still hidden by the edge of the plateau. A night attack would have been safer but this was not a parade ground. There were rocks, fissures, shrubs and all manner of natural objects that would have to be avoided. A Dervish appeared at the top of the slope, just fifty paces from us. I have no idea why he appeared and he was equally surprised by our appearance. He looked at the massed squadrons of Egyptian cavalry and just stared for a moment or two. His shout almost went unheard as the colonel ordered the bugle to sound the charge.

We moved forward. Horses can reach top speed faster than camels and, in any case, our task was to guard the right flank. It was the Egyptian cavalry led by Colonel Kitchener that was the hammer.

The major turned to me, "Sergeant Major."

"Draw your carbines." Every hand slid their carbine from their scabbards. "Advance."

Omdurman

We did not charge but we walked. The Egyptian horses were cantering and, as we saw the Dervish camp hove into view, it was as though we had kicked over an ant's nest. They were racing for weapons and for animals. Ours was the smallest unit and also the one armed with firearms. We kept pace with the major and the lieutenant. Neither had a carbine. While the Egyptians galloped, we trotted. The Egyptian cavalry struck the disordered, milling Mahdists and we closed with the ones on their flank.

When we were one hundred paces from the camp I shouted, "Halt." Our line halted. "Present." We raised our carbines. "Fire." We were facing the flank of the camp. The fighting was to our left and the rolling fire of the carbines slammed into Dervish bodies. Some of the enemy had mounted while others were racing on foot, some wielding twohanded swords towards the Egyptian cavalry.

I fired my carbine steadily. I was aiming but not at an individual, the carbine was not a rifle, but at the mass of men. Our carbines began to take their toll but they also drew the eyes of the enemy to us and some of them, mounted on horses turned to charge the irritant that was the ESEG. This would be a test of the nerve of our men. "Independent volley fire!" I almost smiled at the memory of Lieutenant Bromhead giving the same command at Rorke's Drift. I emptied one magazine and slipped a fresh one in. The barrel was hot already from the sun and the volleys made it even hotter. When I fired the last bullet, I drew my Webley. The Dervish were brave men but the wall of lead sent at them had thinned out their countercharge. The Egyptian cavalrymen were now engaged in fierce hand-to-hand combat with the Mahdists but our unit represented the escape route and more men were joining the charge. One horseman managed to evade all the bullets. He bore a charmed life and he made straight for me. I lifted the Webley and aimed. The pistol was a short-range weapon and he was just twenty feet from me when I fired. The bullet slammed into his chest but did not stop him. I fired again and my second shot smashed into his head, and he fell dead from the saddle. I emptied the pistol at the ones who followed him and then let it drop. The lanyard around my neck held it. I drew my sword. The reckless and fanatical Dervishes were now hurling themselves at us. I would have to test my skills with an unfamiliar sword.

It is a strange thing but, in a battle, any battle, a man only sees what is within thirty feet of him. I daresay the colonel had a better picture however my vision was limited to the wall of spears and swords that came at us. The men were doing well. The Lee Metford's rapid rate of fire did not keep them at bay, but it slowed them. It was when men reloaded that they were in danger. Aisha's back meant that I was higher than the horsemen and soldiers on foot who raced at me. I swept my sword down as they tried to spear and gut me. They wore no helmets, and my sword was sharp. I split the skulls of the first two men who came at me. Aisha was doing her part and was snapping and biting at both the horses and the Dervishes.

It was Colonel Kitchener and the Egyptian cavalry that broke the enemy. The discipline of the cavalry was too much for the wild enthusiasm of fanatics. As the Dervish fell back to Handub the pressure on our line lessened. Sheathing my sword, I reloaded my carbine.

Major Dickenson had lost his helmet and I saw that his sword was bloody. He shouted, "Bugler, sound reform!"

The bugle sounded and the men obeyed instantly. They backed their camels into lines.

"Sergeant Major, have the men reload."

I bellowed, "Reload."

The major nodded and I said, "Present!" Every carbine was raised. "Aim." A moment later I shouted, "Fire!" as I aimed at a Dervish who was trying to rally the weakening warriors. He fell from his saddle. "Independent, volley fire."

The last volley broke them and they fled to the east and the sea. Pursuit was a job for horsemen and the bugle from our left signalled the end of the battle as Colonel Kitcher led the Egyptian squadrons to harry the Dervishes from the plateau. The Battle of Handub was over and the threat to Suakim ended.

Chapter 8

We had lost men. Three troopers were killed and four were wounded. It could have been worse but that did not lessen the feeling of loss as we watched the Egyptian cavalry return. I saw the looks on the faces of the troopers. The ones who had survived looked at the bodies of the three dead and realised that it could have been them. While our wounded were tended to we searched the enemy dead. None were feigning death and that was a relief. We took their weapons and piled their bodies on pyres. Our own dead were buried but there were simply too many of the enemy to do that for them. We burned them. Most of the swords were two handed ones and unusable but some were like mine and the major's. Men took them. One did not look a gift horse in the mouth.

We camped that night in Handub but none of us had an appetite for food. The smell of burning flesh was too great. We heard the sound of the carrion as we slept seeking partly burned bodies.

The next morning the colonel came to see us. He was clearly pleased with the victory. He spoke to the major, the lieutenant and me, "My little initiative has paid off. The gainsayers and doubters have been proved wrong. Now, what do you need?"

The major nodded to the wounded men, "A doctor, sir, and some artillery or Maxims."

Colonel Kitchener shook his head, "I can't give you any of those but I can let you have a medical orderly. That will have to do."

It was better than nothing. The major asked, "And our orders now, sir?"

"Return to your fort. You have proved your worth. Continue to do so. We have begun to reclaim Sudan from the Mahdists but we have a long way to go."

"And replacements for the dead, sir?"

"Send some men to Suakim at the end of next month and you can have your orderly and your replacements."

That was Colonel Kitchener's way. I don't think he intended it, but he was a cold man who expected the best from everyone, including himself. When we left, we were not exactly deflated but having won a battle were not as ebullient as one might have expected.

Fort Desolation looked welcoming as we entered the gates. The men had been blooded and had survived a battle. They did not swagger but their confidence rose. They had stood toe to toe with the Dervishes and emerged victorious.

I was chosen to ride to Suakim. I went with Middy's troop. Since our return, we had noticed more caravans on the road. Many were heading to Ethiopia where Italy was attempting to create their own empire. Perhaps the Mahdists at Handub had more of an effect than we had realised. When we reached the port it was a hive of activity. Corporal Dunn and I went directly to the headquarters. The colonel's adjutant, Captain Baring, greeted us, "Ah Sergeant Major, a timely arrival."

"We were told to come at the end of the month, sir."

"Quite but the colonel has been asked to join General Grenfell. Promotion!" He sounded excited but I wondered what it meant for our detachment. "There are ten men and your orderly, Cowley. We have more supplies for you but you should tell Major Dickenson that there is a new commander here in Suakim."

There was something in his tone that made me ask, "And is that likely to be a problem, sir?"

He leaned in, "Major Bainbridge likes to do things the traditional way. He is related to Sir Wolsey Garnet." His last words told me all that I needed to know. Sir Wolsey had been the one who had criticised us at Rorke's Drift for, as he put it, '*hiding behind barricades.*' "Still, you never know, eh?"

"And where will the colonel and the general be operating, sir?" I did not think it was an impertinent question for it could impinge upon our life at Fort Desolation.

"Up in Egypt, on the Nile." He leaned in again, "Word has come, Sergeant Major, that the Mahdists are seeking to enlarge their empire at the expense of Egypt." He smiled, "At the moment he is here and that is why I am greeting you and not the colonel. They are busy planning the campaign. It should make for a quieter life for you chaps, eh?"

As well as the new men, we picked up the mail. I saw that there was none for me and that disappointed me. I handed a letter over to the postmaster in Suakim. At least they would know I was alive. The medical orderly, Charlie Cowley, was a pleasant man. He had a good sense of humour and, as I came to discover, was a kind man. He was able to deal with all kinds of minor wounds and was a godsend. Once more we gained camels for the supplies had to be carried somehow. The new men were just that, new, and I realised the journey back would be a learning one for them. I was lucky that I had Dunn with me. He was highly responsible and I intended to ask the major to promote him. He had been an officer in the navy, albeit a lowly midshipman, and he could easily cope with the extra responsibility.

The major was equally disturbed at the change in leadership for we had benefitted from Colonel Kitchener's involvement. Indeed, he had created us and the freedom we enjoyed might be curtailed with a new officer in command. However, we put that from our minds as we trained the new men. Charlie Cowley proved his worth immediately. The men wounded at Handub had been treated after the battle but their wounds had still not healed completely. Within three days they were all fit and ready to return to full duty.

Our patrols now took two troops each day. One went north and one went south. The battle of Handub had changed even the rawest of our recruits into a proper soldier and the ten new men were swiftly inculcated into the ESEG. Training became easier and our patrols saw us blend into the landscape. We looked like any other desert travellers. The patrols of eight or nine men did not appear threatening and the keffiyeh wrapped around our helmets disguised our true identity. For a fortnight all that we saw were the increasing numbers of caravans using the road. The battle had given the merchants more confidence.

Corporal Dunn and I were just leading his troop back to the fort one day when the sharp-eyed Middy spotted a movement. It was to the north of us and I decided that we could investigate. It might make us arrive back at the fort an hour or so later but with the prospect of two days off it was worth the detour. It soon became clear that this was no caravan. It was an army on the move. The flags and banners that appeared from the dust cloud meant only one thing. The Mahdists were moving east. Even as I decided that we ought to move a mob of men detached themselves from the main body of hundreds of warriors and hurtled across the desert towards us. "Ride for the fort."

All of us were now expert riders and, more importantly, we all knew our animals. The Dervish horsemen began to close with us and even popped off a couple of ineffectual shots but once our well fed animals got into their stride then a gap began to open. They were keen enough to follow us for three miles but when the fort hove into view they stopped and returned north.

The sentries on the tower had seen our dilemma and we found a fort with manned walls. Our new men meant that our defences looked a little more formidable. I dismounted and saluted the major and lieutenant as they approached, "Sir, a Mahdist army is heading east. They are clearly not coming here…"

Major Dickenson nodded, "They are heading for Suakim and Colonel Kitchener was about to leave." He turned, "Lance Corporal Richardson, take your troop and leave now. Ride for Suakim." He shaded his eyes as he looked at the sun, "If you use the road and ride at night then you can be there in two days. Tell them that we think a Mahdist army is heading their way."

"Sir. Number Three troop, full gear, water skins, rations and ammunition. We are off for a little ride."

The troop left the walls and headed for the barracks. The major said, "Sergeant Smith, you can stand down the men. Come with me, Sergeant Major, you too, Lieutenant."

Once in his office, he pointed to the map, "It will take them two or three days to get to Suakim. I am sure that Richardson will get there first but will the colonel have enough men to hold them off?"

"Don't forget, sir, General Grenfell was there too. If the men have not yet left for the border …"

The major took out a cheroot and lit it, "That is the point, Sergeant Major. It may be that the Mahdists know they have left and hope to take Suakim before it can be reinforced."

The lieutenant said, "We should take the whole unit then, sir, the colonel will need every man he can get."

The major shook his head, "We are needed here. I know what you are saying, Lieutenant, if Suakim falls then we are lost. We would have to make our way north to Egypt." The prospect of a journey of many hundreds of miles was a daunting prospect. Even though it was December and the coolest time of year to travel it would mean many men would die. The garrison and the cooks would have to walk. "I am confident that Suakim will hold."

"How can you be sure, sir? You are gambling."

"No, Lieutenant. If I emptied the fort I would be gambling. I know the colonel well. He has spent too long at Suakim to simply abandon it. Even if he has gone he will have left it well-defended. If nothing else, the guns of the Royal Navy give the port an edge. We will remain at battle readiness but we will not abandon our fort."

We endured a nervous ten days before Lance Corporal Richardson led his troop back to the fort. It was a cooler day than we were used to but the sun still burned brightly. Back in England, they would be well wrapped against the cold and the wet but here in Sudan, even in December, we would not need greatcoats. Syd dismounted and unwrapped his face, "Wyatt, take the animals to the stables." He handed his reins to the trooper who led the troop off.

"Come to the office, Richardson, and make your report there. Sergeant Major, Lieutenant Foster, join us."

Once in the office the major and the lieutenant sat and Syd and I stood, "We made it in time, sir. The general had not left. In fact, they had just received more men. They had the navy as well as the 20th Hussars, The Welsh Regiment, Kings Own Scottish Borderers as well as the Ulster Rifles. With the Egyptian cavalry, they were ready to face the Mahdists, sir. The enemy wanted the water forts and Suakim. They were beaten. The general only lost twelve men and the Mahdists lost more than a thousand. I think their leader, Osman Digna, was wounded. Anyway, both the general and the colonel were more than pleased that we arrived. He used us but we only got to empty our carbines once. The battle didn't last much more than an hour. They are calling it the Battle of Gemaizah."

I know I was relieved and the faces of the colonel and the lieutenant reflected their relief. "Any changes in our orders, Richardson?"

"No sir, but…"

"Go on."

"I got the impression that the colonel was keen to have the ESEG with him. I was there when he boasted to the general of what he called, 'his innovation'. The general seemed to like the idea."

Major Dickenson nodded, "He would do. He is not a Wolsey man. He is an Indian general and knows how to use camels and horsemen." He nodded, "Well done, Richardson, you won't be needed for a day or two. You might get to enjoy Christmas."

Syd shook his head, "You can't do Christmas in the desert, sir. Back home in Newcastle, they will all be wrapped up but it will be against the cold. They will be enjoying hot chestnuts when they do their Christmas shopping. A poker in rum will be the order of the day. No, sir, what I have learned is that out here it is nothing like England. Christmas, Easter, Whit and the like, well they are just fond memories of home, aren't they sir? We just get on and do the same thing every day." He saluted and turned.

He was right, of course. When you were a soldier of the queen the traditions of home were what you fought for but did not enjoy.

Richardson paused at the door, "Sir, there were letters from England. They are in my saddlebags."

"Good, then that will be our Christmas present eh?"

I played Father Christmas and delivered the letters. The ones who did not get one, and that was more than half, put on a brave face. I knew that the ones who had received a letter would read out selected parts just to include them. Mine would be mine alone and read in the cosy quarters I enjoyed. I had a bottle of rum I had bought in Alexandria, and I decided to take a glass while I read Aunt Sarah's letter. Her immaculate hand showed the care with which she had written the letter.

Liverpool, October 1888

Dear Jack,

I don't know when you will get this letter and what might change at home in the

meantime, but I think you should know the news.
Griff is doing well. Mr Myers is delighted with his progress. Griff has added his own letter.

I looked in the envelope and saw a smaller missive. That would be a second treat and worthy of a second glass of rum.

Bet is still in England and your mother lives with her now. Griff and I rattle around here but he doesn't seem to mind his fussy Aunt Sarah. He misses Nan Bet was not well after the baby and even though she is better now she seems fearful of a trip halfway around the world. Billy sends telegrams and letters. He has gone from asking her to come to demand that she does. It doesn't help and she has not agreed to go. I can't see her making the trip in winter so, even if she does go, it won't be until the spring at the earliest.
Your sisters and their families are well. They asked me to say they pray for you each night. Griff wonders when you will be home again. Your letters are most welcome, do keep sending them.
Love,
Aunt Sarah

I read it twice and finished the first glass of rum. Billy would not be happy but I could understand Bet's reluctance to leave England. Two young children were a great responsibility. I wondered if I would have an opportunity to get to visit Billy but I dismissed the thought as soon as it crept into my mind. I was a soldier. The army did not allow for private lives.

I unfolded Griff's letter.

Dear Dad,
Aunt Sarah said I could write to you. Please excuse the
blotches. We only use pencils at school, but I like using a
grown-up pen.
I hope you are well. It is quiet here with just Aunt Sarah
and me. I miss Nan and I miss you. I hope that you get a
leave soon but I know that the Queen needs you more
than me. I am proud of you and I am doing my best at
school so that you will be proud of me too.
Love
Griff xxx

I could see that Griff's teacher, probably Mr Myers, had
worked on Griff's handwriting which was neat and the letters
were well formed. That I was proud of him was an
understatement. I wanted to get home and see him but I knew
that was impossible. The only way would be to resign from the
army. I knew that I could but I still had a job to do. Despite the
rum, I did not sleep well that night. My personal life, unusually,
crept into my dreams and troubled me.

The winter passed and all we did was patrol and ensure that
the caravan route was kept safe. We received one more mail
delivery, in February and as the letters had been sent at
Christmas they were full of Christmas news. Aunt Sarah and
Griff had spent Christmas out at Walton. I felt guilty that he had
not had a present from me and being in the middle of the desert
meant little opportunity to buy anything.

It proved to be the last mail for some time as, in March, a
rider came with orders. He was Egyptian and an officer. The
Egyptian captain came at the head of twenty men who had
marched from Suakim. We were to be relieved.

Any joy at leaving Fort Desolation was replaced by the
prospect of a journey through Mahdist-held land. We were
ordered to join General Grenfell at Wadi Haifa. We had a four-
hundred-mile journey across the Nubian desert. Since the battle
of Gemaizah, there had been no action but none of us thought
that the journey would be an easy one.

Omdurman

It was harder to leave the fort than I had expected. We had dead friends to leave. The original ESEG had attended to the graves so that they looked neat. Sergeant Abdul told us that he would tend to them for us but our departure felt like a betrayal. We had also grown close to the Egyptians. They were friends and the parting was a hard one.

We left before dawn with laden pack camels and all our equipment. We left the Sudanese outpost for the last time.

Chapter 9

Middy was our navigator once more. The major had seen the potential of the ex-sailor and he now had a temporary rank of lance sergeant. It was a step in the right direction. There were only forty of us but we had an extra six camels carrying all the spare ammunition, food, water and the equipment we had yet to issue. We rode with our greatcoats en banderole, and our heads, mouths and helmets covered. The goggles we had procured helped immensely. The bright sun reflected from the sand and the glare could cause temporary blindness.

The first day saw us in familiar territory. We had explored it before, and the oases were marked on the map we had. We knew where the dangers lay in this section of our march. We were heading for the Nile and the major wanted us to reach Abu Hamad. He had chosen that place as it was considered a sort of shrine and, as such, regarded as a neutral place. More importantly, we could fill our waterskins there and give our camels a chance to drink their fill. The two hundred miles, until we reached it, were tough. We used no fires and ate dried rations. We drank the water that had been in our waterskins since Fort Desolation. The camels drank the water at the oases. It took four days to reach the first sign of civilisation. It was a small place but there were more people there than we had seen since Suakim. The river was the lifeblood of Sudan and Egypt. Feluccas filled the river. They sailed between the cataracts and brought supplies and food to the villages and towns that dotted the mighty river.

We bought food from the locals. It was a way of ensuring a warm welcome but we camped away from the houses and kept a good watch. We held a meeting while the men ate.

Middy produced the map he had been making. The river was marked as well as all the oases between Fort Desolation and Abu Hamad. The land between Abu Hamad and Wadi Haifa was empty. The major pointed a finger at the river. "If we take this route, we guarantee water but we add more than one hundred and fifty miles to our journey. In addition, it means that the Mahdists will be in our path. I propose that we use our skilled navigator and cross the desert. It does not mean we will enjoy a journey without danger and we will not have as much water as a journey along the Nile, but we will reach the general quicker."

I liked the major. Some officers would have simply told us and left it at that but he explained his reasoning. The result was still the same but we all felt a little more involved in the process.

"How do you feel about the burden, Lance Sergeant?"

"Not as fearful as I might have been at one time, sir. Sergeant Saeed is a great help. The desert is not as featureless as people think and you can work out where there may be oases. We have two hundred miles to travel and that is a four or five-day passage. The camels can fill up with water here and Sergeant Saeed has told me that they can go four days or so without water so long as their humps are full."

I nodded, "The old water in the skins has been emptied and we can fill them with fresher water before we leave. We have spares and the lads are better now than they once were. I think they will want to get to the army as soon as they can."

"Good, then all we need to worry about is running into Mahdists."

I ventured, "The men are in good spirits, sir. The battle of Handub did their confidence a load of good and Number Three troop acquitted themselves well at Suakim. They won't panic and they each have more than enough magazines. We can keep up a healthy rate of fire if we need to."

We left the next day. We took the precaution of heading due west, along the river until we were out of sight of the houses and only then did we head due north. We had the comfort of knowing that, to the east of us and close, lay the mighty Nile. Should we need to then we had a supply of water. However, we needed to avoid it because we were still in Sudan and any men we saw armed and close to the river would be enemies.

We still rode in the column of twos and that marked us as different from the caravans and Mahdists who either rode single file or in a whirling mob. If our trail was crossed then we would be identified as British. The wind and occasional sandstorms were now seen as a blessing. They temporarily hid our tracks. We were all now more familiar with them. A mild one could be ridden through and a severe one dealt with by the expedient of making a barrier of camels and hunkering down. We only had one of those to endure. The worst part was the sand which permeated every fold of our clothes and pore of our skin.

The encounter, just twenty miles from Wadi Haifa was just that, an unlucky coming together of two bands of travellers. When the camels and their riders appeared from our right, heading for the river, we did not know if they were merchants, brigands or Mahdists. When they charged at us and began firing their weapons we knew that they were not merchants.

"Draw carbines and face the enemy." Their aggressive manner made them an enemy. I drew my carbine even as I gave the order. The major nudged his camel to the left of our line and the lieutenant rode to the right. Both had their pistols in their hands. The three orderlies took the reins of the pack camels and sheltered behind the line of armed troopers. In hindsight, I think that the line of pack camels made the warriors think that we were a juicy caravan, ripe for plucking. I do not think that they would have risked attacking British soldiers. The muskets and rifles fired from the backs of racing camels were wildly inaccurate but, even so, one managed to nick Trooper Golightly. He cried out but did not leave the line.

"Present." The carbines were raised. "Aim." I peered down the sights and chose my target. I waited until the camels and the warriors were just one hundred paces from us and then shouted, "Fire!" I had not told them to keep firing and I was pleased when it was just a single volley. "Fire!"

It was the second volley that broke them. The first one took six men from their saddles but ten fell, as well as one camel with the second. They still outnumbered us but even as I shouted, "Fire!" for a third time they were already turning their camels and heading east.

"Cease fire. Cowley, see to Golightly. Lance Corporal Richardson, take your troop and check the bodies."

The major rode towards me. He was reloading his pistol as he came. "Who were they, Jack?"

I saw Syd turning over a body. The squares of sewn material told me all I needed to know, "Mahdists, sir. We were just unlucky. They were heading for the river and we were in the way. Maybe they thought that we were merchants. The keffiyeh might have deceived them as well as the pack camels. We were lucky."

"That we were. Cowley?"

"A flesh wound sir. Golightly will have a nice scar along his arm to impress the ladies."

Syd returned with the weapons taken from the dead. We would not need them but nor did we want them used again. We would dispose of them at Wadi Haifa. The men without swords would take any usable ones that were found.

"Mahdists, sir. They are all dead. What should we do with them?"

"Just leave them, Lance Corporal. I want to push on to Wadi Haifa. How far to the camp, Corporal?"

"I think we are between twenty and twenty-five miles from the Wadi, sir."

"We can do that. Push on Lance Sergeant and make it a smart pace. The camels can drink their fill at the Nile."

While I was listening I had replaced the magazine. When we stopped for the night, I would refill the one I had used. I was getting used to firing a weapon with a magazine, but I still preferred the range and accuracy of my Martini-Henry.

The Egyptian sentries at the perimeter of the camp were suspicious of the line of dusty camels and armed men who approached them. When the major took off his keffiyeh and cloak they all saluted and their attitude changed in an instant. I could not see why we had been attacked in the desert. We did not look like British soldiers. Sir Garnet Wolsey would be appalled.

We were directed through the camp, to the headquarters, identified with the twin flags of Britain and Egypt.

"Sergeant Major, while the lieutenant and I report, see if you can find where we are billeted."

"Sir."

"Sam, take charge. Atkinson, come with me." I wheeled Aisha and headed towards the far end of the village where I could see horses. Clearly, the buildings that could be used to house soldiers were already occupied. We would be using the tents that lay on the backs of our camels. We had not bothered with them on the way here but that would now change. We were no longer freebooters but subject to Queen's regulations.

I recognised the uniforms of the 20th Hussars and their horses. Their tents were neatly laid out and I reined in Aisha close to a lounging corporal who was talking to a trooper. He looked up and I saw him dismiss me as an Arab. I took off my keffiyeh and then my cloak. I did so slowly. It was the private who saw the stripes and he snapped to attention. The corporal stared at the trooper and started to say, "What…" The nod from the trooper made him turn and when he saw my stripes, he, too, snapped to attention. "Sergeant Major."

I smiled, "Corporal, I assume that this is the camp of the 20th?"

"Yes, Sergeant Major." He pointed further north, "The Egyptian cavalry are to the north of us. The infantry camps are further east." He turned to face the west and gestured with his arm, "We can use the river to water the animals."

I nodded, "Then we shall camp further north too."

He ventured, "Who are you, Sergeant Major? The Camel Corps."

I smiled and said, enigmatically, "No, Corporal, we are the East Sudanese Exploration Group and we have just crossed four hundred miles of desert to get here." I turned to Atkinson, "Let's go Trooper."

I knew that the corporal would race and tell the duty sergeant and officer of the encounter. We passed the Egyptian camps. They were well-ordered but, somehow, not quite as neat as the Hussars had been. We eventually found an open space at the northern end of the vast encampment. I saw that there was grazing and the river was close enough to water the animals. We might be more than a mile from headquarters but, in my view, that was no bad thing. We were used to being away from the scrutiny of senior officers.

"Atkinson, ride back to the column and tell the major we have found a campsite."

He turned and rode off. I dismounted and walked Aisha to the river. There was a reassuring lack of tracks close to the river but as we would be downstream of the other camps the water might not be as clean as we might like. We had passed a well and we would use that to refill our water skins. What I had not seen were the Quarter Master's stores. We would need fresh supplies of food and it was always handy to pick up more ammunition.

I let Aisha drink and as she did so I saw an Egyptian soldier fishing. He saw my uniform and nodded. Sometimes the Egyptians saluted and sometimes they did not. I said, affably, in Arabic, "Any luck?"

I saw the surprise in his eyes that I spoke his language and spoke it so clearly. Saeed had taught me well.

"Yes, Sergeant Major." He pointed to three fish on a rock. "They think they are safe here but my father taught me to fish and they do not escape me." He looked at Aisha. "Are you the Camel Corps, Sergeant Major?"

"No, my friend, we are scouts."

"British scouts? I have never heard of such a thing. How can Englishmen scout in Egypt?" He suddenly realised what he had said, "I am sorry, Sergeant Major, I did not wish to offend."

"You did not. We have been based close to Suakim for a couple of years. We have grown used to the desert but no man ever really knows it, does he?"

He shook his head, "You are a wise man, Sergeant Major. You were at Handub?" I nodded. "We were and we showed those Dervishes that we are trained well. We have English officers and sergeants now." He stiffened, "We are better soldiers than we were and General Grenfell treats us with respect."

"I know that you and your countrymen are good soldiers. One serves with us."

"Ah. We will defeat these Dervishes should they ever venture here."

Aisha had finished drinking, "It was good talking with you. I hope you enjoy your fish."

"You can have a couple if you wish, Sergeant Major."

I shook my head, "You and your tent mates enjoy them but I thank you for your kind offer."

I walked Aisha back to the place I had identified as a camp. She sat down when I commanded her, and I paced out the area we would need for the tents. I took my sword out and marked a line in the earth. I walked further on until I found some grazing and marked the ground with an X. When I reached Aisha, I saw

106

the column riding up from the dusky south. Soon it would be night. By the time we had the tents erected and fires lit it would be pitch black.

I shouted, "Sergeant Smith, I have marked off where the tents are to be placed. Sergeant Saeed, the camels can be tethered where I have marked an x but first take two troops and water the animals."

Both men snapped a salute and said, "Yes, Sergeant Major."

"Right, you lot, dismount. Troop One, unpack the tents."

"Dunn, the major and the lieutenant's tent can go here." I pointed to a place that was far enough from the road so that the two officers would not be bothered by the noise from the road. "I will be here and the rest of you there." I pointed to two places at the end of the marks I had made. The NCOs would be a marker for the troopers.

"Jake, get a fire going." I did not tell Johnson where to light the fire. He had common sense and he would choose somewhere safe.

"Yes, Sergeant Major. Troop Five, let us find some kindling and firewood."

The dried camel dung would be used but the river would furnish flotsam and jetsam. British soldiers were the masters of improvisation. I hefted my bag from Aisha's back and also my rifle and carbine. Trooper Turner took Aisha's reins along with the other four camels. I shook my head, "Aisha has had a drink already."

"Right, Sergeant Major."

I dropped the bags and guns next to the camel that squatted patiently close to the road. Soon there was the sound of pegs being hammered into the ground. I headed for the major. "Sir?"

"We reported in but, it seems, we arrived earlier than we were expected. The general and the colonel were in conference with the senior officers, I daresay we will discover tomorrow what we need to do."

Lieutenant Foster said, "You know I never thought I would miss Fort Desolation, but I do. Here we are just part of this," he waved his arm around him, "a tiny part of a mighty machine."

"Archie, we are a vital part of that machine. We do things that others cannot. We passed the Hussars and if it comes to a battle then they will be the ones who charge at the fore but it will be our men that find the enemy."

Once the fire was going and water put on to boil then the men were able to occupy their tents. The camels were tethered and as the food began to cook, we settled into our new home at Wadi Haifa.

For the first time since we had left Fort Desolation, we ate hot food and although it was just a corned beef stew it tasted like a fine feast ordered by a king. All that was missing was the beer ration we were due. I would send Poulter to find the Quarter Master the next morning. Jackson was an efficient little man, and he had the duty roster for me even before we had begun to eat. He was not a fighting man, but we had grown to depend on his clerical skills in a way I had not imagined.

While the two officers left, the next morning, for their meeting, I gathered the NCOs. We had a camp to organise. Life in the fort had been cosy but a camp was a different matter. We organised latrines and a party to source kindling and firewood. It was not as easy here as in England nor even in Zululand. We did not have the luxury of cooks so I delegated a troop each day to prepare food. I knew that the NCO in charge would ensure that the food was fit for purpose. Another troop was charged with watering the camels each day while another cleared up their mess. We might not be fighting but we all worked hard while the sun burned brightly overhead.

I sat with Jackson and went through all the necessary paperwork. We had not been paid since Suakim and Jackson kept a list of just what we were owed.

"I am hoping, Sergeant Major, that the paymaster is here. It is not right that the chaps don't get their pay."

I nodded. In my case, more than half of my pay went directly to my mother and thence Griff but I knew that most men liked the money in their pockets. "When we have gone through this let us have a wander down to Headquarters." I had already planned on a visit but this gave us a good excuse to ferret around the offices. I had learned that while generals made the important decisions it was often the orderly corporal who knew what was going on.

Private Rose came along while we were speaking, "I wondered, Sergeant Major, if you had any dhobying that needed doing. I am washing through the lieutenant's clothes so it won't be much extra."

I normally did my own but this seemed too good an opportunity to miss. "If you are sure you don't mind, Rose?"

He smiled, "Me and Bert here appreciate that you keep us safe. Call it payback eh, Sergeant Major?"

"My dirty clothes are in my tent in a pile by my blankets."

"Righto. I will pick up the major's stuff too, Bert."

"Thanks, I will give you a hand when I get back from HQ." He stood and donned his forage cap, "Ready when you are, Sergeant Major."

I was also wearing my forage cap and with my swagger stick under my arm, we set off to walk the mile or so to HQ. Soldiers can't help it and we marched in step, down the road. There was no need to other than drills as recruits had made it second nature.

My rank was recognised as we marched, and I returned the salutes of the Egyptians we met. It was clear to me that the only British regiment was the 20th Hussars. I wondered where the rest were. They had fought to defend the water forts and I had expected a sizeable British force. The 20th Hussars were the last camp before the Headquarters. The major and the lieutenant had ridden their camels and I saw them tethered outside the building that was being used. There were horses there too and I guessed they belonged to the senior officers. The animals were watched by a sergeant and two troopers from the Hussars.

"Is there a paymaster's office close by, sergeant?"

"Yes, Sergeant Major. It is three buildings down but if you are hoping for back pay then you will be lucky. They are still waiting for the boat to bring it from Cairo." He shrugged, "Mind you, there is bugger all to spend it on around here."

We headed down the road and Jackson shook his head, "There might not be anywhere to spend it but the men deserve their pay. It is little enough as it is."

We had all the paperwork with us and after the orderly had knocked on the door we were admitted. The recent reforms had reorganised the Commissariat which had performed so valiantly at Rorke's Drift. It was now titled the Army Service Corps. They did not use military ranks, although they were classed as warrant officers, some, and the man who sat in his smartly pressed blue uniform, appeared to regard himself as superior to those who were not officers. He looked down his nose at us and I took an instant dislike to him.

"Yes, what can I do for you, I am an extremely busy man."

He had not given me my title and while that would not normally bother me his tone did. "I am Sergeant Major Roberts of the East Sudanese Exploration Group and we arrived last night after a four-hundred-mile journey through the desert. The men have had neither rations nor pay for two months and as there is a Quarter Master Store here and the Army Service Corps is present, I wondered when either would be forthcoming."

He waved a hand as though trying to swat an irritating fly, "We are all waiting for pay, Sergeant Major, but until the boat arrives from Cairo you will have to wait like the rest of us."

"Jackson."

Herbert handed over the neatly written paper, "Here is a list of the men in the group and how much is owed to them, sir."

He snorted, "You will be lucky to receive all of this. There are other regiments here too, you know."

I knew then that he would withhold the pay if he could. I knew when to walk away from a battle. I would speak to the major and ask Colonel Kitchener to intervene. We were his brainchild. I took a different tack. "Rations, Warrant Officer."

"Rations, Sergeant Major?"

I knew them off by heart and I rattled through them: "On active service, a soldier can expect, one and one-quarter pounds of bread per day, one and one-quarter pounds of meat, half an ounce of tea, two and a half ounces of sugar, half an ounce of salt, half an ounce of rice, one thirty-sixth of an ounce of pepper and half a pound of fresh vegetables or onions." I smiled, "The last rations we received was three weeks ago, Warrant Officer."

I saw Jackson smile as the Warrant Officer flushed, "I am expected to find food out here in the middle of nowhere. It is an impossible task."

I nodded sympathetically, "I realise it will take you some time to gather the supplies, so I will send men down here at, let us say two o'clock?"

His face stiffened, "Very well, Sergeant Major, but there will be more onions than fresh vegetables. They are a commodity that is hard to come by."

"Really, Warrant Officer? I saw many farms along the river and they all appeared to be growing vegetables. Surely, they could be purchased?"

He flushed again and I knew that he was not using all the funds he was supposed to, "Two o'clock then."

I was not finished, "And, of course, ammunition. We expended some when we were attacked just south of here."

That brought a reaction, "How far south, Sergeant Major?"

"Twenty miles or so."

His face fell. He thought he was safe at Wadi Haifa and my news gave him pause for thought. "The ammunition will be here also."

He would cooperate if only because we were one of only two British units and he now knew how close to the border we were."

As we left Jackson said, "You handled him well, Sergeant Major."

I laughed, "Dealing with the likes of the warrant officer is something I learned long ago."

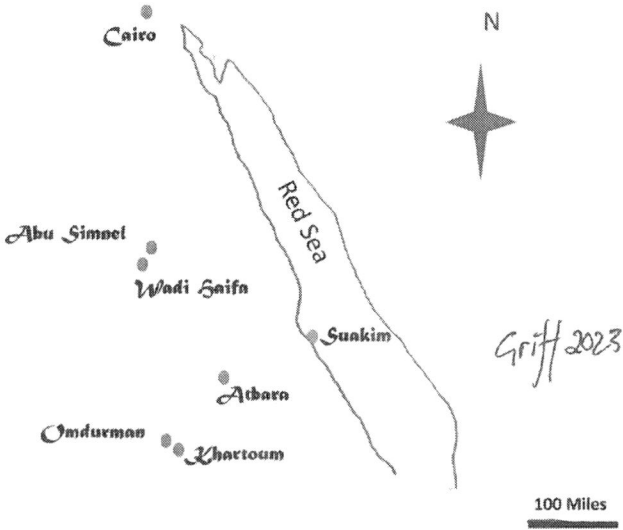

Chapter 10

By the time the two of us returned the camp looked more organised and the men had smiles on their faces. The British soldier likes to be occupied. Sam and Saeed came over to us as Jackson headed to the river to help Rose with the dhobying. "Sergeant Smith, have two troops go to the Commissariat at two this afternoon. Take a camel with you. We have been promised rations."

Sam nodded and gestured to our medical orderly, "Charlie wondered if he could try to scrounge some medical supplies. If we are going into action, then he will need more."

I nodded, "Have him accompany the troops."

"Saeed and I will go with them, Sergeant Major."

"Good. No word from the major?"

He shook his head, "Not yet."

Their camels had still been outside the HQ when we had passed and I took the lack of news as good news. We would not be riding this day but I knew that the colonel would not have sent for us if he did not intend to use us. I looked up at the sky. It was almost noon and while the tents would be hot, they would at least afford some shade.

"Time for a brew and a sit inside, eh? Get someone on it."

Sam shouted, "Lowe, Shaw, get a brew on." Cupping his hands he said, "You can have an hour in your tents." A sarcastic cheer went up and Sam said, "Cheeky blighters."

I smiled, "We might have said worse, eh Sam?"

It was early afternoon by the time the two officers returned. I guessed that they would have eaten. Despite my request for supplies we still had enough for a few days but a soldier always planned ahead for the days when he did not. We too had eaten.

"Officer's call, Brown."

The bugler sounded the call and we made our way to Major Dickenson's tent. His was the largest tent and had an awning. It meant we would all be sheltered from the sun and the major could sit. We stood at attention until the major said, "At ease." We stood at ease. "Well, we now know why we are here. We are the eyes and the ears of the army. There is a rumour that a Mahdist, Emir Wad-el-Nujumi, is planning to invade Egypt. According to intelligence." Sam could not help keeping the wry smile from his face. "Yes, Smith, we all know that, hitherto, the intelligence branch of the army has let us down, but Colonel Kitchener himself has appointed these officers and their information seems to be sound. Captain Wingate knows his business."

"Sorry, sir."

"The Emir is making the move to gain power among the Mahdists. Since the death of the Mahdi, there is a struggle for power and the emir serves Abdallahi ibn Muhammad. As the leader of the Baggara tribe, he is the most powerful of the Mahdist leaders. Anyway, this Emir has between four and eight thousand men. They will be seen from quite a distance away but, as we well know, the desert is empty and they could come from any direction. Our job is to find them. Thoughts?"

I looked at Saeed and nodded for him to speak. "Sir, they will wish to defeat the army but I do not think that they will be ready to face regular British troops. They will try to defeat my people, the Egyptians." He waved a hand. "This camp just has the Hussars and the rest are Egyptian."

"Sir, where are the soldiers we saw at Suakim?"

"The Welsh regiment has been sent to Malta while the Ulster Rifles and the Scottish Borderers have been sent to Aswan to guard the centre there. The railway and the river meet and the Mahdists had been raiding both. We need the supplies that come through there." He leaned back in his camp chair, "There is a famine both in Egypt and Sudan. The people are starving and restless. The Rifles and the Borderers are needed to keep our supply routes open."

I nodded, "It is a big desert, sir, and I would suggest we use the same practice we did at Fort Desolation. We use three troops a day to patrol. It means one troop will have two consecutive days of patrolling, but the rotation will allow the animals to rest. At least here we are close to the Nile."

Saeed said, "And if the army coming here is as large as Intelligence suggests, sir, then they will need to use the river, rather than oases."

The lieutenant nodded, "That makes sense but what if they use the west bank of the Nile? We can hardly ferry our men across every day."

The major said, "A good point, lieutenant, but remember what that chap from intelligence told us. This new Khalifa is stirring up dissent amongst the Arabs both in Egypt and Arabia. There are stories of bands of Mahdist sympathisers attacking along the canal as well as closer to Cairo and Khur Majaj. A push to the east of the river will serve two purposes. Their avowed aim is to take Egypt. The Mahdi might be dead but his dream of the Dervish empire lives on." He looked around and we all nodded. We knew what we would have to do. "Jackson, make up the roster. Sergeant Saeed, you will accompany the lieutenant. Lance Sergeant Dunn, make copies of the maps we have. If we all head south tomorrow and keep five miles between us then the land for twenty miles east of the river can be examined. We are looking for tracks and signs of large numbers. I do not think we need to travel too far south. Let us just watch the land ten miles south of Wadi Haifa. Twenty miles each day will not hurt our animals too much, eh? Dismiss."

As I headed back to my tent, I reflected that the two officers and myself, along with Rose and Saeed, would have the sorest backsides. There would be no respite for us. Sam left with the two troops and the camels for the supplies and I wrote a letter home. One advantage of being this close to the river was that we could send letters home. I knew that the nature of our unit meant more men could read than was normal. The men of the ESEG had more letter writers than the whole of the 24th. I would ask Jackson to collect the letters to have them sent. He was a resourceful man and knew the army inside out. He knew the ways and the means.

It was hot. Although June was the hottest month, July was only a little cooler and, as we headed out in the last week of July, we took the opportunity to leave before the sun had risen. My patrol headed further east and I had Lance Sergeant Dunn and his Number Two troop with me. At night the desert was different but Middy knew how to navigate using the stars and we would reach our allotted patrol perfectly, I knew that. While the major rode due south and the lieutenant south by east, we headed more east than south. Even while we rode in the cool of predawn we still sought tracks. When the sun came up it was almost in our faces and we were all grateful for the goggles.

We were seeking tracks and there was no road in this part of the desert. We rode in a long loose line with twenty paces between each camel. Nor did we ride hard. There was no need. We were alert and as there was more greenery this close to the river we tended to ride toward such places. If the enemy had scouts out then they would use those places too. When we neared them we would have cocked carbines. Once we reached trees we always stopped. We inspected the ground and took advantage of the shade. That first day we saw nothing and, as we headed back Middy and I discussed the day.

"We could be doing this every day for a month, Sergeant Major."

I nodded, "Could be two or three months. Patience is needed."

"Does this life suit you, Sergeant Major?"

I turned to look at him. He was entering territory that was normally off-limits. Syd and I were different. We had many shared experiences. I regarded Middy, however, like a little brother. Indeed, since my falling out with Billy, he was probably closer. I indulged him. "Not really but a man does what he is good at. I joined the army because a man who mentored me had been a soldier. I like being a soldier but if you are saying do I like being out here in the desert then the answer is no. My son is growing every day and I don't get to see him."

"Will you leave the army?"

"One day, I will. I have done all the time I needed to but I don't like to leave a job half done."

"And you think that we can retake Sudan, Sergeant Major?"

I laughed, "Middy, you are believing the newspapers. Sudan was never British nor was Egypt. We took Egypt to protect the Suez Canal and General Gordon chose to make a stand against the Mahdi for religious reasons. We need the canal to maintain the Empire but Sudan is just a drain. Apart from the tiny garrison at Suakim the only British presence here are us and the Hussars. General Grenfell and Colonel Kitchener command the

Egyptians. When Sudan is safe I will think about asking for a transfer back to England. And you?"

"Major Dickenson thinks that I am officer material. He has spoken to me about getting me a commission. Since the reforms, it can be done but there is paperwork involved. He seems to think that if I transfer to an Egyptian regiment it might be easier." He shrugged, "I speak the language and I think I have learned a lot from you."

"You would be happy to be out here?"

"If it means I get to be an officer then, yes. If I can get promoted, then I might be able to transfer to an Indian regiment. Who knows, I could transfer to a regular British regiment eventually."

I smiled, "You are doing the right thing, Middy, and not narrowing your options. Well, anything I can do, let me know."

We had three days of patrol where nothing happened. What did enliven our lives was the arrival of back pay. A boat arrived with the pay for both the Egyptians and us. I guessed that the powers that be worked out that the last thing they needed with famine in the land was a disenchanted fighting force. There was little to spend the money on but the men felt happier knowing that they had been paid.

The three of us had the same patrols each day and even without Middy, I was able to recognise our route. He had learned from me and I had learned from him. I could now use a compass. Four days after we had begun, I was with Syd and Number Three troop. We stopped at the first stand of trees, as normal and it was there that I spotted signs of horses' hooves. They had not been there the previous day. After the men had been watered, I said, "We head due east and then south."

We had not gone more than two hundred yards when we saw clear evidence of the enemy. The sand was disturbed for a huge swathe. Horse and camel dung proliferated. The Mahdists were on the move.

I waved my arm and we turned north to follow the signs. The tracks kept going in a straight line. There was no mistaking them but we saw no signs of enemy horses or camels. They were well ahead of us. We had some dried food with us and were well supplied with water. I took a decision. "Lance Corporal, I want you to ride back to camp and report to the major. Tell him that we have found the Mahdists and are trailing them. We will camp out here in the open."

He lowered his voice, "Are you sure, Jack?"

"Syd, we both know that if a sandstorm blows up then we might well lose these tracks. We have to keep on their trail."

He nodded and turned his camel, "I will get back with help as soon as I can, lads."

Now that we were following tracks, we adopted a different formation, we rode in pairs. One advantage we had was that while the Mahdists were a huge force and covered a large area, the handful of men I led were almost invisible in comparison. As dusk approached I spied in the distance the green of an oasis. I led the men there. After ensuring that it was unoccupied, we dismounted. There was water and the men filled their waterskins before the camels drank it dry.

"Two men will be on watch all the time. Dawson and Peters, you two will be first. Get to the edge of the oasis and keep your eyes peeled. I will have you relieved in a couple of hours."

Dawson said, "Can we smoke, Sergeant Major?"

"Here? Yes, on sentry duty, no. We can disguise the glow but not at the edge. It is just a couple of hours."

He nodded glumly, "Aye, Sergeant Major, but the flies."

"Keep your puggaree around your face and your hands covered. You will be fine."

We used the saddles to make a camp. We could use our greatcoats as blankets and, if the worst happened and we were attacked, we could use them for defence.

"You can eat but remember, until the major joins us the food has to last us." I saw the men look at the meagre rations to hand. A couple of days of such fare would do them no harm. The flies were bad. They seemed to have followed the camels. I lit my pipe, keeping the bowl shaded with my hand and the smoke worked. The flies kept away from me. I took the middle watch and did so alone. The desert appeared silent but that was an illusion. If you listened carefully, you could hear the creatures of the night as they fought their own war, a war of survival.

I roused the men before dawn and we headed back, east, to pick up the trail. Trooper Dawson felt emboldened enough to ask, "Where are they heading, Sergeant Major?"

I gestured west with my thumb, "Well clearly not to Wadi Haifa. They must know that the army is there. We are almost in Egypt now so I am guessing that they will look for a target. If I was a gambling man I would put money on Abu Simnel or Aswan. Neither has a garrison and the Mahdists could cut the Nile in two."

He nodded to the tracks we were following, "How many men do you reckon, Sergeant Major?"

"More than General Grenfell has at his disposal, that is for sure." I saw the fear on his face. "Don't worry about strategy, Dawson, or numbers. You just listen for my voice and face your front. If there is one thing I have learned it is that the British Army is better than most of its enemies."

"But it will be the Egyptians who will be fighting the Dervish, Sergeant Major."

"I served with them and they are better than the Mahdists. They have British officers and Sergeants. Sergeant Saeed was an officer in their army and he is as good a soldier as I have ever met. Stop worrying and just do your duty."

It was after the sun reached its zenith that we spied the dust cloud ahead and slowed. We had caught up with them. I had the men take out their carbines. The last thing I wanted was to be surprised. The dust cloud, however, kept heading north and west. They were heading for Abu Simnel. The map Middy had made showed me that the small town was just fifty miles ahead. We found a dried-up wadi which we used for our camp. There was no water but we still had half-full skins and the camels had drunk well the previous day.

The rest of the troop arrived after dark. We heard them before we saw them. Sound carries a long distance at night and the sentries heard them. I had heard the hooves already and I took my carbine to join them at the edge of the wadi. Middy and Saeed were leading them and I whistled to attract their attention. They stopped and then turned their animals.

"Nicely navigated, Lance Sergeant."

As he dismounted Middy said, "Quite easy, Sergeant Major, I just used angles and the speed of camels."

The Major reined in, "Well done, Sergeant Major. General Grenfell has the men on the march. They are twenty miles behind us."

I knew that although there were four Egyptian cavalry regiments, a camel regiment and the Hussars there were also six infantry battalions and artillery. They would not move as fast as the Dervish.

"The enemy warriors are just ahead. We have followed their dust cloud all afternoon. I think they are between five and ten miles ahead. What are our orders, sir?"

"To keep in contact with them." He turned, "Lance Corporal Richardson, have the camels with the supplies and water brought up. I dare say your men and the Sergeant Major will need them."

I smiled, "Just had to tighten our belts by a notch, sir."

I confess that I was relieved to have the security of the rest of the men. Only Jackson was absent and he would be busy at our camp. Syd's troop was given the night off and they deserved it. I sat and spoke with the major and the lieutenant.

"Sir, what if they continue north? I mean Abu Simnel and Aswan make sense to me but if there is trouble further north then this could be the fuse that lights a revolution."

"You are right, Jack, and if they do go further north then the Colonel wants us to alert them to our presence."

I stared at him. The lieutenant did not see the implications of his words, "You mean sacrifice ourselves, sir?"

The lieutenant shook his head, "It would not come to that, Sergeant Major."

I shook my head, "Lieutenant, there are more than six thousand men ahead of us and they are mounted on horses as well as camels. If they wanted to head north and we were close they would turn and swat us like an annoying fly. Oh, we might make them bleed a little and slow them down but make no mistake, Lieutenant Foster, if we obeyed the colonel's orders then the ESEG would be sacrificed to buy the general the time to get close to them."

The major's silence told me that he agreed with me. Eventually, he said, "Anyway, that is in the future. Tomorrow, we keep following and see where it leads us."

The next day we closed a little so that we could see the rearguard and baggage train of the Mahdists. It was a risk but I knew why the major did it. He wanted us as close as possible to the enemy. What became clear was that they were heading for the river. That made sense to me. They would need water. They were heading for Abu Simnel. Of course, it could have been just a stopover, but the major sent Corporal Dunn and his troop back to the main column to tell the general. They might be able to save five or ten miles by heading directly for the river.

The enemy camped at Abu Simnel. Saeed took two troops north in case they continued on their way. The major wanted us to be able to get ahead of them and warn any British and Egyptian garrisons of the danger. A refreshed Dervish army could strike quickly and with devastating results.

We also used the river. The major let us camp upstream from the Mahdists. We watered our camels and used thorn bushes to make a barrier around our camp. We would keep a good watch but the thorn bushes would give us an early warning of a surprise attack. At dawn on the next day the major, Lance Sergeant Dunn and I rode closer to the camp. It was a risk but the general would need to know the layout. The Mahdist army had found some rocks, there were three groups of them and they were using them as a sort of fortified camp. We saw that they had huge flags fluttering from their tops. They were coloured red, white and blue. As we had learned the white did not mean surrender here. To the north of them lay the small village of Toski. I wondered if they had left any men at Abu Simnel, which lay across the river.

Middy had just used the binoculars and as he handed them to the major he said, "Sir, what I don't understand is why they are just waiting there. Their animals must be well rested now as they have been there for two days. Surely a cavalry army keeps moving."

The major nodded, "You may be right, Lance Sergeant and it worries me too. Sergeant Major, any thoughts?"

"If that was British soldiers then they would be making their position a defensive one. British soldiers would use their fire to destroy an enemy attacking them."

"But these are not British soldiers, Roberts."

"They are expecting Egyptians to attack them. I think they hope to break the attack and then use their camels and horses to destroy the ones who flee."

"But these are led by British officers, now, Roberts."

I shrugged, "You asked me, sir, and the only reason I can see for them to squat in the rocks is to make us bleed when we attack." I pointed at the rocks. "They can see us, sir, can't they? I mean we are not hiding and the light must have reflected from the binoculars."

"Yes, Roberts, they can see us. What is your point?"

"Why aren't they sending men to chase us off? They know that their horsemen could reach us before we could get very far. They are happy for us to watch them. I think they want a battle."

We rode back to our camp and the next morning the Hussars, the Egyptian cavalry and the camel regiments arrived. The single squadron of British horsemen was commanded by a captain and was outranked by the major.

"The Mahdists are a few miles north of us. What are the general's orders?"

"He wants us to make a camp as close to them as we can."

The major waved an arm, "This is as close as we can get that is near the river. They are slightly inland from the river occupying a small piece of high ground."

The captain turned, "Ensign York, ride back to the main column and tell the general that the Mahdists have occupied the high ground and we are making a camp."

"Sir." The young officer whipped his horse around and galloped back down the road.

"Thank you, Major. We will make our camp. The horses need the water."

The five squadrons of horsemen and the single squadron of camels dismounted and led their animals to the river. A soldier learned in this hot part of the world that you either looked after your animal or faced the consequences of going afoot.

By late afternoon, the infantry and the animals pulling the artillery pieces march in. There was still light in the sky and the general wasted no time, "Dickenson, show us the enemy."

I mounted Aisha without being ordered to and accompanied the major, General Grenfell and Colonel Kitchener. I rode ahead with my Martini-Henry across my saddle. There was a bullet in the breech. If the Mahdists had binoculars too, they might see the two senior officers. The major might not be a risk worth taking but a general and a colonel were. The major explained what we had seen. When we found the place we had observed the enemy the general asked to move closer. I did not dismount when we eventually stopped but I raised my rifle and used Aisha to steady it. We were less than half a mile from the Mahdists and I saw their camps. The smoke rose from fires cooking their food.

I did not take my eyes off the crude road we were using but I heard the conversation from the three officers.

"What are they doing, Dickenson? I thought we would keep chasing them until they did some damage but you say they have not yet raided?"

"Yes, General. Sergeant Major Roberts seems to think that they want us to attack."

"Does he, by God? Well, if he is right then the Emir is in for a rude shock."

Colonel Kitchener asked, "How many men, Dickenson? I assume you have a rough count?"

"Six thousand, sir."

"And we have less than four thousand."

"Don't forget, Colonel, we have two batteries as well as three thousand men armed with Martini-Henry rifles. Their little safe haven might prove to be a death trap."

Just then I spied two dozen horsemen who mounted their horses and galloped from the camp. "Sir, there are horsemen coming for us." The sun was dipping in the west but there was still enough light for them to see us.

The three men, unlike me, had dismounted. Our lack of guards now made us vulnerable. We were more than a mile from safety. I aimed at the leading rider. The range was too long but it paid to track the man. The three officers seemed to take an inordinately long time to mount. I suspected that was the fault of the major on the camel. The horsemen were less than two hundred yards from us when the major said, "Ready, Roberts."

I fired and my bullet hit, not the man, but his horse. Without looking to see the effect I whipped Aisha's head around and urged her on. The general and the colonel were mounted on horses and they had already extended a lead over the major. I was the last man and the one at risk. I sheathed my rifle and drew my pistol. Aisha was the best camel in the troop and she began to catch up with the major. The angry buzz of bullets and balls fired from the Mahdists made me turn. They were less than one hundred paces from us. I pointed my Webley under my arm and fired. It was a blind shot but, as I glanced behind I saw that it made them move to the side. It was a small thing but it allowed Aisha to gain a yard or two. The general and the colonel would be safe. They were more than fifty yards ahead but the major and I were in danger. The major's camel must have been nicked for it was slowing.

I heard from ahead, a familiar voice, "Present!" It was Sam. "Aim!" I saw the thin line of men from the ESEG. They were using the camels as a barrier and there were two sections whose Lee Metfords pointed towards us. I trusted the men and knew that the major and I were in no danger. "Fire!" The carbines bucked and I saw the flare from the barrels in the darkening gloom of dusk. "Fire!" The disciplined volley made me proud of what we had done with the raw clay that had come to us. I looked over my shoulder and saw that five saddles had been emptied and the survivors were racing back to their rocks.

The Major reined in, "Well done, Sergeant Smith."

He sheathed his carbine and said, in a matter-of-fact manner, "Just thought I would give the lads a bit of exercise and when we heard the Martini-Henry we knew that Sergeant Major Roberts was firing." He turned, "Lance Corporal Richardson, take your troop. Collect the weapons and any animals you can."

We rode into the camp where there was a buzz of excitement. They had heard the firing but the coming on of dusk had hidden the action from them. We walked our animals into camp and Jackson and Rose led our two camels to the river. The bugle from the main camp told the major and the lieutenant that the general had sounded officers' call.

We had eaten by the time the two of them returned. The major was grinning, "The general, it seems, is impressed by the ESEG and the quality of its men." The other NCOs all beamed. Hitherto we had, seemingly, been ignored. "Tomorrow the general intends to attack before they get a chance to run. We will be with the Hussars on the left flank. The Egyptian horse and camels will be on the right. We are there to prevent them from attacking our infantry and artillery. The general intends to make a long line of infantry and after the artillery batteries have softened them up, march them close enough for their rifles to destroy the enemy."

It sounded simple but I knew it was anything but.

"We are to be in position at dawn."

I nodded, "Right, have the lads clean their guns and load any empty magazines. We water the camels two hours before dawn and I want the men to have hot food. It may be a long day tomorrow."

The nights were never cold but it was always easier moving in the relative cool before the sun rose to make the desert bake. We had an easier task than the Egyptian cavalry for we were closer to the river. It lay half a mile from us. We stopped four hundred yards from the rocks. We had seen no evidence of artillery and the muskets and rifles that the enemy used were out of range. If they made the mistake of attacking then there would be more than one hundred and twenty carbines that could send a thousand bullets at them.

We dismounted and watched the dust of the infantry battalions and breech-loading artillery pieces. The tanned faces of the British officers and sergeants were reassuring. It told me that the battalions were British-trained. They would stand. I watched as they were marshalled, in their battalions, into three lines. It took less time for them to do so than when I had first served with the Egyptians. They were good soldiers but their Turkish officers had not led them well. Four of the battalions that I saw were Sudanese. They too had British officers and sergeants. This would be the first time I would see them fight at close hand. I saw General Grenfell, his staff officers and Colonel Kitchener. It was the general's sword sweeping down that began the battle. The cannons belched smoke and their shells whistled

125

in the air. When they struck the rocks I heard screams. The falling shells would shatter rocks and send shards and splinters to scythe through the waiting men. After an hour the infantry were moved forward into range. The Mahdists responded and opened fire but it was not the disciplined volleys that destroyed an army's will to fight. When the Egyptian and Sudanese volleys rolled across the desert the difference between the two armies was clear. The Mahdists had more men, but we had the discipline. I knew, at that moment that we would win.

The Dervishes were brave, but they were not fighting in their natural way. They were cavalrymen and hiding in rocks and sniping was alien to them. After two further hours, the fire from the rocks had lessened and it was then that we saw some horsemen mount their animals.

Major Dickenson had been placed in command of this flank and he was decisive. "Captain, mount your men. Sergeant Major."

"ESEG, mount."

When we were all mounted the Major said, "We stop the Mahdists getting to the river." He waved his sword and we moved forward in two lines. We trotted towards the three hundred or so mounted men who had decided that they had endured enough. We were charging them obliquely and despite their horses, we would strike them before they could reach the safety of the river.

The Hussars had already drawn their sabres. I waited until we were two hundred yards from the nearest warrior before I shouted, "Draw swords." I drew my own. It was not standard issue. I had taken it from a dead officer when I had first come to Egypt. It was longer, straighter and heavier than the ones used by the others. We had rarely practised with swords and I hoped we would have no disasters.

The Hussars were the first to make contact for they were slightly faster than we were and there were more of them. They were well trained in the use of swords and striking at unprotected backs began to reap a harvest of Dervishes. Aisha afforded me a higher position and I had to lean from the saddle to sweep down and split open the skull of the warrior who was to my right.

The men who had fled were not the bravest of the warriors and as they were hewn from their saddles the last of their bravery evaporated. They shouted that they wished to surrender.

The Major shouted, "Throw down your weapons first."

Lieutenant Foster shouted, "Hussars, they are surrendering."

Some of the Hussars had the fire of the fight in their bellies and it took their own Sergeant Major to make them halt.

Our little action had not gone unnoticed by the rest of the Mahdists and a short while later, as we herded our prisoners, we saw that they had surrendered. The Egyptian and Sudanese soldiers had shown that they were now a force to be reckoned with. They had won the battle of Toski and we had taken four thousand prisoners. Their leader was killed while trying to rally them and the invasion of Egypt was short-lived.

Chapter 11

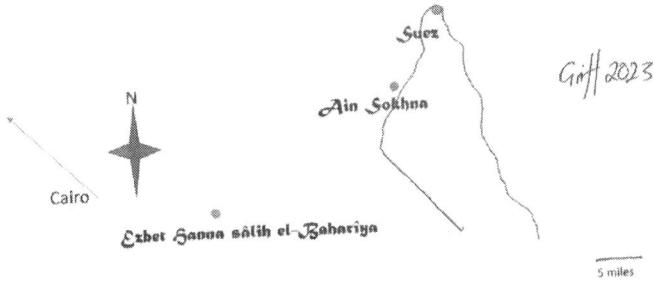

We marched the prisoners back to Wadi Haifa. Saeed and his troops returned to us having sat for two days waiting for an enemy who never came. After a month at Wadi Haifa, Colonel Kitchener came to see us. He was in an ebullient mood.

"You have all done especially well and my brainchild has made those gainsayers take note. The ESEG will be sent back to the north where you will train others in the tactics you have demonstrated so well." He nodded to the Lance Corporals. "All of you will be promoted to the rank of sergeant. Lance Sergeant Dunn and Sergeant Saeed, General Grenfell feels that you two have shown that you are true leaders. He offers both of you a commission in an Egyptian battalion. Would you accept the transfer?"

In Saeed's case, I knew that he would accept the promotion immediately, but Middy was another matter. However, both snapped a salute and said, almost as one, "Sir, yes sir."

"Good, then when you have said your goodbyes come to HQ. Major Dickenson, you will take your men to Suez. There is where you will train the new men. You will be the only military unit in the area, and you can act as a defence there. We have heard of bandits who are trying to cause unrest amongst the locals."

"Sir. How many men will be in the new unit?"

"You misunderstand me, Dickenson. Your written orders will be here tomorrow, but your task is to make another four versions of the ESEG. When they are trained they will be sent back to Wadi Haifa and they will join British units. I want you, Lieutenant Foster and Sergeant Major Roberts to create copies of the ESEG."

With that, he left. There were, of course, great celebrations but I was not sure that I wanted to be stuck at Suez and become a teacher. If I was destined to no longer fight in Africa and just train soldiers then I would rather be back in England. It was after we had eaten and were enjoying a smoke that the others turned to the major and me. Syd was the one who spoke up, "It doesn't seem right, sir. I mean you and the Sergeant Major, well you made this troop what it is and yet we have all been promoted. You and Jack have not. It is not right."

The others nodded. I could see that the major was disappointed with the lack of promotion. In my case, I had not even thought of that. I was just happy for the others. The major tried to put a brave face on it, "When we get the orders then things will be clearer. For my part, I do not begrudge any of you the promotion. I feel that you deserve it." He looked at me, "I would have hoped that Sergeant Major Roberts would have been offered the rank of lieutenant too but…"

I tapped my pipe out in the palm of my hand and threw the ash away. I shook my head, "Saeed was an officer before he joined us as was Middy. I never expected a promotion and, besides, I have served in an Egyptian regiment already. To be honest, sir, if I am going to train men then I would rather do it in England. I have a son."

Silence greeted my words. I had not meant to say it so soon but when Syd nodded and smiled, I knew that it was the right time.

When the orders came they also came with the news that Major Dickenson was to be a brevet colonel, he would be Lieutenant Colonel Dickenson and Lieutenant Foster would be a brevet captain. When I clasped arms with Saeed and Middy I felt both proud and sad at the same time. Both were friends. I had helped them and they had both helped me. The army saw many such partings but that did not make it any easier.

"Sergeant Major, Jack, you will always be my friend and I will hold that friendship here." Saeed patted his heart.

"And you, Lieutenant Saeed, will forever be in mine."

I turned to Middy, "You deserve this, Archie, no one more. I just hope that you will be happy here."

He smiled, "You know, Jack, I think I will. I loved the sea but the sea did not love me. Here I can sail the desert like the ocean. I am a good navigator and I can do something here I couldn't do in England. I am just sad that your talents have not been recognised."

I shrugged, "Archie, I joined this army to be a soldier of the queen. I joined without any expectations. I am a sergeant major and that is a rank I never thought I would achieve. I am content."

He lowered his voice, "But you won't stay in Africa."

"No, Archie, I won't. I will help the Major do what he must and when it is all organised I will go home and see my son."

"Good."

The rest of the troop was excited as we headed north. We would follow the river until we reached the Pyramids and then turn east. The orders told us that the men we would be training came from India. They were all volunteers and unlike the first tranche, these had experience of heat. In theory, it would be easier to train them. It explained why we had been sent to Suez. The troopship bringing them would be able to unload there. While the others were excited to be part of this venture I was reflective. I would be there for the start but I made it quite clear to the major, when we camped at night, that I wished to return to England. After a few abortive attempts to dissuade me, he promised me that he would do all that he could to secure me a posting close to Liverpool. "The army owes you that much, at least."

We were heading north and we passed the Tropic of Cancer but the temperatures rarely dropped. I knew that we had become well-acclimatised to the heat in a way that few British soldiers managed. We were helped by the new khaki uniforms which, unlike the red woollen ones, were fit for purpose but the ESEG had adapted. We rode camels as well as most Arabs and we could cope with the desert. We reached Suez at the end of November. The year would soon be over and my son would have grown once more. Next year would mark the twentieth anniversary of joining the army. That was quite a milestone.

Suez was a busy place. Ships waited patiently to use the canal and a thriving little town had grown around the port. The locals sold things to the crews of the ships travelling in both directions. If they were heading south then the next place they would land would be India. The trade with the ships was profitable. I saw warehouses, for some ships landed their goods and then simply headed back to India, Australia, New Zealand and the southern seas. They were the faster ships for the voyage along the canal was slow.

The major headed for the Union Flag flying over the guarded building close to the port. He and the lieutenant entered and we watered the camels. The men's eyes sought the places where they could buy a drink. This was civilisation and that meant alcohol. It might be a Muslim country but it was ruled by the British and it was not only gallons of tea which kept the Empire running but beer, rum, gin and whatever other alcohol the British soldier could buy. I looked for somewhere to buy tobacco. They grew tobacco in Zululand but Sudan did not. The last of my tobacco, brought by Syd from Suakim, was almost gone.

The two officers were in the building longer than I had anticipated. When they emerged, with some papers in his hand, the major's face was dark. "We have arrived, it seems, somewhat propitiously." He pointed to the west, "The camp is over there. We are lucky, there is a well and a couple of buildings. The soldiers we are to train have not yet arrived and so there are just a handful of Egyptian soldiers guarding it and the equipment that is there."

As we headed along the road that would, eventually reach Cairo, I knew better than to ask for more details. This was not the place to talk but I wondered what had upset the major so much. He was clearly shaken.

There was a well and four simple wooden buildings and a building with a roof but without walls; clearly, it was a stable. They were little more than wooden barracks. The Egyptian soldiers had their weapons ready as we neared them and only relaxed a little when they recognised the uniforms of the officers.

"We are the ESEG and we are here to take over this depot."

"Thank you, effendi, it has been a great responsibility to guard it for there are guns, ammunition as well as other supplies. We have had to deter many who wished to take them."

Major Dickenson nodded, "Sergeant Major, have the camels taken to the stables while I examine the buildings."

"Sir." I dismounted and led Aisha towards the primitive stable, "Right, lads, you heard the officer."

Lowe grumbled, "Not much here, is there, Sergeant Major?"

"And what did you expect, Lowe? The Ritz? We are here to do a job and as there are no distractions we will be able to impart what little knowledge is in your head to the new chaps."

Chastised and with the others chuckling he was silent. Jackson and Rose had brought the officers' camels and when we had taken off their saddles we piled them neatly to one side, the side facing the desert. They would act as a sort of windbreak. We had all grown close to our animals and anything that we could do to make their lives easier, we would.

The lieutenant pointed to one building and shouted, "This is the barracks for other ranks." He turned and pointed to a second building, "This is officers and NCOs."

"Righto sir. Move your gear into the barracks. I will give you a shout when I need you."

"Right, Sergeant Major."

Sam and Syd flanked me as I hefted my gear and walked towards the building. Syd said, "We can soon tart it up, Jack. We have endured worse. Remember what Fort Desolation looked like when we first arrived?"

Sam nodded, "Aye, I wonder if the bread ovens are still working well. They baked good bread."

I pointed, "There is plenty of empty space here, Sam. We can build one here."

I saw that the building was compartmentalised inside. There were eight small rooms and a larger area. Major Dickenson was seated at the table, studying the papers he had been given.

Brevet Captain Foster pointed to the two nearest rooms, "Those are ours. Take your pick from the rest, Sergeant Major."

There did not seem much difference so I went to the nearest one and threw my bag onto the canvas cot. There was no wardrobe but I spied some nails hammered at regular intervals. I hung my clothes from them. They were off the floor and to hand. I made up the bed. That meant putting down my blanket on the bed. I liked something next to the bed so that I could see the photograph of Griff, Aunt Sarah and my mother. I would see what I could pick up in Suez, the next time we were there.

I stepped outside and Major Dickenson, now a brevet colonel, waved me over. He was smoking a cheroot and Brevet Captain Foster was smoking a pipe. The Major, I still thought of him as such, waved me to a seat. "We have, Jack, a problem." He pointed to the map. "Three weeks ago, just about the time we were setting off from Wadi Haifa, a group of merchants, all Englishmen, were on their way back from Cairo. Their caravan was attacked west of here and six prominent businessmen were taken as hostages. A local emir fancies himself as a Mahdist. He has demanded a five-thousand-pound ransom for their safe return. He is little more than a warlord but this is a way for him to become rich and gain a reputation. He has taken them to a place south of here, Ezbet Hanna sâlih el-Baharîya. It is a piece of high ground about seventy miles south of us and carefully selected. According to the locals, it commands a view for miles around so they would easily see if we attempted to rescue them. We don't know the numbers involved nor their weapons but our orders are to rescue them. There are eight Britons." He looked at me, "One of them is your brother, Jack. I recognised his name from the list, William Roberts."

Had he slapped me I could not have been more shocked. I knew Jack was in Egypt but I had assumed he was in Alexandria. I was stunned but I was a professional. My face did not change as I nodded, "Do we take the whole troop, sir?"

He shook his head, "The Egyptian sergeant tells me that there have been many suspicious characters scouting out the camp. The ammunition and guns are worth a fortune. Not everyone is a fanatical Mahdist, there are still criminals out there. I was going to leave Poulter and his troop along with Jackson. He can get this place organised and Poulter is the QM."

"Now that Middy has gone that leaves us with Number 2 Troop, sir."

"We haven't the time to appoint another NCO, Sergeant Major. You will have to command them."

I had detached myself from Billy's plight. Worrying about him would avail me nothing. I put my mind to the problem ahead. We had thirty-six men and an unknown number of enemies. We did not have Dunn and his maps. This would not be easy.

"When do we leave, sir?"

"The sooner the better. The abductors are expecting their money in a week from now."

"I take it the ransom will not be paid, sir."

"Her Majesty's Government does not bow to criminals. We are to rescue the hostages and bring the perpetrators back for trial and execution."

I was aware that the other NCOs had been listening to the conversation. I stood, "Right, let us get organised. Poulter, see what supplies we have. I want every man with at least one hundred rounds. We don't know if there will be oases or where they will be. I want double the number of water skins." I looked at the officers, "I reckon we can get there in two days, sir."

The major nodded, "That will give us a chance then as they are not expecting the ransom for a week."

"The rest of you, brief your troops and we leave before dawn. I saw a road heading south and we can make good time while it is still dark. If we can travel twenty miles while it is dark, we might cover forty miles tomorrow, maybe even more."

They nodded and began to leave, Syd stopped at the door, "It is your brother, Jack, the lads will get him back. This is like family."

I shook my head, "We can't think like that, Syd. The other men are someone's brothers, husbands, and sons. We owe it to them all."

As we were eating, my mind distracted from the food, Syd said, "You know, Jack, if we took the spare camels and rode like the Arabs, if we are seen we might be taken for a caravan."

Jake nodded, "And we might need transport for…" He did not finish the end of the sentence. We might find corpses. There was no guarantee that the payment of the ransom would result in the freeing of the captives.

I nodded, "We do this like every other job we have been given. We try to get as many of the prisoners out as we can and we don't take chances. I don't want to have to write any letters home, right?"

Everyone nodded. I saw Major Dickenson scrutinising me, "You know, Jack, that if you want to sit this one out we will all understand."

I looked back at the officer, "I know but I am still the Sergeant Major and until I go home I will do my duty, no matter what." I had a sudden thought, the word 'home' triggered it. "Have the families been informed?"

He shook his head, "No, the powers that be thought it was unnecessary. The commander at Suez informed Cairo and he was waiting for us to arrive. It is a good thing that we made such a speedy journey. He seemed to think that sending half a battalion of regulars might just result in the recapture of corpses. We are the best chance to take them out alive."

I did not sleep well. It was not the fault of the cot but the dilemma. Billy was young and I prayed that he would have survived but as we all knew he might be dead already along with the others. I rose in the middle of the night to make water and to pray. It helped a little. My lack of sleep meant that I rose first and I ate a little. It was only because I knew that I would need food. The others rose early too and we left two hours before dawn, taking the road south. There was a moon and the road was clear. We made good time and when we stopped at Ain Sokhna, an hour before sunset, we had covered thirty-six of the seventy-five miles. We did not rest there. We watered our horses, paid for bread and after half an hour pushed on south. Ezbet Hanna sâlih el-Baharîya lay to the west of us. Five miles south of the village, according to the map we had, there was a fork in the road. One fork headed south, down the Red Sea and the other went west to Cairo. There was no road to Ezbet Hanna sâlih el-Baharîya. Once we left the road any watchers would know where we were going. Our plan was to leave the road at the fork and disappear into the rocks and scrubland that we hoped lay to the east of the stronghold. We would have the next day to scout it out. It was a rough plan but our advantage lay in the skills of the men with whom I rode. They were the best.

We used the time on the road west to plan. The major had his ideas but he was a good officer and listened to advice. I confess that we missed Saeed. His knowledge of the desert was second to none but we had all learned. "When we reach a camp then we use hand signals. Johnson, you will have your troop guard the camels and the camp that we will make. I don't know where that will be until we find it but I want one hidden from the top. Foster, Rose can stay with the camels too."

"When do we attack, sir?"

"Night, I think, Archie…"

I shook my head, "Sir, that is a mistake. While it would hide us we would have no way of knowing who the captors are and who needs to be rescued. If we approach in the dark but attack at dawn we will see which is which."

Major Dickenson looked ahead as though visualising the attack and eventually nodded, "It might work in our favour. The night guards will be ready to come off duty and the ones relieving them will be tired."

Sam asked, "Prisoners, sir?"

The major shook his head, "If we can then yes but we take no chances. The priority will be the captives. These are important men. They are the lifeblood of the empire and besides, the bandits murdered every man with their caravan. They are ruthless men, and we must be just as ruthless as they are." Sam nodded. He had just wanted clarification. "So, we reach a place to camp, Jack, Sam and I will go to scout out the defences while the rest of you make a cold camp. We rest during the day and then the three troops will approach and rescue the prisoners." He smiled at me, "Your brother will have a shock when you are with the rescuers." I said nothing. It was bad luck to assume success.

We reached the foot of the rocky, natural fortress after dark and we picked our way around the side to approach it from the south and east. We had decided that would be the direction they would least expect a rescue attempt to be made. The huge outcrop of rock that rose at an acute angle was the perfect place for us to shelter from the sentries that would be watching for us. Its disadvantage was that it faced south but we reasoned it would still give some shade from the sun.

We dismounted and the three of us discarded everything except for our uniforms, keffiyeh, blades and pistols. The keffiyeh wrapped around our heads would disguise us and, if we were spotted, might delay an alarm. The other two deferred to me. I had shown, many times over, that I could pick my way over rocks and loose sand without coming to grief. I had helped Lieutenant Bromhead track the deserters in Zululand. That had been my education. The defended top of the stronghold was less than a mile away and we had all night to get to the top and back. We could sleep during the day. There was a path, of sorts, I guessed it was made by animals. We passed sheep and goat dung although we saw and heard no animals at all. The path wound up the side. Goats are clever beasts and use the line of least resistance.

It was when I heard voices that I raised my arm and stopped the others. A rock was close to my right and I pressed myself into it. There were men ahead but I could not make out how far away they were. It became clear that they were emptying their bowels from their words and when silence followed, I risked moving. The smell told me that I had been right and identified their latrine. It was a slightly more open area just one hundred yards from the top. I could smell horses and hear them. There was the smell of woodsmoke and although the night was dark I caught a glimpse of a crude building and some tents. The other two joined me and lying close to the rocks we scanned the skyline. There was one rock that was taller than the rest and stood proud of the camp. I spied two figures there perched precariously at the top. It was like our tower at Fort Desolation. During the day it would afford a view over the land that surrounded the camp and even at night would be the best place to see an attack. There were other sentries too. I counted four. They walked around and chatted with one another. I could not see directly into the camp as there were rocks in the way. Any attempt to get closer risked discovery. Having seen enough the major pointed down the slope and I led the way down. Knowing where the rocky eyrie lay helped me. And after an hour of careful stepping, we reached the camp.

As much as we wanted to speak we knew that sound travels at night. We would wait until dawn. The watches had already been set and I rolled into my greatcoat and I tried to sleep. I knew that what we planned was possible but what I could not know was how the prisoners were held. I eventually fell asleep realising that this was, for Billy and his fellow captives, the best chance of rescue. A battalion would guarantee the death of the bandits but would probably result in the captives dying. A battalion was a blunt weapon. We were a scalpel.

When I woke I heard nothing. We had trained our animals to be silent and as they had been well watered and they had food they were content. I drank water. You learned, early on, that you drank regularly in the desert. You were always thirsty, but you took just enough to keep you alive. The overhang of the rock made a shelter from the worst of the sun but, as I discovered, any noise was echoed. The men had realised that and were as still as could be. The major had already woken, and he waved me, Sam and the lieutenant out of the shelter of the outcrop where we would be able to talk. We found a rock that sheltered us a little from the sun in the east and also hid us from the mountaintop. We squatted.

"Jack, those two men on the rocky tower are the problem. What do we do about them?" The lieutenant had not been with us and he frowned. The major explained, "There is a natural tower of rock and two men watch from it. We can get to within a hundred yards of the camp but once we go beyond it we will be seen and they will give the alarm."

I had pondered the problem when I had wrestled with sleep. "There is no easy solution to that problem but if we have men take out the other guards we saw then if I use my Martini-Henry, I can shoot the two sentries and then they will be blind. We will be attacking at dawn and the rest should be asleep."

Sam said, "What we don't know, Jack, is what time they rise."

The major said, "Then we get there in plenty of time. As soon as there is enough light for Jack to shoot then we take out the sentries." The major took out his knife and drew in the sand. "This is rough. We know where the building is and a couple of the tents but that is all. Archie, you will lead Number Two troop and approach from the south. Take Cowley with you. Keep him safe as he might well be needed for any injuries. I will go with Richardson and Number Three Troop. We will go around the camp and come from the northwest. Sam, you bring your men from the northeast. We will take care of the sentries. It doesn't matter when we take them out but Jack will have to wait until dawn before he shoots to ensure he hits them."

Sam looked at the lieutenant when he said, "It will have to be knives." The two officers nodded. It would be execution but the lives of the six Englishmen hung in the balance. We had not signed up for it but we would do whatever it took and live with our consciences afterwards. I had no qualms but then again my killing would be at a distance. It would be Sam, Syd and another two men who would have to sink their knives into the throats of the bandits.

We went over the details a few times. Each of them would have to brief the men that they led. One advantage we had was that the Lee Metford carbines would give a good rate of fire. Even though we might be outnumbered we would have surprise on our side.

"The captives, sir, what about them?"

"Once we have overcome the bandits, we try to secure them."

I shook my head, "When I have shot the sentries sir and while the rest of you overcome the opposition, I will find the prisoners."

"That is a risk, Jack."

I nodded, "Sir, it is my little brother with the other prisoners. I know that I will be taking a chance but I have taken chances before when it was not as important as this. I am not asking anyone else to risk their lives but once I have shot the guards then I will drop my rifle and find the prisoners." I smiled, "It is not as though the men don't know me, sir, is it? I trust them not to hit me."

He nodded, "I suppose you are right."

They went back to speak to their men. There were whispered conversations. I joined Jake's troop on watch and I was gratified that I could not hear the conversations. The major marked off Syd's troop to watch for an hour while we slept. I stood a watch and Sam took over from me. It meant we all rested during the day and yet the camp was guarded and watched.

As darkness fell we prepared. The others had carbines, but I had my Lee Metford. I would take my sword but instead of hanging it from my belt, I wore it diagonally so that it would not catch. With my Webley and knives, I felt I was well-equipped to deal with whoever I met.

I led the way up the slope. We had more men this time and the other leaders were well-spaced to keep a steady pace. We moved slowly. The reason was twofold. Rapid movement might be seen and haste might make a slip and create noise.

When we reached the latrine we stopped. Sam and the major led their troops away and we waited. I laid my rifle against a rock. I would lead the lieutenant to the place where we would watch when I spied false dawn. I was just about to lead them off when I heard footsteps. Someone was coming to use the latrine. I waved the men to the rocks and picked up my rifle. The bandit sniffed and peered at the ground. He was seeking a clean place to use. As he looked down I lifted my rifle and then brought it down hard on the back of his head. I mimed for Lowery and Ashcroft to secure him and raised my rifle. There was no further noise. I did not know if the man was dead or alive but the two troopers had trussed and silenced him. I led the troop and the lieutenant closer to the camp. We had been lucky. The man I had clubbed must have been a sentry for there was no one close by. I saw no movements and deduced that the other sentries had been silenced. I nodded and the lieutenant mimed for the men to prepare their weapons.

I moved through the rocks until I had a good view of the two shadows at the top of the rock. It rose fifty feet in the air. I idly reflected that the men who stood a watch there had to be good climbers. I could have risked shooting at their shadows. So long as they were hit then they would die as the fall would kill them but we needed some light to identify the captives. I raised the rifle and rested it on the rock. I took two more bullets from my pouch and held them in my left hand. I waited as the sky began to lighten. I aimed the rifle at the top. I was patient. As soon as I could make out their features I prepared to fire. I aimed at the older man, the one with the grey-flecked beard. I aimed at the large target that was his chest. Squeezing the trigger, I fired and as one bullet was ejected I loaded the second. The first man fell and the second turned and began to raise his own rifle. He could see the smoke but it was the last thing he saw. My bullet slammed into him and, like the first guard, he fell from his perch. I reloaded the gun, rose and ran towards the camp.

Considering the sound of the two shots the bandits were slower to react than I had expected. I saw a man emerge from a tent before me and I fired from the hip. He was less than ten feet from me and the force of the .303 threw him back into the tent. I dropped the rifle and drew my pistol and sword. I ran for the building. There was enough light to make out faces and, all around me, as bandits rose and left their tents the Lee Metfords rattled out their song of death. The troopers knew how to use the carbines to best effect. I ran the gauntlet of friendly fire and bandits appearing before me. I was heading for the building. It was little more than a mud edifice but it had a roof and a door. I reasoned that it would be the place they used to keep the prisoners. The bandit who ran at me with a sword took me by surprise but before he could skewer me he was struck by a bullet. A warrior appeared from the building. My Webley was in my left hand and I fired. The bullet hit him but did not stop him. I took another two steps and slashed my sword down across his face. The sounds of battle were all around me. Bullets buzzed alarmingly close to my head but I ignored them. I trusted my troopers' skills.

Stepping over the dead warrior I kicked open the door and peered into the dark. An English voice shouted, "Watch out, behind the door!"

I turned as the bandit thrust a sword at me. I used the pistol to deflect it but it still scored a nasty cut down the back of my hand. I punched at his face with the hilt of my sword and then fired the Webley at point-blank range. The flash lit up the room and the noise deafened me. I barely had time to turn as the third guard from the room ran at me. He, too, had a sword and I fired the Webley. He was a big man and although I hit him, he kept coming. I fired a second bullet at his head. He was dead.

The flashes from the gun had made my night vision disappear. I said, in the dark, "Is that it?"

The English voice said, "It is."

Then I heard a second voice, "Is that you, Jack?"

It was Billy and I smiled, "Aye, it is, our kid. You sit tight."

I went to the door and, after sheathing my sword began to reload the Webley. I witnessed a furious fight. The troopers were still in the rocks and the flashes from the carbines' muzzles were all around. The bandits lay in groups but there were still some alive. This was a needless slaughter. I shouted, "Lay down your weapons. You are surrounded and we have the hostages. It is over."

Just then a figure turned. Unlike the rest, this one had bejewelled fingers and a fine sword. He shouted, "Die!" and ran at me. I fired three bullets and he fell at my feet.

That signalled the end of the fight. The survivors dropped their weapons and raised their arms.

A figure appeared next to me. It was a middle-aged man. He was unshaven and looked gaunt. He pointed at the body, "Thank you, sir, that evil creature was their leader. You gave him too swift an end. He deserved to suffer."

I nodded and shouted, "They are giving up. You can come in now," I turned to the man, "I am Sergeant Major Jack Roberts of the ESEG."

"Then you are William's brother. You may be too late."

Just then someone in the room lit the oil lamp and it was bathed in light. I saw the other men but my eyes were drawn to the figure with the bandaged leg. It was Billy. He was smiling but, as I neared him, I could smell the stink of putrefaction. He had gangrene.

Chapter 12

I knelt next to him and cradled his head in my arms. "Cowley!"

"I knew you would be the one. Isn't that daft? I mean Egypt is a huge place but I knew that the one who would come through that door would be my big brother."

"Of course, I came. Cowley! What happened? Did they do this to you?"

He shook his head, "My own fault. I tried to run when they were bringing us. I fell and broke my leg. It has gone bad. The smell makes me sick."

I forced a smile, "Don't worry. We have medical help." I turned to shout again and I saw Cowley appear with his medical kit in his hand.

"I came as fast as I could, Sergeant Major."

I looked up, "This is my brother, Billy. He has broken his leg."

He looked down and I saw, from his face, what he thought of it. He took his bag and said, "Sergeant Major, if you could clear the room…"

"Of course."

"Right, gentlemen, it is quite safe outside. You can leave my brother with me. He is in safe hands."

As I turned, I saw that Cowley had given Billy his water skin. He was taking a bottle from his satchel. "Right, young man. If you have a drink of this then I can have a look at the wound."

Billy drank the spoonful of mixture and lay back. He looked up at me. "I am sorry we parted so badly, Jack." He shook his head, and his eyes began to close. I thought he was asleep but he opened them again, "Bet wouldn't come, you know. I was lonely here and..." His eyes closed.

"Bill!"

"He is just asleep, Sergeant Major. I need to look at this wound." He began to unwrap the bandage. The smell was even worse. I saw the two bones peering from the angry red flesh. The orderly turned to me, "Jack, he has blood poisoning. If I had found him a few days earlier, then we might have saved him. He would have lost the leg but he would be alive."

"Charlie, there must be something you can do."

In answer, he took off Billy's trousers and pointed, "He has a compound fracture of the tibia and fibula. You can see the ends of the bones. Had they been joined and cleaned there might have been a chance but the blood is infected. The blood poisoning is in his body. If he was a horse or a dog..." he left the words unsaid. "I can make him comfortable and ease the pain but he won't see Suez, let alone England. When he wakes then make the most of the time you have with him." I nodded. "You can cut along if you like. This will take some time."

"I am not leaving." I took Billy's hand in mine and held it. It was a good job he was asleep for Charlie had to clean away dirt and dried blood. The ends of the bone looked jagged and I knew that it was too late to try to splint it properly. He took out a splint and, as gently as he could, secured it to the leg. He bandaged it.

Just then the major and the lieutenant entered. Major Dickenson said, "The other survivors told us. How is he, Cowley?"

I answered, "My brother is dying, sir."

Silence filled the stinking, foetid chamber.

"I am so sorry, Jack."

"So am I. This is the sort of end I envisaged for myself, not my little brother."

Cowley saw my hand and shook his head, "And you need tending to as well." He cleaned up the wound and bandaged it.

The major said, "Some of the men have scrapes too, Cowley."

"Righto, sir." He rose and said, "Just be there for him."

I nodded.

"I have sent for the animals. I hoped to leave today but..."

The officers left and I sat close to Billy. Like the middle-aged man, he looked gaunt and thin. His fine clothes were in tatters. He had not seen an end like this when he had accepted the offer of promotion. He had gone for the money and this was the result.

He slept for an hour. When he woke, I made sure I was smiling. "Well, you had a good sleep. Do you feel better?"

"Your chap has made it less painful." He looked up at me, "I know I am dying, Jack. I am not a fool. The smell told me that days ago. I have hung on to life because… well I knew you would come."

"And here I am."

"Look after Bet and the bairns for me, will you?"

I could not speak. Words would not come and I simply nodded.

"I can see now that this whole venture was a mistake but it seemed to guarantee a fine future for my family. How could I have foreseen this? I will never see my family again, will I?"

You don't lie to a dying man and I shook my head, "No, Bill, but Charlie will keep you comfortable and I will stay by your side."

He looked at me, "You were the one who came in here to rescue us. Why you?"

"I am a good soldier, Bill, and I was chosen. I am glad."

Charlie came back in. "We have a shelter rigged up outside, Sergeant Major. The air is cleaner and we have food." He waved forward four men. I saw that they had a stretcher they had made. "Be gentle with him." He smiled at Bill. "I have more medicine to ease the pain, son."

"Thank you."

We lifted him onto the stretcher and I helped them to carry him outside. There was a shelter. I smelled the smoke from the fire. The prisoners were being watched. The camels were tethered. All the troopers were staring silently at me and my brother. I saw Syd detach himself, "I am Syd, one of your brother's mates. It is good to meet you, Bill. If you need anything then just ask. Me and the lads will try to make you as comfortable as we can."

Bill gave a thin smile, "Thank you, Syd. I will try not to be a burden."

That day was a hard one. I ate just because Bill wanted me to. He slept most of the time for Charlie kept up the medicine doses. That night I slept next to my brother. No one asked me to do a duty and I am not sure I was ready to do one. When we left the next day Billy was slung between two horses on the stretcher. Charlie and I led the horses down the slope. It took half a day to reach the road and, thankfully, Billy slept for most of it. The major sent a rider back to Suez to tell them of our success. It felt like a failure to me but I knew I was wrong.

The others spoke to the rest of the captives but once we were on the road I rode next to Bill on one of the captured horses. Charlie led the pair of stretcher-bearing animals. When he was awake and lucid, I spoke to Bill about home, Mum, Aunt Sarah, Bet, his children and Griff. There were no more words of the past and of regrets but only of hope and the future. By the time we reached Ain Sokhna, it was almost dark and all of us were ready for a rest. I felt no sympathy for the bandits who had been forced to walk, barefoot, first down the mountain and then along the road. They had kidnapped innocent men and while they had not directly caused Bill's wound, they were responsible. I ate but Billy just drifted in and out of consciousness. We had made the journey south in two days but it would take a little longer to get back to Suez. Our pace was determined by the bandits' progress and, more importantly, the need to keep Bill as still as possible.

After Charlie had given him a larger dose than normal and my brother slept, Sam and Syd came to speak to me. We smoked a companionable pipe each. Sam used his stem to point at the other captives. "They had been to Cairo for a party. A nabob wanted to wine and dine them. Bill didn't want to go but a telegram from Head Office said he had to go as it would increase their business."

I shook my head. Once again, I saw his promotion as a poisoned chalice.

Syd said, "This lot," he pointed to the prisoners, "want hanging. They butchered the servants who were with your Bill and the others. It was all for money. One of the businessmen speaks their language and they were just using the Mahdist cause as an excuse to line their pockets."

Sam asked, as I tapped out my pipe, "Do you still want to go home, Jack?"

"More than ever. I have to. I promised Bill I would watch over his family and I can't do that in Egypt. Besides, I have done what I said I would do. If they won't give me a posting home, I will take the pension and get a job back in England."

Syd nodded, "I won't be far behind you. I intend to save what I can from my pay, do a year or so over here, and then back to Newcastle. I might have forgotten her by then."

"And you, Sam?"

"I like it here and when you go I become Sergeant Major. The money is good and I like the job. We are good at what we do, Jack."

"I know but can we ever win?"

"That depends on what you mean by win. Can we make Egypt and Sudan safer places to live? I reckon so. I don't think I will die out here..." he suddenly realised what he had said, "Sorry, Jack." I waved a hand to dismiss any offence he thought he had caused. "A few more years and I can go home well set up. I can open a bakery. I would like that."

We left before dawn. Billy had barely spoken but he had tried to smile. Charlie was doing his best to help my brother. His supply of drugs was rapidly running out and, in many ways, they were wasted. It was merely palliative care but Charlie was one of the kindest men I knew.

Billy died at noon when we stopped to rest the animals, water them and eat some food. I was next to him and holding his hand when he died. His back arched as though he had a spasm of pain and I said, "Charlie!"

Bill smiled and squeezed my fingers, "No, it is fine. You know I have always been proud of you. I could never be you and I wanted to be the best that I could be but I was always singing your praises. Thank you for looking out for me."

I did not even have the chance to reply. He gave a soft sigh and his eyes closed.

Charlie had raced over and seeing his eyes closed he felt his pulse. He shook his head, "Sorry, Jack, he has gone. It was a mercy. He is in no more pain and he is with God."

I nodded, unable to speak.

The major came over and put his arm around my shoulders, "The camp is just a few hours away, Jack. We will take him there."

I croaked, "Sir." I was not in Egypt for the last few miles. My thoughts were in England and the family who would get a telegram they had always expected for me but now it would be for Billy.

When we reached the camp Sam had the men dig a deep grave. My medals were back in England but I took the medal ribbon and placed it in Billy's hand. The heat meant that we had to bury him quickly. I understood that but it did not help. I was too distraught to speak and it was the major who said kind words as he was interred in a little patch of Egypt. I cannot even remember the words but the looks on the faces of the survivors told me that they had been well said.

The two officers and Number Four troop escorted the prisoners and the rescued captives back to Suez. The condolences from the other former captives were well meant but felt empty. I went to my cot and lay down. The others gave me space. When I rose, after they had all eaten, the other NCOs were sitting around the table. There was a bottle of rum on the table and they poured some in my mug. I took a deep swallow.

Sam lit his pipe and said, "I know it is not important right now, Jack, but we will put a cross on Billy's grave and I promise that so long as the ESEG is here we will tend it. We will not forget him."

I took out my pipe and began to fill it, "The hardest thing about leaving Egypt will be saying goodbye to you lads. It was hard enough with Middy and Saeed but you, well, you are like brothers." I realised what I had said, and I winced. I lit the pipe to stop my hands from shaking and sucked in the aromatic smoke.

I raised the beaker, "Here's to Billy and to the ESEG, both are close to my heart."

Before I went to bed, I went outside to the freshly turned desert soil and I just stood. The moon came out and my shadow spread across the grave. I don't know how long I stood there but, eventually, Syd took my arm and said, "Come on, Jack."

I went to bed.

The others returned at noon the next day. They had with them the first twenty recruits from India. The businessmen had been grateful to us and promised food, tobacco and alcohol to thank us. Everyone, it seemed, was happy and I feared that Billy was forgotten, another casualty of war. I was still the Sergeant Major and work was the best way to heal my hurts. Over the next few days, I threw myself into the training of the new men. Every time I passed the grave it was a reminder of how parlous life was. The others walked around me as though I was a ticking bomb about to go off. I was not. I was a soldier of the queen and I knew how to detach Jack Roberts from Sergeant Major Roberts.

A messenger arrived in the second week and he had with him the confirmation of the promotions. Lieutenant Colonel Dickenson, Brevet Captain Foster and Sergeant Major Smith all had their ranks confirmed. The sergeants had received theirs when we had first arrived in Suez. There was a promotion for Cowley, who, in my view, richly deserved it. I am not sure if the confirmation would have come as quickly but for the rescue, however, I was pleased for the others. There was talk of a medal for me but that seemed inconsequential in the grand scheme of things.

There were also orders for me. The Lieutenant Colonel called me into his office. He had a bottle of brandy open and poured us both a good glassful. "You have your wish, Jack. You are being sent home to England. There is a regiment that needs you. The Loyal Lancashires are based at Fulwood near Preston. They were formed eight years ago by the amalgamation of the Loyal Lincoln Regiment and the Lancashire regiment. Colonel Grafton is the commanding officer and he has approved of your appointment. You are promoted to RSM."

"Thank you, sir."

He shook his head, "He is a friend of Colonel Kitchener and he thinks very highly of you. I think he wants you where he can get at you. I don't think he has forgotten you."

I shook my head, "I am done with Egypt, sir, I will go home and train men so that they have a chance of surviving."

I had a week to hand over to Sam and for the goodbyes. To be truthful I was touched. Some of the troopers, like Atkinson, Lowe, Shaw and Lowery were genuinely upset at my departure. They threw a party for me before I left and the food and drink were provided by the rescued captives. I suppose the cost was a fraction of what the ransom would have been but it was a kind gesture. I rode Aisha for the last time. Sam and Syd accompanied me as I headed to Suez to take a ship to Alexandria and then a troop ship home. I had back pay in my pocket and I now had three children to buy for. I took my responsibilities seriously. I had promised Bill that I would watch over his family and I would.

I now had too much gear for a kitbag and I bought a chest made of cedarwood. Sam and Syd carried it aboard while I said farewell to my camel. I found it hardest to say goodbye to Aisha. There was a chance I might see Sam and Syd again, both promised to visit when they had a leave, but the animal I had ridden for so many years would now be ridden by another. I stroked her ears as I nuzzled her, "It won't be me riding you, old girl but one of the troopers. He will be lighter that is for sure. You have been more than my camel, you have been my companion and friend. I shall miss you."

They say camels are dumb and nasty but when Aisha bowed her head to touch mine I knew that they were anything but dumb. The boat was waiting and after a firm handshake for I did not wish to risk words, I boarded. As the ship headed north I saw the three camels and my two friends. I was leaving Egypt.

Chapter 13

I saw the canal for the first time and it was as impressive a piece of engineering as I had ever seen. It was certainly a more pleasant way to travel. The desert was hot and even trains were smoky, smelly, and hot. I was not the only passenger but I wanted to be alone with my thoughts. I had one night and a day in Alexandria and I used the time to buy for those in England. As I boarded the steamship I said, "Goodbye, Egypt. You are keeping more than a little part of me here."

This was not a troopship. It was a cargo ship with cabins for passengers. The English soldiers who had helped to hold back the Mahdists were now back in England or India. Some were heading down to South Africa where the Boers were beginning to become a nuisance. The result was no troopships commandeered by the war office and my chit afforded me my own cabin and service in the mess with the other passengers. There were just thirty of us but there were six stewards to tend to our needs. As I sat down to dine in a salon with tablecloths and silverware, I reflected that this was how Billy would have travelled on his way out. I could see how it might seduce a man. The stewards were attentive to the point of fawning. I suppose they were used to being tipped by the richer clients who used the service.

I was not the only soldier. There were four soldiers from India. They had the tanned, leathered skin of veterans. All were sergeants and all were heading for retirement. We naturally sat together. That, in itself, caused a problem. The tables were for four and they naturally sat together having travelled from India as a group. I sat alone. They saw my uniform and waved me over and, whilst I was at first reluctant, I moved my chair to join them. The chief steward did not like it and asked for me to return the chair to its table. I might have obeyed for I was never one to cause trouble but Jim Aitcheson, the informal leader of the group, would have none of it.

"Listen, little man, we have ten days aboard this ship and all of us are soldiers of the queen. We don't mind being a little cramped, do we, lads?" I found myself nodding with the others.

Jim was, as I came to realise, a force of nature. "You now have a cosy table over there." With that, he turned to me, "Jim Aitcheson, formerly a soldier of the East India Company and latterly, a counter of beans." I nodded, intrigued. Before I could answer he went on, "This is Bert Milligan," an almost completely bald man nodded, "Angus McCoy," the man to his left beamed a smile that showed me that he had lost his two front teeth. The man was a pugilist. "And Joseph Bell. We have all done our time in India and we are taking our pensions to go back to England."

The chief steward had given up and resigned himself to having to deal with soldiers. His face told me that he preferred a different clientele.

"I am Jack Roberts. I am on my way back home to start training men of the 1st Loyal Lancashire Regiment."

Jim nodded, "A sergeant major, eh? You have done well. You are, what, thirty?"

I shook my head, "Thirty-six."

"Even so, you must have seen action."

"A little." I was reluctant to speak of my wars and I left it enigmatically at that.

Jim was having none of it. As the soup was brought and served, he said, "We have had a long voyage from India already and as we served together for the last twenty-five years we know all that there is about each other. I can sum it up quite quickly. Until 1874 we served as soldiers in the East India Company. Like you, we wore red uniforms and used British weapons. Then the Government nationalised the company and we were transferred to an Indian regiment. We were all promoted to sergeant and we fought in little wars against bandits. For the last three years, we have run the stores in Calcutta. You, I can tell, have led a more interesting life."

Sighing I nodded, "I was in the 24th at Rorke's Drift and served in the Zulu wars…"

Over the next three days, I told them about life in England and South Africa. I told them about Hooky and then my transfer to the Egyptian Army. They too had met officers like Harding-Smythe and my tale was interrupted as they told me of equally obnoxious young officers who had come to India and ruined men's lives.

In many ways, it was good to talk about the past. I realised, in telling the tale, that my life had been a good one. Billy's death had made me despair and fall into a depression. As I told the story of Jack Roberts, soldier of the queen, I realised that Billy had made his own mistakes and that there was nothing I could have done to stop it. Even had I never joined the army and worked my whole life in a glass factory, Billy would still have gone to work at Hargreaves and Winterbottom. His potential would have been recognised and he would have been manipulated into the man he became, not the one God intended him to be. By day four of the voyage I had come to terms with Billy's death. I was able to comfort myself, as I sat by the stern looking east and smoking my pipe, that I had been there at the end and I had not left his side from the moment we rescued him until he slipped away. I could have done no more. I became, at that point, a better companion for the four men. They had amassed a larger amount of money than any other soldier I had ever known. I quickly realised that they had done so partly through criminal activities, selling army supplies, but also by trading themselves. They would not be as rich as a nabob but they had the money to set themselves up with a pub or a business. Jim especially was an enterprising man.

As we passed the coast of France he and I were by the stern where we were sheltered from the wind and we smoked our pipes. The four of them had a large quantity of tobacco that they intended to sell in England, along with some spices and silks. They had planned their retirement well. I had been given a couple of pounds of tobacco by my new friends. Jim said that it was payment for my stories.

As we talked, he tried to persuade me to resign my commission, "Listen, Jack, you know that you will be used by the army until you are a dried-up and desiccated shell of a man. They will hand you a pittance of a pension that won't even put a roof over your head. You will end up having to work for someone else who will not see your worth and give you the least that he can. Come and work with me. I am heading for Manchester. The town is growing." He leaned in, "I heard that there are plans to build a canal to the sea. Liverpool's days are numbered. This is not public knowledge and before property prices go up I intend to buy a pub and start an import-export company. With my contacts in Calcutta, I will make a fortune."

"Jim, that is a fine and generous offer, but I am just a soldier."

He laughed, "Do not do yourself down. Me and the others just wore the uniform but you made a difference. Men like you can be relied on. I don't know yet how I might use you but I am willing to gamble that you would be an asset."

I confess that I was tempted and I gave Jim an acceptable answer. I said that I would think about it but first I had to see my family and discuss matters with them. "Fair enough. It will take me a year to get set up in any case. They haven't even announced the start of building work yet. I have time."

As Jim was travelling to Manchester we travelled together on the train from London. Angus was heading for Glasgow and he also came with us. They parted from Joe and Bert at Waterloo. The name of the station seemed an appropriate place to part. The four had divided their goods on the ship and ended their association. My chest was placed in the luggage car along with Jim and Angus'. We would part at Crewe where I would get off the train and take the one to Liverpool. This time it was not a through train. A change was necessitated.

Jim leaned from the window, "I have your address, Jack, and when I am sorted I will write to you. Don't delay in your reply. Chances like this only come once in a lifetime. Do not spurn it."

I nodded and waved as the steam from the engine billowed around me. I wondered if the chairman of Hargreaves and Winterbottom had said something similar to Bill.

My chest meant that I had to take a hackney carriage from the station. Aunt Sarah knew that I was coming home; I was expected. The change of trains meant that it was after eight in the evening when I pulled up outside Aunt Sarah's house. It was spring in England, but I wore my greatcoat for I was freezing. It would take some time to become used to the lower temperatures.

Griff was now nine and when the door was thrown open at the sound of the hooves on the cobbles I saw that my son had changed. He was taller and leaner. He had lost the puppy fat of the boy I had left. He also looked more like Annie than ever. I was pleased for he would be a reminder of my lost love. As the chest was unfastened and Aunt Sarah's hand brought a handkerchief to dab a watery eye, Griff stood wondering what to do.

I grinned, "Not too big to give your dad a hug are you?"

He hurled himself into my arms and squeezed me tightly. He said, in my ear, "I am glad you are home, Dad. Are you staying, this time?"

The taxi driver stood with his hand open and as I paid him, I said, "I hope that I am and I can watch you grow day by day and not year by year."

Aunt Sarah had recovered her composure, "Get your things in the house, Jack. I have tea on the stove."

Griff and I manhandled the chest into the hall. It filled it. "I will take it upstairs to my room, Aunt Sarah."

The chest was clearly too big for the room, however, I worked out that if I emptied it, stood it on its end and fashioned a rail, it would act as a wardrobe. As we lifted it upright Griff asked, "Is this new, Dad?"

I nodded, "I have left Egypt and I had too much for my kit bag. I had a local carpenter make it. He did a lovely job. He used Lebanese Cedar. No moths here and look at the joints. This is a well-made piece of kit."

"But I thought you were home for good."

"I am, son. This was just a way to get my gear home and it only cost me a few bob. Craftsmanship like this is always worth keeping." I took out the guns and placed them beneath the bed. I saw Griff studying them and I said, "A simple rule, Griff. I don't mind you looking at them and, if I am present and allow it, for you to handle them but if I ever catch you touching them when I am not here…"

"I won't, Dad. Can I touch them now?"

I shook my head, "Let me get unpacked. Besides, you want your present, don't you?"

He nodded eagerly.

I had sought the maker of lead soldiers in Alexandria, and he had some new figures. They were British soldiers wearing khaki.

I paid extra for him to paint stripes on one of them so that it looked like me. Griff's eyes lit up, "Is this you?"

I smiled, "Could be. The uniform and the stripes are right."

"They mean I can fight even more battles. Thank you, Dad." He threw his arms around my neck and hugged me. I was home and this was what I had been missing.

I descended wearing just my trousers and shirt. I would need to buy civilian clothes, but I had four weeks in which to do so. I also took my pipe and bulging pouch.

There was a fire in the hearth, and I sat in my chair and began to fill my pipe.

"Griff."

My son obeyed Aunt Sarah's command instantly. It was a good sign. When he returned he had a glass filled with foaming ale and Griff carried it as carefully as though it was a crown jewel.

"I bought a few bottles from the off-licence. You still like brown ale, don't you?"

I laughed as I took a swallow, "After the beer I have drunk in Egypt it is like nectar. Thank you."

I had half finished the beer and not even lit my pipe when the stew with the suet crust was fetched to the table. This was hearty provender. Griff brought the pickled onions, beetroot and piccalilli. Aunt Sarah had pulled out all the stops to give me a feast worthy of a returning soldier.

We had a rule in our house that we didn't talk while we ate and the only sounds to be heard were the click-clack of cutlery, the crackling of the fire and the slurping of my beer. I was in seventh heaven.

When we had finished and after the apple crumble had been devoured I sat back and patted my stomach. "Many more meals like that and I will need a bigger uniform."

There were some things we could talk about, especially with Griff sitting there and others that were taboo. Billy was clearly taboo.

"Your telegram just said that you had been posted home but not where."

I pointed the stem of my unlit pipe north, "Preston, Fulwood Barracks."

Her face lit up, "Why that is just up the road. Will you get leave?"

"I am sure I will but in any case, I won't be a world away, will I?"

"And you are home?" There was an underlying message in the question and her eyes bored into me.

I nodded, "I reckon another five years and I can leave the army. I will have a nice pension and I will still be young enough to work."

She smiled but Griff looked sad, "I like having a dad who is a soldier. All the other boys in the class are envious of me." I smiled at his vocabulary. I did not think that many other boys would know such a word. "Their fathers are dockers or work in factories. You are a hero."

I shook my head, "That is too strong a word, Griff. I just do my duty."

He shook his head, "No. Mr Myers did an assembly about Rorke's Drift and he mentioned you by name. He talked of how a handful of men held off a horde of Zulus. I was so proud when all the other lads asked about you and what you were like."

As we couldn't speak about Billy then Bet, my mother and Billy's children were also off limits and so we spoke of England, Griff's schooling and Sarah's life outside Hargreaves and Winterbottom. I took Griff upstairs and prepared him for bed. He read to me from a new book he was reading, *'Count Robert of Paris'* by Walter Scott. It was a story of knights fighting in the Crusades and he seemed engrossed in it despite the vocabulary. Aunt Sarah's influence was clear. I tucked him in and descended. The table was cleared, the dishes washed and dried and Aunt Sarah was seated close to the fire with a small glass of sherry; her indulgence.

I went to the sideboard and took out the half bottle of rum I had brought back with me. I poured a large one and sat by the fire. We looked at each other, without saying a word and then I lifted my glass. Looking up I said, "Here's to you, Billy. I hope you are at peace now."

Aunt Sarah said, "To Billy."

I put the glass down and began to fill my pipe, "Now tell me the tale, Jack. The telegram was, perforce, basic. He died but how and why?"

I shook my head, "It's not a pretty tale and I wouldn't want to upset you."

She sighed and downed the sherry in one. That was unusual for her. She shook her head, "When you tell your mother what happened and Bet, then give them a sanitised version. I want the truth, I need the truth. Imagining what it was like has kept me awake."

The pipe was filled and I took a taper and lit it. When I had the pipe going, I nodded, "I will tell this the once and then that is it." I told the story but I did not give her the details of the pain of Billy's end. I just said that we rescued him but the blood poisoning killed him.

She stood and went to the sideboard where she poured another small sherry, another first. She sat down and sipped it, "I can tell that you have spared my feelings but at least I know that his big brother was with him at the end. That you risked your life for him speaks volumes, Jack."

"But it was all in vain. I suppose our rescue meant that the others survived but …"

She shook her head, "Jack, he did not die alone. You were meant to be the one who rescued him."

We sat in silence for a while. I smoked my pipe and watched the fire dance. Aunt Sarah sipped her sherry. She was an eminently practical woman, "Now we have to put our minds to Bet and Billy's children. They can't afford the house."

"Billy had investments and he told me, once, that it was Hargreaves and Winterbottom who made the loan to him."

She frowned, "And in that way, they had their claws in him. I worked for them for years and I believed I was well thought of. When I got Billy the job, I believed I was doing the right thing but when old Mr. Hargreaves died and his son, Willoughby took over, things changed."

"Changed?"

She nodded, "We began to expand. When I first worked there we were a small office with just eight of us. Billy got his job because young Mr. Hargreaves started to expand into new markets. Mr Winterbottom was quite happy to be given the dividends and profits. He never questioned what Willoughby was doing."

"Did he have a will?"

She sipped the sherry and her forehead furrowed in a frown, "I know that when he said he was going to Egypt I suggested he write one." She looked up at me, "Do you have one?" My guilty look told her that I did not. "Oh Jack, what would happen to Griff if you died? What about your pension? It will cost a few shillings, but we will get yours written and when we go, tomorrow, to Walton, we will ask Bet."

"How is she?"

"I am not sure that it has sunk in yet. She was ill for a while after the baby and then she decided not to go to Egypt. I know that she had a couple of letters from Billy but, well, you know better than any about the problems of the post in the tropics. I think that he was out of sight and out of mind. She and your mother were upset, of course they were, but it was as though it had happened to someone else."

"The children?"

"Jack can barely remember his dad and Victoria, well, she is still a baby." She smiled, "She is a pretty little thing and Jack dotes on her." She stood, "Having you home might help me sleep a little easier and you have comforted me. Knowing that Billy did not die alone will destroy the night terrors." She came over and kissed the top of my head, "Make sure the fire is damped down before you come to bed."

"I will, and if I have not said so before, thank you for looking after Griff."

She smiled, "He is the light of my life, Jack. He brings me so much joy that my heart feels as though it is breaking." She shook her head, "I know that sounds daft but it is how I feel. No one wants to die but now I want to live forever to see this fine young man grow up into a man. I want to be there when he walks down the aisle. I want to see his children." She stopped speaking and I watched her face as she gained control of her emotions. "And now that you are home, you can be the father he misses so much."

I smoked another pipe and watched the fire slowly die into ashes. When the pipe was out, I raked the coals and put the fireguard around. This was life at home and the simple things were a pleasure.

Chapter 14

I still had no decent civilian clothes and had to wear my uniform when we got the bus to Walton. Egypt seemed a long way away and I think that people had, by now, forgotten Khartoum. I was just another tanned soldier home on leave and, as such, not worthy of comment. Before Khartoum, we had all been heroes. Afterwards, we were forgotten men. We were the same men but the newspapers had other news to sell. It was as we walked to the house that I noticed how tall Griff was getting. When I had left he was still a little boy but now he was taller and leaner. He did not need to run to match my stride.

We rang the doorbell. This was the suburbs. For some reason they kept their front doors locked. Mother opened it and, even though I knew she was expecting me she burst into tears, "Our Jack. Our Jack. You are home."

If Griff had grown, Mother seemed to have shrunk. I had to bend to hug her, "Aye, back in England now."

She looked up and I saw the joy on her face, "No more gallivanting off to fight the heathens. Sarah told me, good." She linked my arm, "Come inside, Bet and the bairns are desperate to see you."

The house was much larger and grander than Aunt Sarah's and I wondered how Bet would manage. How would she repay the loan? I wondered if four weeks' leave would be enough to do all that I needed to do.

Bet had recovered and now, positively bloomed. I don't know what I expected but this was a pleasant surprise. Victoria was toddling and Jack was playing with her. My sister-in-law stood and threw her arms around me. Like my mother, she burst into tears, "You are home, Jack. Our prayers have been answered."

Aunt Sarah said, "Come on, Mary, let's go and put the kettle on. Griff, play with your cousins. You are the big boy remember?"

"Yes, Aunt Sarah." He dropped to the floor and joined in the game that Jack was playing with his little sister.

There was a sofa and Bet sat down and patted it, "Next to me. Tell me everything."

I sat and she took my left hand in her two. "Do you really need to hear this, Bet?"

"Billy was my husband and I loved him dearly but when he went to Egypt it broke my heart. I felt abandoned."

"He wanted you to go with him."

She nodded and waved an arm, "I never wanted all this. I was happy just being a typist and cooking Billy's tea." Her face furrowed into a frown, "It was that Mr Hargreaves. He kept pushing Billy. So, yes, Jack, I need to know how my husband died."

I sighed, "He was on his way back to Suez when he and his companions were captured by bandits. During the fracas, he broke his leg. It was the broken leg that killed him. It was not set properly, and he got an infection."

She nodded, "He died alone then?"

I shook my head, "I was with the men sent to rescue them. We made them all comfortable. When he died, Bet, he wasn't in pain."

"And you were with him." She squeezed my hand.

"I was with him at the end."

She nodded and then said, suddenly, "His body! Where is his body?"

"We buried him at our base. His grave will be tended by the men who served with me."

She smiled, "That is a comfort and once again Billy's big brother comes to the rescue. He looked up to you, you know. When you and he fell out he was upset."

"I know and I can't undo that. There is something you should know, Bet. Before he died, he made me promise to look after you, Little Jack and Victoria. I am here to tell you that I will keep that promise."

I should have known that Griff would be listening. He was a clever boy and although his hands were playing his mind was working. "Did you kill the bandits?"

I looked at him, "A soldier does not speak of such things, Griff, especially not when ladies are present. I did my duty."

My mother and Aunt Sarah came in with the tea things. As they laid the cups and teapot on the table Aunt Sarah said, quietly, "I told your mother. You don't need to go through it twice, Jack."

The tea poured, we sat and silence filled the room. I say silence but Little Jack and his sister were oblivious to the tension in the room. Griff was watching his cousins but his attention was on us.

Aunt Sarah was ever the practical one and she broke the silence, "Bet, did our Billy have a will? I asked him to write one."

My mother shook her head, "Our Sarah, there is a time and place."

"Mary, you can't hide your head in the sand. There is a mortgage on this house. How is Bet going to pay it?" It was clear that my mother had not thought of that. "Jack said that Billy told him he had investments. Do you know where they are, what they are, Bet?"

She shook her head, "He kept that side of our lives to himself. He thought I was too pretty to bother my head about such matters." She sipped her tea, "Perhaps the manager at the bank might know. Billy visited him often before he left for Egypt."

Aunt Sarah asked, "William and Glyn's?" Bet nodded. "Then it is Walter Critchley. He is a good chap. We will see him on Monday. Is there a will?"

"I know he wrote one but I have no idea where it is."

Aunt Sarah was in her element. She was organising. "And Jack and I will see Mr Hargreaves too. Has the company been in touch?"

Bet shook her head, "Not a word."

"Then before we leave you can write a letter giving Jack and me permission to speak on your behalf. Hargreaves and Winterbottom have a duty and I will ensure that they do it." She looked at me, "We will use your red coat, Jack. Let them all know what this family has done for England."

I smiled, "I know that I am the soldier, Aunt Sarah but you would have made a wonderful Sergeant Major."

The business out of the way I gave them their presents. Like Griff, I had soldiers for Little Jack and the two of them played happily with them. The other gift was a teddy bear for Victoria. I bought it in London when I was between trains. I had felt guilty about such an afterthought until her face lit up into the most beautiful smile. We left it as late as we could to leave and with Bet's letter in her handbag, Aunt Sarah and I caught the last bus back to Liverpool.

Monday was a school day for Griff, and I took him to school while Aunt Sarah cleaned the house. Mr Myers gushed when he saw me. I was dressed in my red uniform and he called over other children as they arrived, "This, children, is a hero. This is a soldier of the queen and we are all safer for his service." He stood to attention and saluted, "We thank you, Sergeant Major." The children all cheered and I felt embarrassed. Griff just stood taller. He was proud of his father.

I had much to do and the sooner I started the better. Aunt Sarah and I went to the offices of her former employers, Hargreaves and Winterbottom. They now had a large building rather than the cosy little one Billy had first joined. Had it been back then we would have been able to enter and get our business done. As it was we had to make an appointment with his secretary. She was a cold woman who looked down her nose at the two of us. I was still in my uniform and she was less than impressed by us. It took some time to be given an appointment and even then it was given with reluctance. We had two days to wait.

Walter Critchley, in contrast, saw us immediately and was most sympathetic. He had his secretary bring us in tea and biscuits and, even though it was a Monday and a busy day, listened as we spoke. When we had finished and he had read the letter written by Elizabeth he nodded, "William did make a will and he left it with me." He smiled, "I will have it fetched but I can remember that he left everything to his wife." I was relieved. That would make life easier.

Aunt Sarah was more practical than me and she asked, "His accounts, they are still held here?"

His face became serious, "They are but it took some persuasion by me for him to do so. Someone at his office, a Mr Hargreaves I believe, advised him to use a Turkish bank as it would afford him the opportunity to receive more interest and access his cash quicker." He stood, "I will fetch the letter and the statement of accounts. If you would excuse me."

Left alone Aunt Sarah shook her head, "Willoughby
Hargreaves is a snake. When he came to the office as a child, he
was rude and obnoxious. When my time was ended at the firm I
missed everyone but him. He made leaving a pleasure."

When the bank manager returned, he confirmed what he had
thought. He handed the will to us and gave us a written
statement. "As you can see his wife and children inherit more
than a thousand pounds."

I looked at Aunt Sarah and she smiled at the shock on my
face. Smiling she said, "One thing about Billy, he knew how to
save." Turning to the manager she said, "And the deeds to the
house?"

"Yes, we hold those. I believe that the outstanding amount on
the mortgage is six hundred pounds."

I did some calculations, "So Bet could pay off the mortgage
and own the house."

Aunt Sarah said, "And what would she live on, Jack? We
must see what Hargreaves and Winterbottom will do. Mr
Critchley, could we close Billy's account and transfer it to Bet?"

"Of course, but she will need to come in and sign papers."

I nodded, "That is understood. Should we say, this Friday?"

He looked at his diary, "Shall we say eleven?"

"Perfect."

Once outside Aunt Sarah said, "And now you need to be
dressed appropriately. The uniform might impress many people
but not Willoughby Hargreaves."

We went to Dunn and Co. They were not the cheapest of
tailors, but they were the best and I went to buy clothes to wear
immediately and to have a suit made. I had never had one before
but now I would need one. I saw my time in the army drawing to
a close and even though the purchases ate into my dwindling pile
of coins it had to be done. I also needed shirts, shoes and, of
course, a hat. It took until noon and by then we were ready for
food. We found a place to eat and it was there that we spoke, for
there were few diners in the room and we could be more
intimate.

"She should sell the house and buy something less grand."

Shaking her head Aunt Sarah said, "The house is perfect for the children and the area is quiet." She sighed. If anything I should sell my house and move in with them but…"

I nodded, "Griff. He would find the move from Mr Myers too hard." I understood that Mr Myers had the same influence on Griff as Trooper had on me.

"I think your idea to pay off the mortgage is a good one but she needs an income to provide for them all. Billy said they had investments but the bank account just showed his savings and there looks to have been no payments from Hargreaves and Winterbottom for more than a year. Since his death I could understand it but what about the rest of the time?" Wednesday cannot come quickly enough for me.

It felt strange to be wearing civilian clothes. The suit would not be ready for a week or so but the jacket, waistcoat and trousers I had bought were good ones. My new shoes were polished until I could see my face in them and I had trimmed my beard and, on the advice of Aunt Sarah, waxed my moustache. She said it was all the fashion. She wore her best clothes and we were at the offices early. As Aunt Sarah had surmised, we were left waiting beyond the appointment time. To many people that would have been hard. When you have stood watch in the desert for six hours then it is an easy duty. It was Aunt Sarah who drummed her fingers on her handbag and glowered at the hatchet-faced secretary.

Eventually, a smartly dressed young man with slicked hair opened the door and beamed a smile, "Sarah, so good to see you, it has been too long. Come in."

The office had a huge desk and was there to impress as was the leather swivel chair upon which the young man sat. I noticed that he did not wait for Aunt Sarah to sit first and it told me much about him. His secretary closed the door. Unlike when we had visited the bank there was no tea.

He gave us both the falsest of sympathetic smiles and said, "I was devastated to hear of William's death." He shook his head, "Savages."

I had a whole raft of questions in my head but, at that moment I just wanted to slap the smoothly dressed man who faced us.

Aunt Sarah must have been on the edge already for she suddenly said, "And no words of sympathy for his wife and family! His death was caused by you and this firm, Mr. Hargreaves."

The false veil was lifted and his eyes hardened, "I am offended by that statement. We had nothing to do with William's death. He was working for the company it is true, but the rest was not of our doing."

I had been ready for this, "That is not true, Mr. Hargreaves. Billy did not wish to travel to Cairo," but you ordered it."

"That is a lie." His face coloured. "You are the brother, are you not? The soldier."

"I am, Sergeant Major Jack Roberts."

"If you soldier boys did your duty instead of shirking behind walls then William would be alive. I did not order him to go to Cairo."

I nodded, "The men whom we, '*soldier boys*' rescued say otherwise and they gave me the telegram that you sent to Billy. It is safely in my possession and is clear evidence of your order. It was they who told me that Billy did not want to travel to Cairo."

He was defeated and he took a cigar from a box, struck a match and lit it to give him thinking time. It was rude. A gentleman always asks a lady before smoking.

Aunt Sarah seized the moment, "Billy had investments and, I believe, shares in the company." She was on more comfortable ground and her temper was now under control.

Her question took the officious young man by surprise, and he coughed as he swallowed smoke, "What?"

"He has shares and I believe a pension due to his wife." Before he could speak she said, "There are company accounts and records of payments, we are more than happy to pay a lawyer to take this to court. With the evidence Jack has and his firsthand account of the rescue I am sure that any court would find in favour of the widow and her children, or we could see Sir Charles Lowther the chairman."

It was, of course, a bluff. We had seen a lawyer but that had been simply to do as Billy had wished and make me the guardian for Bet and her children and to make me a will. Mr Hargreaves did not know that and I knew that adverse publicity was the last thing he wanted. Perhaps he had hoped to keep Billy's money. The threat of speaking with the chairman was also a good one. Sir Charles was known to be a supporter of widows and orphans charities. He would not look kindly upon the cavalier attitude of Willoughby Hargreaves. It was Aunt Sarah's words that won the day. He was defeated but he did not take the defeat with any grace.

"Mr. Lowther is far too busy to deal with such inconsequential matters." He waved a dismissive hand, "If you would wait without I will have Pemberton from accounts deal with you. I don't have the time to deal with such trivial matters." He stood. The meeting was clearly over. There must have been a bell on his desk for the door opened and the secretary appeared, "Miss Jones, have Mr Pemberton bring up the records of William Roberts and ask him to see me. These people can wait in the waiting room downstairs."

"Of course, Mr Hargreaves." She held an imperious arm for us to walk out. We were now, 'these people'.

I let Aunt Sarah go first and then, when I was at the door, I turned, "And what you should know, Mr Hargreaves, is that the British soldier is not there to help you make profits but to protect the queen's empire. The men who went with me to rescue your brother and the other businessmen risked their lives and faced odds that would have you running back to Mama, weeping like a baby. Remember that when you next send some poor soul into the world that is not and never will be England."

His eyes glared at me but I gave him my sergeant major stare and he backed down and averted his gaze. It was a petty victory but I took it anyway.

We did not have to wait long in the public waiting room on the ground floor. Ronald Pemberton, in contrast to his employer, was a nice man. He remembered Aunt Sarah and was both sympathetic and civil to her. He took us to his utilitarian office and had tea brought for us.

When we were alone, he said, "Sergeant Major, Sarah, we were all shocked at the manner of Billy's death. We all liked him. I had been up for the promotion too and I am glad that I refused it." He realised what he had said and shook his head, "Sorry. That came out wrong."

I shook my head, "You made the right decision and Billy did not."

Aunt Sarah was the practical one. "Ronald, is there a pension?"

"There is. Billy was quite careful in that regard. In the event of his death, his wife receives a pension of £50 a year. It can be transferred to his children, but you would need to see a lawyer about that."

I said, "Back pay?"

He looked at me and was clearly confused, "Backpay?"

"When we were at the bank we found no pay for the last year. I assumed he would be paid up to his death, at the very least."

He looked down at the papers he had and eventually sat back and shook his head, "I shall have foreign accounts hauled over the coals for this. They omitted to pay him." He scribbled figures on a piece of paper and then said, "His widow, Elizabeth, is owed £350. I shall have it transferred immediately."

Aunt Sarah said, "The shares and their certificates?"

"Billy owns two hundred shares. Their present value is ten shillings each." He looked around as though he was afraid of eavesdroppers and said, quietly, "Their value is rising as the company has just acquired a trading station in West Africa. They will rise in value. There is also a dividend due." He gave an apologetic smile, "But do not let on that I told you."

Aunt Sarah smiled, "Of course not." She leaned forward, "Ronald, you are a good chap and I give you this advice because I don't want the company to corrupt you like they did Billy. Do not be seduced by silken words."

"Don't worry Sarah. Billy's death was a lesson to us all. Mr Hargreaves now hires men from outside this building. They are the ones who take the risks."

"The share certificates? No offence, but I would rather we held them than Hargreaves and Winterbottom."

He handed the bound documents over, "Of course." He took a pen and dipped it in ink and wrote out a receipt. "If you would sign for them." He waved the pen upwards, "Keep everything in order, eh?"

As we left, I shook Ronald Pemberton's hand, "Thank you, Ronald."

He shook his head, "No, thank you, Sergeant Major. Mr Hargreaves may have little time for the British Army but Billy was proud of his big brother and we all appreciate what you do for us. Thank you."

We left and walked back to the house. Elizabeth was now financially secure. The mortgage could be paid off and the income from the shares and the pension would give them all peace of mind. Aunt Sarah would manage the shares and make the decision as to the best time to sell them. They were secured in the bank and I could spend the rest of my leave with Griff and my family.

Chapter 15

The rest of the leave flew by and it seemed barely days before I headed to Preston and my new posting. I donned the uniform again. I had grown used to my civilian clothes. I did not take my trunk; my kitbag would do and I left after taking Griff to school for the last time. I arrived the night before I was actually due. My reasoning was two-fold. I did not want to risk arriving late and whilst the train service was a good one, I would not gamble on creating a bad impression. Secondly, I would see the NCOs and other ranks before they were prepared for their new sergeant major. I was not to be the Regimental Sergeant Major, my orders had made it quite clear that this was a secondment and I was still in the ESEG.

The barracks were large and clearly important. It was getting on for dusk when I arrived and in England that meant the air was filled with smoke as people lit fires to warm houses and to cook food. This was not the woodsmoke smell of Africa but the smoke from coal. There were many coal mines in this part of the world and a lot of the men were miners. I stopped at the end of the street to watch the two sentries at the gate. They were lounging against the wall. It told me that either the duty NCO had just passed by and they thought they could get away with it or that the discipline was lax. I waited and sure enough, when the corporal and a second private arrived there was no change in the two soldier's demeanour. The four of them chatted for a while and then the corporal and private disappeared inside.

I had my bag over my shoulder and my swagger stick under my arm. I marched from the end of the road down to the barracks and was thirty yards away before they saw my approach. My chevrons were clearly visible, and they snapped to attention. It was laughable for one managed to do it before the other. I dropped my bag to the floor and took my swagger stick. As I had expected they had not buttoned up all their uniforms. I tapped the unfastened button of one and as he fastened it the other did the same. I walked around their rear. "Those boots are not polished enough."

"Sorry, Sergeant Major." This time they managed to chorus it together.

I stood in front of them. "What is the purpose of this duty, Private?"

"What sir?"

"Is that your name or do you not understand the question?"

"Sorry, Sergeant Major, the purpose of our duty is to ensure that all those who enter the barracks have a right to do so."

I nodded, "And if I had been some fanatic wielding a bloody great sword, what would you have done?"

They looked at each other and then the one who had been speaking to me said, "Stop you, Sergeant Major."

I nodded and tapped his Lee Metford rifle with my swagger stick, "As you have no bayonet on the end and I doubt that you have a bullet up the spout, that might have been a trifle difficult as I was just thirty yards away before you saw me." I leaned in, "Have you a round up the spout?"

He shook his head, "Sergeant Major, this is Preston and not Africa."

I gave him the smile that Middy had called my wolf smile, "And you assume that you will spend your whole career here, eh, is that it?" They had no answer and so they kept at attention. "It seems I have arrived at just the right time."

Just then the corporal of the guard and the private double-timed from the orderly office. They had clearly seen what was going on. They were both attired correctly but were unfit. They had run just fifty yards and were huffing and puffing like steam trains.

They snapped to attention and the corporal said, "Corporal Booker, Sergeant Major, Corporal of the Guard. We weren't expecting you until tomorrow."

"That is obvious. This won't do. Sentries lounging around and failing to keep a close watch is a dereliction of duty. Do you understand me?"

They all nodded. I pointed my swagger stick at my kitbag, "You," I flicked it towards the private standing next to Corporal Booker, "fetch my bag."

He hefted it to his shoulder, "Yes, Sergeant Major."

"Is the commanding officer available?"

172

The corporal shook his head, "No, Sergeant Major, he has not yet returned from his weekend leave. Captain Dawson is the officer of the day and he is in the mess."

It would have been a courtesy only to speak to the colonel and the next day would do. I said, "What is your name?"

The soldier with my kitbag said, "Private Cunningham, Sergeant Major."

"Well Private Cunningham, how about you show me to my quarters and then give me a tour? I am sure that the corporal can spare you. He and your two friends have much to talk about."

"Yes, Sergeant Major."

"Which way?"

He had slung his rifle over one shoulder and had my bag over the other. He was struggling to hold them both and he had to nod, "Over there, Sergeant Major."

The barracks had been there for some time and were solidly made of bricks. My quarters were in the first building and we passed one door before the private said, "This is yours, Sergeant Major."

Whilst not as big as the one at Fort Desolation I would be comfortable there. "Drop the bag and then take me to the mess."

He pointed out all the important buildings as we walked. The mess was a short walk away and I saw that there were three. The one for NCOs and warrant officers was bigger than the one I had first joined in Wales. The private waited at the door. I said, "Expecting a tip, Cunningham?"

"No Sergeant Major."

"Well, off you go then and smartly."

I removed my forage cap and tucked it into my belt. I had eaten at Aunt Sarah's but this would give me the opportunity to meet the other NCOs and see what the food was like. Army food was never wonderful but better cooks tried to make it palatable.

Entering the mess, faces turned towards me as I headed for the food. A quick glance told me that I was the senior officer there. They had cooked sausages and mash and there was black pudding. It was more interesting fare. The senior cook smiled, "Welcome, Sergeant Major, we weren't expecting you until tomorrow."

I nodded, "So I discovered." I nodded at the black pudding, "Not the usual fare for the army."

"Local sir. The colonel likes to feed the men the food they know."

That was a good idea. This regiment had recently amalgamated, and I knew from speaking to other soldiers I had met during my leave that there was a recruitment drive. The government was going to do something about Sudan and needed men.

I approached a table with three sergeants sitting around it, "Do you mind?"

"Of course not, Sergeant Major."

I put down my plate and said, "Sergeant Major Roberts, formerly of the 24th and latterly the ESEG."

One of the sergeants held out his hand, "Sergeant Highcock, Albert, first platoon B Company."

I shook it.

A second said, "Sergeant George Ramsay, third platoon C Company."

I shook his hand.

The last one said, "Sergeant Edward Thomas, Ted, second platoon D Company."

I detected a Welsh lilt and asked, "Are you Welsh by any chance?"

He grinned, "Yes, Sergeant Major, Trearddur Bay, Anglesey. I came to show the English how to fight."

I liked Ted from the first. "I know how well they fight, Ted, believe me." I smeared mustard on a piece of sausage and black pudding and ate it. The food was not overcooked and that, in itself, was a miracle. "Who is the RSM here?"

Ted said, "RSM Bert Sanders but he is in the infirmary in Manchester. There is something wrong with his insides."

"Who is the senior NCO then?"

"Before you arrived it was Sergeant Callow of A Company. He has just left."

I nodded and continued eating. They had all finished their food but were clearly wanting to speak to me. I did not like gossiping behind the backs of others and I would let them ask what they would. It would be my decision to divulge or not.

174

"Your arrival has been eagerly anticipated, Sergeant Major."

"Jack, off duty it is Jack." They smiled. The exchanging of Christian names was an important step. "Why is that?"

"Your reputation precedes you. We all know you fought at Rorke's Drift." Ted beamed, "That was the day I decided to join up when my countrymen defeated a Zulu army."

"It was harder than the papers made it sound."

George said, "And then Captain Dawson told us how you had fought against the Mad Mahdi and led men behind the enemy lines." He waved a hand, "We have not fought a battle since the Crimean War."

Albert said, "We weren't this regiment then. The lads are hoping that your arrival presages a trip abroad and the opportunity to serve the queen. We are fed up with marching up and down and having inspections. Some of those who joined up want to avenge Gordon."

I had finished and I wiped my mouth on my napkin. I spooned some sugar into my tea and sipped it. It was cold. Ted said, "Let me warm it for you, Sarn't Major."

He hurried off, poured out the tea into the slop bin and after refilling it with tea and milk came back. It was good tea. I hated cold tea.

When I had swallowed a steaming mouthful I said, "If you haven't served in Africa, the West Indies or India then you cannot possibly imagine the heat, dust and the challenges they bring. It is easier now that we wear khaki, the red wool and stiff collars were a nightmare. The Lee Metford is a better rifle because it has a magazine but, certainly in Sudan, the Dervishes are fierce warriors and I have seen good men run. All that we can do is to teach the men to trust us and that our officers know their business."

The mess had emptied and we were the only ones left. I stood, "Tomorrow I will report to the colonel and my time here will begin but I thank you gentlemen for your company and your welcome." I returned my plate, mug and cutlery and headed for my quarters. I could see that I had my work cut out and after organising my room and laying out my uniform, I went to bed.

I was up and dressed well before reveille. I donned my cap and took my swagger stick. I headed for the orderly room and found it all in order. My arrival the previous night had been effective. They snapped to attention as I walked in. "Carry on." They relaxed. "Report."

It was a sergeant, one that I had not met and he handed me the clipboard with the notes of events in the night. It would be written up during the day. I nodded and handed it back. I walked around the barracks and all was silent. That, in itself, told me something. The men were not rising early but clinging to their cots. For the older hands that was understandable but the younger ones should have been eager and keen to become soldiers of the queen.

I headed for the other ranks' mess. The cook sergeant saluted as I entered, "Do you want to taste, Sergeant Major?"

I nodded and he put some of the porridge in a bowl and handed me a spoon. It was tasty. He had added salt as well as milk to the water and oat concoction. "Good. Carry on."

I was the first one in the NCO's mess. From what I had seen the previous night there would soon be a need for a division into Sergeants' Mess and Corporal's mess. I mentally made a note to speak to the colonel. In the grander scheme of things, it was not important. The NCOs would all get on but overcrowding caused conflict and that was to be avoided. I chose porridge followed by bacon butties. With a mug of hot tea, it was the sort of breakfast that would see me through to lunch.

The sergeants I had met the previous night were the first to enter and it was moments before reveille. Perhaps they thought to keep on my good side. I judged men by what they did and not by how they impressed me. I had finished by the time the mess filled up and after returning my eating irons I headed out to the new day. The colonel would be at breakfast but the orderlies in the company office would be arriving soon. My guide had pointed them out and I entered the office. It was, as I had expected, empty. I looked around the room and saw a map of Sudan and Egypt. Khartoum was marked with a red pin. I also saw another map of South Africa. I remembered that there had been another war there when I had served in Egypt; the Boer War and I idly wondered what that meant. The inspection of the office told me that it was well run and efficient. After picking up my helmet and donning my Sam Brown, sword frog, Webley and sword, I headed for the parade ground. It was, of course, empty. I stood, at ease, and watched. As men finished their breakfast, they raced to their barracks to fetch their equipment. There would be no packs, but they would have their rifles and bayonets.

The bugler, Bates, arrived first. He was young and I liked his keenness. "Nice and prompt, bugler, I like that."

He grinned and nodded, "I wanted to make a good impression, Sergeant Major."

"And you have. Let's see you keep it up."

Surprisingly, the next ones to arrive were the colonel and the adjutant. The colonel was an older officer than I was used to. His skin showed that he had spent time in hotter climes. He smiled, "You must be Sergeant Major Roberts, welcome to the regiment. I am Colonel Grafton, and this is my adjutant. Captain Bellerby."

I snapped a salute, "Sir."

"When the parade is over you and I will go to the office so that we can have a chin wag, eh? We have much to discuss."

"Yes sir. Looking forward to it."

As we watched the men emerge, like so many ants, from their barracks, I was observing their movements closely. I saw which sergeants and corporals arrived first and which ones were tardy. I ignored the officers. A regiment succeeded or failed based on the NCOs. I saw which companies were the slowest to arrive. They would need gingering up.

The colonel nodded to me and I said to the bugler, "Sound parade."

The notes rang out and the lines straightened. The colonel said, "Sergeant Major, if you please."

I shouted, "Atten.....tion!" The sound of the regiment's boots on the cobbles echoed as they stamped to attention.

The colonel, despite his age, had a voice that carried. Once you had learned how to make your voice sound you never lost it. "Men of the 1st Loyal Lancashire Regiment, we have a new Sergeant Major today. Sergeant Major Roberts is here to make this the finest regiment in the north. He will help us make what were two regiments, one. When you are dismissed the order of the day is to prepare for months of hard training. Tomorrow sees the birth of a regiment."

He nodded to me and I dismissed the regiment.

When the colonel and I were in his office with a mug of tea brought by his man, Jennings, he lit a pipe, "Smoke if you wish, Roberts."

I shook my head, "No thank you, sir."

"I have been waiting for your arrival eagerly. Colonel Kitchener is a friend of mine or rather his father and I were close friends and Herbert seems to look up to me. This regiment recently returned from India for the first time in sixteen years. When we passed through Suez I spoke with the colonel and he told me about you. When I told him what I needed he said that there was no better man to make this a cohesive fighting formation."

I realised then the reason that Kitchener had allowed me to leave so easily.

"When we reached England, we lost many men who had served their time and left the regiment. We had two regiments to amalgamate and RSM Bert Sanders," he smiled, "Sanders and I go back a long time but he is not a well man. Let us say that we are both old warhorses. I fear that I, too, will not be with the regiment when we are sent abroad but by then you and I will have honed them into a sharpened weapon."

"Sir."

He pointed behind him at the map, "Sudan and Khartoum, we shall be sent there, I dare say. The regiment is below the numbers we shall need and the men are ill-prepared. India was hot but most of the men who served there are now gone. Many of the NCOs and officers are India hands but it is the rank and file who are new or served in the Lincoln regiment. You need to prepare them for life in the desert." I was about to say that it would be difficult to replicate those conditions in the north of England but the colonel anticipated me. "They will listen to you. You have experience. You have fought in battles." I nodded, "And that brings me to the other, equally important role that you will fulfil. We are desperately short of men and I want you to spend one week in three touring Wigan, St Helens, Bolton, Leigh Preston and Ormskirk. I want new men to be recruited. You need to sell the life of a soldier."

The first part of the job I could do but this was something else entirely, "Sir, with due respect, I am a simple soldier."

He smiled and put his pipe down, "Do not underestimate yourself, Sergeant Major. It might be more than ten years since Rorke's Drift but it is still spoken of. Ulundi was a bigger victory but the courage of the red line at Rorke's Drift is legendary. You will take your red uniform and Bugler Bates. I will give an experienced orderly to you for the paperwork. You will sell the regiment." He smiled, "His youth and your experience will have men flocking to the ranks. For the first month, I want the training procedures established. Work with Captain Bellerby on that. Make the last week in the month when you tour the towns. We need two battalions and, at the moment, we have just one."

I resigned myself to a role I did not know. However, there were benefits. When I recruited new men, I could stay at home. There would be payment for lodgings which I could save. I also remembered that day, long ago, when I had walked into a pub and seen the red uniform. I would use him as my model.

"Right sir, well I had better speak to the adjutant. I can see that I have my work cut out."

"Don't worry, Sergeant Major, Colonel Kitchener thought that you were the perfect man for this job." He smiled, "And remember, this is just a secondment. When you are needed you will return to Sudan. Our work there is not yet ended."

Chapter 16

My life found a pattern and a rhythm that was unlike my time in Africa. My enemies were not Zulus or Dervishes waiting to ambush me but incompetent and sometimes corrupt NCOs. I soon discovered who they were and within a year had managed to encourage most of them to seek a transfer or a pension. I recognised talent and had those men promoted. I was patient and I scoured my memory for clues as to how best to prepare men for a life so unlike that in Preston as to represent a huge challenge.

The recruiting was harder to learn. I wore my red uniform with the medals sewn on. That part was easy. The wool was more comfortable in England. I learned how to smile and be enthusiastic. I was better at the task than I had anticipated, and a regular flow of men joined us. The best part was seeing Griff and my family for one week every month. I was able to extend my time by using the weekends as well and I became an expert on the train timetables. Life was good and I felt guilty thinking about Syd and the others still baking under the Sudanese sun.

I followed events in Sudan and East Africa through the newspapers. I knew to take the jingoism from the papers with a pinch of salt but I learned that the Mahdists had enjoyed success against both the French and Italians. They would be emboldened. The British were not there yet. It was the Egyptian army, officered by the British, who were keeping them at bay.

During that time Bet and I became close. It was not in a romantic way but more like brother and sister. I felt closer to her than my two sisters and when I went home, I spent the weekends in Walton. It suited everyone for Griff liked the garden and playing with his cousins. Our visit to Hargreaves and Winterbottom had resulted in a healthy income for Bet and she would never need to worry about money. My mother was worried about a fall in the value of the shares but Aunt Sarah assured her that there was more than enough in the bank account to keep their heads above water.

Colonel Kitchener was made Sirdar in 1893 and took charge of the Egyptian army. I knew it would mean a more aggressive policy. The British Army was still not yet fully involved but I had seen the Sirdar as a young officer. He would harangue and harry Horse Guards until they sent British troops. Kitchener wanted Khartoum. The Mahdists might have abandoned it, but he had not forgotten the loss.

It was the year after that my mother died. She had been ill for some time. The illness was simply a slow debilitation and slide into death. She became forgetful. It was fortunate that little Jack and Victoria were young children and Bet could easily manage on her own. She moved back into Aunt Sarah's home where her sister could spend more time looking after her. Aunt Sarah, Griff and I were with her at the end. She had taken to her bed. Aunt Sarah was a trooper and it was she who dealt with the commode and incontinence. When she woke Mother was always lucid, for a short while at least. I was with her the last time that she awakened.

She opened her eyes and put a thin, blue-veined hand on mine, "I am so proud of you, our Jack. Your father was taken too soon but you have become the head of the family. Watch over them when I am gone. I fear it will be sooner rather than later."

There was something in her voice that made me stand and stamp on the floor. "Don't worry, Mother, I always will."

Aunt Sarah burst in and I shook my head.

Mother said, "Sarah, you have been the best of sisters and I go to meet my maker, husband and son knowing that I leave everyone in good hands."

Sarah bent down and taking my mother's hands in hers she kissed them, "Your family has been mine. God chose not to give me my own but yours are as dear to me as though I had borne them myself. I will look after them."

Mother nodded, "I am tired now. We will talk when I wake." She closed her eyes.

Aunt Sarah had tears in her eyes and I put my arm around her. The door opened and a fearful Griff entered.

"Is she....?"

I shook my head, "She is sleeping but you need to prepare yourself."

He came over and I put my other arm around him. I had seen men die before and knew the signs. She gave a soft sigh and her mouth lolled open. I let go of the two of them and Aunt Sarah put her arm around my son. I put my hand on my mother's neck. There was no pulse.

"She has gone." I shook my head, "I never got to say goodbye."

Aunt Sarah put her arms around me and pressed her salty cheeks against my chest, "She knew."

"But I never got to tell her how much I loved her."

Griff put his arm around my waist, "She often told me, when you were in Africa, that she could feel your love even though you were oceans away. She knew that you were alive,"

I shook my head, "But I should have told her."

Aunt Sarah said, "Her soul is but a little above us. Say it now. She will hear."

"I love you, Mother."

It felt better.

We had a fine stone made and carved. The funeral was attended by just our family but I wore my red tunic and as Bugler Bates was with me he played the last post. She had not been a soldier, but she deserved that send-off.

She had not left a will for, outside of her personal belongings, she had nothing. We each took what we wanted and then Aunt Sarah donated her clothes to the poor. My mother had always been a kindly soul who did not like people to suffer. Mother's death left a huge hole in my life. I had been away many years but since returning from Africa we had become closer and I would miss her. I could tell that Griff missed her even more. Until she had left to care for Jack and Victoria he had shared a room with her and I knew that there was a bond there that transcended death.

When Griff passed the entrance exam to the grammar school close to Walton then it seemed as though Fate had taken a hand. There was more than enough room for Jack and Aunt Sarah at Bet's house and she was able to sell her house. It guaranteed that Bet would have financial support even if the worst came to the worst. The weekends and my recruitment drives were easier to manage.

I was summoned to the colonel six months after Mother died. He had a serious look on his face and I wondered if he was ill, too. The colonel and I got on well. If I was to be honest he was the best officer with whom I served. He cared for the regiment above all else even though the reforms had amalgamated it. In the event, it was nothing to do with him and all to do with me.

"Jack," we had grown close over the last years, "Herbert Kitchener has sent for you. You are recalled to the ESEG. I am sorry for you have ensured that the men are ready to go to Sudan or South Africa and do the regiment proud. You have weeded out the tares and recruited fine young men. It has been an honour to serve with you." I nodded as I took it in. "I am also leaving the regiment as I am being pensioned off. It is understandable and my wife will say high time. I dare say the rigours of Africa would not have suited me."

In many ways that made it easier to leave. "Sir, do I have any choice in the matter?"

He shook his head, "And you would be foolish to refuse and resign for you are to be promoted to second lieutenant." He smiled, "I confess that I had a little to do with that. When Herbert first contacted me I said that you were so valuable to us that I was considering promoting you. You will have rank, better pay and a much better pension."

I knew at that moment that I would accept the promotion and the offer. I had to for Griff, if for no one else. I could not help but glance skyward. Mother and Trooper would be so proud of me. "When do I leave?"

"Immediately, you are given a month's leave to make all necessary arrangements and the troopship will take you and reinforcements from Southampton."

I nodded. A month was not enough time but better than nothing.

"See the regimental tailor today and he will make your uniforms. It is the least that we can do for you."

"Thank you, sir."

"One word of advice. When you are in the officers' mess be proud. You have earned the right to be there more than the young officers from privileged backgrounds. As you know, probably better than anyone, some of them are arrogant young...pups," He smiled, "Anyway, as you are returning to the ESEG it will not be a problem, eh?"

I was also taken aback by the warm reception in the Sergeants' Mess. The separate mess had been my suggestion and was cosier than the larger one I had first experienced. I think one reason for the joy in the mess was not my departure but the manner of it. I had broken the barrier and climbed the rung to an unbelievable height. It had happened in the past. Colour Sergeant Bourne was an example but that had been as a result of valour. Mine was a result of just surviving.

The tailors worked hard to finish my uniforms. Officers often paid private tailors to make them and I think that the regimental tailors, both of them, wanted to prove that they could do as good a job as any civilian. I think it was better. The colonel presented me with my pips and he also gave me a sword. I still had the one taken from the Egyptian officer but the one I was presented with was a better one. The day I left, the colonel held a parade and the two battalions I had trained passed by me and I was given my first salute as an officer. I had travelled a long way from the Welsh barracks I had joined all those years ago.

I had not sent a telegram home and so, when I arrived in Walton, the joy of seeing me in my officer's uniform was clearly visible. Aunt Sarah insisted upon going into Liverpool and buying a bottle of champagne from a reputable wine merchant. I thought that it was a waste, but Aunt Sarah and Bet were adamant. I had never drunk champagne. When I was toasted, I was disappointed in the taste but astute enough to act as though I had enjoyed it.

I slept on the couch. Griff offered me his bed, but I insisted that he retain it. I was the guest. I knew I had a limited time in England and I had much to do. I spent the first days putting my affairs in order. I saw a lawyer and amended the will I had made when I had returned from Egypt. My circumstances and finances had changed. I wrote a letter to inform any who needed to know that in the event of my death Elizabeth and Sarah would become Griff's legal guardians until the age of twenty-one. That done I was able to spend time with my family but, primarily, Griff.

Since I had been at home I had begun to teach Griff more Arabic. He was keen to learn new things and each time I saw him I taught him new phrases. We even tried French although I was never particularly fluent in that language. My time in the

184

desert had shown me that I might need another language. I was impressed by Griff's skills. He was also good when it came to figures. He was a clever boy and I was now just realising how clever he was. He had a neat hand and a thirst for knowledge that was impressive. He asked questions but they were all asked with a purpose. It was a delight to be with him.

The countryside was just a mile or so away and I began to walk it with Griff. I was teaching him skills that he had not acquired in school and passing on what I had learned as a soldier. I drank in the local pub and Griff came with me. He just drank small beer and listened more than he spoke. It was there I met old Joe who was the gamekeeper on Lord Stanley's land that lay a few miles away. He was fascinated by my tales of Zululand and the Sudan. We spoke of the guns I had used. One day he said, "Do you fancy going shooting? Tomorrow is my day off and there is a copse that needs clearing of bunnies. I could bring a spare gun. What do you say?"

I grinned, "Nothing nicer than rabbit stew. Can Griff come too?"

"Of course, he can."

It was like being back with the regiment. We rose before dawn and, wearing old and serviceable clothes, silently slipped out so that we would not disturb anyone. We met Joe and tramped the three miles to the wood. It was more and more like being on active duty. The shotguns were Joe's and both double-barrelled. They were not Purdeys but were well-made weapons. Joe had his dog with him. Molly was a cocker and a good retriever. She started the first rabbits within twenty minutes of our arrival and Joe and I shot six. I missed with my first shot but that was understandable. I had never used the gun before.

When we neared the second burrow Joe said, "Do you fancy a go, young Griff?"

His face answered the question. Joe was a good teacher and I let him instruct my son. He showed him how to nestle the stock so that the recoil did not break any bones. Like me, Griff missed with his first shot but managed to bag two others. When we headed for home we had eight bunnies for the pot.

Joe nodded to Griff as we parted, "If you want to go shooting when your dad is away just let me know. That is my cottage there."

"Thank you, I should like that." Griff was a well-mannered and polite boy and I was glad that there was another Trooper as a mentor while I was away.

Back at the house I took Griff to the potting shed and showed him how to skin and gut the rabbits. "If we treat these skins then we can use them. The guts we burn. They will attract vermin."

These were more skills to be passed on and the days to the end of my leave flew by. I did not want to leave but I knew that I had to go back, even if it was for a short time. One day we walked to the woods, mainly because it was a pleasant day. We were alone and I decided to ask Griff how he saw his future.

"So, Griff, you will have a few more years at Grammar School and then the big wide world of work. What do you see yourself doing?"

His answer told me that he had been thinking about this already. "I suppose that I would, if I could, go to university but that is an impossible dream. The family cannot afford the expense."

He was right but the realisation that he could not have the future he dreamt of hit me harder than a punch in the solar plexus.

"I suppose I could get a job in an office but to be truthful that does not appeal and I saw what it did to Uncle Bill." He was no fool and whilst we had not discussed my brother's death he had been close enough to see it all.

"Not everyone who works in an office suffers the same fate as my brother. Indeed, most don't." We had reached a small clearing with a lightning-struck log lying as a convenient bench and we sat down. I took out my pipe and began to fill it.

"I know but the work does not appeal. I don't mind working indoors although an outdoor life appeals more. I think I would like to be an archaeologist but that is an impossible dream. You have seen the Pyramids, were you filled with wonder when you saw them?"

I nodded, "It is their age that impressed me. Even today such wonders are rare."

He nodded, "Perhaps I could be a writer but how would I become published? The family has no connections, and the pay is uncertain. When you retire from the army, I shall be the one earning the money to keep the whole family."

My mouth dropped open. Griff was prepared to take on the support of the family. I was so proud of him. I shook my head, "You need not worry on that score. Aunt Sarah and Aunt Bet are both well set and when I leave the army I will have a pension to keep me. You just choose the job that you think you would like."

"You didn't. Nan told me how my grandfather made you go to work in a factory and how you hated it."

I took out my penknife and scraped some ash from the pipe and loosened the tobacco beneath. It began to draw better. "I wouldn't say I hated it but I knew it was not for me."

He nodded and picked up a stone. He threw it towards a distant tree and smiled when he hit it, "So you joined the army."

I nodded.

"I can see me in the army. I could see me being a soldier of the queen."

I did not want that. I saw now that my promotions and my medals had given him a false idea of army life. I shook my head, "Life as a private is not easy, Griff. Do not be so hasty in your choice of a future. You have a talent for languages, and you are clever. I know not what career that might lead to but then all I know is life as a factory hand and a soldier. Keep your choices open."

"Have you enjoyed your life?"

I looked at my son and knew that I could not lie. He would not be here but for the army. I would not have met his mother otherwise. I nodded, "Aye, I have but I know that I have been lucky. I have buried friends and that memory hurts."

"But you have also done much good."

I shrugged and tapped the last of the ash into my palm. As I spread it to the wind I said, "I am not sure about that. I did not bring peace to South Africa and now more men will be going to fight there. Some will die."

I stood and he did so also, "I will keep my options open but I know that I can join the army if all else fails."

That thought haunted me for the rest of my leave.

Omdurman

The last night before I left Sarah and Bet laid on a feast for me. It was a celebration. I had done all that I could to be there for my brother's family and for Griff. If the worst should happen then they would be provided for. Billy's investments were doing well as were the shares in Hargreaves and Winterbottom. Aunt Sarah sold half when they were at their peak and that money was placed in a solid savings account. The profits from that would not be as great but they would be more than secure. Jack and Victoria were doing well at school and were helped by Griff tutoring them. He had few friends in Walton but seemed happy to be there for his cousins. Annie would be delighted in the son she had borne but never met.

The farewells were after the meal. Bet and Sarah wept. Griff looked as though he was frightened to say a word in case he broke down. I would be leaving before dawn to catch the first train to London and thence to Southampton. I had been ordered to report to Horse Guards first and that appointment could not be missed. I hugged Griff and said in his ear, "I am so proud of you, son, and I know your mother and your nan up in heaven are equally proud. When I return we will enjoy more walks and talks. The ones we have had shall keep me warm on the cold nights in the desert. I will not ask you to do anything for I know that you are made of the finest metal and your natural instincts are good ones."

We pulled apart and he said, simply, "Come back safe, Dad. You need no more medals."

Chapter 17

My train warrant was for the 1st Class compartment. My new uniform brought me respect from all that I met and envy from the soldiers I saw who crowded into the 3rd Class. I was still the same man, but the uniform seemed to make a bigger difference. My compartment was empty for the train was too early for the civilised folk who travelled 1st Class. I was able to reflect on my life and my promotion. I suppose it was inevitable that Griff would see my life as glamorous. It was not. I knew that the heady heights I had attained might afford a better life but Griff was not well-connected enough to become an officer. When I had the chance, I would speak to Colonel Dickenson. He would know how to make Griff an officer although I hoped that my son would change his mind over the next few years.

My chest was in the luggage compartment, and I had paid for it to be taken to Waterloo Station. The cost was minimal and an officer did not lug around his own chest. I also took a Hansom Cab to Horse Guards. I had never been there and it was an imposing building. I had been sent a letter and I proffered it to the sergeant at the desk.

"Nice and early sir." He waved over an orderly, "Take Lieutenant Roberts to Colonel Dickenson. He is on the third floor."

The use of my title meant I did not react immediately to the name of the officer I was to meet. My old major had now been permanently promoted and was no longer in Egypt. Colonel Dickenson had been given a brevet rank in Egypt but it was clear from the nameplate on his door that the promotion was now permanent. He beamed when I entered and held out a hand, "Congratulations, Jack, a well-deserved promotion."

"And to you too, sir."

He tapped his leg, "Sadly, Jack, I am now desk-bound. A little incident with a falling camel meant I could no longer serve actively. Instead, I sit here and plan the future. Sit. Fotheringill, tea!"

A disembodied voice shouted, "Sir."

"Now I know you do not have much time. You have a ship to catch and as we both know time and tide wait for no man." He took out a manilla folder and pushed it over to me. "Your homework and reading for the voyage. The ESEG is no more. Instead, General Kitchener has organised the unit into smaller scouting forces each one attached to a British brigade. Major Baden-Powell has spoken to the general about the benefits of having men make maps and discover the enemy's intentions. He was in Zululand, did you meet him?"

I shook my head.

"Baden-Powell is a very clever man. The unit is now called Kitchener's Scouts. The sergeants that you trained now each lead one such unit. You are to be their commanding officer and liaise with General Kitchener."

The orderly came in with the tea and I used the time it took to pour the milk and the sugar to get my mind in the right place. "Sir, I am just promoted. How can I be a commanding officer?"

"Jack, you are a natural leader. I know that. You can do this. There are just six troops and there are ten men in each troop. Their names are in the folder." He smiled, "Sergeant Major Richardson is in temporary command." He leaned forward. "Listen, Jack, the general wants to retake Sudan and end the Mahdist threat once and for all. He knows the value of having scouts. Your job will be to find the enemy and let the general know. Every troop has a Sudanese scout. The lesson of Saeed was well learned."

"Sir, it has been some years since I was in Egypt."

He smiled, "You never forget. One more thing. There is a batman waiting on the troopship. You are an officer now and the model of someone like Private Jackson was not wasted on me. Private Adams has served in Egypt before. He is not a wet behind the ears recruit."

"Then why is he still a private, sir?"

He smiled, "You can ask him on the voyage." He looked at his watch. "And you will have to fly." He stood and held out his hand, "Good luck, Jack, and who knows, you may get your second pip before this is all over."

It was only as the cab headed to Waterloo that I realised I had not asked the colonel about Griff and officer training.

I barely made the train. I was unsure if I had given the taxi driver a big enough tip. This new world was all a little strange to me. The guard assured me that the chest was in the luggage compartment, and I was relieved. I did not read the contents of the manilla folder. I had three weeks aboard a steamship to do that. Instead, I enjoyed watching England's green fields fly by as the train headed towards the coast, it was a farewell to the land which, for the last couple of years, had been home. I missed it already. I was envious of Joe who would be able to take Griff out hunting. My son's skills would improve. He would be hunting for food whereas when I used my rifle it would be to take a human life. Did I want to impose that sort of life on Griff?

The soldier who waited for me at Southampton station was an older soldier. He had the tanned skin of a soldier who had served time in India. I knew immediately that it was my batman. The porter carried my chest on his trolley and I strode towards the start of a reawakened life. He saluted smartly, "Lieutenant Roberts?"

I saluted back and said, "And you must be Private Adams."

"Yes sir, but if it pleases, I prefer Ged or Gerald." He smiled, "I know your story, sir and how you were at Rorke's Drift. I am an old soldier and this will be my last posting. It might be easier, as I am your man, if you used my first name."

"Of course, Ged."

He looked relieved, "I have a cab waiting outside." He gestured for the porter to follow us and I fumbled in my pocket for some change. Being an officer had unexpected expenses. The extra pay would not go as far as I thought.

The chest loaded, Adams and I sat in the back. "I have our berths all sorted, sir. Mine is a cosy little bunk. My gear is stowed so I can sort yours out while you have a stroll around the deck. We leave at ten tonight on the tide."

I smiled, "Very efficient, Ged, and I am impressed. You seem to know my life story, tell me yours."

"Nothing much to tell, sir. I served with the 5th Bengal European Cavalry. I suffered a wound, sir, not from action but from a building collapsing. They wanted to send me back to England but, well sir, I have lived in hot countries since I was eighteen and I am now forty-five. All my family are dead and the

lads in my troop were all transferred to the 15th Hussars. There
was nothing for me in India. It was when I was in Alexandria,
waiting for the ship home that Colonel Dickenson met me." He
beamed, "He is a proper gentleman, sir. Spoke to me like I was
an equal and seemed interested in my story. When he offered me
the chance to be an officer's servant and still do something
useful, I jumped at the chance." He became serious, "I promise,
Lieutenant Roberts, that I will not let you down."

"I don't think you will, Ged, but as my servant, you will not
be placed in harm's way. I think we shall get on."

He nodded, "So do I sir. The colonel said that we would."

I learned that he had been in Southampton for three weeks
and that was how long Colonel Dickenson had been in England.
That told me the decision to have me return to active duty had
been taken in Egypt. General Kitchener was, indeed, the reason
for my recall.

I had a porthole but my cabin was not a huge one. That
reflected my rank. I was the lowest-ranked officer aboard. While
Ged attended to my trunk I familiarised myself with the ship.
The old soldier in me found the mess first. This was in what had
been the 1st Class dining room. It was being prepared for dinner
even as I peered in. I waved over a steward, "Excuse me, but can
you tell me if it is formal dress for dinner?" Colonel Grafton had
ensured I had a good dress uniform and I wanted to know if I
should wear it.

The steward shook his head, "Not the first night aboard, sir,
but I dare say the president of the mess will let you know."

That done I strolled along the deck to have one last look at
England. Soon it would be dark and by the time the sun rose
England would be a speck on the northern horizon. Other
officers were doing as I was doing but many seemed to be in
pairs or even threes. This was a troopship taking men to Egypt to
fight for General Kitchener. I was the stranger although I would
be the one with the most experience in Egypt.

By the time I had returned to the cabin, my trunk was
emptied. "If you would take off your boots and tunic, sir, I will
give the boots a polish and the tunic a brush. First impressions
and all that."

I did as he had said and took out my pipe. "Do you think they will dress for dinner tonight, Ged?"

He shook his head, "Not the first night but the rest? Probably."

I sighed. I hated formal dressing.

He smiled, "Just a new skill to learn, eh sir? I am sure that you will manage."

I made sure that I was early and Ged had ensured I was groomed immaculately. I felt like Daniel walking into the lions' den. There was a smart orderly sergeant at the door and he smiled, "You are new aboard sir." I saw him glancing at my uniform. Officially I was still in the 24th and my collar reflected that.

"Lieutenant Roberts." I left it, enigmatically, at that. I did not need to get into a conversation that explained I was a scout and an officer who would be operating behind the enemy lines.

He nodded, "Unattached, eh sir? There are other officers who are returning from leave. I shall seat you with them."

Whilst walking along the deck I had seen that most of the officers were from the Staffordshire Regiment or the Connaught Rangers. He took me to a table with four chairs. The table was at the side and I liked that. I chose the seat with my back to the side of the ship. "Can I get the steward to bring you a drink?"

This was my first test. Ged had said that most officers began with a sherry or a short. I was never a sherry drinker and so I said, "Whisky, with ice." He nodded and left.

As I sat there, watching the officers arrive, I realised that this was a learning experience. Just as I had learned to cope with the desert, the heat and Aisha, so I would learn. I sipped the whisky. It was a good one. I would nurse it through the meal.

The officers who arrived and were brought to my table had the tanned look of men who had served under the sun. That they entered together told me that they knew each other and their rank, captain, that I was the lowest-ranked officer. I stood smartly as they approached. The older of them, still a good ten years younger than I was said, "May we join you, Lieutenant?"

"Of course, sir."

They sat, as did I. The officer held out his hand, "Peter Radcliffe, the 9th Egyptian Battalion and this is Ralph Howard of the 10th and Geoffrey Critchley of the 13th." As he introduced them each one shook my hand.

I knew that I would need to give an explanation of my unit. "Jack Roberts of Kitchener's Scouts, formerly the East Sudan Exploration Group."

Their faces broke into smiles. Just then the steward arrived, and Captain Radcliff said, "Three large whiskies, with ice. Would you join us, Jack?"

"I have one, sir."

The captain waved a hand at the steward, "Now I can see why you have the tanned skin of a veteran and yet we did not know you. Your chaps did excellent work."

I inclined my head.

Captain Howard said, "Did I not hear that you chaps rescued some businessmen from a mountaintop? Were you there?" Again, I nodded, "From what I was told you all deserved medals for what you did."

I shrugged, "The men needed to be rescued and we were handy." It seemed to make Billy's death insignificant, but I did not wish to open that particular wound again.

The drinks came and Peter raised his glass, "Here's to victory against the Mahdists and promotion in battle."

"Victory against the Mahdists and promotion in battle."

The mess was filling up and a waiter came with a menu. I chose the soup, the roast beef, sponge pudding and custard.

When he had gone Peter said, "Excuse my bluntness, Jack, but you appear a little old to still be a lieutenant. What is that story?"

Knowing that these men had all been lieutenants who had chosen to be promoted by joining the Egyptian Army made it easier for me to be truthful. I tapped my single pip, "These are less than a month old. I was a private at Rorke's Drift, a sergeant in the Egyptian Army at Alt Klea and a Sergeant Major at the Battle of Toski. The Sirdar has sent for me." I gave a self-deprecating smile, "I thought my days in the sun were over. I was wrong, it seems."

Peter leaned over and proffered his hand, "Jack, let me shake the hand of a hero. My God man, your climb has been filled with glory and you have a just reward. I shall enjoy this voyage."

I was relieved and knew that I owed much to the steward sergeant who had seated us together. We sat at the same table for every meal and I got to know well the three officers. The voyage would not be as daunting as I had expected.

When we retired to our cabins I could tell that we had left the land for the motion of the ship was rolling. Some of the younger officers from the other regiments had clearly drunk too much and had no sea legs for I heard, from the deck beyond my cabin, the sound of retching long into the night.

After breakfast, I took the manilla folder and began to read. The rain on the porthole told me that a perambulation around the deck was not a good idea and the sooner I got to know what was expected of me, the better.

I looked, first, at the list of men. One name leapt out at me, Sergeant Major Syd Richardson. I idly wondered what had happened to Sam who had been senior to Syd. I also saw that Brian Wyatt and Stan Shaw had been promoted to sergeant and Ashcroft and Lowe to Corporal. There was another name I did not recognise and that was Sergeant Philips. Jake was also a sergeant but there was no sign of Poulter. It meant that there were four very small troops. The colonel had said six and I wondered if there were plans to enlarge the unit. A troop of cavalry normally had one hundred men while a Camel Corps troop could have one hundred and thirty. The four troops did not total more than fifty. We were the silent stiletto of the army. I saw that we were still based at the camp close to Suez. The orders reflected General Kitchener with every stroke, full stop and comma. He was being precise. I recognised Major Dickenson's hand, but it had been directed by the Sirdar. The four troops were to range ahead of the army when it eventually headed down the Nile, and to find the Mahdists before they found us. We were to create problems for the enemy and I saw that our role would be more aggressive. There was an Egyptian scout attached to each troop. The four men each had the rank of corporal. I saw that Major Dickenson had remembered the lessons learned at Fort Desolation. We had spare camels as well as our own tents. What we did not have were men to guard our camps or to lead the pack animals.

After three days of reading, I felt sufficiently confident to put the manilla folder in my chest. I had everything I needed in my head. The next day, after breakfast, I wrote a letter to Griff, another to Aunt Sarah and a third to Bet. They would be posted at Gibraltar when I landed. There was little to say but just the arrival of a letter would mean much to my family. I did not expect a letter in reply for six months, if at all. The postman did not deliver along the Nile.

My circle of acquaintances, I would not yet call them friends, remained small. The other African officers and I kept to ourselves. Sometimes we would play cards, normally whist, and at others share a companionable pipe after dinner. The pattern remained the same until we reached Gibraltar. There we were joined by four officers who had been in the hospital in Gibraltar recovering from wounds and illnesses incurred in Egypt. They were known to my three new acquaintances and sometimes I was left to my own devices. I did not mind. It was a warm, balmy night halfway to Alexandria when unpleasantness reared its ugly head. We had enjoyed a good dinner. The closer we came to Africa the more the cuisine represented Africa. The food was spicy and I enjoyed it. The problem was the spiciness made those who were unfamiliar with it drink too much and, as I smoked a last pipe by the stern, the loud and raucous voices told me that the approaching officers were drunk.

I turned and saw that there were three of them. Their collars were open and they staggered down the deck, half carrying one who was clearly incapacitated. I took in their pips. One was a 1st Lieutenant and the other two were the same rank as I was. I had to move sharply out of the way as they lurched towards the rail and the drunk hurled the spicy food over the side. The other two laughed as though it was the funniest thing that they had seen. I tapped out my pipe and made to head back to my cabin.

The 1st Lieutenant put out a hand and said, "Do you not know when to salute a senior officer or do you Indian chappies not do that sort of thing?"

I snapped my heels together, "Sorry Lieutenant but as neither of us is wearing a hat I deemed that a salute was unnecessary and as you were busy helping your friend I thought to get out of your way."

I turned to go and he put his hand on my shoulder, "I am not done with you yet."

I took his hand and removed it from my shoulder, "Lieutenant, your friend needs your help and I wish to retire."

"Are you the monkey they promoted from the ranks?" He laughed and turned to the lieutenant who had not been sick, "Breeding will out, eh, George? You can't take men from the slums and make them officers. It simply isn't done."

I think that George had seen the look on my face for he said, "Algernon, let it go. Percy needs cleaning up."

"Perhaps we should ask this fellow to do it. I am sure he is more familiar with cleaning up mess than we are."

I stood straight and said to the one called George, "You seem like a good fellow. Get them both to bed, eh, and we shall forget this ever happened."

Even as George nodded, Algernon swung a haymaker at me. He was drunk and I was not. I simply swayed backwards. He missed and lost his balance. His head cracked on the rail and he fell on the floor.

I knelt. If he was sick in such a position, he might choke. I turned his head to the side. The drunk sat with vomit down his tunic resting against the rail and George looked terrified.

"Sorry about Algernon. He drank too much."

"Clearly. I will send someone to help you. Make sure his head is kept to the side."

I left them and descended to the deck below. I saw two sergeants from the Staffs having a smoke. When I approached, they snapped to attention, "A couple of your officers need your assistance on the deck above."

"Right, sir. Thank you." He turned to his companion, "I bet you a shilling that one of them is St. John-Browne."

As they climbed the steps behind me the other said, "Do I look like an idiot? No takers."

I retired but there was a bad taste in my mouth. The friendly Anglo-Egyptian officers had lulled me into a false sense of security. I would find more St. John-Brownes.

We had almost finished our breakfast when the three officers from the previous night entered. One looked green still but the one who had swung at me now sported a bandage around his head. His fellow officers all jeered as they headed for their table. The bandaged officer glared at me. He clearly blamed me for his accident. I sighed. The sooner we landed, and I could get to Suez the better.

Chapter 18

Once we landed I was in familiar territory once more. While the newly arrived officers looked lost, I found a cab and had the Egyptian load our trunks and we were on the road to the railway station before the pale-skinned officers had reached the quayside. I had wondered how much of my Arabic I would have lost but my lessons with Griff had kept it in my head. The Egyptian took us the quickest way and I wondered how much extra the new officers would pay as they were taken around in circles. The result was that we made the train to Cairo and thence Suez before any other officers. Run by the British Army, the train, which was not quite full, left on time.

No one was expecting us in Suez for we had made such good time. I reported to the office there. The captain, who was in the office, said, "If you just head on to your camp, lieutenant, I will let the general know you have arrived. He was anxious to meet with you." He looked at my pith helmet, "I will send you one of the new helmets, the Wolsey. You need to stand out as an officer, eh?"

I paid an Egyptian to transport our trunks and ourselves to the camp. We rode horses but the Egyptians used donkeys for our trunks. The camp had grown. The thorn fence had been replaced by a barbed wire one. It looked uglier but I knew it would be more efficient. As we approached, I saw that there were now five barrack blocks and four stables. Sergeant Smith's oven still stood apart but there was a mess and a kitchen. The other addition was a bigger office.

As we neared it Ged said, "Our home, eh sir?"

I shook my head, "For our trunks, perhaps, but you and I will be with the army. Make the most of the cot while you are here."

He grinned cheerfully, "You know what they say, sir, if you can't take a joke then you shouldn't volunteer. I asked for this and I am well happy about it."

The sentry and I did not recognise each other but he knew my rank and saluted smartly, "Sir. What is your business here?"

A pair of familiar faces appeared at the guard house door. Syd shouted, "Let him in, Wise, that is the new commanding officer, Lieutenant Roberts."

The sentry stood aside as we entered, and his face reflected his curiosity. I saw that Sam Smith was also a sergeant major. As I dismounted, I said, "I didn't know you were still here, Sam."

He smiled, "I was asked to wait, sir, to hand over, as it were. I am back to England, and I shall use your animals to do so."

"Of course." I paid the Egyptian and then asked him to wait for Sam. He was delighted as he had doubled his pay for the day.

Syd gestured for us to head to the mess. There were still too few to need more than one but at this time of day, it was empty. Ged hovered at the door, and I said, "This is Private Adams, he is my batman."

Syd grinned, "Pleased to meet you." He shouted, "Thompson."

A soldier appeared, "Yes, Sarn't Major?"

"Show Private Adams where to find Lieutenant Roberts' quarters."

"Righto. Come on, old chum, let me give you a tour of the palace of sand and bugs."

As they left I cocked an eye, "Palace of sand and bugs?"

Syd shrugged, "You know the lads and their sense of humour. It is still better than Fort Desolation. At least we are too far from the Dervishes for us to be under threat."

I had the manilla folder in my hand, "Is this still an accurate picture of the troops?"

He glanced at it and nodded, "The colonel and I wrote that together, sir, before he left."

"Good, if the men are all trained and ready to go we just await orders."

"And they may be forthcoming sooner rather than later, sir. The Sirdar passed through here two days ago on his way to Suez. He said he might call in on the way back."

"Right." I smiled at Sam, "Is it a posting home or..."

He beamed, "I have done my time, sir, and served my queen. I am back to England. Once I land I become a baker. My sister has found me a little place in Macclesfield. My brother-in-law died and she has no one. I can bake and look after her at the same time."

"Your dream come true, eh, Sam?"

He smiled and filled his pipe. He did not need to ask my permission. Our friendship was an old one. "You know, sir, I never would have thought I could do it if it hadn't been for Fort Desolation, but once I knew I could make bread that the lads liked then the future became clearer."

Sam left an hour after I had arrived. He was not a fool and had managed to acquire supplies that would both help his baking and make money for him. Spices were cheaply acquired in Suez and he could make a tidy profit when he reached England. I toured the camp with Syd and found that they had improved it both as a home and as a place we could defend. He told me that Poulter had suffered a bout of malaria and the MO in Cairo had invalided him back to England. It was a shame for he had been a good soldier. The malaria would haunt him to the end of his days and was hardly the mark of a soldier. He nodded to the Egyptians who toiled in the small garden that the men had created. "The colonel found these ten old soldiers. He persuaded the powers that be to pay them to guard the barracks. They are happy little bunnies, sir. They served for twenty years as fellahs and army life is in their blood. They like the order and the saluting. When we go on campaign the camp will be well looked after."

I looked around. I had met my sergeants but there was one face that was missing, "Cowley?"

"Retired, too, sir." I had not seen his name on the list of troopers and had wondered about that. "He left a year ago. His arthritis plagued him but before he left he trained one man in each troop as a first aider. We are alright."

"And the Egyptian scouts?"

"Good lads, sir, and we have a reputation that means we are well respected. They think that it is an honour to serve with us."

After we had eaten and while the last rays of the sun were highlighting the camp I went to Billy's grave. It had been tended and tended well. I had seen where they had tried to plant some flowers but they had died. The wooden cross we had made still looked sharp. I knew that over time it would erode and I would have to have a stone one made. I knelt next to the raised earth and touched the cross, "I am back, Billy. Bet and the children are doing well, and I have made sure that they will be looked after should the worst happen. You must know about our mother. She will be in heaven with you now and at peace." I sighed. "I wish you were not lying here and that you lived still in England. This is no place to die, Billy. You died for a man's greed and having met Willoughby Hargreaves he is not worth the spit to curse his name. You cannot change the past but I shall harbour a grudge against him until my dying day. I know not how long I shall be here but while I am I will speak to you each night. I pray that you can hear me but prayers and words to the dead are never wasted for in their utterance comes remembrance. While we live we shall speak of you. Griff, Jack and Victoria will speak your name and gaze upon your photograph on the mantlepiece. It gives me a comfort." I stood, "Goodnight and God Bless."

I turned and saw Ged Adams watching me from a discreet distance. He said, "Sorry, sir, I didn't wish to intrude but the corporal of the guard wanted to know if the standing orders had changed."

I nodded, "Thank you, Adams. No there are no changes yet. It will take me a day or two to get back into the rhythm of life out here."

"Sergeant Major Richardson told me about your brother. I am so sorry. It must have been hard."

"The hardest thing I ever did. How are your quarters?"

"Fine, sir." He turned to walk back to the barracks with me. "Sergeant Major Richardson is a good bloke, sir. He is firm with the men and yet you can talk to him. Rare qualities. Most of the sergeant majors I knew had one volume and that was full blast."

"That might work in a big regiment but this one is more like a band of brothers. We rely on each other."

"I am glad I took the colonel's offer, sir. I feel like I might actually do some good out here."

The next morning I went with Syd, Ged and Number 1 Troop, to familiarise myself with the desert and my new camel: Lady Jane. It was not an Arabic name as the animals had been bought as young animals and named by the troop. She was a good mount but not Aisha. I missed the old camel. Syd told me that she had simply died, a year after I had left. That saddened me too for I had been fond of her and her death was a harbinger, I feared, of my own.

The column of horsemen riding from Suez were spotted by Corporal Hill who was in command of the sentries. He had been a raw recruit when I had left and now was a seasoned trooper. Syd's words had warned me that the Sirdar might return and I took no chances. I had the troopers ready and armed as the twenty horsemen approached. It was Kitchener. He had not changed but was now surrounded by a larger staff.

Syd had the men snap to attention as they dismounted. General Kitchener had the hint of a smile on his face as he came towards me. Herbert Kitchener was not one for over familiarity and the hint of a smile was as much as I could expect. "Roberts, the uniform suits you. Let us get inside the office, out of the sun. My visit here is a brief one to water the animals. Hunt, water the animals."

"Sir."

Adams must have put the kettle on as soon as the riders were seen for as we entered the office he said, "There is a pot of tea there, sir. Shall I be mother?"

The general grunted, "Good fellow, three sugars in mine and no milk. When that is done leave us."

"Yes sir."

Once alone the general said, "I arranged for your promotion and had you expedited out here for a reason, Roberts. We begin to retake Sudan. My aim is to retake Khartoum. This unit has proved its worth and now that it is fully trained with no weaknesses, then I wish to exploit it. When we head south you and your men will be with the advance guard commanded by Colonel Burn Murdoch. These will be Sudanese camels, horsemen with six companies of the Camel Corps as well as two Maxim guns and a battery of guns. They will have teeth. You will be their eyes and ears. They will all be mounted. I will not be surprised by the Dervishes. I need not tell you that they are a fast-moving army and have caught others out before. You will ensure that we see the enemy before they see us. Once we are in a position where we can give battle then your unit will be assigned to British brigades."

I nodded, "And when does this offensive begin, sir?"

"In the spring, or what passes for spring here in the desert. You have three months to get down to Wadi Haifa and familiarise yourself with the land between there and Dongola. You will leave here in the next week. Supplies will be arriving from tomorrow. You need to be self-sufficient. I know that you chaps are good at keeping yourself safe. It matters not if the Mahdists know that you are sniffing about but I want no losses. Your unit must be intact when we leave."

He took his pocket watch from his pocket. He had finished his briefing and was working out when he should leave. I decided to broach the question of my future. His words told me that we would not finish this task in six months. It would take a couple of years. "General Kitchener, while I am grateful for the promotion I have to tell you that once we have taken Khartoum then I would like to resign my commission and retire from the army."

He cocked an eye, "Found a woman, Roberts?"

"No, sir, but I have a son and he is growing up. The last couple of years have given me the chance to get close to him and..."

He drained his mug of tea, "Hmnn, I thought you were single. I prefer single men. Marriage, women and children complicate things, still, if we get to Khartoum then you will have done what I wish and by then Colonel Dickenson should have trained up the men to carry on where you left off." I thought he had finished, "Your son, how old is he?"

"Fourteen, sir, why?"

"You are a good soldier, Roberts. If your boy has your blood in him then he could be a soldier. We shall always need good soldiers if we are to maintain the empire. You are an officer now and there could be a place at Sandhurst for him. You will never rise above the rank of Second Lieutenant but your son..." He stood, "Anyway, it is something to think about. I shall see you and your unit at Wadi Haifa at the end of February."

He stood and left. Syd entered as did Ged. Brown was still the bugler but he was now a corporal. "Have Brown sound officer's call. We have our orders."

204

As Syd left Ged said, "Be a little crowded in here, perhaps if you used the mess? I can fetch your maps and the like."

"Good idea, and put on a dixie of tea, eh?"

"Righto, sir. Sergeant Major's tea coming up."

He was efficient and I began to use him like a crutch from that day on. Considering that I had only recently met him we formed a bond and had a rapport that normally came from brothers in arms who had fought together. I think in our case we had similar experiences and just liked each other.

After he returned with the tea, he took out a cardboard box, "This was left for you, sir. Your new helmet." He took it out. It was larger than the one I had used since I had first come to Africa and had a flared bottom.

I shook my head, "Leave it in the box, Ged. I shall continue to wear this one."

"When we reach the main army there might be comments, sir."

I nodded, "Comments, I can take. I know that General Kitchener will not object." I saw the question in Adams' eyes, "When we ride with our puggarees and keffiyeh, we all look the same. The helmet would mark me as an officer and a target. I have no death wish, Ged, I want to survive and get home to my family."

"A good enough reason sir and this will make a nice souvenir."

When we left, we looked like a huge caravan. The camp was guarded by the handful of old soldiers and our trunks were in safe hands. I would need no dress uniform in the desert nor fine shoes. We had no Egyptian servant and so the troopers led the camels that carried our tents and supplies. We had plenty of ammunition and magazines. The food was largely dried but we had fresh fruit and vegetables for the first few days. Until we reached Wadi Haifa and the Sudanese border we would be in a relatively safe country. We would be able to cook and enjoy hot food. We would be following the Nile. I had read the orders left by the Sirdar and knew that when the campaign began the foot soldiers and artillery would be transported down the Nile by boat and by train. With just one British, mounted unit, the 21st

Lancers, the bulk of our mounted force would be Sudanese and Egyptians.

The two who needed the most adjustment were Adams and me. I was used to England and the cold while Adams had never ridden a camel. He seemed to enjoy the challenge of mastering the beastie. He rode just behind me with Corporal Brown. Syd and I rode together. He gestured behind him at the troopers, "The new lads who joined us after you left us are trained up, sir, but the trouble is all that they know is how to ride and to cope in the desert. We have seen no action since…well, sir, the rescue." He nodded at the mountain, "We have scoured that of bandits. They won't return."

"There will be another hole for them to occupy. As for the lack of action, we have enough men who have had the whiff of cordite. If the new lads are a bit slower to react they will learn and learn quickly. These months ahead will give us time to hone their skills."

Although the two of us were speaking our eyes were constantly scanning the desert and the skyline. Even though any travellers we met might be friendly the skill of spotting them was a necessary one.

"An officer, eh, sir? It is the dream of all of us."

I nodded, "But it comes at a price." He cocked his head to one side. "There is more pay but more expenses and some of those officers that you and I came to fear for their incompetence are still there. I still have to salute them and obey them. I have to give orders to men that I might not agree with." I lowered my voice. "When we have taken Khartoum I will resign my commission and head on home. I will not be promoted any further, I know that and I am content."

"That could take a couple of years, sir."

"I know, Syd, but let us hope we can do it quicker this time. Kitchener knows his business. Our role shows that. We went blindly through the desert last time and hundreds of men paid the price. We will not let that happen."

The first week saw my body and mind get into the rhythm of the desert. We rose whilst it was dark and travelled until two hours before noon. We ate, drank water and kept watch until two and then headed off again to arrive at a camp just before sunset.

206

Once we reached the Nile then water was not a problem but we made sure that any water we drank was boiled. The camels seemed immune to the impurities in the lifeblood of Egypt. The second week of travel saw us becoming more alert. The border was guarded at Wadi Haifa but it was an Egyptian infantry battalion. They did not venture from their defences and, as we had discovered in the past, mounted Dervishes could simply slip past.

The fort at Wadi Haifa was a comforting sight. It had been improved since we had camped there before the Battle of Toski. They had two Maxim guns as well as four artillery pieces. That they had not been attacked since arriving told me that the Mahdists were no longer trying to take Egypt. The war with Italy had diverted their attention. The French and the Belgians were also making inroads in the southwest. For the first time since I had returned to Egypt, I began to think that it might be less than a year before I could return home.

The fort was supplied by river and we were able to commandeer fresh supplies. When we left we were ready for whatever the desert and the Dervishes threw at us. Once we left the fort I sent out the four Egyptian scouts in two pairs. One pair rode further east than the other and I alternated them each day. Syd had trained them and assured me that they could easily range two or three miles ahead of us. They were normally waiting for us at the end of each day at the campsite they had selected. We would only see them earlier if they spotted anything.

We were ten miles from Firket when Ali and Mohammed rode in. They saluted and Ali pointed, "We have found the Mahdists, Lieutenant Roberts. They are south of Akasha at Firket. We did not close with them."

I nodded. They had obeyed orders. It was not that they were not to be trusted but I would need to estimate numbers for the general. "Then we make camp here. Sergeant Major Richardson, I will lead Number 2 Troop out tomorrow. We will leave at 3 a.m. You will make a defensive camp here."

"Sir." My orders meant that Jake and his men would not be asked to do anything in the way of cooking or sentry duty. They would be allowed to get their heads down.

While Ged saw to my camel I took out my weapons. I had cleaned and oiled them at the Palace of Sand and Bugs but now was the time to check them. Ged had been curious about the Martini-Henry which now seemed like a museum piece but when I told him of its range he understood. It might be slower at firing but its accuracy gave me an advantage. The Lee Metford would probably be the weapon I would need if we got into a firefight, that and the Webley. I made sure that I had plenty of bullets in my cartridge pouch and that my five magazines were easily accessible. That done I had Ged put them in the scabbards on the saddle.

He made up a bed for me. The greatcoat that I rarely wore these days would be the base with the keffiyeh rolled up as a pillow. The blanket was neatly folded. Ged was an old soldier and trained in the way of the army. I ate with the others and, after smoking a pipe, snuggled into my bed. I slept like a baby until Ged shook me awake.

"Sergeant Major has a brew on, sir, and Sergeant Johnson is sorting out his men."

I looked up and saw that the sky was clear. Stars filled it. I missed Middy. He could navigate by the stars and gave us confidence that we would never be lost. Ali and Mohammed were at prayer and I let them have their privacy. Once we left they would lead and we would ride in silence. Hand signals would be the order of the day. I knew that Jake would ensure that the men had loaded weapons and that they would obey his orders instantly. I smiled as I ate the dried fruit and drank my tea. I was not some gung-ho, keen young second lieutenant. I trusted my men and my NCOs for I had been one. It made a difference.

We made good time down the Nile Road. When we neared Akasha, Ali took us to the east to bypass the silent, sleeping village. Our two scouts had assured us that there were no Mahdists there but it paid to be cautious. Closer to Firket, Ali signalled for us to stop and dismount when we smelled the smoke from their woodfires. He pointed and I saw, in the distance, the barricades that the defenders had made. I gestured for Jake to join Ali and me. Along with Mohammed, we headed across the scrubby desert to get a better view of their defences. Ali had told me that they had seen the defences and identified the enemies' position but not the numbers. We would have to get close enough to do that. The fewer of us the better. The cover was made up of half-derelict buildings and scrubby weeds, bushes and stunted trees. Our khaki helped to disguise us and we made it to the wall of what must have been an ancient farm. It slightly overlooked the camp and I took out the binoculars that had been issued to me. There was no moon and therefore no reflection from the lenses.

I peered through them. Jake had his head close to mine and he had a notepad and pencil. I scanned the camp and identified the four sentries. I could see no guns. Inside the camp were tents. I used them to estimate numbers. I checked twice and hissed, "Thirteen hundred." That was the number of warriors that I estimated. I did so by counting fires and flags. Their makeup was impossible to gauge. I heard the sound of horses and moved my binoculars. They had a horse herd and there were another four men watching them. This was easier and I counted close to a hundred animals. "One hundred horses."

We had seen all that we needed to and Ali led us back to our men and the horses. By the time the sun was up, we were back at our camp. I transferred Jake's notations to my report. I sat with my NCOs and drank tea while I filled them in.

"I estimate between twelve and fourteen hundred men. One hundred are cavalry and there are no guns. This is their forward base and I think they are doing the same job as we are. They are early warning. We will leave after the sun is at its peak and get to the south of Firket in the dark. They must have a bigger base further down the river."

Syd gave a smile, "This will be a test of the lads, eh sir?"

"Aye, and if we are spotted then we will be behind enemy lines. We all know what that means."

They all nodded. Any wounded men would have to be left behind.

We found no more signs of the enemy until we neared Dongola. It lay south of the 3rd Cataract and this time, when Syd and I scouted it we found a more formidable force there. This time there were more than seven thousand men with five hundred cavalry and eight guns. I suppose we could have returned to Wadi Haifa there and then but the general would not thank me for returning with half a report. We continued south until we reached Debba. There the Nile's course took us north and east towards the Nubian desert. There were, surprisingly, no defences or a garrison at Debba. We still used the maps made by Middy and they were a godsend. We had a far better idea of where we were and if the worst came to the worst we knew that we could head across the seemingly featureless desert knowing we could get back to the river.

Abu Hamad was familiar to us and it was there we saw a smaller outpost like the one at Firket. The difference was that this one was now defended and, in addition to men, had four artillery pieces. When Jake and I returned to our camp I held a meeting. I took out the map and pointed to the defences we had found. These three camps look to be the only defences south of Wadi Haifa. We could go further south to Berber." I smiled at Jake and Syd, "We know what that place is like and it is safe to assume that it is still well-defended."

Syd said, in explanation to the others, "Solid walls protected by the Nile and at least six guns."

"So Dongola and Berber will be the harder nuts to crack. What I propose is to head north from here along the caravan route to the border. It will mean a one hundred and fifty mile ride across the desert but we need to know if there are desert camps. We know that they used to use them."

We left before dawn and headed up the packed sand that had been used since the times of the pharaohs. This time our four Egyptian scouts were there to look for signs of enemy horsemen. If we found signs of camels then that would more likely be the evidence of caravans. I estimated that our pace meant we would be back at Wadi Haifa about a fortnight before the general expected us.

We were just forty miles from the border when we heard the sound of firing ahead of us. The haze from the desert and the sun always made it harder to see too far. Syd had trained the men well. Carbines were drawn and the troopers formed two lines. The second lines held the reins of the dismounted men in the front rank. I slid my rifle and chambered a round. I hoped that Ged would cope with whatever was coming our way. Two camels burst over the small rise that lay ahead of us. It was Ali and Mohammed. Two riderless camels told me that the other two scouts had been either wounded or killed. If the former then the latter was inevitable.

Syd shouted, "Mark your target. Wait for the order."

I saw dust behind and Baggara tribesmen mounted on good horses. There was too much dust to give an accurate estimate of numbers but I reckoned there had to be more than fifty. After drawing my rifle, I aimed at the leading rider. I would wait until the main body was in range of the carbines but mine was the more accurate weapon. I was confident that I could hit my man. Ali and Mohammed were old hands and they took their animals in a loop to allow us to fire. It put them in danger as the horses closed with them. I waited until the horsemen were about one hundred and forty yards from us and shouted, "Fire!"

My rifle cracked and the leading rider was thrown from the back of his horse. The carbines' volley followed.

"Rapid fire."

I sheathed my rifle and drew my carbine. In that time the horsemen had closed to within fifty yards and I aimed and fired as fast as I could. The twenty odd carbines had done their job and enough saddles emptied so that the survivors took to their heels and fled.

Syd shouted, "Cease fire. Reload." It was good practice to replace half-empty magazines with fresh ones.

Ali rode next to me, "We found a Baggara camp, sir." He nodded to the two riderless camels that had followed the two scouts back. "Mohammed and I were on the flanks and the other two were spotted by hidden sentries. The ones who followed us were less than half of the men we saw."

In the desert, survival was often down to instant decisions. I pointed to the northwest, "We leave the caravan route and go across country. Mount." I saw the fearful look on the faces of those who were newer to the desert. We would be using a compass and a map. We would have to survive on the water we had with us. "Corporal, secure those two camels, we might need them."

Syd said, "Do we check the bodies, sir?"

I shook my head, "We have no time. You are the rearguard, Sergeant Major. I will take the lead."

I reloaded my carbine and sheathed it. I took out the compass
and took a sight. I identified a point to aim at and waved my arm.
We left the solid ground of the caravan route and headed across
the desert. The map was now a guide only. This would be down
to my skill as a navigator and not for the first time I wished that
Middy was with us.

We did not ride hard for we knew not what lay ahead. I
peered at the distant marker trying to identify any hazards that
we might encounter. Every few minutes I would look at the
compass to see if we were headed in the right direction. I was
now an experienced rider and while Lady Jane was no Aisha she
was a good camel and I kept my saddle despite the uneven
ground over which we rode. I did not look back. I had placed
Syd at the back because I knew he would ensure we left no one
behind. I was the navigator. Once we reached the spot I had
marked I stopped. The camels would appreciate the rest and any
slower riders would have the chance to catch up. I sought
another marker and spied, in the distance, what looked like a
tree. That meant water.

I pointed and said, "Follow me."

An oasis was like a sanctuary but could also pose a danger.
The enemy could be there. It was on our route to the Nile and so
I took it. My Webley was still unfired. If a threat manifested
itself, I could empty the Webley as fast as I could blink.

We reached the oasis as the sun was setting in the west. I did
not gallop nor did I slow to a walk. My pistol was in my hand as
I descended to the patch of vegetation. It was, mercifully, empty.
I spied a puddle of water. It would do for the animals but not us.
We would have to eke out our canteens.

"Set sentries but no fires. Water the camels."

"Right, sir. Number 2 Troop, sentry duty." Syd would see that
everything was organised equitably. I dismounted and handed
my reins to Ged, "Holding up, Adams?"

He smiled, "Exciting, sir. Had nothing like this in India.
Makes me feel like a youngster again."

He would do. I took the map and, using a pencil, roughly
marked the oasis as well as the place where we had fought the
Baggara. It was all estimated, but I knew, roughly, how far and
fast we had travelled. We still had more than one hundred miles

to go across an unknown desert. Syd came over to me and Ged brought us both some dried fruit and dried meat. Syd gestured at the two scouts, "Ali feels guilty about the ambush."

I shrugged, "It couldn't be helped and we have been lucky so far. Our luck had to run out some time. I am just sorry we couldn't recover their bodies."

That was always hard. In my case I imagined myself lying there, alone in the desert waiting to die. Ali did not know if the two had been dead when they fell from their camels.

"I'll just make your bed up Lieutenant."

"Thank you, Adams. Get some rest yourself. It will be harder tomorrow." He went to fetch the bedding. "They will try to find us tomorrow. We emptied too many saddles for them to simply let us go."

He nodded, "The lads did alright though, sir. Their first action and none of them froze."

I took out my pipe. There were insects close to the rapidly shrinking water. The smoke could clear the insects and help to calm me. "They know the desert better than we do."

"Aye, sir but we have a head start."

"Not necessarily, Syd. Their camp was north of us and less than half chased our scouts. The rest will be well rested. They know we will head for the river and could get ahead of us. I want us away from here by the middle of the night."

He gave me a sceptical look, "Sir, no offence but can you navigate by night?"

I smiled as I got the pipe going, "None taken. I know that I am not as good as Middy but if it is a clear night I shall use the stars. I watched Middy do it. Besides which, we have to use the dark to maintain what little advantage we have."

He was right, of course, and our night flight would be a test of me as much as anything.

When the sky was clear and the air cold, I breathed a sigh of relief. All I had to do was to find a fixed star and use it. Middy had taught me about the North Star, and I took a compass bearing on it. I then took a route north and east towards the Nile. I was alone at the front and felt the weight of responsibility lying heavily on my shoulders. There was no one above me to blame if things went wrong. The fact that I had never hidden behind anyone before was immaterial. We ploughed on through the night. I had to watch the ground as well as the star and the compass. It was exhausting. I stopped at the top of a steep climb. There had been sand to the left and right and I deemed that it might hide danger. The rocky path up the escarpment had been trodden by goats and sheep.

"Let the men drink, Sergeant Major."

"Sir."

Adams ghosted up next to me and handed me a canteen, "Here you are, sir, you need to take care too." I took it and drank three swallows. He shook his head, "I don't know how you do it, sir." He pointed in the distance. You could see the prints left by the camels and they were arrow straight."

"There is more luck to it than you can imagine, Ged."

The short rest helped the camels and we headed down the slope. As the stars disappeared, I waited for dawn and something I could use as a fixed point. The compass gave me the direction but like the sea the desert could be deceitful. Once again it was the hint of an oasis that gave me my point. We headed across the desert and into a rising temperature. The clear skies of the night had forecast the day and without a cloud in the sky, the air began to feel heavy, as though we were wearing thick coats. We had to keep going longer than was wise just to reach the partial shade of the trees. It was another puddle, albeit a little larger than the last one.

As I dismounted, I waved over Syd, "Better make sure that they are husbanding their water. We still have a long way to go."

"Aye, sir. You get your head down and let me keep an eye on things. It is you who have had all the pressure."

Surviving on dried fruit and dried meat was all very well but without liquid our bodies would soon begin to complain.

We saw the dust cloud raised by our pursuers as we prepared to move after our noon halt. There was little we could do about it. As we mounted Syd asked, "How far to the river, sir?"

"We will reach the river either late this evening or by dawn." I gestured with my thumb, "It all depends on how determined they are. I estimate that we should hit the river somewhere between Sarras and Wadi Haifa." I did not need to spell out that the further we were from Wadi Haifa the smaller were our chances of survival.

It was a long afternoon. I focussed on my job but I was aware of the growing noise in the distance. As they closed with us the anticipation of vengeance grew. I saw in the distance the green of the fertile land that bordered the river. Salvation was in sight but still tantalizingly too far for comfort. The sudden depression ahead gave me an opportunity, albeit a risky one. I shouted over my shoulder, "When we drop into the depression turn in one line, draw your carbines and prepare to fire a volley as the enemy comes over the rise. Form your line with me in the centre. Make sure the Sergeant Major knows my intent."

Jake shouted, "Yes, sir." I heard my order repeated.

I drew my carbine and leaned back in the saddle as Lady Jane took the slope. I whirled her around and rested my forearm on the saddle. I cocked the carbine and waited. The troopers took their places. Corporal Brown was next to me. "Be ready to sound retreat if I order it."

"Sir."

Ged took his place behind me and shouted, "Give those spare camels to me."

The troopers with the two spare camels would be able to add their firepower. None of us knew how many men pursued us and they would be depending on me making the correct decision. The sound of the Baggara grew as their horses' hooves pounded on the sand and rock and their voices shouted and screamed as they closed with us.

I waited until the first four men had begun to descend before I shouted, "Volley fire!" I had gambled but the gamble paid off. We all fired as twenty men joined the first four to descend. The smoke from the carbines briefly obscured the enemy. I chambered another round and lowered my carbine slightly. I fired at the Baggara horseman who had survived the volley by dint of his speed, and was charging at me. He was so close that he was thrown from the saddle by the force of the bullet.

I chambered another round as Syd shouted, "Cease fire." As the smoke cleared I saw the dozen or so bodies and some horses meandering along the ridge.

"Brown, sound retreat."

Omdurman

As the bugle sounded, I wheeled Lady Jane. We had bloodied their noses and, so far as I could tell, not suffered a wound. They would be warier when next they approached. In the event, our turning and snapping had the desired effect. We reached the river and there was no sign of pursuit.

Chapter 19

We spent the next couple of weeks patrolling closer to Wadi Haifa. The Baggara had taken away their dead and their wounded. One of the horses had been killed but when we found the carcass carrion had already begun to devour it. The Sirdar's army started to arrive and I saw relief on the face of the fort's commander. He had been isolated and although he had not been attacked, it had been a threat. Colonel Burn Murdoch arrived overland but the Sirdar and the bulk of the army arrived by gunboats towing locally sourced boats.

Before I even had the chance to introduce myself to the colonel, I was summoned with the man who would be my superior to a meeting with General Kitchener. There were just three of us present. "Colonel, the lieutenant here has been scouting out the land ahead and I thought that you should hear his report at the same time as I did."

I liked Burn Murdoch, who was of a similar age to me and had also served in the earlier war. The difference between us was that he had been brought up as a gentleman and had always been an officer. I was still learning how to be an officer. I had written down everything in chronological order and although I did not read from my handwritten report, it was a nice aide memoir.

When I had finished General Kitchener held out his hand, "Give that report to me, Roberts."

"Sir, it is just a scribbled account."

He shook his head, "I do not need a tome written by Charles Dickens. This will do. A sound report. It is clear to me that we need a fort at Sarras. I will deal with that. Secondly, we need to rid the river of the men at Firket. It will take another couple of weeks to assemble all the men we need. I want you, Colonel, to lead your brigade across the desert so that when we attack along the river you can prevent the enemy from escaping." As the Scot nodded the Sirdar turned to me, "You can navigate through the desert?"

"Yes sir. When we fled from Abu Hamad, I learned how to sail the camels through the sandy sea."

"Keep it simple, Roberts. I care not how you acquired the skills merely that you have them. In a fortnight, we will head for Akasha. You said it was not fortified when you last visited," I nodded, "Colonel, your first task will be to occupy it while I fortify Sarras. That will be all."

We were dismissed.

The colonel smiled and shook his head, "The Sirdar can be a blunt fellow but by God he gets things done. I am happy to have your chaps with us. The Camel Corps are excellent in their own way but they have yet to be tested in combat and your handful of men have experience. I take it that you are happy to be isolated at the fore?"

I nodded, "Yes sir. When we were under the Sirdar's command before we learned to be self-sufficient. You will have plenty of warning of the enemy and we will not tarry returning as fast as we can to the safety of your column."

"Good, we cannot afford to be profligate with good men. Have your troop bivouac with the rest of the column and you shall dine with my officers and me. It is important that we get to know one another."

The officers I met were not the same as the drunken young men I had met on the ship. These were men like me who had taken promotions in the Egyptian and Sudanese armies. We got on well. Many had heard of me and the ESEG. Our exploits at Fort Desolation had become almost legend. The men also got on well and that helped. Ged proved to be very resourceful. His time in India had been well spent and he acquired all manner of things we needed. Before the time that the rest of the army arrived my only disappointment was the lack of letters. None arrived for me and I sent my bundle back up the Nile. My family would, at least, know how I was doing but I was in the dark about home.

When we left for Akasha, my troops were the four fingers that led the desert column. The two thousand seven hundred mounted men, and two machine guns, with whom we served were the most potent force since Alt Klea. It was comforting to know that just a mile behind us were soldiers who were ready to fight. It helped to give us confidence.

The Dervishes had sent men to Akasha but the sight of almost three thousand mounted men made them flee to Firket. We were given the task of following them. As we neared the camp I could see that they had been reinforced. There was a piece of high ground to the north and east of the camp, the Jebel Firket, and we positioned ourselves there. It afforded a fine view south and west. I sent Sergeant Johnson and his troop back for the colonel. I thought that he should view the position for himself. We dismounted and I used my binoculars to spy out the defences. From what I discerned there were almost three thousand men as well as five hundred horses. I wondered if our scouting expedition had warned them of the presence of British troops. In any event, it could not be helped. When the colonel arrived I let him judge the position himself before I spoke.

He smiled, "I expected the Mahdists to send men out to shift us, Roberts. I wonder why they do not."

I patted my carbine, "We have met the Baggara before and they have learned to respect the Lee Metford, sir. We can send almost two hundred bullets at them in a short time." I pointed to the narrow track that bordered the river, "The River Column will struggle with that, sir."

The colonel nodded and used his glasses to look south and east, "We can skirt the high ground and use the land to the south. It looks perfect for mounted men."

Having seen enough we returned to the column and then the army. General Kitchener listened patiently. With him was General Hunter who would lead the River Column. The Sirdar said, "So my basic plan still works. We use the artillery to give us cover and the infantry can advance in battalion formation to hold the enemy. Colonel, your men can block the escape?"

"Yes, sir, Roberts and I scouted that out today but the road along the river is narrow, sir."

"We will attack at night. I want complete surprise. There will be no smoking on the march, no bugles and bayonets only. I want us to fall upon them at dawn. Any questions, gentlemen?" There were, of course, none. "Very well, rejoin your units and prepare for the morrow. We begin to retake Sudan. Firket may be only a small step but it is one which is in the right direction, towards Khartoum."

We would be closer to the rest of the desert column, but we would still be the eyes and ears. I had my sergeants and corporals gather around me and Ged took notes. "The general has said that he wants silence. That means cold steel. We don't have bayonets. If we find sentries, it will have to be knife work. You know your troopers better than I do, do we have men who can creep up on an enemy and use a blade?"

Syd nodded, "The assault on Ezbet Hanna sâlih el-Baharîya showed us the right men." He smiled, "As I recall, sir, you are pretty handy with a knife yourself."

The memory of Billy's death came back as I remembered the night assault up the slopes. "Then when we near their position I will lead the men with blades and we will walk, leaving our camels with the rest of you."

Syd shook his head, "No, sir, I didn't mean for you to risk yourself."

"Sergeant Major, these pips don't change the man beneath them. You are right about my skills and I will lead."

We headed through the desert as a single column with my troop as the vanguard. We were well to the east of the river and although there was no moon my men and I were used to travelling by starlight and we did not lose the path we were to take. Once we had passed Khor Firket I led us more south-westerly than south. When I spied the reflective sparkle from the stars on the Nile I halted. I rode back to the colonel. "I will lead my men to silence the sentries, sir. My Sergeant Major will fetch you when it is safe."

"Good luck, Roberts, and don't take chances."

"Don't worry, sir. I won't."

Once back with the troop I dismounted and handed my reins to Ged. The four men chosen by my sergeants were ready and I drew my sword. I smeared some soil on the blade to dull it. "I will send Carter back when it is clear."

Knowing an argument was futile Syd said, "Sir."

The men followed me in a loose line as we headed through the rocks that led to the low escarpment that overlooked the shingle beach to the south of Firket. I was not sure if they would have sentries but it cost nothing to check. I smelled smoke and knew that, ahead, someone was smoking. It had to be an enemy. Some smoked tobacco while others smoked the leaf they called hashish. I held my sword out to halt the others and listened.

There was a mumble of conversation from behind the rocks ahead. I waved Trooper Atkinson to my right and Trooper Carter to my left. I gestured for the other two to wait. Trooper Atkinson was a small soldier and I let him move alone. I went with the burlier Carter. As we edged around the rock I detected two, perhaps three voices. The rock behind which they sheltered gave us little option, we had to creep around it and hope that we had quicker reactions and sharper blades than they did. It was Carter who stepped out first and I followed a heartbeat later. The three Mahdists were squatting on the ground and smoking. There were no horses and I guessed that they were an outpost. Carter was slower than I was. My sword darted to take the Mahdist on the right. The long, sharp sword entered his throat and he died silently. Atkinson had his arm around the neck of the one in the middle and had slit his throat even as the first was dying. Carter's knife missed the throat, for the warrior turned a little. The dagger went into the man's shoulder. Even as his mouth began to open in preparation for a shout of alarm I lunged with my sword. The tip entered his eye and before he could scream, his brain. He died.

"Sorry, sir," whispered Carter.

"Get the other two and scout out the rest of the rocks. I don't think there will be others but check, eh?"

"Sir."

I wiped my sword clean on the keffiyeh of the dead man and said, "Good work, Atkinson."

He cleaned his own blade, "I would love a sword, sir."

I nodded at the one in the dead man's belt, "There is one, take it but don't let it trip you up."

He looked amazed and said, "Really? I can have it?"

"Of course."

"But it is not in Queen's regulations."

I chuckled quietly, "And when has that ever stopped us? We do what we can and the name of the game is to do our duty and survive, any way that we can."

Carter came back, "All clear, sir."

"Head back and tell the Sergeant Major to bring up the others and send a message to the colonel."

As he headed back we searched the dead men. As I expected there was neither paper nor money but they had food and we shared it. It was a kind of cake made with honey, raisins and nuts. It was delicious and I knew that the energy we would get from it would help us.

By the time the troop and then the column arrived, it was getting close to dawn. The Maxims were set up to enfilade the beach and the exit from Firket. The camels and the cavalry formed two lines. This would be sword work although my troop had the firepower of their carbines. I smiled as Atkinson rested his sword on his shoulder. He looked like one of the Queen's Guards outside her palace. We saw the muzzles flash and heard the cracks as the Egyptians and Sudanese advanced upon the Mahdist camp. It was both too dark and too far away for us to make anything out but the wave of smoke and men moved closer to us showing us that we were winning. MacDonald's company appeared from the east and soon the men who had survived the initial assaults were driven into Firket.

It was then that the Baggara horsemen took to their mounts. It was not cowardice but the need to fight as they had been trained. With rifles and machine guns to the north and east, they took the only route that they had left, south. There we waited. This time it would not be me who gave the command but Colonel Burn Murdoch. He timed the bugle to perfection and as the Baggara began to climb the gentle slopes that offered them the chance to get up and around the advancing columns of infantry then the two thousand cavalrymen were ordered to charge. Had this been some years ago then the men of my troop might have struggled to both control a camel and fire a carbine. They could now do both. My troop was on the extreme left of our line and as I waved my sword to lead them forward so the Baggara saw the wall of camels and horses charging down at them. They were brave men and they drew their swords to charge up at us. Carbines cracked before contact was made and some Mahdists fell. Atkinson and I, along with my sergeants and one or two others all had swords and we slashed at the Baggara from the lofty backs of camels. The wounds we risked were to legs whilst our swords cracked down on unprotected skulls. When there were no warriors close enough for sword work I sheathed my sword and took out my carbine. We had forced the Baggara closer to the centre and our carbines reaped a harvest. While some of the men in Firket surrendered the Baggara did not. They either died or fled through our lines to return to their main army and tell them of the disaster of Firket.

Two hours after it had begun it was over. We had killed or wounded a thousand and over six hundred were prisoners. The Desert Column had lost not a man but the total deaths amongst the Egyptian and Sudanese Battalions was only twenty-two. It showed what could be done with officers and NCOs who were British and had served as a soldier of the queen.

As we rode back to Firket Colonel Burn Murdoch said, "We know one thing, Roberts. The Egyptians and the Sudanese are now more than capable of standing up to and defeating the Mahdists. The days of them rolling over are long gone."

That night in our camp there was a mood of high excitement amongst the troopers. They had acquitted themselves well. I sat with my sergeants and we smoked our pipes and enjoyed the rum provided by Burn Murdoch. Ged hovered nearby until Syd said, "This is not the Guards, Adams. You are one of us now. Sit down and enjoy the rum with us."

The old soldier looked at me and I nodded, "We are brothers in arms, Ged. We have won a great victory and rank is now immaterial."

He did as we had asked and from that moment on whenever my sergeants and I enjoyed a quiet time together, he was with us. Of course, whenever the bottle was empty or someone needed food then he would rise and scurry off to fetch more.

"Do you reckon it will be as easy for the rest of the campaign, sir?" Shaw was one of the younger sergeants and had grown since joining the troop.

I shook my head, "Firket had the smallest garrison we saw and they had reinforced this one. Dongola, Abu Hamad not to mention Berber, are all tougher nuts with artillery. We have a hot summer ahead of us."

I did not say so but I knew that it meant we could not possibly complete our task before the next year. Colonel Burn Murdoch had told me that General Kitchener wanted a railway built across the desert and before the Nile shrank, gunboats were brought up.

With quick firing twelve pounders the armoured vessels would give us control of the river and therein lay our best chance of victory. It was like having the most mobile of artillery.

The Desert Column occupied Suarda, where the Nile turned east while General Hunter, with the North Staffordshire regiment along with the Egyptian and Sudanese battalions, returned to Wadi Haifa to haul the gunboats over the rocks to be refloated south of them.

It was our presence in Suarda, I think, that saved us from the disaster that was the cholera outbreak. It raced through the North Staffs as well as the native battalions. None were immune. That and the heat meant that the work to both bring the gunboats and finish the railway across the Nubian Desert slowed to a crawl. Along with the Camel Corps, we were detached to guard the men building the railway and they seemed to suffer less than the other units.

The work was dull but necessary. We stood watches at night and during the heat of the day watched the desert for raiders. If the boot had been on the other foot, we would have raided and it seemed that it was more than likely that they would try to disrupt the building of a railway that would surely presage the ending of the Mahdist rule. It was not the enemy who thwarted us but nature itself. Back in England, we were used to unseasonal storms in August but here in the desert, they were unheard of. That August we suffered, in just two days, storms that were truly of Biblical proportions. First came a wave of searing heat followed by a sandstorm that was the worst I had ever endured. I was just grateful that Sergeant Saeed had shown me how to deal with them. When we finally emerged from the piles of sand around us we saw the devastation the sand storm had caused. The telegraph lines were down and when my troop and I rode along it to inspect the damage we discovered that twenty miles of recently built track had been destroyed. Even as I gave my report the next storm struck. This time, and for the first time since I had been in the desert, the storm that had brewed up in the far south was wet and there was thunder and lightning. Horses were terrified but thanks to our close relationship with our camels, we were able to quiet them. Even so, we were soaked to the skin and thoroughly miserable. Others were not so lucky and our campaign was set back even further.

It was such a disaster that General Kitchener brought five thousand men from Firket to spend twelve days rebuilding the railway. It was as we guarded the men toiling to replace sleepers and rails that the Baggara began to raid us. They took advantage of the storm to get closer to us, and although they were outnumbered, their intent was clear. They wished to make the men repairing the railway cease their labours and defend themselves. General Kitchener sent for me. Captain Thomas of the Camel Corps was also in the meeting as was Colonel Burn Murdoch.

"Roberts, find the Baggara camp and lead the Camel Corps to destroy it."

He said it as though it was the simplest task in the world. It was not and while I thought it an unfair task I merely saluted and said, "Yes, sir."

"If they are looking over their shoulders for you then they cannot attack my builders. We have been delayed by three disasters let us not compound this one."

As we left the meeting I said, "Three disasters?"

Captain Thomas nodded, "Yes, lieutenant, the cholera, the storm and the blowing up of the boiler on the Zafir, allied to the major problems of getting the gunboats to Firket really upset the general." He smiled at me, "I have heard much about your troop and I look forward to working with you. Can you find them?"

On our walk back to the camp I had put my mind to the problem, "The Baggara have to be within twenty or thirty miles of us and they need oases. We find the one they use and then it will be up to your chaps to chase them off."

We were the only British force now that the North Staffs had been decimated by cholera. The Staffs had only lost nineteen men but the North Staffs would not be a fighting force until the new year.

It took three days to find the enemy. The first two oases we discovered had been used and drunk dry. The third one was clearly occupied. I used my glasses to identify the horses and warriors. Numbers were impossible to determine. Men naturally took shelter from the sun. I sent a rider back to the Camel Corps. Syd ordered the men to take out their carbines.

Captain Thomas looked relieved that we had found them. Riding every day in the desert sun sapped both camel and trooper. "You take the right flank, Lieutenant. I will take the centre and Lieutenant Price can take the left."

"If you can shoot or take their horses it will weaken them almost as well as killing or capturing the men, sir."

Captain Thomas was a proper officer, a gentleman and he scowled, "It goes against the grain to kill an animal, Roberts."

I shrugged, "So long as it shortens this war then that is all I care about, sir."

I drew my Webley as I joined my men. Adams rode behind me. When the bugle sounded I dug my heels in and we leapt forward. We had been seen, of course, and the guns of the Baggara rattled from the vegetation. Mahdist powder was poor and their aim even worse. We closed the ground quickly and I waited until we were almost upon them before I shouted, "Fire!" I aimed my Webley and fired six times. I dropped the pistol to hang by its lanyard and drew my sword. It was unnecessary. The thirty survivors had fled. There had only been seventy or so in the band but as my troop had proved you did not need large numbers to be effective.

Dongola was guarded by five thousand men and their leader was clever. Emir Wad Bishara had his defences on the west bank of the river. The gunboats pounded away at Dongola and the defenders but they were resolute. It was only when General Kitchener occupied the island in the river, opposite Dongola and used artillery there to pound the defences that Dongola was abandoned. We had taken a major Dervish stronghold and few men had fallen in combat. We could now turn our attention east and the next target, Berber.

Chapter 20

Before an attack could be started on Berber, first the general wanted a railway built across the Nubian desert. I had thought it an impossible task if, for nothing else, the lack of water, however the engineers and Kitchener himself came up with a solution. A water station with water tanks was built every twenty-three miles as the railway progressed. At first, the building of the railway was slow as Kitchener was in London trying to find the funds and Lieutenant Maxwell, the officer in command of the operation was limited in what he could use. He only had one engine at first. We were assigned to guard the rail head. I was happy to do so as the outbreak of cholera had terrified me more than action against the Mahdists. A soldier felt he could do something about bullets and blades but an insidious illness was something quite different. The open air seemed safer than a camp and so we became the eyes, ears and protectors of the engineers labouring to build the railway.

It was not hard work but it drained a man as we sat in the winter sun watching the desert for any signs of the enemy. We rarely had to ride far although I sent a patrol out every day for a ten-mile ride around our perimeter. It exercised the camels and varied the diet of the men. We looked for signs of the Baggara who were the horsemen we might expect to find. We found no signs as what passed for spring came to the desert and February tiptoed towards March.

We received letters from home, although I was the only one to be a regular recipient. They all brought relief that my family was safe. Griff was excelling at Grammar School although my Aunt's letters hinted that while his academic studies were going well he was struggling with the social niceties of an education with the sons of gentlemen. Those thoughts disturbed me, all the more because I could do little about them. Bet, Jack and Victoria thrived. My son and aunt's letters told me that but a rare letter from my sister-in-law confirmed it. The letters were a lifeline and kept me sane. I was used to the desert but she was an unforgiving mistress.

The dangers were manifested most clearly when Trooper Ball died. It was not enemy action but a snake. He had not checked his blankets before sleeping, something we all did but the elusive reptile hid and bit him. His cries brought us all to his bivouac and the reptile was hacked to pieces. Such was the men's anger, for Ball had been so popular that they scoured the camp and killed every snake that they could find. The young man was given a lonely grave next to the railway and I had to write my first letter home to a grieving family. I found it hard to write.

It was while we were at the railhead that I met Lieutenant Percy Girouard. He was a Canadian railway engineer and the general had brought him to build the Nile railway. That had now been stopped as all our efforts were on the Nubian railway. He had been given the rank to make life easier but he was no soldier. He was an engineer. I got to know him well as I was often asked to take him into the desert to seek the best route. He did not know the desert but he had an eye for the best route for the tracks. We got on well for the rank was new to both of us.

It was in the new year and, for the desert, the weather was a little chillier than we were used to. It was not exactly cold but the wind was a chilly one and whipped the sand up into our faces. I had Syd and Number 1 Troop with me. Adams was back at the camp. We had developed a routine whilst guarding the railhead and Ged seemed to enjoy the life. The camp edged further south each week and he was able to break and make camp quickly and efficiently. Percy and I rode at the fore. It had taken me some time to persuade him to ride a camel rather than a horse but once he mastered the technique it made desert movement easier as well as conversation as we rode more comfortably.

"Well. Jack, when this railway is finished, we shall be able to supply our army and be ready to assault Abu Hamad. How will the general attack do you think?"

I smiled, "Percy, I was just a plain soldier and then a sergeant major. Such strategies are beyond me. I would not have the first clue how to take a fortified town. If the Dervish have artillery then it could be bloody." I shrugged, "This is my world."

It was at that moment that Corporal Ali shouted, "Baggara!"

I switched my attention to the Egyptian and followed his arm. There was a band of horsemen galloping across the desert toward us.

"Skirmish line. Percy, take shelter behind me."

Percy had a Webley but if he had to use it then we would have failed for the Mahdists would be too close to us.

We formed a thin line and I drew my carbine. I rarely used my old rifle now. The rapid firing of the carbine was more effective as I could fire at the same range as my men. We could all fire from the backs of camels and our animals had been trained to endure the sound of the guns and our forearms resting upon them. They were as solid a platform as was possible.

Syd commanded, "Mark your targets and wait for the order. Nice and steady, eh lads?"

Corporal Brown had his carbine too. We would not need the bugle for we were alone in the desert. The nearest help was more than ten miles away. As I aimed at the whirling mass of men I wondered if we should have used two troops to guard the lieutenant. As always hindsight was perfect. I waited until the Baggara, swords waving in the air, were just one hundred and twenty yards from us. I had learned, over the years, to judge such things. It was closer than many would have liked but I knew that rapid volleys would empty more saddles. The Lee Metford did not penetrate well at a distance. The shorter range made it more likely that our bullets would be effective.

"Fire!"

The carbine bucked and I aimed at another target and fired. There were many Baggara warriors, and I emptied the magazine quickly. Holding the carbine in my left hand I drew my Webley. I aimed carefully and emptied its chambers. We were wreathed in thin smoke. One Baggara warrior, luckier than the rest had made it through the maelstrom of bullets and falling warriors and horses. He had a sword and was coming directly for me. I dropped my Webley to hang from its lanyard and even as I drew my sword I had to block his sword strike with my carbine. The blade scraped and scratched along the barrel.

I heard Syd shout, "Shoot him, sir!"

As the warrior raised his sword for a second strike I lunged with the tip of my sword. I hit his eye and as he screamed and reeled I ripped the sword across his skull. One of my men, probably Syd, had reloaded and he fired a bullet into the brave warrior's head.

"Reload!"

As men slipped fresh magazines into their carbines the smoke cleared and I saw that the survivors had fled.

Behind me, I heard, "Sorry, Jack, I just froze. I thought I might hit you. Sorry, Sergeant Major."

Syd was unsympathetic. "Sir, if you have a gun then learn how to use it. We can't afford passengers out here you know."

It was one thing for Syd to speak like that to me but not another officer, "Sergeant Major Richardson, that will do. Have the Baggara horses gathered, check that the warriors are dead."

I sheathed my sword and holstered my guns. "Sorry about the Sergeant Major, Percy, but we are close."

"No, Jack, he is right. I know I am an engineer but out here everyone is a soldier."

That was the only attack we endured but the next time that Percy needed to explore I used two troops. The Baggara did not bother us again.

A message came to the advance camp along with a Camel Corps company. They were to take over the guarding of the railhead camp and we were ordered to scout out Abu Hamad. When last we had done so I had found it formidable. The general was obviously planning an attack and that meant we were closer to a battle for Khartoum, the ending of the war and a return to England. That it might be dangerous seemed immaterial to me. Ball's death and the Baggara attack had shown me that death could come at any time and I did not want to die.

Adams had to come with us on our patrol as we needed every man but I did not like to put the old soldier in jeopardy. I put him in command of the pack camel. We had one hundred and twenty miles to travel and it was hot. We travelled at night when we could. Unlike most British soldiers we were able to sleep during the day. We were used to the heat. We managed more than twenty miles a day and that was remarkable. We were helped by the proximity of the Nile and so our animals were refreshed more than we might have expected. Each morning when I viewed the land, I realised what a daunting prospect it was. It looked like a stormy ocean which had frozen into solid red rock. To me, it looked as though it had baked for centuries and shards of red shale had fallen to make treacherous footing. When General Hunter attacked he would find it almost impossibly hard.

We found a place where we could hide and I used the glasses to peer into the town. I realised immediately that there were fewer defenders. I passed the glasses to Syd to confirm and he concurred. There were less than eight hundred men and they had neither guns nor horses. It was the best news I had heard.

When we reached the railhead we heard that General Hunter was making his way along the Nile and that he was supported by gunboats. We left the railhead and I bade farewell to Percy. I thought that I would see him as soon as I returned from my meeting with the general but I was wrong.

The general was delighted with my news. "Roberts, I have heard good things about you. I want you seconded to my flying column. I need your eyes, ears and your experience. You shall lead us to Abu Hamad."

We left at the end of July when the desert was unbearably hot. We covered the one hundred and thirty-three miles in just over two hundred hours; most of it at night. One advantage was that the Mahdists had no idea of our approach. The disadvantage was that the marching cost the column three men dead. The desert was unforgiving. They were not from my troop but that did not mitigate their loss. I led the general to the place we had observed the town and we watched in the slightly cooler air of dawn. We spied the town below us. There were watch towers and as soon as the general began to deploy then we would be seen.

"Any horses, Roberts?"

"Not that I saw, sir."

"Hmnn," he was speaking aloud but I do not think it was for any other purpose other than to clarify his thoughts, "We will use a thorn hedge just in case and camp the four brigades in a semi-circle. I concur with your estimate. We outnumber them by at least four to one but there are others in the town who can fight. I will not risk losing more men. We shall use the two Maxim guns and the ancient machine guns to clear the field and then send the men in with bayonets. You will join my single troop of cavalry. I cannot stop any survivors from escaping down the river but you shall ensure that they do not flee across land."

Lieutenant Cross was the officer in command of the Sudanese cavalry. He was a seasoned officer and, like me, had been a sergeant. Neither of us was young any longer. We were positioned behind the 9th and 10th Sudanese brigades. We had the high ground and had a clear view of the battlefield. The machine guns, especially the two Maxims, did the damage. They scythed through men and mud walls alike. When the general ordered in his infantry it would be there to mop up and take prisoners. We were mere spectators in the brief action.

As soon as the town was occupied we were given more orders. "Roberts, I want you to ride to Berber. It will take time to bring the gunboats here but I want to be ready to march as soon as the Sirdar gives us the orders."

I felt obliged to give the officer a warning. "Sir, there is another cataract between here and Berber." If he planned on using the gunboats for support then he would have a problem.

He gave me a curious look, "That is right, you were stationed here for some time. Your local knowledge will be invaluable."

"Sir."

This time we had less than a hundred miles to go and we would have the river for water but we would be deep in the heart of Mahdist territory. We would be within two hundred miles of Khartoum. The Khalifa might have abandoned Abu Hamad and Dongola but Khartoum and Omdurman were a different prospect. I used the lack of direct command from the general to rest the men and camels for two days before we left for Berber.

As we rode down the river Syd and I spoke, "It seems a lifetime ago, sir, since we had that running fight from Berber. As I recall they had cavalry and artillery."

I nodded, "You know the old maxim, Syd, look to your front and do your duty. We just have to see who is there. We do our duty and then head back."

He nodded, "You know sir, I am coming around to your way of thinking. When we have Khartoum then I will hand in my papers."

I shook my head, "Don't make the mistake of thinking that because we took Abu Hamad so easily the rest will be plain sailing. We have still to meet an army that is our size. Kitchener has been lucky thus far and faced men he outnumbered. The Khalifa will dredge every man he can for Khartoum."

Syd chuckled, "Aren't you a little ray of sunshine, sir?"

I laughed, "I am a realist, Syd."

This time we would be approaching Berber from the north and we were unfamiliar with the caravan route. When we saw the shadow in the distance that was the old fort we left the road and I took us, by instinct, through a labyrinth of twisting gorges and wadis. I used my compass to keep us in the right direction. When I had deemed we had travelled far enough I stopped and dismounted. Ged took the reins of my camel and I ascended the rocks. Without being ordered, Syd followed. Once near the top I took off my helmet and crawled up. We were above the caravan route by some forty feet and half a mile from Berber. We had a good view. I did not risk the glasses but peered into the heat haze.

Syd joined me and after a few minutes said, "That is odd, sir."

I knew what he was going to say for I had just noticed it too, "There is no flag, and I can see no sentries either in the tower or on the walls."

"Yes, sir, but there are people coming and going. The town has not been abandoned."

I hunkered down a little so that the rock to my right shielded me from the rays of the sun and I risked the glasses. Suddenly, it was as though I was next to the walls. There were no sentries and the lack of a garrison was confirmed when, on the far side of the town walls I saw boys running and playing along the fighting platform.

"It has no soldiers." We returned to the camels and I made an instant decision. "Ali, you and Brown come with me. Sergeant Major, stay here with the men. I spied a caravan approaching. We will tag along behind it."

"Risky, sir."

I shook my head, "I don't think so. We are armed and well-mounted. If there is trouble then we can simply turn around and flee. If it is safe, I will send Ali back. Either way, we will know for certain."

We all headed down the gorge to the flatter land closer to the caravan route and while Syd hid the men from the town and fort's walls, I led the other two to follow the caravan heading south to the town. The man at the rear turned and I gave him a cheery wave. He waved back. With our cloaks over our weapons and keffiyeh covering our helmets we looked like any other traveller. A close inspection would have revealed our identity, but the man seemed unconcerned. There was no guard on the gate which lay invitingly open. We trotted in and no one gave us a second glance.

We rode into the main square where they held their souk. Men were chatting there, and I dismounted. I handed my reins to Brown and strode over to four older men who were smoking a hookah. I took that to be a good sign.

"As-salamu alaykum." I made the appropriate gesture.

They replied, "As-salamu alaykum."

"Where are the soldiers and warriors?"

The older of the four smiled and said, "Those parasites have left us and now dwell in Omdurman. Our lives are simpler now. We can trade and we fear not the fanatics who seem to live for fighting." His eyes narrowed, "You are English?"

I decided that there was little need for pretence, "Lieutenant Roberts of the Egyptian Army." It was not a lie, technically, General Kitchener was Sirdar of the Egyptian and Sudanese armies. Saying the British army would make me sound like an imperialist.

"You are coming here?"

"We are."

He nodded, "And you will pay for food and accommodation?"

I could not answer for the army but I could for my troop, "I will send for my men and yes we will." I turned, "Ali, fetch the Sergeant Major and the troop."

Grinning he said, "Sir."

I turned back, "Is there a barrack block and stable?"

He pulled a face, "There is but those animals who used it made it stink. You will not like either, Englishman."

"If you could point me in the right direction?"

The man shouted, "Boy, show these soldiers the barracks and stables."

A street urchin ran up and taking Lady Jane's reins I followed him. He was a cheeky enough youth and said, cheerfully, "Are you here to take the town?" He looked up at Brown, "Both of you?"

I smiled, "We are here to free Berber from the Mahdists."

He nodded, "They did not pay. Englishmen have money. You will pay, I think."

"Perhaps."

The old man was right. The barracks stank of urine and the stables were equally disgusting. I slipped the boy two copper coins, "Now I think you and your friends would like to earn more money, am I right?"

"Yes, effendi." He wanted money and it paid to be polite.

"Then bring over as many of your friends as you can and if you clean the stables and the barracks, then I will pay you." The money I had was not my own. Some coins were taken from dead enemies and some had been given to me for just such an occasion. It would be money well spent.

"Five coins for each boy."

I knew that they had to haggle and so I said, "Three."

"Four."

I held out my hand, "You drive a hard bargain."

"And if we do a good job then there may be an extra reward... for the foreman, of course."

"Perhaps."

Brown had dismounted and led the two camels to the water trough. It was the cleanest object that we saw. The boy returned with half a dozen fellows and he smartly ordered them to find brushes and brooms as well as cloths. Remarkably they found them quickly. It was not in our nature to do nothing and so Brown and I helped the boys. We moved the heavier tables and righted them. They swept. By the time the troop arrived, it was a hive of activity.

I looked up, "Water the camels and then help us. Shaw, find an oven and get some hot food on and a brew. Johnson, you and your troop will ride back to the column tomorrow and tell them that we have captured Berber, without a fight."

He grinned, "Yes sir."

Syd just shook his head, "We shall have to start calling you Lucky Jack, sir."

I smiled, "I think Fate owed us this one. Tonight, we will mount a guard on the gates and the walls and tomorrow we buy food. If nothing else it will show the locals that we are not bandits."

The boys did a good job and I gave them a bonus. For the rest of our sojourn in Berber they were our constant shadows offering to do all manner of jobs in return for the tiniest remuneration.

Chapter 21

The flying column arrived two weeks later. By then we had become a fixture in the town and not only accepted by the locals but, I think, welcomed. Partly it was because we paid our way but also, I think because we were respectful to all and spoke their language. We became part of the garrison of Berber. We were a small number, just three hundred and fifty men, compared with the thousands in the main Dervish army less than one hundred and fifty miles further along the river. The railway had yet to reach Abu Hamad and with the 5th cataract still an obstacle we had fewer gunboats than we would have liked. It became a bigger version of Fort Desolation which lay closer to us than Khartoum. While General Hunter and his men built a better fort and gunboat base along the river my men and I scouted out the land around. The twelve thousand people who lived in Berber were happy, it seemed, to be Egyptian once more but we were still very vulnerable and when the gunboats began to arrive, we breathed a sigh of relief.

Another New Year arrived and passed before reinforcements began to swell our numbers. By February we had the Lincolns, the Royal Warwicks and the Cameron Highlanders. Another Scottish regiment, the Seaforths was on its way. There was nothing wrong with the Egyptians and Sudanese, but the British troops were equipped with Lee Metford rifles. They had a five-round magazine and a much higher rate of fire than the Egyptians. However, the British reinforcements also brought typhoid and it raced through the town. Once again, we were spared the worst by dint of being in the desert more than we were in the town.

We spent the next weeks travelling down the Nile and the Atbara. Here the Mahdists were not welcomed, and we were. We discovered the names of the villages, and I added them to the map. We spoke to the headmen and I knew that when the Mahdists arrived we would be warned.

The new general, Major General Gatacre had interesting ideas. He believed in exercise as a way of defeating illness and making a unit efficient. He had the new brigades exercise in the

desert. His men nicknamed him backache. The running did not
help the appalling boots issued to the men. We had suffered from
them in Zululand and they had not improved. The stitching was
poor and the soles came away from the uppers. We, riding
camels, did not suffer as much but we had found cobblers
wherever we went and they repaired the boots. The Seaforths had
marched from Suakim and when they arrived their boots were in
a dreadful state. General Hunter tried his best to dissuade
General Gatacre from making his men endure forced marches
but the new general was of the opinion that Hunter was an Indian
officer and therefore not as good as he was. He did not listen.
That said, the men he led were good soldiers and despite the
typhoid, poor boots and pointless exercise, they performed well.
Kitchener ordered a fort to be built at Atbara and they built it in
an impressively short time.

We had been assigned to patrol the road south. We knew that
the Mahdists had a sizeable force at Metemma on the west bank
of the Nile. The gunboats patrolling the Nile now reported that
elements of the Mahdist army had crossed the Nile and were on
the opposite bank, at Shendi. We were still under the command
of General Hunter and it was he who sent us south to scout out
their new position.

Normally I would have sent out a single troop but with
typhoid in the camp and the prospect of the return of cholera, I
took the whole unit out, even Ged. Having all my troops with me
gave me the luxury of covering a larger area and because of that
when we encountered the Baggara horsemen, we not only
surprised them but we were also able to attack from two sides.
Syd and his troop attacked the head of the patrol, I led the men in
the centre and Jake, with the supply camels, the rear. The heat
haze meant that when we found them they were less than a
hundred and twenty paces from us.

I had Brown sound the command to charge. Any hesitation
would have allowed the Mahdists to gain the upper hand. I drew
my Webley and led the charge. The carbines did not fire in
volley but rippled along the line. It mattered not for the Baggara
horsemen had rifles that were hard to fire from the back of a
horse and once fired could not be reloaded. Some of the
horsemen were young warriors and keen to show their prowess.

Three turned to charge us. They seemed to bear a charmed life until Corporal Brown brought down one and I raised my Webley to pluck a second from his saddle. The third was five yards away when my bullet struck his skull. Our sudden attack made them run and they headed west.

I had the bugler sound the recall and then, when my sergeants and Syd arrived gave the command, "Follow them. They are obviously an advance guard of some kind. Let us see what sort of opposition we face." I had ascertained that we had all survived. As we followed the fleeing horsemen, we all reloaded. None needed to be given the order to do so. We were veterans.

When we were just five miles from the place we had met them we saw the Mahdist army. I raised my arm and we stopped. We needed to go no closer for the army was huge. There had to be fifteen thousand men. I saw the Black, White and Green Flags that told me these were better troops than we had met hitherto. I drew my glasses and peered through them. I saw the survivors from our attack conferring with leaders and pointing at us.

Syd said, "Sir, they will send men after us and we are a long way from home."

"Start the men back. I need to check something. Brown, you stay with me."

"Sir."

I had spied men on foot who did not look like the normal Dervishes. I saw they were wearing metal chains, shackles. These were conscripted men and they had been chained together to make them fight. I had heard of such things but this was the first time I had seen it. Some of the Sudanese battalions were formed from prisoners who had been thus chained and chosen to fight their former masters. It was a small thing but an important one, nonetheless.

"Sir."

I dropped my glasses as Brown pointed to the four riders galloping towards us. They rode horses. "Take out your carbine, Brown."

I drew my Martini-Henry. There was a bullet chambered already. I used Lady Jane to make me stable, aimed and fired. The rider I struck was two hundred yards from me and obviously felt safe. I chambered another round and shot a second. When

Brown fired three shots from his magazine and a third was wounded, the last man decided that discretion was the better part of valour. "Now we can rejoin the others."

Grinning, Brown put in another magazine, "Sir."

When we reached Fort Atbara, the Sirdar had arrived. To the surprise of Major General Gatacre we were admitted immediately. The English general snorted, "My lord, cannot the news from this…camel man, wait?" Kitchener had recently been made KCB and this was the first time I had heard him thus addressed.

Kitchener shook his head, "This camel man, as you call him, is one of my most trusted soldiers. When he speaks General Hunter and I listen. Go on, Roberts."

"We have found a Mahdist army of fifteen thousand men, sir. They are heading for the Atbara." I took out my map, complete with pencil marks and tea stains. I jabbed a finger at a point about fifteen miles from us. "If I was to guess I would say this village, Nakheila." Our first patrols had not been wasted ones.

"Good work, Roberts. Dismissed." As I left, I heard the Sirdar say, "We cannot use our gunboats on the Atbara but we have more than enough men to defeat them; if we can avoid the sun. Here is my plan."

Once back at the camp I warned Syd and the others, "We will be in action soon enough. The Sirdar is pleased with our news and proposes to act upon it."

Syd said, "Sir, you have to stop taking chances."

I frowned, "I beg your pardon?"

"Sir, you had no need to stay so long today. If they had sent more than four men you and Brown might be dead or prisoners."

"But I am not and the result means we have valuable intelligence for the Sirdar."

He lowered his voice, "Sir, with respect, how many times have we risked our lives and then the generals have not used the information well?"

I smiled, "Syd, I want to go home. Omdurman is where the Khalifa is waiting and it is so close I can almost taste it. Bringing the news I did means that the Sirdar will be more willing to let me leave."

That night as Adams brought me my tea and I smoked my last pipe he said, "The Sergeant Major is right, sir. You can be…well sorry to say it but reckless. Your son wants to see his dad return from this oven and not mourn the memory of a hero. A medal cannot give comfort like the arm of a father, can it, sir?"

They were right but I had endured enough of the desert and the army. I would do all in my power to defeat the enemy because that was the only way I could see myself getting home.

Once more we accompanied General Hunter as he reconnoitred the Mahdist position. He was impressed as they were exactly where I said they would be. They were making a zareba, a sort of fort. They had used thorns and stakes to make a perimeter. They had a good defensive position.

I used my glasses to survey the ground, "Sir, by my estimate they have three thousand cavalrymen."

"Have they, by God? That is a problem. Still the ground does not suit cavalry and we have guns this time."

The Sirdar was not deterred by their defences but he planned well. We made night marches to head south along the river. Once more we and the Jaalin Irregulars under the command of Major Stuart-Wortley were the scouts. We encountered no vedettes. I wondered at that for had they used scouts as we did then they would have been forewarned. It was General Burn Murdoch, recently returned to the army, who explained.

"The Mahdi was a unique character. His charisma held the Dervish army together. Since he died there has been infighting and plotting. None of the enemy leaders trusts any of the others. We have managed to either kill or capture their better leaders. I take this as a good sign, Roberts."

I liked the general. He chose to ride with the scouts to give himself a feel for the land. Like me he had learned to use the land to his advantage.

It took some time to get into position. The Mahdists obliged by doing nothing to stop our preparations. The artillery and machine guns were placed without any interference. We would be spectators for this battle. We were with the Sirdar and Burn Murdoch on a piece of high ground in the centre of our line. The cavalry was well to the south of us for we saw the massed ranks of their horsemen were also to the south of the thorns and trenches of the Mahdist zareba. It was like a game of chess. The two sets of cavalrymen might be the decisive blow or they might just watch.

The Sirdar nodded and the lines moved forward. When they were six hundred yards from the first of the thorn defences the guns and machine guns opened fire. The thorn defences were simply blown apart and the lines of British, Egyptian and Sudanese battalions marched steadily. It was the presence of British officers and NCOs that made the whole army one. The commands were given in English. As they neared the thorns the bugles sounded the charge and I could hear, above the screams, bullets and cracks of machine guns, "Avenge Gordon."

"Remember Gordon!"

"Death to the Dervish."

The Egyptians and the Sudanese had been silent at the battles before but these were British soldiers fired up by newspaper rhetoric. The smoke wreathed the battle and made it hard to see clearly what was going on but when the end came it was clear for all to see. Their cavalry first fled and then those that could raced south. We had won the Battle of Atbara.

General Kitchener looked happy. We had defeated a numerically superior army and more than half of our army had been Egyptians and Sudanese. We were ready to take Omdurman and then Khartoum. The other senior officers congratulated the Sirdar and as he mounted his horse I said, "Sir, when we have defeated the enemy I would, respectfully, like to resign my commission and return to England."

I thought he might have been angry but perhaps the joy of victory had mellowed him. He nodded, "I had hoped you would stay with me for we have much to do but, unlike me, you have a family and I do not. You have my permission." He waved his aide forward, "In case I forget, Carruthers, I give Lieutenant Roberts permission to resign his commission and return to England once we have defeated the Dervish."

"Sir."

I was relieved. The words could not be unsaid. I would go home. I had one more battle to fight.

More than three thousand were killed or wounded but we also had two thousand prisoners. Many of them had been virtual slaves and they happily joined a Sudanese Army that did not chain them as well as feeding and clothing them.

We headed for Shendi which was soon abandoned by the Dervish. Metemma had already been emptied and we knew that the enemy was concentrating their forces at Omdurman. That meant an army in excess of fifty thousand men. We would need more men and we waited as the railway to the Atbara river was finished and reinforcements arrived. They were good troops too. The Grenadier Guards, the Northumberland Fusiliers, the Lancashire Fusiliers and the Rifle Brigade were all excellent soldiers. Even more welcome was a British Cavalry Regiment, the 21st Lancers. It brought our army up to twenty-two thousand with forty-four artillery pieces, twenty Maxim guns and a fleet of gunboats.

As we waited in our camps for the order to march south there was a high level of optimism. One of the Seaforth officers had become friendly with us, mainly because we had a good mess and Lieutenant McIntire would sit at night and enjoy a pipe with us.

"Atbara showed what we could do. We shall repeat the same at Omdurman."

I looked at Syd who shook his head. I was the one who would have to disillusion the keen officer, "Donald, they have concentrated every warrior in Omdurman. They have had a long time to prepare their defences and they will have superior numbers."

"Look, Jack, I accept that you know this land better than I do but we killed three thousand and took two thousand prisoners. With our reinforcements, we will simply roll over them."

Along with the Jaalin Irregulars and the Camel Corps we had been scouting since the battle and reporting to Kitchener's head of intelligence Major Wingate. He liked me and, thanks to the information he had shared with his men, I had a better picture of what we faced.

"Donald, we face fifty thousand infantry as well as five thousand cavalry men, and their cavalry are good. You did not see them at their best. Atbara did not suit a cavalry charge. Our only superiority comes from our guns. They have but a handful. Remember, Donald, how hard they fought at Atbara?" he nodded, "Think how much harder they will fight for the place they regard as their capital and under the eyes of the Khalifa."

"You do not think we can win?" He sounded deflated.

"Oh, I think we shall win but it will not be easy. Think of it as hard and you will not be disappointed.

Chapter 22

The Battle of Omdurman September 1898

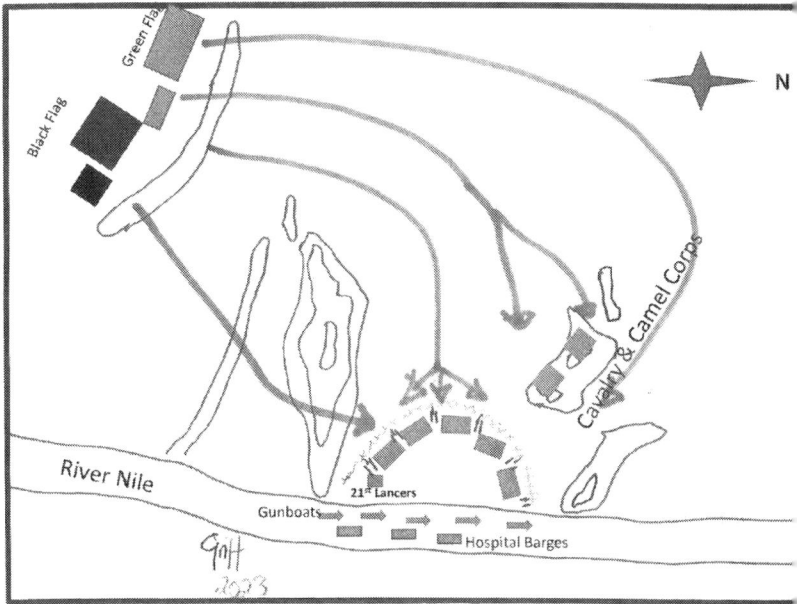

We did not leave our camp until the end of August. We had two columns and the men marched, at night, in brigades. Wad Hamed, Jebel Royan, Wast el; Abid, Sayal, Sururab and finally Egeiga were cautious moves that ensured we lost no men before the mighty battle. The Sirdar showed his normal close attention to detail and all the plans that we followed were made by him. General Hunter was used to him, as were other leaders like Burn Murdoch, but General Gatacre was bemused by the planning of General Kitchener. I think he thought that having such a decisive victory at Atbara we should simply race down the river and attack Omdurman. I knew that the Sirdar was right.

We would be attached to the Egyptian and Sudanese cavalry. The recently arrived 21st Lancers would operate separately. I think they were eager for the opportunity to show their skills with a lance on an open battlefield. I remembered Trooper telling

245

me about the 17th Lancers at Balaklava. They too had been keen for glory. I did not mind for we were used to the other regiments. It helped that we were held in high esteem. We were few in number but we had shown that we could handle ourselves.

We camped each night in defensive camps. The Sirdar sailed down the river on his own gunboat. The flotilla of armoured ships was very reassuring. The Dervishes had no answer to them and both their artillery and powder had proved to be inadequate in dealing with the leviathans of the river.

It was when we camped at the village of Egeiga, south of the Kerreri Hills that the Dervish made their move. We had our normal camp, and a thorn fence was in place, but the number of men who appeared made me realise just how inadequate it was. There was a wall of warriors three miles wide and eight men deep. The Sirdar had made his plans known and we knew what to do. We headed with the cavalry and Camel Corps to the high ground of the Kerreri Hills. The rest of the army formed a huge semi-circle anchored at the river and with gunboats protecting the flanks. Hospital barges were ready in the river to take the wounded to safety and we waited for their attack.

It became clear that there would be no attack that first day and I watched as our infantry and gunners made their thorn fences more formidable. We ate, drank sparingly and waited nervously. There were just two thousand of us and we all felt isolated. A messenger came from the Sirdar. It warned of a possible night attack, and we took it seriously. I divided the men into three and each took a third of the night watch. Captain Thomas of the Camel Corps saw what I did and he copied me. He was a much younger officer and my experiences in the last twenty odd years in Africa had given me an insight into how to survive. Dawn broke and there had been no night attack. One advantage of the watches in the night was that my unit had hot food. If a man went into battle with hot food inside him he fought better somehow. We fried corned beef and had it between slices of the stale bread we had toasted on the open fire. Covered with mustard and served with hot sweet tea it was as good a preparation for battle as any. We ate in the cool of pre-dawn and the start of the battle was announced when the vedettes of the

Egyptian Cavalry were attacked by overwhelming numbers of Mahdists.

Captain Thomas looked at his watch, "Six thirty."

I nodded, "Now it begins." I took out my binoculars. I saw that we had the men of the Green Flag against us. Major Wingate had appreciated the information I had brought him, and he had given me details of the enemy leaders. The Green Flags, light green and dark green, were led by Uthman al-Din and Ali wad Ullu. They were largely horsemen who faced us and we would be well outnumbered. Beyond them, I saw the Red Flag and the enormous body of men that was the Black Flag. They considered themselves the best warriors in the enemy army.

Ten minutes after the wave of men and horses poured from the south towards us the artillery fired. Howitzers as well as the naval guns sent their shells into the packed enemy ranks. We did not have the luxury of artillery. Lieutenant Colonel Broadwood commanded the brigade and he knew that we could not stand against such a formidable body of horsemen. He ordered two squadrons of horsemen to dismount and use their carbines to discourage the enemy while the Camel Corps negotiated the steep and rocky slope to reach the safety of the river and the gunboats protective fire.

"Roberts, I know you have less than half a squadron of men but if you would dismount and add your firepower…"

"Of course, sir. Dismount. Tether your camels. Adams, stay with the animals."

He shook his head, "Sorry sir, but you need every man you can get." He produced a Martini-Henry and said, "Who knows the extra bullets may make a difference."

There was no time to argue and I led my men down to the rocks where we joined the Egyptian cavalry. They were led by Lieutenant Wallace. He was incredibly young, "Rum do, eh? I thought we would have had a glorious charge and not skulk back to the river."

I smiled, "Look to your front and do your duty. That is my maxim." I shouted down the line, "Mark your targets and wait for my command." I had both my rifle and carbine. One would have the range and accuracy I wanted while the other would have the firepower I needed. Ged found a niche next to me. The

Egyptian pickets were riding as fast as they could but the Dervishes had the joy of battle. This was their chance to drive us from their land and were hurling themselves at us. For once they outnumbered us. I glanced to my left and saw that the two attacks to the centre of our lines had stalled but the cavalry charging us had been reinforced with some Black Flag warriors. Camels might have struggled in the rocks but the Baggara horsemen coped with the problems easily. I aimed at a leader who was exhorting his men on and my bullet ended his heroic gesture. I dropped the rifle and picked up the carbine. My shot, killing a leader, had inflamed the horsemen and they urged their horses up the slope to get at us.

"Open fire!"

There were too few of us and too many of them for me to hope to stop them but we emptied saddles. We kept firing and changing magazines with a regular rhythm that was impressive. My men kept up the steadier fire but the Egyptians gave a good account of themselves. We could not stop them but we did slow them and every moment we did so enabled more of the Camel Corps to descend the slope and make the safety of the river. The rest of the Egyptian cavalry were firing their carbines from the backs of horses. Their fire was not as accurate as that of their dismounted colleagues but the odd bullet found its mark.

Some of the Dervish warriors had been unhorsed and they made their way through the rocks. The mass of men before us were still mounted and it was only when a Dervish warrior suddenly appeared with a spear not three paces from us that I realised the danger. He thrust his spear at Lieutenant Wallace. It might have been a killing blow but for Ged who fired his recently reloaded rifle at the Dervish warrior. The .303 bullet smashed into the warrior's face. Just then Colonel Broadwood sounded the fall back.

"Get the Lieutenant to safety. Brown, sound the fall back."

My men would wait for our own bugle and we had done enough.

"Well done, Ged."

"I feel useful, sir."

Three more men rose and their rising coincided with the Camel Corps moving back to their animals. My men were still firing. Two of the Dervish warriors had swords and one a spear.

It was the one with the spear who lunged at me. I swung my carbine to fire at the spearman who represented the greatest danger. Ged raised his rifle forgetting that he had not reloaded. It had been a long time since the old soldier had been in combat. I hit the spearman as one of the swordsmen swung his sword to hack into Ged's side. Even as I fired the third swordsman took his chance and the sword sliced into my left arm. I was able to reload and fire before he could strike a killing blow. I had been lucky.

Brown appeared with my camel, "Sir, we are the last."

"I can't leave Adams."

"Sir, he is dead."

He was right. The old soldier had died but he had a smile on his face. I nodded and rose to salute. "Farewell, old friend. We will fetch your body when this is over."

I emptied my magazine at the warriors who saw their opportunity. Suddenly there was a volley from behind me as I climbed onto Lady Jane's back and sheathed my carbine. Saddles were emptied by a volley from my men and I was able to wheel my camel. We hurtled down the slope to follow the Egyptian cavalry and I saw the problems presented by the ground. Horses could cope but camels struggled. Had we all not been superb riders then we might have come to grief. As it was, we made the safety of the rest of the brigade whose carbines, allied to the two gunboats brought up to provide extra support, drove the Mahdists back.

Brown said, "You are wounded, sir."

I had almost forgotten the blow to my arm. "Put a bandage on it, Brown. This is far from over."

It was as he did so that I realised I had an empty scabbard. The rifle I had used at Rorke's Drift lay with Ged. It was fitting somehow for the weapon was as much a soldier as Ged. I glanced down the line of men and saw that Ged had been our only casualty. There were others, like me, sporting wounds. Some were facial injuries caused by flying chips while Hill looked to have been speared in the leg. That might prove to be a danger.

"Sir, I think we should get you to the river and put you on a hospital barge."

I shook my head, "Now that it is bandaged it will suffice until this is over. The men need me, Corporal Brown."

"They need you, sir, but they need you alive."

"It is a scratch."

Colonel Broadwood chose that moment to ride towards us, "Thank you, Roberts, that was well done."

I nodded and pointed to the two gunboats and the five hundred or so warriors they had killed, "Thanks to the gunboats, sir, they saved our bacon."

"Quite. Have your men form up behind the Camel Corps. The Dervishes are falling back and I believe that the Sirdar will order an attack."

Just then we heard a bugle and saw the 21st Lancers, to our left, forming up. They were going to charge. I knew from their officers that this would be the first charge in their history and they were keen to gain honour. They moved off at a smart pace with bugles blaring and pennants fluttering. They made a fine sight. The back of a camel gives a man a good view over the heads of marching men and I saw the lancers as they ploughed into a body of Baggara horsemen. They scythed through them only to disappear down a hidden slope. The charge was the only sound of battle, except for the artillery and gunboats which continued to rain death on the Mahdists. I heard the clash of arms and then the sound of gunfire.

Syd shook his head, "That doesn't sound good, sir. The lancers have pig stickers. You can't fire a carbine if you are holding a pig sticker."

The fate of the 21st was a moot point for the Sirdar ordered an advance. We held the right flank and the infantry marched in echelon. I looked up and saw the mass of Jebel Surgham before us. At least its slopes were too uneven for horsemen and afforded some protection.

My left arm now ached. The blow had been below the elbow and I rested my forearm on the saddle. It seemed to help. I held my reins loosely in my left hand. Lady Jane was well schooled and she seemed to know I was hurt and looked after me. It was mid-morning and we had fought for some hours. I needed water but I knew I had to keep all my attention on the field before me. We had not lost a large number of men but there had been deaths amongst the Egyptian cavalry and others had been wounded. The Dervishes were not yet defeated.

Suddenly, from behind the Jebel Surgham came the army of the Black Flag supported by the two Green Flag armies. The enemy had kept a mighty force in reserve and, by my estimate seventeen thousand men were now charging the Egyptian Brigade commanded by Colonel MacDonald. There was a gap which the Black Flag warriors intended to exploit and I saw the British 1st and 2nd Brigades hurrying to their aid. I had seen Egyptian troops fight many years earlier but the ones who turned to fire volley after volley into the charging horsemen were a different breed from the ones that had fought at Alt Klea. They were Birish trained and led and as doughty and steadfast as any. They fired volley after volley and were wreathed in smoke.

Colonel Broadwood said, "Form lines." He intended to charge.

I did not draw my sword but took my Webley from its holster to hang from its lanyard. Some of my men, like Atkinson, had acquired swords and they drew them. Others had acquired pistols. In a regular unit, such acquisitions would have been frowned upon but in mine, it was encouraged. Only a handful of our men would have to use a carbine.

"Forward!"

I repeated the colonel's order, and my sergeants did the same. We moved smartly out behind the Camel Corps. We walked at first but seeing the Mahdists swarming around the Egyptians made the colonel increase our speed. The Black Flag warriors were so intent on charging the Egyptians that they failed to see our approach. Perhaps our paltry numbers made their leader dismiss us. Whatever the reason they did not turn to face us but continued to scream their way to the bayonets and rifles of the Egyptians. When the British brigades halted and poured their fire into the flanks of the Dervishes, so the Dervish attack spread to charge them. The British soldiers had a five round magazine and the volleys were continuous.

The bugle sounded the charge and we began to gallop. A camel can reach a prodigious speed although the morning's exertions had taken their toll. The horses, led by Colonel Broadwood would reach the enemy first. I drew my pistol as we neared the enemy. We would strike in the second rank and my pistol would be of more use than my sword. The Camel Corps struck first, and their swords slashed down. The enemy horsemen and camel riders were more than competent and many of them wheeled their animals as they heard our bugles. It was not just the Dervish who fell but some of the Camel Corps. I saw a Baggara raise his sword to strike at the back of a Camel Corps sergeant. I fired the Webley and hit him. I fired at a second who rode towards me with a lance. My bullet threw him over the back of his camel. It was now a frenetic fight with horses and camels from both sides intertwined. From my left I heard the regular volleys of the British and Egyptian brigades as they harvested the enemy cavalry.

I emptied my Webley and let it drop. I drew my sword. My left arm complained as I pulled on the reins to turn Lady Jane to go to the aid of Syd who was fighting two Dervishes. She was a good animal and raced to Syd's side. Standing in my stirrups I brought the sword down to smash through the skull of the warrior. The time I had spent, as a youth in the iron gang, meant even without an edge my blow would have crushed the warrior's head. Syd slashed with his sword and ripped open the warrior's middle. He fell writhing to the ground.

"Thanks, sir." Syd sheathed his sword and drew his carbine. He began to fire at the men closest to us, clearing a space.

I shouted, "Reform and reload!"

One advantage of our small number and our position in the second rank was that we were still together. I emulated Syd and as there was no immediate threat sheathed my sword and reloaded my pistol. I did not trust my left arm to support my carbine.

Syd said, "You should be in hospital, sir." He nodded towards my arm which dripped blood.

I smiled, "And do you think I can get there without harm, Sergeant Major? The battle is not over yet."

It was at that moment that some Green Flag warriors fell upon us. No doubt they had been delayed by the terrain but whatever the reason their appearance was both unexpected and a danger as we were defending the right flank of the Camel Corps. If we did not stop them then they might be routed.

"Face your front!"

We wheeled and with reloaded weapons fired bullet after bullet into the mass of mounted men who flooded towards us. My Webley emptied, I drew my sword, and seeing my men reload urged Lady Jane towards the enemy. I found myself facing three men. I blocked the first blow but felt a spear stab me in my right leg. A bullet from behind took the spearman and I heard Syd shout, "Help the lieutenant."

I slashed sideways and was rewarded when my sword hacked into the head of the swordsman. The other warrior used two hands to swing his sword at my unprotected left side. The blow struck to the bone on my left arm and hurt more than any wound I had ever endured. His head disappeared as my men's bullets struck him. Even as I began to slip from Lady Jane's back, blood flowing freely from my arm, I heard the sound of Maxim machine guns. Someone must have brought two Maxims up and as their bullets scythed through the Dervishes I succumbed to darkness.

I came to when the motion of being carried jarred my arm and I cried out. Syd's voice rang out, "Be careful you dozy bugger. Clear the way there."

"Did we win, Syd?"

His face, covered with specks of blood, dust and cordite broke into a smile, "Aye, we did. Colonel Broadwood is chasing the enemy over the desert. I thought you had left us, Jack. You hang on in there. We are almost at the river. The doctors will sort you out."

"Did we lose any men?"

He sighed, "Ged was the only one killed and you have the worst wound." He shook his head. "You took too many chances, Jack. You were always too brave for your own good."

I was thinking of a witty reply when darkness took me once more.

When I came to it was to the smell of antiseptic. A white coated doctor leaned over me, "Well, Lieutenant, you have more wounds than a living man has a right to. Let us see what we can do. Nurse, the chloroform. Fetch me the saw."

Epilogue

I woke and felt sick. I looked up and saw a doctor standing over me. He was studying a chart. "Well, Lieutenant, you are alive and that is more than can be said for some of the others who came through this hospital. Still, you will be going home soon."

I smiled, "Thank you, doctor."

I closed my eyes and lay back. I heard his footsteps recede. "Ready for a drink, sir? It will clear away the taste of the anaesthetic." An orderly stood over me with a jug of water and I tried to sit up. My left arm would not support me. He gave me a sad smile and put the jug and the mug on the table next to me. "Here, let me help you." He put his hands under my arms and raised me. He said, "Afraid they had to take your left arm at the elbow, sir. Still, it was better than losing your life and according to the doctors you nearly did."

I looked down at the stump where my arm should have been. I was going home but doing so as less than a man. What would I do with one arm? How would I make a living?" I drank the water but it did not remove the feeling of nausea.

Syd and Brown came to see me a few days later. The wound was healing, it had begun to itch and amazingly it still felt as though I had a hand and fingers. They both looked happy. "Thank God you are alive. You were more dead than alive when the doctors got you. They did a good job."

"Syd, they took my arm!"

He shook his head, "This is not like you, Jack, the glass is half full. You have your right arm, don't you? This means you are invalided out. Colonel Broadwood reckons you will get a pension for the wound." He looked around to see if he was observed and slipped a bottle of run to me. "This will cheer you up a little and if not you can drown your sorrows. You are going home. You will see Griff and he won't care that you only have one arm, will he?"

He was right and I nodded, "You are a good friend, Syd and I am sorry. What will happen to you and the lads?"

"We have been given a choice, we can either transfer to the Camel Corps or take a boat and go home. We have taken Omdurman and Khartoum and they will try to save money now. Brown, Johnson, Shaw and Brian Wyatt and me are all taking the pension we have been offered. We hoped to go home with you but you will have a more leisurely journey than us. You go by boat to Atbara and then a train to Wadi Haifa, from there you head to Alexandria. Three months from now and you will be home."

"And you lads?"

"The ones going home are heading for Berber. We take the caravan route to Suakim and then a boat to Suez and England." Syd smiled, "I will get to see Fort Desolation one more time." The orderly came in and frowned. "Looks like Florence Nightingale wants us to go." He took a notepad from his pocket and a stub of a pencil. "Here, write down your address, and I will try to get to see you when things are sorted out."

For some reason, the thought that an old friend would see me in England raised my spirits and I smiled, "Looking forward to it and you, too, Brown, any of the lads are more than welcome." I scribbled down Bet's address.

They left and my happiness evaporated. I was alone.

I left the hospital a week later. I needed a stick because of the wounded leg. They had offered me a wheelchair, but I would not endure the indignity. It was in Cairo, where my stump was examined for signs of infection and gangrene, when Sir Herbert Kitchener visited with me. I was in a better mood for there was no gangrene.

He gave me a rare smile, "I am pleased that you live, Roberts. You are a good fellow and I wish there were more like you. You have your wish and you shall go home. I hope the pension that they give you is commensurate with your efforts."

"I am going home, sir, and I am happy."

"I put your name forward for the Victoria Cross, you know, but I have enemies back in England and it was refused. You deserve it, you know." He waved forward the aide who had hovered since he had entered the ward. The eyes of the other patients were all on the Sirdar. He took out three medals, "These medals cannot be denied and I present them to you now, the

Khedive's Sudan Medal, the Queen's Sudan Medal and the Egypt Medal." He stood back and saluted me, "It has been an honour to command you and if your son should choose to follow his illustrious father then there is a place at Sandhurst for him. You have my word."

"Thank you, sir, but..."

He shook his head, "You are bitter about the loss of the arm. I understand that but you are a hero, Lieutenant Roberts and your son will see it that way also. Do not try to stop him. The Empress will need soldiers like you in the future and it is, I think, in your blood."

The aide said, "Sir, the Governor..."

"Yes, I know." He held out his hand and I shook it, "Good luck."

I looked at the medals on my chest. Kitchener was right, Griff would see the medals as vindication that his father was a hero. I had done the same with Trooper. I knew that no matter what I said, Griff would want to be a soldier of the queen.

The End

Glossary

Butty (pl butties) - 19th-century slang for close friends

en banderole – worn diagonally across the body

Cataracts – rapids and rocks that impede the passage of boats

Dhobi (n)– washing (from the Indian) dhobying (v)

Fellah- An Egyptian soldier, the equivalent of a private in a British regiment

Half a crown - two shillings and sixpence (20 shillings to the pound, 12 pennies to a shilling)

Laager- an improvised fort made of wagons

Jibbah – short white blouse worn by the Mahdists

Lunger - nickname for the sword bayonet

Nabob – someone from India who has made a fortune

Puggaree – a cloth tied around a helmet

Historical Background

Like many people my age I first came to know about Rorke's Drift through the superb film Zulu. It inspired Keith Floyd to join the Guards. That too came alongside a British disaster, Isandlwana. Both the charge of the Light Brigade and the disaster at Isandlwana have much in common. Whilst the leadership and planning were appalling the behaviour and courage of the ordinary rank and file could not be questioned.

This book is about life as soldiers, ordinary soldiers. The soldiers of the Queen did not care who they were fighting they just knew they were fighting for their Queen and country. That idea may seem a little old-fashioned now, but I am not rewriting history, I am trying to show what it might have been like to live in 19th Century Britain. The British Army saluted with their left hand until the First World War. The weapons used are, according to my research (see book list) the ones used in the period.

Many men joined the army as a softer option than the incredibly hard and dangerous work in the factories. I worked in an iron gang in the 1970s and I can attest to the hard work even then. I tended presses that reached 3000 degrees and needed the consumption of gallons of squash during each shift. How much harder would it have been a hundred years earlier? I was working an eight-hour shift while ten and twelve-hour days were the norm a hundred years earlier.

Anyone who has researched their family history in the nineteenth century and looked at the census records will know how even relatively well-off factory workers rented or boarded. Four and five to a bed was the norm. We take so much for granted today but even in the 1950s life was hard and had a pattern. With coal fires, no bathroom, an outside toilet, no carpets and little money for food it was closer to life in the 1870s. Offal was often on the menu and you ate what was there. Nothing was wasted. Drinking beer and smoking were not considered unhealthy pastimes. There was a teetotal movement but it was only in the latter part of the nineteenth century that the water the people drank became healthy. Until then it was small beer that was drunk.

Omdurman

Abu Hamad is named after a celebrated sheikh buried there, by whose tomb travellers crossing the desert used formerly to deposit all superfluous goods, the sanctity of the saint's tomb ensuring their safety.

This series will continue but unlike my British Ace Series and my WW2 one, I will not be working my way through wars. I intend to look at how British soldiers served this country and how their lives changed as Britain changed.

One reason why the attempt to relieve Khartoum failed, apart from the usual vacillations of the politicians, was that the main army travelled by boats which had to be unloaded and carried over the cataracts and the smaller, allegedly faster relief force led by General Stewart, marched in square and took ten days to cover one hundred miles.

The British NCOs who were recruited to retrain the Egyptian army were the Sergeant Whatsisnames made famous by Kipling. They did a good job. Every officer who volunteered was given the rank of major so that no Egyptian officer could give them orders.

Berber was, indeed, without defenders. It was an irregular troop that discovered that fact. I have allowed Jack and his men to gain the glory.

Books used in the research:

- The Oxford Illustrated History of the British Army- David Chandler
- The Thin Red Line- Fosten and Fosten
- The Zulu War- Angus McBride
- Rorke's Drift- Michael Glover
- British Forces in Zululand 1879- Knight and Scollins
- The Sudan Campaign 1881-1898 -Wilkinson-Lathom
- Onwards to Omdurman- Keith Surridge
- Omdurman- Donal Featherstone

Griff Hosker
September 2023

Other books by Griff Hosker

If you enjoyed reading this book, then why not read another
one by the author?

Ancient History

The Sword of Cartimandua Series
(Germania and Britannia 50 A.D. – 128 A.D.)
Ulpius Felix- Roman Warrior (prequel)
The Sword of Cartimandua
The Horse Warriors
Invasion Caledonia
Roman Retreat
Revolt of the Red Witch
Druid's Gold
Trajan's Hunters
The Last Frontier
Hero of Rome
Roman Hawk
Roman Treachery
Roman Wall
Roman Courage

The Wolf Warrior series
(Britain in the late 6th Century)
Saxon Dawn
Saxon Revenge
Saxon England
Saxon Blood
Saxon Slayer
Saxon Slaughter
Saxon Bane
Saxon Fall: Rise of the Warlord
Saxon Throne

Omdurman

Saxon Sword

Medieval History

The Dragon Heart Series
Viking Slave *
Viking Warrior *
Viking Jarl *
Viking Kingdom *
Viking Wolf *
Viking War
Viking Sword
Viking Wrath
Viking Raid
Viking Legend
Viking Vengeance
Viking Dragon
Viking Treasure
Viking Enemy
Viking Witch
Viking Blood
Viking Weregeld
Viking Storm
Viking Warband
Viking Shadow
Viking Legacy
Viking Clan
Viking Bravery

The Norman Genesis Series
Hrolf the Viking *
Horseman *
The Battle for a Home *
Revenge of the Franks *
The Land of the Northmen
Ragnvald Hrolfsson

Omdurman

Brothers in Blood
Lord of Rouen
Drekar in the Seine
Duke of Normandy
The Duke and the King

Danelaw
(England and Denmark in the 11th Century)
Dragon Sword *
Oathsword *
Bloodsword *
Danish Sword

New World Series
Blood on the Blade *
Across the Seas *
The Savage Wilderness *
The Bear and the Wolf *
Erik The Navigator *
Erik's Clan *
The Last Viking

The Vengeance Trail *

The Conquest Series
(Normandy and England 1050-1100)
Hastings

The Aelfraed Series
(Britain and Byzantium 1050 A.D. - 1085 A.D.)
Housecarl *
Outlaw *
Varangian *

The Reconquista Chronicles
Castilian Knight *

Omdurman

El Campeador *
The Lord of Valencia *

**The Anarchy Series England
1120-1180**
English Knight *
Knight of the Empress *
Northern Knight *
Baron of the North *
Earl *
King Henry's Champion *
The King is Dead *
Warlord of the North
Enemy at the Gate
The Fallen Crown
Warlord's War
Kingmaker
Henry II
Crusader
The Welsh Marches
Irish War
Poisonous Plots
The Princes' Revolt
Earl Marshal
The Perfect Knight

**Border Knight
1182-1300**
Sword for Hire *
Return of the Knight *
Baron's War *
Magna Carta *
Welsh Wars *
Henry III *
The Bloody Border *
Baron's Crusade

263

Omdurman

Sentinel of the North
War in the West
Debt of Honour
The Blood of the Warlord
The Fettered King
de Montfort's Crown

Sir John Hawkwood Series
France and Italy 1339- 1387
Crécy: The Age of the Archer *
Man At Arms *
The White Company *
Leader of Men *
Tuscan Warlord *
Condottiere

Lord Edward's Archer
Lord Edward's Archer *
King in Waiting *
An Archer's Crusade *
Targets of Treachery *
The Great Cause *
Wallace's War *
The Hunt

Struggle for a Crown
1360- 1485
Blood on the Crown *
To Murder a King *
The Throne *
King Henry IV *
The Road to Agincourt *
St Crispin's Day *
The Battle for France *
The Last Knight *
Queen's Knight *

Omdurman

Tales from the Sword I
(Short stories from the Medieval period)

Tudor Warrior series
England and Scotland in the late 15th and early 16th
century
Tudor Warrior *
Tudor Spy *
Flodden

Conquistador
England and America in the 16th Century
Conquistador *
The English Adventurer *

Modern History

The Napoleonic Horseman Series
Chasseur à Cheval
Napoleon's Guard
British Light Dragoon
Soldier Spy
1808: The Road to Coruña
Talavera
The Lines of Torres Vedras
Bloody Badajoz
The Road to France
Waterloo

The Lucky Jack American Civil War series
Rebel Raiders
Confederate Rangers
The Road to Gettysburg

Soldier of the Queen series

Omdurman

Soldier of the Queen
Redcoat's Rifle
Omdurman

The British Ace Series
1914
1915 Fokker Scourge
1916 Angels over the Somme
1917 Eagles Fall
1918 We will remember them
From Arctic Snow to Desert Sand
Wings over Persia

Combined Operations series
1940-1945
Commando *
Raider *
Behind Enemy Lines
Dieppe
Toehold in Europe
Sword Beach
Breakout
The Battle for Antwerp
King Tiger
Beyond the Rhine
Korea
Korean Winter

Tales from the Sword II
(Short stories from the Modern period)

Books marked thus *, are also available in the audio
format.
For more information on all of the books please visit the
author's website at www.griffhosker.com where there is a

Omdurman

link to contact him or visit his Facebook page: GriffHosker at Sword Books or follow him on Twitter: @HoskerGriff

Printed in Great Britain
by Amazon